He paused at her impulsive cry, one eyebrow cocked in question. "Yes?"

Looking at him as he held the halter of another man's horse, Tamasin searched the muddle of her own feelings.

"Why did you come back?" she asked suddenly, surprised by her own vehemence, by her burning curiousity. "Why did you come back?"

As if the question angered him, he turned away, his hand clenching the thoroughbred's reins more tightly.

"Why?" Tamasin demanded again, her emotion building. "You could've gone anywhere in the world, for heaven's sake—America or Canada. You could've made a life for yourself there, been *free*. Why didn't you, Hunter? Why did you come back to Ireland?"

He paused just long enough to give her a long look, his beautiful mouth slightly curved, saturnine. When she continued to give him a flushed and serious stare, he smiled suddenly, broadly, then turned and continued to lead Sir Harry's pampered horse down the hill toward the forge.

Tamasin followed, wanting an answer, determined to get one even if she had to trail him all the way home and pester him for it. *"Why, Hunter? Why!?"*

At last, with his eyes fastened on the horizon where green met blue, the groomsman halted, his shoulders rigid, the fragrant green breeze ruffling his hair. He spoke through his teeth, curtly, as if she should have known the answer all along, knowing his mind as he knew hers. "Because I belong to Ireland, Tamasin. And because Ireland belongs to me."

DAMSEL

Debra Hamilton

Zebra Books
Kensington Publishing Corp.
http://www.zebrabooks.com

ZEBRA BOOKS are published by

Kensington Publishing Corp.
850 Third Avenue
New York, NY 10022

First Printing: April, 1997
10 9 8 7 6 5 4 3 2 1

Printed in the United States of America

To Rita Arnn Brightman—
for all the wrong that you made right . . .

Prologue

With wings upon her heels she fled over a landscape of emerald blades and cloud-mist, veering to avoid a sacred mound of stone where the fairies jigged at night. In case they watched and planned some vengeful prank, the blithe child of Ireland cried out a breathless greeting as she passed. "God speed ye gentlemen and spare me yer mischief! I've got enough trouble in this world already!"

Her mud-stained legs flew like whirligigs, while her slender arms pumped and black hair whipped across her shoulder blades. Nimbly she bounded across a brooklet, zigzagged over a patch of sod, and raced across a potato field. Hearing the bay of hounds, she increased her gallop while her fingers tightened over a dirty string, at the end of which a curious object danced.

A fox's hide it was, recently skinned, its neck and tail adorned with pink and purple ribbons. The pelt looked alive as it undulated over the ground with its white-tipped tail wagging.

"Just a wee bit further," the girl gasped, talking to the pelt while she yanked it forward.

Behind her, the yap of hounds created a terrifying cacophony accompanied by the thunder of churning hooves, and whimpering, she darted into a woodlet, where she searched for a likely tree. Finding a hawthorn, she scurried toward it, shimmied up the mossy trunk, and crept out along a branch. When she had balanced herself, she looped the string ends over a limb and tied them fast.

Pausing only a moment to catch her breath, the girl then jumped down to survey her handiwork, watching the fox pelt with its fancy bows dangle from the tree like a puppet.

"Perfect!" she pronounced with a breezy laugh.

A second later she was off again, her feet disturbing last autumn's leaves and stirring up the scent of ancient withered things. Glancing over a shoulder, she spotted the line of hounds scurrying over the top of the hill, so close now she could see the pink of their lolling tongues, and just at their heels, a bevy of half-drunk huntsmen in vivid coats galloping on lathered horses, one tooting a rallying cry upon his curled brass horn.

Desperate to be out of sight, she sprinted away from the grove and splashed across a flooded field in the direction of a hedgerow, where, like a hare going to ground, she dived beneath its foliage and, tucking her legs under her body, burrowed deep.

Once secure in her hidey-hole she drew her knees up and rested her tousled head upon their shelf, too exhausted to mind the prickling of furze against her bottom.

"God's blood—," she gasped. "I earned me prize today. 'Twas the hardest job I ever did."

Not far away, she heard hooves crash through the underbrush, their noise orchestrated with the yapping of dogs and the curses of inebriated men. She scooted closer into the safety of the hedgerow, her elfin mouth curving into a mischievous smile.

After dusting both hands upon her skirts, she pulled a square of linen from her pocket with dainty and exaggerated care. Edged in costly lace with a design of love knots embroidered in the center, the white lady's handkerchief seemed to shimmer against the rustiness of her old black clothes.

"Ah," she whispered, her eyes radiant as she beheld it. "Fine, it is . . . so fine. And me very own to keep forever."

She turned the handkerchief this way and that, scrutinized its every angle in the same way she might a thing of mystery, letting the pale sun shine through its invisible weave to touch her face. So absorbed did she become in admiring her fancy treasure, so lost in her world of dreams, she failed to hear the approach of a passerby.

Although he was garbed in the rough corduroy frieze coat and breeches of a workingman, and his top boots had seen better days, the traveler led a magnificent thoroughbred stallion the color of terra cotta, whose high-held tail brushed the ground like a length of ragged silk. Even before the nervous horse shied as the scent of the girl reached its nostrils, the young man's sharp eyes glimpsed her huddled like a mole in the hedgerow.

Putting his hands upon his hips, he grinned, and in a loud voice drawled, "Have you started conversing with yourself in ditches now, Tamasin Cullen? Or are you only speaking with the fairies again?"

Startled out of her wits, the girl snatched the handkerchief to her breast as if to protect it, then squinted to stare up at the face framed by the backdrop of pearl-colored sky. She relaxed a bit, for his was a familiar visage—or, at least, it had been once.

Hunter Kinshella was getting to be a man, Tamasin thought in rapt surprise, eyeing the breadth of his shoulders and the taper of his flanks, the long limbs and angular jaw that epitomized the dark breed of Irishman renowned for reckless charm and whipcord strength. Staring up at the underside of that jaw and its bristly shadows, she revised her first opinion; Hunter Kinshella *was* a man.

She had not seen him in some time, and in the interim he had metamorphosed into quite a different being than the one she had known. His dark features were fine-drawn yet bold, and although his stance was not the obnoxiously cocksure one peculiar to the other young village men, it suggested Hunter Kinshella possessed no lack of confidence in himself.

He had always been a popular lad in the village, a natural leader of the boys, and recently the desired suitor of every marriageable lass in the county. Tamasin knew he was away a great deal these days racing Sir Harry's horses, for it was said he had a way with the high-strung beasts, a skill inherited from his grandfather. When she was younger he used to give her stolen rides behind the stable until she grew to love the saddle, and when he had a spare hour or two away from his duties, he had always seen to it that Mam had enough turf for a fire when Da was too drunk to provide it. Hunter was always doing things like that about the village, always putting his healthy young back to use for others.

Flushing, not quite understanding the tensing of her belly as she examined the interesting changes in her companion, Tamasin ducked her head and, fastidiously taking hold of the handkerchief's corners, held it up for view. Pride caused her face to glow. "Look, Hunter—isn't it the finest thing ye ever saw?"

He regarded it with one black brow raised, unimpressed by her hard-earned treasure. "Does that scrap of frippery have anything to do with the ballyhoo going on over yonder?" he asked. He jerked his head toward the confused knot of riders and hounds still milling about on the distant brae.

Feeling at a disadvantage crouched beneath the towering height of her interrogator, Tamasin uncurled her legs and stood up, squaring her thin shoulders. She had learned long ago that the best answer to an uncomfortable question was an indignant demand, and gave one now. "And what if it does?"

"Good God,Tamasin! What mischief did Little Lord Tyrant put you up to this time? Everyone in the village knows you do his dirty work."

"Don't be calling him that!" she snapped in defense of her lofty acquaintance. "He's *Master Avery*—as well you know— son of your grandfather's employer, who just happens to own that fine racing animal yer holding there. Ye should be more respectful."

"I'd likely be more respectful of an ass with long ears than one with pantaloons," he snorted.

Ready to argue for the young gentleman she idolized, Tamasin threw back her shoulders and glared. Hunter's greenish gaze flicked over her with sudden interest. He realized she hovered between the states of childhood and womanhood, and likely hedged closer to the latter. His eyes narrowed, tarrying upon the too-tight jacket whose laces strained across her maturing chest. He said irritably, "Doing his bidding will land you into trouble, Tamasin. A baronet's son doesn't associate with a cottier's lass for any purpose save that of using her. And, anyway, you're getting too old for such shenanigans, I should think."

His voice lowered as his eyes scanned her willowy length and he felt his vitals tighten with unbidden interest. "Ere long he'll be paying you for something else."

Tamasin dropped her lashes and squeezed her bare toes into the green earth, failing to understand all that Hunter's words implied. But the deepened sound of his now manly voice disturbed her, spoiled her triumph of the day.

"It's just that I like fine things, Hunter," she trailed, impulsively confiding in this self-possessed presence because she wanted to divert his condemnation. She was only just beginning to realize her own power of persuasion, her ability to make her actions appear purer than they were.

"I always have," she went on with a touching breathlessness that might have softened a less discerning listener. "I don't seem to be able to help meself. When I was six, I had the most wondrous dream. I dreamt I was a damsel living in a marble house filled with treasures. The halls were long—endlessly long—and so polished they gleamed like the pebbles by the river when the sun shines. And there was food in every room, long tables full of food so cleverly cooked it might have been something the fairies conjured up. I've never forgotten it. Every chance I get, I go and peek through the windows of the Hall. I stare at all the grand furnishings in there—they're almost as wondrous as those in my dream. I imagine myself touching the crystal and the silver, sitting in the little satin chairs like a lady. And dancing!''

She whirled around, then took a few mincing steps, her muddy feet graceful and light upon the soggy turf. ''I've watched, and this is how they do it.''

''Nay, Damsel,'' Hunter said, taking her hand in his, closing calloused fingers over her small, thin ones. ''I believe 'tis done more like this.'' Putting an arm about her waist, he led her in a few swirling, elegantly maneuvered steps that made her dizzy with delight.

''Why, Hunter Kinshella!'' she cried, laughing and breathless when he released her with a gentle twirl. ''However did ye learn to dance like that?''

''The fairies taught me.''

At first she believed him, and her jaw dropped in envious amazement. But when his black-lashed eyes twinkled, she scoffed. ''Och, ye're only teasing me!''

Then, with her gaze shining with both the wonder of youth and the passion of maturity, she asked him a serious question. ''Don't you ever wish to own one of the fine horses you curry and feed, Hunter? Don't you ever *ache* to possess it, yearn to tell everyone it's yours, ride it to Dublin? Surely you do! When I see something beautiful,'' she went on in a dreamy way, clutching the fine handkerchief, closing her eyes so tightly her lids wrinkled, ''I want to put me hands upon the thing and *own* it, no matter what I have to do.''

The simple, not so childish confession gave Hunter cause for consternation, and for several seconds he considered the ragged peasant's daughter who stood on solid Irish turf with her head in the clouds.

At his silence Tamasin glanced up to meet his eyes, which had always been the keenest eyes, so keen the other boys used to choose him to watch for the mail coach on the crossroads at Three Rocks. But now, besides the sharpness, they held a man's awareness of life and reality.

"Fine things cost plenty, Tamasin," he said with a level gaze.

"And what if they do?" she cried. "Look at me, Hunter! No shoes upon me feet, because leather's too dear to wear except to church. Not a new scrap of clothing since springtime a year past, and me growing like a weed. Look at me hands, red from stacking turf to get us through the winter. Have you been out of Sir Harry's fine stable lately and visited a cottier's cabin? Mean, nasty places they are. The thatch is so poor rain seeps in. Pigs and chickens soil the place, and the smoke of the peat fire blackens all the walls—me mother is near blind from it, like half the other cottier's wives."

She sighed and raised her own violet eyes to the sky, and they glistened with a sudden trembling of tears no less bright than the rain beads on the hedge. "Me da had to pawn me Sunday bonnet this morning, just to pay the agent's rent. 'Twas a fine bonnet too, with a feather stuck in the brim. Ah, 'tis a wretched life," she finished, her face suddenly appearing more mature than her years.

And then, in the passage of a second, she seemed to lapse back into childhood again, taking hold of her dirty skirts and twitching them with a precocious flip of her hand. "I'm meant for something grander, Hunter. I know I am. That's why I do Master Avery's bidding—to get things. I'm hiding them, and one day I'll be leaving County Wexford, be going off to Dublin or London."

Hunter braced an arm atop the high arch of the thorough-bred's neck and grinned, knowing that all the girls of the village vowed the same thing at one time or another. In a serious voice he asked, "And what do you think you'll be finding there, Tamasin?"

"Happiness," she declared without a second of hesitation, pronouncing the word with the same pretension as a lady entertaining in a drawing room. "I want to be happy. And I've decided I *shall* be, even if I have to be doing Master Avery's bidding half me life or more.''

A flicker of compassion touched Hunter's eyes at that, just before he grinned again in the slow affecting way of a man who possesses unconscious charm and a whimsical sense of humor. ''Have you ever heard the legend about *Tir-na-n-Og,* Tamasin? It's the favorite city of the fairies, land of eternal youth. 'Tis said you can buy happiness for only a penny there.''

On the brink of condemning him for falling to treat her ambition with proper respect, Tamasin paused. He was smiling. Critically, she measured the expression with a budding feminine ability to interpret a man's look. But Hunter Kinshella's smile was not one that mocked; it might even have been given in sympathy.

He reached out a hand rough from work and laid it atop her shoulder, speaking with sudden seriousness. ''I guess we're at opposite ends, then, Tamasin. Where you're content to do another man's bidding, I am not, and never will be. I'll be my own man soon, beholden to none, not bound to curry horses— or favor. I'll not be like the rest of these poor Irish fools, forced to break my back for the gentry and live half-starved. No.'' His voice lowered, and he no longer looked at her but out to the fields, his eyes as hard as agate. ''I'd rather die first.''

Tamasin shivered, and it occurred to her in a flash of insight that Hunter Kinshella possessed something Father Dinsmore said everyone should seek to have regardless of their faith or station in life. She had not pondered it much before, but the word integrity came to mind.

''Are you going away then, Hunter?'' she asked with disappointment, liking the pressure of his fingers against the ridge of her collarbone. ''Something tells me that you are.''

''Then something must be telling you wrong, Tamasin,'' he said with a sudden change of mood, a lighter attitude, as he gave her hair a teasing tug. With his eyes strangely soft, he stared out across the rough green landscape with its dark peat stacks and huddles of wooly white sheep, a landscape mystically overlaid with timeless legends. "Ireland is where I belong. I would only be existing anywhere else. Life is here. My soul is here."

At his words a curious chill of forebodement chased down Tamasin's neck for the second time, but before she could speak of it, Hunter's younger brother hallooed to them from the lane.

Hot-blooded, always brawling and guzzling ale with the men, Brendan Kinshella was what disapproving matrons called a 'bad un.' According to rumor, the young man with the swaggering loose-jointed frame and shaggy golden hair had already got a lass with child. The general opinion of the villagers was that he would come to a violent end one day, despite the fierce and ready defense of his more levelheaded—if occasionally hot-tempered—older sibling.

Tamasin liked Brendan, though, for he did the most audacious things, like putting a lace cap on his head and mimicking old Mrs. McDeary. At his ridiculous antics she often thought her sides would split with laughter.

"Halloo!" Brendan called again, waving and vaulting over the hedgerow in one gangly bound. "Are you idling away the mornin' with Miss Cullen, then, Hunter? A shame it is, if you've already stolen her heart, for I had her marked for meself in a year or two."

"I'd not be surprised," the brother returned, imperturbed by the raillery. Gathering the reins of the sleek-coated chestnut, he swung a leg over its saddle and added drily, "A dandy pair the two of you'd make. One always finding trouble and the other—" he curved a lip at Tamasin, "always looking for it."

Tamasin averted her eyes in pique at the insult while Brendan jumped up behind Hunter to catch a ride, nearly pulling his brother off the polished saddle in the process.

"Go easy," Hunter admonished, ignoring his sibling's playful jabs while he regained his balance. "The stallion's recovering from a bruised fetlock. I don't want him taxed."

Even as he spoke, a magenta-coated rider detached from the

huntsmen on the hill and cantered toward them upon his steaming mount.

As he approached, Tamasin observed him minutely, part in
worship, part in fear. Straightening, she slipped the handkerchief back into the safe depths of her pocket with a furtiveness
that had become second nature.

Avery Hampton spurred his heaving horse forward. It leapt
into their midst with a flurry of iron-shod hooves. Foam dripped
off its snaffle and lather gathered beneath its mane and trickled
down the dappled gray shoulder. The young rider, no older
than Hunter, wore a cockaded hat, curled wig, and milk white
scarf tied in meticulous folds about his neck. The cut of his
clothes and the silver buttons at the knees of his breeches
suggested no expense had been spared on fashion. He had
perfected the half-lidded stare that a young gentleman always
reserved for Catholic peasants.

"You there!" he said, addressing Hunter and his brother
with the pointed tip of his riding crop, flaunting his authority.
"Get down from that horse and give him to me. Mine is spent."

Hunter gave him a steady look. "This stallion has a bruise
and cannot be ridden hard. I was just taking him back to the
stable."

Avery never suffered the disobedience of those who worked
for his father; he considered their status barely above that of
the exhausted beast he sat astride. Jabbing spurs into its blood-
flecked sides again, he guided it so close to Hunter's horse that
the gray laid back its ears and nipped at the other stallion.

"*Get down*, Kinshella," Avery repeated through his teeth in
a way no less vicious than his steed. "I order you to dismount."

"We'll be gettin' down when we damned well please!"
Brendan cut in with a sneer.

Infuriated, Avery leaned close and snapped, "Then perhaps
I'll have to knock your lowborn ass off the saddle then." Before
anyone could react, he raised his crop and brought it forcefully
down atop Brendan's head.

In a flash Hunter hurled himself toward the gentleman, unbalancing him so that both young men jolted to the turf in a tangle of limbs. Hunter emerged straddling the baronet's son and, hauling back a fist, plunged it deep into the soft belly of his adversary. The weaker man could do no more than deliver an ineffectual cuff to Hunter's lip.

Although accustomed to seeing spirited brawls among the townsmen, especially outside the alehouses on Saturday nights, Tamasin stood transfixed. The sight of a mere groomsman seizing the fine, London-made coat of one of Wexford country's most auspicious heirs, then delivering another blow so forceful that Avery's breath left him in a mighty *whoosh,* appalled her beyond speech.

For once, Brendan kept out of the fisticuffs, remaining in the saddle while encouraging his brother to greater acts of violence.

When Hunter had done his work and straightened, his frieze coat hanging off one shoulder and blood trickling from his lip, he leaned to snatch his cap from the ground. Looking with contempt at the slumped and groaning form of Avery Hampton, he said, "Now you know that a highborn ass hits the ground just as hard as one lowborn—maybe harder when it's fed on boxes of French bonbons."

Avery raised his head and stared with malevolence at the man who had beaten him. "I'll have you flogged from this village like a cur, Hunter Kinshella! You'll go begging on the road before I'm done with you!"

Hunter did not grace the threat with a reply, but merely set his jaw, mounted behind Brendan, and turned his green eyes in Tamasin's direction. "Mind what I told you, Tamasin," he said.

At the sound of the thoroughbred's retreating hooves, the girl shifted her feet and looked with unease at the gentleman who was just managing to push himself up on all fours. His immaculate coat was soiled, its gold lace torn from the lapel, and his disheveled wig sat atop his head like a dislodged bird's nest. She saw that his pate was shaved bald beneath it, and almost giggled.

"Go and get my horse," he ordered thickly, sitting on his heels and holding his battered middle.

Obediently Tamasin hastened to retrieve the gray beast who stood a few yards away cropping grass.

Staggering to his feet, Avery snatched the reins from her, his lip curling with wrath. He resented the fact that she had witnessed his humiliation, and his hands in their grass-stained gloves trembled with a need to retaliate against Hunter Kinshella.

"I have something else for you to do today," he growled, clamping his teeth together in order to control his voice. Jerkily, as if he could not do it fast enough, he reached to remove the ruby stickpin from his neckerchief. The large red gemstone winked with sunlight. Fumbling at his waistband for the silver pocket watch tucked inside its pouch, he drew it out. Then, to Tamasin's astonishment, he seized her hands and slapped both of the precious possessions against them.

"Put the stickpin in Hunter Kinshella's belongings and the watch in his brother's," he commanded. "Do it today, discreetly—without their knowing it."

She stared at him, at the twitching corner of his right eye and at the pulsing vein in the center of his forehead. Suspicion assailed her, and for the first time, the niggling voice of her conscience made her hesitate to follow Avery's orders.

Avery raised his chin and sighed as if pained, then shifted his feet and began to tap his riding crop against the top of his boot. Staring up at the sky, he spoke with feigned contrition. "You'll obviously not be satisfied until I apologize for my actions toward your friends. Very well. It was wrong of me to strike young Brendan as I did—it was below the dignity of a gentleman. These gifts will make it up to them. I would deliver them myself, except that my regret does not run so deeply as to prompt a personal delivery of anything to my father's stable."

He finished with an airy wave of his gloved hand. "I'm certain you can manage it for me."

Still unsure of his sincerity, Tamasin examined the shiny treasures resting in her palm, then shifted her gaze to the silk scarf knotted round his neck. Lastly, she raised her eyes to judge the expression of her superior; his face was hard with impatience, his head cocked in an attitude of unmistakable disdain.

"Oh, for God's sake," he growled suddenly, furious that she hesitated. He yanked the scarf from his throat and thrust it at her chest. "What a bloody little prostitute you are."

Beyond its derogatory implication, Tamasin did not know precisely what the word meant. But as she grasped the silk scarf and felt its texture against her small rough fingers, she ceased to care whether or not she had been insulted.

"It's mine to keep . . . ?" she breathed in wonder. "If only I put the pin and the watch in the brothers' belongings—nothing more . . . ?"

"Aye," he said through tight lips. "As long as you do it without anyone knowing." Collecting the reins of his horse, Avery mounted with an awkward lunge. "I'll be waiting at the end of the park. When you've done it, come and tell me."

Tamasin watched as he retreated, but the scarf in her hands quickly claimed her full attention. For several rapturous moments she stood threading its silky length through the spaces between her fingers.

She had learned to be quick in her accomplishment of the various escapades that the bored and often vindictive Avery Hampton masterminded. Within the space of an hour, she had invaded the tiny garret situated above the stable of the lodge, cleverly inserted the watch and stickpin in the pockets of the extra set of work clothes hanging on wooden pegs, and crept out to meet the impatient young gentleman in the park of his estate.

"I've done it!"

"Good lass!" Avery said with a smile. Leaving her without

another word, he sprinted down the pathway to the great house. Tamasin stood rooted in place. She felt uncertain and oddly afraid, and toyed with a half-formed notion of finding Hunter and confessing her sly deed.

Finally, still undecided, she turned and ran back toward the lodge where he worked, hoping for a divine revelation of moral direction along the way.

The gabled structure built for the dual purposes of hosting the pleasures of the baronet and housing his prized thorough-breds lay quite a distance over the fields, and by the time Tamasin arrived at its drive, her legs were flagging and her face flushed. Darting through the hawthorns to avoid the gardener stooping in the rose beds, she circumvented the timbered lodge and sprinted round to the cobbled stable. In the paddock a few horses lifted their heads curiously. Nearby an old man whitewashed a fence. Skirting the perimeter of the stable, Tamasin searched for Hunter to no avail. Then, hearing an echo in the glen, she scurried off in that direction, rewarded at last with a glimpse of the tall young man.

He labored hard, building a high stone wall to enclose land which once had provided a meager living for a tenant family; now it would contain the baronet's cattle. Shirtless, with the sun spreading its bronze light over his shoulders and the wedges on either side of his spine, Hunter hefted a stone. With muscles straining, he hoisted it to a height level with his chest. Sweat put a lustre upon his flesh, dampened his black hair so that it clung to the back of his neck in short snaking tendrils. As he bent again, Tamasin heard his deep intakes of breath. With rugged hands he lifted another stone and set it straight. Mud crusted his boots, grass stained the knees of his breeches, and wisps of hay stuck to the moisture on his forearms. As Hunter worked, he sang an old tune, deeply and privately, in the poetic words of the Gael that the English called a barbaric tongue.

Squatting behind a rowan bush, Tamasin watched him for a spell, her interest seized and held captive all at once. It struck her suddenly that the vital young body of Hunter Kinshella was a thing of coarse but excruciating beauty. Somehow, he shared an affinity with the fine spring day, shared a constancy with the fertile smells and quickening branches, with the earth which gave her own naked feet an enduring home. He was a part of Ireland, she thought. No. *Hunter Kinshella was Ireland.*

Something fluttered inside her, a burgeoning that made her ache with the familiar hunger to touch, hold the thing whose beauty she admired, as if through holding it, she could absorb into her own body the seed of its essence. And as if to find an ease to the ache, she stroked the scarf knotted at her throat. But the ache did not diminish.

She stood up, knowing all at once that she must speak to Hunter about what she had done, vow never to behave so wickedly again. But before she could open her mouth to confess, the sound of galloping horses invaded the peaceful glen.

Tamasin would never forget the vision of it. A half dozen mounted men circled Hunter like hungry wolves on the scent. He paused, a stone in his hands, the soil of Ireland smeared across his chest, his face ruddy with sunshine and happiness.

Avery Hampton drew his horse up with a jerk of the reins, followed by the local magistrate and three soldiers wearing uniforms of the Irish militia. One of the soldiers stayed mounted, leading a horse ridden by Hunter's brother; Brendan sat atop the saddle with his hands manacled.

"Hunter Kinshella!" the bewigged magistrate called in an ominous tone. He dismounted and strode toward the young man who stood with his feet planted at the half-finished wall. "Come forward!"

After Hunter took a few steps forward, the magistrate continued. "You and your brother have been charged with thievery. Not a quarter hour ago my men found Master Avery's stickpin and watch in your belongings at the lodge. And thirty guineas besides. What do you have to say for yourself?"

Hunter clenched the stone in his hand as if to use it as a weapon, but after a moment of consideration, let it fall to the ground.

All at once Tamasin thought he looked young and vulnerable as he faced the representatives of the Irish law. But when he noticed his brother sitting battered atop the soldier's horse, his expression hardened, took on the fierce look of a man.

"The guineas are mine," he stated loudly, rebelliously.

Tamasin drew in a surprised breath. How had Hunter managed to get such a fortune? Thirty guineas were enough to buy him passage to any city in the world.

"The guineas are mine," he repeated, then added with a clear reckless disrespect, "As for Master Avery's stickpin and watch, I'd say they must have flown out of his jewel box and into my room on wings."

The soldiers snickered. Beside them, Avery stiffened. "Insolent bastard! No one here doubts that you are guilty of thievery. How fortunate you are that the magistrate has agreed to give you a choice in sentence."

Hunter stepped forward, his handsome young face instantly wary. "Sentence? I've not even been tried yet."

"Ah, but you have," Avery countered. "And we'll give you your choice of sentence, as I said. You shall have the option of either rotting in Kilmainham jail or taking the King's shilling."

As the dire choices were pronounced, two of the soldiers rushed forward with their pistols cocked, demanding that Hunter put out his hands to be fettered. When the young man only cursed them, they shoved the pistol at his temple, then seized his arms and hurled him against the wall.

In horror Tamasin watched from her hiding place while Hunter was manacled at gunpoint. The sight terrified her. She wanted to jump up and scream that she had been the culprit, admit that Hunter was innocent of any crime.

But Avery stayed her with a sharp, significant look. He reminded her without saying a word that she was a peasant girl; her speaking out against a baronet's son in defense of an Irish laborer would be an utter waste of words.

With a whimper, she hid her face in her treacherous hands

and listened as Hunter was carried off on the back of a soldier's steed.

Avery headed for the stable yard. Suddenly shaken out of her misery, Tamasin ran after him. Tugging at his sleeve, she demanded, ''What will happen to Hunter Kinshella?''

The young gentleman shrugged as if the matter were of no concern to him. ''Rather than rot in jail, I'm certain he will opt to take the King's shilling.''

''The King's shilling? What does that mean?''

''It means he'll be wearing a red coat and a cross belt for the rest of his life, doing the bidding of the Crown.''

''He'll be a soldier? But where will he be going?''

''To face the open end of a cannon, I should hope. That should strip the insolence from his peasant tongue. England is crying for fresh meat to replace her recruits dying from fever in the Indes. It looks as if Kinshella's carcass will provide it. At any rate, he and his brother will not be coming back here.''

''But he loves Ireland,'' she protested, as if it mattered to the baronet's son.

''Then Kinshella will miss it, will he not?'' Avery shrugged again. ''Ah, well, Ireland has plenty left just like him—more's the pity.''

Left standing alone, Tamasin lifted a hand to caress the white silk scarf noosed about her neck. ''A soldier . . . a soldier. Forgive me, Hunter . . .'' she whispered plaintively, her panic rising. ''I couldn't help meself, I swear I couldn't! I wanted the scarf, you see . . . felt I *had* to have it. Aye, I wanted it more than *anything*.

Chapter One

Tamasin strolled through the fair goers in her new skirt of green-and-cream-striped silk. Occasionally she executed a pirouette amidst the press, watching the skirt whirl about her legs in a flash of color that resembled the paper pinwheels sold at the toy maker's stall.

She loved the fair for its life, for its boisterous sounds and pungent smells. It amused her to see the children gallop between the flimsy tents made of quilts and wattle frames and beg for bits of peppermint. Amid the clamor, village women clustered in knots and tapped their bare feet to the fiddlers' melody, while their menfolk either drank spirits, bartered the price of a pony, or brawled good-naturedly over a feigned insult.

With a flounce of her skirts Tamasin passed the victuals tent where an old crone hawked spooleens, the local concoction of salt beef and cabbage boiled over an open fire and served in wooden bowls. Hungry families sat at makeshift tables and consumed the plain but nourishing fare washed down with whiskey, while, garbed in colorful rags, jugglers meandered through the bustle of young couples gathered to participate in the long dance. Some dancers were so inebriated they could scarcely perform the jiglike steps and had to be supported by their fellows, but their antics only increased the general hilarity.

Tamasin paused at a tent that sold whistles, popguns, and toy drums, and observed the merrymaking. Earlier in the day several cottier's lads had asked her to dance, some bowing and posturing as if she were a peer of the realm, but she knew they had only issued the invitation on a wager, having bet their fellows that they could win a turn with "Lady Tamasin" about the grounds.

Just to annoy the braggarts she had chosen the homeliest village oaf and danced with him while watching the others scowl and whisper, maligning her, no doubt, for putting on airs and thinking herself above them. She knew that any one of them would give a precious month's earnings to spend an hour behind a hedge in her company, kissing her mouth and fumbling clumsily at her skirts. But she did not intend to give herself to any of the coarse, cottage-bred louts; she had set her sights on higher prospects.

An elegant carriage with brass accouterments glided over the turf and halted near the huddle of stalls, where the postilion in his livery hastened to pull out the step and hand down a lady. Her pale tangerine gown slithered over the turf sumptuously; her dainty slippers, lace sleeves, and elaborate coiffure lent her the appearance of a porcelain figurine, while the gentleman who accompanied her in black velvet made a perfect foil.

Tamasin's fascinated eyes devoured every detail of their appearance, for the gentry and their mode of life still obsessed her in the aching way it had always done; they preoccupied her, inspired her to new and more grandiose dreams that begged to find fulfillment. She noted the precise angle of the lady's plumed hat, and the way she stepped through the peasant throng with the train of her skirt trailing carelessly over the muddy ground, suggesting her confidence that someone else would launder the stains. The couple purchased salted herring and delicately consumed it and, afterwards, the gentleman snatched a cheap trinket from a stall and pinned it to the lady's bodice.

"Tamasin! Yer mam's wantin' ye!"

Having been caught in a daydream, she tore her eyes away from the couple and frowned at the lad who tugged like a terrier at her sleeve.

"Yer mam's wantin' ye," he repeated, pointing over his shoulder.

She turned her eyes to the table where her mother sat with two of her neighbors. All three were dressed in rusty black skirts, their faces seamed from poor diet and their eyes squinty from the peat smoke that blackened their cottage walls. Indeed, Dora Cullen could scarcely see at all, so feeble had her vision grown these last few years.

With a sigh Tamasin obeyed the summons. "What are you wanting with me, Mam?" she asked.

"Ye didn't get over yesterday," came the accusing whine.

"I know. But Sir Harry had guests at the lodge and I was needed in the kitchens. And then . . ." She paused, remembering the honor that had befallen her, relating it proudly. "And then Miss Eushanie called me to Hampton Hall to bathe her spaniel. She doesn't trust anyone else to do it."

The truth was that no one else could be persuaded to touch the ill-tempered dog, who had buried its teeth in the hands of more than one faithful servant.

Tamasin's mother stared at her through cloudy eyes. "Bathe a dog? That's the queerest thing I've ever heard. And I'll wager that uppity Miss Eushanie didn't pay ye a penny for doin' her the service, did she?"

Tamasin lifted her chin and, significantly caressing the fine striped skirt, spoke in defense of Avery's younger sister. "She gave me *this.*"

Dora shook her head, reaching out with a finger to flick the delicate fabric stained with wine at the hem. "Another bit of frippery ye have no use fer. Pity ye won't sell it to the gombeen man and put the coin to good use.''

"It wouldn't fetch much," Tamasin argued stubbornly. "Besides, Da would only be spending what coin I gave you on drink."

"Och, Tamasin," her mother lamented. "Yer always findin' excuses. I don't know where ye come by yer high-hatted notions. None of the other village lasses fancy themselves so fine. They wouldn't want to be hobnobbin' with the gentry. The *gentry*. Huh! Despised lot of wastrels they all are, turnin' half of us out of our cottages in order to graze their cattle, leaving decent people to starve on the road."

Her two cronies nodded their capped heads in tandem and gave Tamasin censorious stares.

"Oh, Mam," she sighed, weary of hearing the constant complaints against the landowners, which, recently, were being echoed in every cottage and alehouse. "I'll be coming over to help you later. But now I've got to go to the lodge."

" 'Now I've got to go to the lodge,' " her mother mimicked, jabbing an elbow in her neighbor's ribs. "I've got to serve the master his tea."

Tamasin bit her lip against the sting of her mother's mockery. She labored daily at Sir Harry's hunting lodge, keeping it tidy and helping to serve the baronet and his guests whenever they happened to amble in from hunting or boating or watching cockfights. And when Miss Eushanie required her for a special chore, Tamasin ran to the Hall as if on wings, relishing the privilege of spending a few hours in such a grand, storybook place. Even though she was led through the back entrance and up the servants' stairs, she still caught glimpses of the drawing room and library, literal treasure chambers filled with looking glasses, leather-bound books, china figurines, vases, sculptures, and chandeliers. Miss Eushanie's bedchamber was no less magnificent than the rest, for Tamasin had seen it once when she had been permitted to carry up a ball gown pressed in the laundry.

She received a meager wage for her work, which was often erratically paid, but at least a frequent hearty meal came her way at the lodge. The work was hard, however, for Sir Harry deplored having servants afoot in his masculine retreat, and allowed only a valet, two footmen, and cook to work there during his residence, along with Tamasin, who served as housemaid. He seemed to have no care or understanding that such an establishment needed at least three times the staff.

After finishing at the lodge every day, Tamasin tramped dutifully over the fields to do the chores her mother could not manage at the cottage, and although she kept her carefully hoarded money to herself, she brought along a bit of food to supplement the insufficient diet her father provided. But still her mother whined and wheedled, finding fault with her as she had always done, and Tamasin yearned for the day when her savings would be great enough to allow her to leave the village. She had determined long ago that she would not stay and become like Mam and her cronies. She would not watch her own face grow dark and lined, grub in the soil until her back was bent, nor go half-starved in the winter like the others. Nor would she bear a dozen children for some heavy-handed cottier who spent his nights drinking at the alehouse. She was pretty—almost beautiful—and she would use her beauty. By dressing herself in fine clothes with the money she saved, and by learning the manners of the gentry, she could surely attract the notice of some wealthy young man who would cherish her. And love her, too. He would not strike her and curse her as Da did to Mam, and then grunt over her in the darkness with no more tenderness than an animal.

"I heard that Master Avery is comin' back home soon," her mother commented, and when Tamasin glanced up sharply, Dora added with a sly smile, "Did ye not know it, Daughter? I heard it from the gardener's son. He said the young swine is returnin' from his travels next week. What foreign place did ye say he went off to?"

"He went on a Grand Tour, Mam. And then he was to stay

with his kin in Italy. 'Tis common for sons of the gentry to travel the Continent. It makes them worldly."

"Does it now?" Dora intoned, raising her brows. "And does it make them less mean as well?" Her companions cackled at her disparaging wit.

Tamasin ignored them and thought of Avery, who had embarked upon his sojourn three years past. In the years just before his departure, his prank playing had decreased, but he had still maintained his compelling influence over her. Whenever he had invited his peers home from the university and engineered some trick against them, it was Tamasin he employed to aid him in the deed. He continued to reward her with tokens, usually some inconsequential item filched from his younger sister's wardrobe. Rarely did he give her money.

She dreamed of catching the notice of one of his friends, perhaps a bright student from Dublin or a landowner's son who would offer marriage—or even a position slightly less respectable, but still worthwhile. Mindful of her looks, she bathed her face in milk whenever she could siphon a small measure from Mam's meals, washed her hair in rainwater scented with wild marigolds, and pinkened her cheeks with crushed red roses. She knew that she had caught the interest of more than one of Avery's guests, but, much to her dismay, the young master had always discouraged their advances.

At the prospect of seeing Avery again, Tamasin experienced both fear and anticipation. It was as if a part of her—that part that always constricted in an odd way during Father Dinsmore's lectures—warned her that her association with the baronet's son would lead her down a road of trouble, or at the very least, a prickly path. After all, it had already caused a young man's exile . . .

Hastily, just as she had always done, Tamasin shoved the distressful thought away, for even after so many years, her sin against Hunter Kinshella harrowed her, grew more burdensome as she matured and realized the full significance of what she had done to the groomsman and his brother. Even when she

tried to excuse her deed as youthful folly, her conscience was
not much eased. So she simply did not allow herself to dwell
too often upon the fate of the unfortunate pair.

Nevertheless, sometimes at night, curled upon her pallet, she
could not stop the vivid nightmares of a young soldier outfitted
in a scarlet tunic, nor could she stop envisioning a pair of
handsome eyes with the soft green of Ireland mirrored in them.
*"Ireland is where I belong. I would only be existing anywhere
else. Life is here. My soul is here."* Tamasin had not forgotten
a word of what the groomsman had said on the day of his
forced exile.

"Tamasin!"

She turned to see a trio of village girls idling at the adjacent
stall, eating salted herring, wiping the oil from their lips with
the backs of their wrists.

The leader of the three stepped forward, tossed her head,
and with a soiled hand reached down to fondle the folds of
Tamasin's skirt. "What a fine new gown you're wearin' today,
Your Ladyship," she mocked with exaggerated words, curtsey-
ing deeply. "Will you be going to a ball tonight? Mayhap
you'll put on your gold crown and grace us with a visit."

Laughing, she circled Tamasin with mincing steps that mimicked the motions of a lady. "Will you be dancin' with a
handsome duke tonight? Come on, tell us! They say that you're
grander than a queen. And," she slanted her eyes at her companions, anticipating their appreciation, "the boys say you're purer
than the Virgin, too!"

Despite the warning in Tamasin's violet eyes, Noreen sidled
even closer, attracting the attention of the young couples who,
having just concluded their dance, were alert to entertainment
in any form. They all knew that the spirited Tamasin Cullen
was not one to passively suffer any insult.

She gave her adversary a threatening glare as the heavy
butcher's daughter snaked out a hand to clutch the sash of the
striped shirt. When Noreen pulled the end of it, Tamasin shoved

her shoulder with such force that the girl lost her balance and nearly toppled over.

"Go after her, Tamasin!" one of the young men urged, admiring the blazing eyes of the cottier's lass. "Don't be takin' her guff!"

The onlookers were quick to choose sides. Most of the boys aligned with Tamasin, but the females, envious of the arrogant cottier's daughter, sided with her opponent.

"Knock her backside in the muck, Noreen!" one yelled shrilly. "That'll teach her to raise her nose at us!"

Encouraged, the stout village lass faced off with Tamasin, who stood with her slender fists balled in challenge. She had watched the men brawl often enough, and with her talent for imitating behavior, affected such a menacing fighting stance that the lads whistled in appreciation.

Noreen flew at Tamasin, who nimbly stepped aside to elude the first attack, but did not escape a second, for when Noreen lunged, the weight of the butcher's daughter unbalanced the slighter girl so that she fell with a jolt to the ground. Yet Tamasin clutched her adversary's ankle on the way down, and when she yanked, Noreen joined her on the turf in a flurry of yellow petticoats.

Tamasin squirmed from beneath her attacker, who seized her long black hair and yanked it spitefully from its knot. Grimacing in pain, the cottier's daughter managed to deliver a jab to Noreen's ribs before rolling quickly to the side. Then, lunging forward, she straddled the butcher's girl and pinned her arms to the ground.

Noreen squealed like a fettered pig and struggled to free herself, but Tamasin leaned far forward on the girl's bucking body and pressed her flailing wrists against the turf.

The spectators cheered and laughed uproariously, shouting taunts at Noreen while declaring Tamasin the victor. One boy tossed a wreath of posies atop her head and shouted, "You're a fighter, Tamasin Cullen! I'd like to go a' you meself!"

"God in heaven!"

The bellowing voice caused everyone in the crowd to freeze. With guilty glances, each watched as an old, lion-maned priest stumped up the hill like a vengeful angel, his papery-skinned face flushed with anger and his sandaled feet slapping against the ground in a furious rhythm. No one relished the lash of his merciless tongue, and in a skittish flock, his sheep scurried away through the rows of stalls, leaving Tamasin and Noreen to endure the brunt of his fury.

"Shame on ye all!" the newcomer called after them, waving his black-sleeved arms in the manner of an irate crow. " 'Tis bad enough that the men brawl like brutes, but to see lasses at it now is a pure disgrace!"

With the ends of his black frock flapping, Father Dinsmore hobbled forward through the quickly dispersing press and frowned at the two young women still grappling with each other upon the ground. The old man carried a crooked staff in his hand and, with all the aplomb of Moses, stabbed the earth so hard the tip disappeared. "Get up the two of ye! Ye'll be confessin' for hours tomorrow or I'll know the reason why! Rolling about in the dirt like mad cats. I've never seen the likes of it before. Noreen Fitzdenning, get along home with ye! And Tamasin Cullen—"

He leaned down to grasp her arm and yank her up from the grunting butcher's daughter, who hastily shoved down her skirts and scampered off without daring to meet the priest's fiery eyes.

"Tamasin Cullen," he repeated, glowering at her while, with great care, she brushed soil from the precious striped skirt, "I never expected such a spectacle from ye. What in the name of heaven were ye doing?"

Beneath the fierceness of his gaze, Tamasin's eyes lowered. But her chin remained high in ill-concealed defiance, and with innocence, she answered, "I was protecting my dignity, Father. After all, 'tis what you're always telling us to do."

"Bah! Ye were protecting yer pride, more like," he retorted.

"There's a difference, a very big difference, and 'tis time ye learned to distinguish between the two."

Her shawl had fallen in the scuffle and he stooped to retrieve it, examining its fine green and cream weave with a suspicious frown before returning his scrutiny to her face. "What were ye fighting about?"

"Noreen provoked it." Tamasin raised her chin a notch higher. "She was suffering from the sin of envy."

"Was she, now?"

"Aye. And the sin of blasphemy, too."

Father Dinsmore snorted. "In another minute ye'll have me believing that Noreen was fighting by herself. Come along with ye."

They passed a huddle of laborers who were swilling poteen and gambling so intently that they failed to notice the priest's approach. Limping forward, he went to stand in their midst, his black sandals nearly trodding upon the dice. It was a fearsome stare he gave them; his right eye protruded more than the other and the brow above it arched higher than its mate, giving him the look of a medieval gargoyle.

Flustered, the men abandoned their dice and skulked off like beaten hounds to join their wives.

"They've barely enough to eat, and still they wager," the priest grumbled. "And tonight they'll be takin' oaths to join the secret society of rebels."

Tamasin looked at him.

"Aye, there are uprisings all over the county, lass. And mark my words, their rebelling 'twill come to naught but bloodshed and a terrible waste of life. These mullet-headed peasants think they can fight the aristocrats and the whole English army with nothing but pikes in their fists and high-sounding words. Bah!"

Having no desire to hear more talk of politics, Tamasin made no reply. After a moment of silence the priest said, "Master Avery is coming home."

"Aye. I can scarce wait to see him again."

"Ah, Tamasin Cullen. Ye are a bold and naughty lass." The

priest sighed and pointed to the soft hillside where farmers paraded bobtailed horses for potential buyers. His voice changed from an ireful tone to the softer one he saved when offering grandfatherly advice. "Do ye see the ponies—yonder, Tamasin?"

"Aye," she said with reluctance, wondering what moral point would follow.

"Well, God in His wisdom created those ponies to work. Aye, indeed. 'Tis the only thing they're suited to do, and they do it well if they put their minds to it. Across from the ponies are the thoroughbreds. There—" He pointed, prompting her to look. "God in Heaven designed the thoroughbreds to do nothing but run fast enough to win wagers for all the misguided fools who bet money upon them. Sleek and elegant they are, I'll grant ye that, but bred for man's vanity. Do ye know what I'm getting at, girl?"

She knew very well, but stubbornly refused to answer.

Father Dinsmore regarded the rich, raven hair trailing down the girl's back, and shook his grizzled head. "The ponies are not meant to run in races, Tamasin. And the thoroughbreds are not fit to work. Do ye understand what I'm saying to ye?"

"Aye, Father. I understand."

"But are ye paying heed?" he persisted fractiously. "Must I say it outright? Mastery Avery will be coming back to the Hall any day now. Ye must keep yerself away from him. No good can come of your association with a baronet's son."

"Father! Father Dinsmore!" A small lad trotted toward the priest. "Mrs. McDeary needs ye! Quick! She thinks her time has come."

"Again?" the priest muttered, irritated that his lecture had been interrupted. "Not a day goes by that the woman doesn't believe she's dying. Ah, well." He turned back to Tamasin and wagged a finger at her nose. "Ye'll remember what I told ye?"

Tamasin forced a smile and was careful to promise nothing. "I'll remember.

"That's a good lass." He put a hand on her shoulder, and after bidding farewell, limped off to do his duty elsewhere.

Free at last, Tamasin lifted her skirts and ran with abandon down the green brae past the horses, past the pens of sheep for sale. The turf beneath her feet was as soft as velvet and as colorful as Isolde's robe, the air heavy with mist, but clean-smelling, inviting her to breathe deeply of it before slowing her pace to hum a lively Gaelic tune. All at once, the steep, elegantly pointed gables of the hunting lodge appeared above their circle of protective hawthorns. How welcome was the sight after the view of thatched cabins, wattle-frame stalls, and overworked fields!

She began to run faster, dashing through the spiny gorse and whirling around so that her skirt belled around her knees. Snatching up a handful of the yellow blooms, she tucked them in her hair and laughed with nothing more than the simple pleasure of being alive.

Although she had been given the whole afternoon off to enjoy the fair, she yearned to return to the lodge. It was not nearly as grand as the Hall, of course, but contained many fine objects which Tamasin handled with reverence whenever she applied her feather duster. They were mostly masculine things—shields and swords, ancient mail, antlers and fox brushes mounted as trophies—but she loved them almost as well as she did the fragile, gem-colored china and porcelain at the Hall.

An open landau was just turning onto the lodge drive, and recognizing Sir Harry's coat of arms emblazoned on the door, Tamasin shielded her eyes against the sun to examine it. Her face brightened with a smile, for sitting beside the baronet was the great brown bear he had bought from a London circus last month, a beast he occasionally allowed to take a turn with him around the estate. His eccentricity outraged his aristocratic neighbors, and the peasants condemned him for his excesses—even called him mad—but Tamasin defended him, arguing that his sense of humor was endearing.

Two other carriages trundled along in his wake and, speculating that they were filled with guests who, for several days at least, would drink and gamble and hunt with their host, she hastened on, knowing that every pair of hands would be needed in the kitchen.

As she rounded the back of the house and cut through the herb garden, she saw old Seamus Kinshella leading a thoroughbred out of the paddock. Although nearly eighty years of age, Hunter Kinshella's grandfather still trained Sir Harry's prized racehorses. Each time Tamasin saw him she yearned to ask if he received letters from Brendan and his brother, to ask if he knew how they fared and in what country they were stationed. But she never did, fearing that their circumstances would be worse than her grim imaginings.

A few hours later, after Sir Harry and his guests had been served an excellent if hastily contrived meal, and lounged in the drawing room sipping claret, Tamasin readied the bedchambers. From the stair landing she paused with a clean bundle of linen in her arms, observing the gathering of gentry, whose waistcoats were now half-unbuttoned over paunches well filled with beef and bread pudding. Some guests already lay sprawled and snoring on the sofas, while six nervous greyhounds nosed about hunting for bones tossed on the rug during dinner. In the midst of the mess, discarded newspapers lay crumpled beside overturned chairs whose damask upholstery was stained with squashed chocolate bonbons. Spilled wine shimmered in pink pools on the sideboard, where a red Chinese vase lay shattered from a rowdy game of billiards.

Standing in the midst of the lounging, pie-eyed company, Sir Harry attempted to sing, while one of his equally inebriated peers tried to play a fiddle.

Tamasin marveled that Sir Harry and his peers seemed oblivious to the dark political undercurrents swirling all around them like a gathering menace, and, shaking her head at their innocent hilarity, went to fluff their pillows.

When evening approached and the afternoon light grew dim

from the clouds that had unfurled themselves across the sky,
Tamasin and Sir Harry's valet moved silently amongst the
dozing guests and the debris of the gentry's merrymaking. They
snuffed the sputtering wax candles and replaced them with new
ones while Sir Harry snored in a chair, still clutching a wine
goblet. The valet gingerly slid the cup from between his fingers
before laying a rug across his velvet-covered knees. Earlier
the baronet had kicked off his shoes, and his stockinged toes
protruded from the cover like two overturned sauceboats, while
scanty hair stuck up from his pink scalp to give him the look
of a disheveled infant.

Tamasin surmised that, like a child, the baronet could not
have cared for himself alone; he depended upon those who
served him, and, if asked, would likely admit his dependence
with unashamed arrogance.

Arching her back against its ache, Tamasin sighed and picked
up a discarded wig festooned with paste curls, which she
perched atop the back of a chair, well out of the way of the
roving greyhounds who would make sport with it. The thought
of trudging across the soggy fields to the cottage oppressed her
and, procrastinating, she made one last trip upstairs to assure
herself that the windows were shut against the storm.

Finding one open, she stood for a moment breathing in the
air.

Below, pearly rain drifted in a fine-spun mist, veiling the
landscape, giving it the blurred look of a wet canvas dabbed
with diluted emerald tempera. Evening had not yet descended,
but heralded its approach by washing lavender blue over the
Irish green, whose vividness was dimmed only by the storm.

All was still except for the rain that dripped off the eaves
and ran in silver rivulets over the flower beds. Even a stable
cat sat on the dry stoop as motionless as a statue on a plinth.
Only a pair of horseman who traveled down the lane interrupted
the tranquility of the scene, and Tamasin observed them idly,
her interest roused when they guided their mounts down the
drive. Both were plainly dressed in surtouts and breeches, and

both wore black bicorne hats pulled low to shield their faces
from the drizzle. As if impatient, one of the men spurred his
horse forward and in a reckless canter rounded the house to
the stable yard. Even before his mount's hooves had ceased
slithering upon the cobbles, he dismounted and tossed the reins
over a post. Then, resting his hands upon his slender hips, the
golden-haired man stood surveying the grounds with a puckish
grin that slowly split, broadened, and brightened his face in a
peculiarly radiant way.

Something in his pose pricked Tamasin's memory like a
dart; she stiffened and raised an unsteady hand to her throat.
"Sainted Mary," she breathed, "I must be dreaming . . ."

In disbelief, she watched the newcomer as he left his steaming
horse and sauntered toward the stable with his riding crop in
hand, then bounded up the narrow outside stairs to the garret
room he and his brother had once shared with old Seamus.

When he disappeared through the portal, Tamasin glanced
back at the drive, pressed her cheek flat to the windowpane
in order to see the second rider, who did not enter the yard
precipitously as his brother had done, but kept his mount's
pace checked with a firm hand on the reins.

Beneath the dripping surtout his shoulders were squared
smartly, and his legs, encased in top boots and tan breeches,
were bent in the formal posture of a correctly schooled and
seasoned rider. The straightness of his bearing suggested not
only a self-possession lacking in his companion, but a soberness, almost an unnatural rigidity of bearing. Not an ounce of
his brother's carefree airiness marked his attitude or expression.
He sat grimly astride the saddle, and after halting the horse,
stayed mounted, staring through the downpour at the emerald
fields spreading beyond the stables to meet the river like a
velvet carpet unrolled for a long-awaited guest.

With a sudden painful insight, Tamasin knew that he was
remembering all the years he had spent away from the place
he loved. He was remembering all the years she had caused
him to lose after his banishment from home.

Shutting her eyes, Tamasin breathed deeply, raggedly, not only with guilt, but with a kind of uneasy fear.

Several seconds passed, and unable to help herself, Tamasin opened her eyes again, looked down, and saw Hunter Kinshella swing his leg over the saddle to dismount. The movement, though graceful, seemed almost brittle. She had not yet been able to get a good view of his face, but as he moved to stand at the head of his horse, she saw his profile clearly. The sight of it caused her to bite down on her lip in sharp, breathless reaction.

Hunter Kinshella's visage, strong of line, bore the rough strength of his Celtic ancestors, and the fine arched Norman nose completed the picture of proud manhood. But, still, it was a profile changed from the one Tamasin remembered. Every last trace of its boyishness had been erased by the hardness of the lost years. No smile hovered at the corners of Hunter's mouth, no insolence tilted his head, and no humor flashed in his keen, long-lashed eyes, which had once watched for the mail coach at Three Rocks.

Trembling, Tamasin clutched the windowsill and felt her heart twist as she observed the man she had so terribly wronged. She wanted to look away from him, but could not; so she simply watched, stared, pressed her hot face more closely against the windowpane while her stomach churned. And while she stared, he did an extraordinary thing.

With his gaze still fastened upon the fields, Hunter Kinshella removed his hat and, tucking it beneath one arm, stood in the manner of a soldier at attention. He held his chin high while water trickled off his brow, dripped down to the point of his jaw, and splatted from the bottom of his surtout to his boots. Even when the horse nudged his hand, which was clenched in a fist against his thigh, Hunter paid no heed. His eyes scarcely blinked against the rain as he continued to stare at the landscape of Ireland, and Tamasin knew that in his own way, wordlessly and with eloquence, he paid homage to his birthplace.

Ashamed to witness his private homecoming, she turned her

head away, even while tears—not the first she had shed for him—gathered on her lashes. Lifting a hand to dash them away, she experienced a compulsion to shift her eyes again to the man standing on the flooded drive, and saw him mouth a few words to himself—or to Ireland—in such a way that suggested the voicing of a vow.

Suddenly, as if sensing her presence, Kinshella jerked his head up and with unerring direction found her face framed in the casement window.

Tamasin's breath caught in her throat, and she could neither smile nor move her hand in greeting. In that instant something passed between Hunter Kinshella's eyes and hers, a flicker of the past, a flicker of the present, and of the future, a realization that destiny had not yet finished with the intertwining of their lives.

And something else shone clear in the cold green eyes of the man whose life Tamasin's greed had altered: the knowledge that she had been the one to help banish him from Ireland.

She forgot to shut the window in her haste to turn around and flee the lodge. Down the curving stairs she tripped, breathing hard while she stumbled through the sprawled forms of drunken gentlemen and dozing greyhounds. Dashing out into the downpour, she did not even bother to grab a shawl to cover her head.

She didn't stop running until she had reached her parents' cottage. Slamming the flimsy door, she crossed herself and muttered a prayer for God's protection.

"He's home," she whispered through stiffened lips, putting her arms around her waist and closing her eyes, rocking slightly on her heels. *"Hunter Kinshella's come home."*

Chapter Two

The next morning, for the first time, Tamasin did not want to leave the prickly comfort of her pallet and go to Sir Harry's lodge. She lay with a quilt pulled to her nose and stared up at the bogwood rafters and the weeds that grew out of the thatched roof, and at the chinks of carmine light that shimmered through the handfuls of heath Da had used to plug the drafty holes. She hadn't slept a wink all night.

Her glimpse of Hunter Kinshella and the eerie spark of recognition that had flashed between them had frightened her. In the few seconds that he had stared at her face through the rain, his eyes had seemed to penetrate her brain and read the intricate workings of it.

She shuddered. Hunter was no longer the boy with whom she had grown up, but a wronged stranger whose anger she had a right to fear. She could scarcely believe he had returned, and wondered at the circumstances that had left him free to do so. Was he back to stay, or only on some term of leave from his regiment? Thoughts of him churned round and round in Tamasin's head until she grew frantic, and for a moment, she wished she could stay abed forever. Dawn arrived in its gold and copper glory, peering over the edge of the brae that arched like a cat's spine in the distance. She could see it through the window of the cottage when the breeze swayed the tattered curtain, and used its brilliant light to study her surroundings, which was part of her morning ritual. By examining the dreary place she reinforced her determination to leave it forever. How she loathed the crude mud walls overlaid with oily soot, the old, poorly made cupboard propped up on one side with a stone, the huge black kettle hanging empty, more often than not, over the moldering hearth. The one-room hovel was freezing in winter and stifling in summer.

After splashing water on her face, she arranged her hair in the loosely knotted style she had seen Miss Eushanie wear, then pulled the striped skirt out of an old trunk where she kept every item she had ever received from the Hall—the handkerchiefs, combs, hairpins, ribbons, and scarves that were her treasure trove. Hopefully she would be able to hoard enough objects to pawn someday, and thereby purchase her freedom from the crude cabin. The skirt was the greatest gift of all, of course. She stroked its weave, put it to her cheek, and relished the softness. She could not resist wearing it a few more times before it was carefully folded away between layers of lavender and stored for a future purpose.

While nibbling an oatcake, Tamasin threw more turf on the dying fire and wielded the bellows to stir up the embers, mindful of the fairies, who grew disgruntled if a fire went out. All cottiers kept their animals inside their cottages at night, and the pig rooted around her feet hoping a crumb would fall.

Da was still abed as usual, and Mam was carrying in a pail of water. After bidding her good day, Tamasin set out for the lodge, shivering as her feet tracked through the glaze of dew. She had been given a pair of shoes upon employment, but she always carried them by the laces until she arrived at the lodge, where she sat down behind a privet hedge and slipped them over a pair of woolen stockings. Economy had been bred into her nature, and good leather was not to be ill used. The shoes were precious to her and she kept them polished with lampblack and rotten eggs, a concoction that smelled vile, but kept them shiny.

She approached the lodge warily, staying close to the tall hawthorns while keeping an eye out for Hunter Kinshella, whose path she did not intend to cross. If he caught sight of her, he might curse her for her part in his exile, or even strike her down. Even if he said nothing at all, but remained cold and remote, she knew that confronting him would be like confronting her own guilt, and she was not in the habit of examining her conscience too closely.

As Tamasin crossed the smooth green park, Sir Harry's fox hounds began yapping, and she veered wide of their kennels toward the stable yard, suddenly freezing in her tracks when a tall man wearing corduroy breeches and a long trusty coat appeared beside the open double doors. In each hand Hunter Kinshella held a dandy brush, and with energetic strokes, began cleaning the hide of the nervous, long-legged black thoroughbred who was one of Sir Harry's champion racers. Tamasin drew in a breath, awed by Hunter's splendid looks.

Although soldierlike in efficiency, his movements were naturally easy, an indication that his body was conditioned to much activity. His black hair was cropped slightly above his collar. Tamasin noted that dried mud covered his top boots and wondered if he had taken an early morning walk along the riverbank he had so intently pondered the day before. When the horse stamped impatiently, he laid a hand upon its neck and soothed it with a few murmured words of Gaelic, the same low and musical words Tamasin had heard him speak in a green glen many years ago.

Fortunately his back was turned and Tamasin was able to dart through the servant's door, where, breathless and flushed, she rushed into the kitchen, nearly tripping over the dozen pairs of boots freshly blacked by the valet.

"You look as if you've been chased by a goblin, Tamasin,"

the cook remarked. "Your eyes are as big as saucers." Casting the girl a curious look, the old woman turned to stir her pan of bubbling custard.

The valet and footman were seated at the kitchen table eating breakfast, and at Tamasin's entry, looked up from their plates with unconcealed interest, always eager to ogle her figure or hear a tidbit of gossip.

She made an effort to compose herself, tying an apron around her waist and busily washing up the pans Cook had left beside the stone sink. Inhaling to steady her voice, Tamasin affected a conversational tone, wanting information, but cautious lest her inquiries sound too curious.

"Did you know that Hunter and Brendan Kinshella have come back?" she asked the servants over her shoulder. "You remember them, don't you, Loftus? They're Seamus's grandsons. I saw the two of them myself when they rode in last evening."

The footman grunted. "I hardly recognized them this morning. They've been gone a long while. Eight or nine years, isn't it?"

"Ten," Tamasin corrected automatically, knowing the precise number—down to the months and days—of Hunter's exile. " 'Tis strange. The brothers weren't wearing soldier uniforms. I wonder if they're no longer with His Majesty's Army."

" 'Tis not likely they're out of the military. When a fellow takes the King's shilling, he's bound for life."

"Have you spoken with them?"

Loftus took a bite of bread and scowled. "Nay. And I likely won't be havin' the leisure to talk with anyone as long as Sir Harry and his guests are here, will I? We could use another dozen pair of hands for all the work they make."

"At least none of them are out of bed yet," she commented, disappointed that the subject of the Kinshellas had been dismissed.

"Nay. But when the lazy bastards do manage to fall out of

their beds, they'll have sore heads as usual and be as ill-tempered as bears.''

"Speaking of bears,'' the valet said, "that poor animal that the master keeps as a pet is tethered in the malt house and howling like it's hungry. I've been given no orders to feed it. I wonder what it eats.''

"I roasted three beefsteaks for the creature last week when Sir Harry brought it over in the landau.'' Cook spoke through tightened lips. "Can you imagine such a waste?''

The footman, Loftus, wolfed the last of his breakfast and spat, "Mad old bugger. Feedin' beef to such an animal when there are cottiers half-starved and livin' in ditches right beneath his nose.''

" 'Tis said a house of servants up in Kildare murdered their master and mistress,'' Cook whispered, stirring her custard so energetically that the room grew redolent with vanilla. "Stabbed them in their beds.''

The footman rose from the table and shrugged into the livery coat adorned with silver braid. "Aye. And ye can be sure it won't be the last ye hear of deeds like that. There are plots all over Ireland to bring down the landowners.'' His voice lowered. "Thirty more tenants took the secret oath last night, and the blacksmiths are forging pikes and guns as fast as they can. We'll have a rebellion soon.''

His words chilled Tamasin. Wanting to hear no more of his dire predictions, she grabbed a pair of buckets and began lugging water from the well to the kitchen, pouring it into the huge kettles suspended from cranes over the blazing hearth fire. Each time she emerged from the door she glanced warily toward the stable, but saw nothing more threatening than the usual domestic scenes. Hunter Kinshella and his brother were nowhere in sight.

The sun broke through the clouds in warm saffron rays and she paused in her labors, setting down the buckets to roll her aching shoulders and admire the honeysuckle that twined like jade ribbons over the well. A fresh breeze spun the weather vane atop the stable roof and whipped Tamasin's skirts. Dismayed, she realized that water had sloshed over the sides of her buckets, wetting her shoes and the hem of the striped skirt.

"Do you need some help, miss?"

Startled by the sound of the voice, she whirled around.

Except for the natural maturing of his features over the last decade, Brendan Kinshella had scarcely changed. His hair was still thick and gold, the glint of devilment in his blue eyes undimmed, and the sensual charm that had been evident even in adolescence had intensified, enhanced by the dimples in his cheeks. Only the puffiness beneath his eyes and the slight rounding of flesh beneath his chin—both suggesting a fondness for food and drink—marred his youthful good looks.

For a moment Brendan's unexpected appearance rendered Tamasin speechless, and she glanced anxiously past his shoulder to assure herself that his older brother had not followed.

"Do you need some help with the buckets?" Brendan inquired again, grinning at her discomposure, assuming that his attractiveness was the cause of her confusion.

"N-no," she stammered, still staring. "I can manage, thank you." Her eyes scrutinized every feature of Brendan's face again. After she had completed her examination, she took comfort in the fact that he looked no worse for wear from his term in the military. Indeed, he appeared quite well.

"Good Lord!" he exclaimed all at once, putting a hand on her slender arm to stay her. "You look deuced familiar. 'Tis not young Tamasin Cullen, is it, turned into a goddess with sparkling eyes and rosy cheeks?"

She blushed beneath the praise, which, although nothing more than Irish blarney, flattered her more than the clumsy compliments of the village louts ever had. "Aye. I'm Tamasin Cullen—the same lass that you used to see running over the fields."

"Not wed yet, are you?"

She laughed. "Nay."

"Ah, that's to my good fortune." Brendan gave her a wink

and, snapping a sprig of honeysuckle from the vine, presented it to her with a courtly bow.

Unable to resist, she smiled while Brendan glanced around the yard to view the quaint timbered lodge, the malt house, the whitewashed dairy, the brewery, and the kennels where three dozen hounds whined to be let out. "The place hasn't changed much in the years I've been away, has it?" he remarked conversationally.

"Nay. Nothing at the lodge ever changes, not really." She hesitated, eager to know where he and Hunter had been, what hardships, if any, her greedy mischief had caused them to endure. Above all, she wanted to know how long they would be staying before the army called them back. "Are you and your brother on leave from your regiment?" she ventured.

Brendan laughed. "You might say that we're on permanent leave. We've been discharged from the army and are as free as birds."

"Really?" she said, her voice breathless.

"Aye. Thanks to my brother and his handy presence of mind, our discharge was even an honorable one."

Tamasin twirled the honeysuckle stem between her fingers and frowned. "But I thought when a man took the King's shilling, it meant he was enlisted for life."

"It does, unless you have friends in influential places—or in this case—one friend in one influential place." Brendan's tone was amused. "When you see him next, ask my brother about his daring act of heroism."

Tamasin did not admit that she planned to avoid Hunter Kinshella at all costs. But she was relieved by Brendan's hearty good looks; she was beginning to think that the brothers had not suffered at all during their years in the army. Brendan certainly seemed unscathed. Perhaps the pair had even appreciated the opportunity to travel and see the world at the expense of King George. Hoping to ease her conscience even further, she asked, "Did you enjoy your time in the army, Brendan?"

The young man squinted his eyes as if he could not quite

believe she had asked the question, then guffawed, and, leaning to pick up a pebble, dropped it down the well to listen for a splash. "No one *enjoys* marching about in a horsehair stock and goatskin pack, Tamasin. Not unless he's half-witted or mad. But I managed well enough. With plenty of drinking, gambling and—well, let's just say that there are diversions to be found in the army if one is so inclined. Of course . . . Hunter is a different breed than I."

"Different?"

"Aye. He's grown serious, intensely defiant upon principle. I, on the other hand, have no principles at all. I'm rarely serious about anything but cards, and defiant only when I'm drunk—which is admittedly half the time." Brendan shook his head, his eyes growing unfocused with some unpleasant memory. "No, things did not go so smoothly for Hunter in the army."

Tamasin gave Brendan a sharp glance. "What do you mean?"

The young man dropped another pebble in the well and waited until it had made its splatter. Then he shrugged, letting her know that the discussion of sober topics chafed his carefree nature. With a sour expression he asked, "Have you even heard of a tripod?"

She frowned, "Nay."

"Well, it's a structure about eight feet tall made of split rails. Every soldier hates to see it. Even one glimpse is enough to make a fellow's stomach turn."

"What is its purpose?"

Brendan smiled without humor. "Persuasion, you might say. When a soldier displeases his commanding officer, the whole regiment is paraded out, including the drummer—who's often required to perform the dubious honors. The soldier is stripped to the waist, and then tied by his wrists and ankles to the tripod."

"And then . . . ?" she asked in dread.

"He's disciplined, you might say. A leather thong is put in

his mouth to keep him from yelling." Running his slender fingers over the rusted well chain, the young man peered into the well. "Hunter spent more than a few times tied to the tripod. When that failed to achieve the desired results, they sentenced him to solitary confinement. For six months he stayed in a cell so small he couldn't stand up. He wasn't allowed to see or speak to a soul. And was scarcely fed."

Tamasin shook her head, confused and appalled. "I don't understand. What had he done to deserve such a punishment?"

Brendan straightened, dusting his breeches as if he had had enough of the conversation and intended to go in search of a livelier pastime. "He was insubordinate, you might say. But the army finally broke him down. They always do. They have their ways."

When Tamasin continued to stare at him in chagrin, Brendan smiled to erase the grimness from his expression. Snatching the mangled honeysuckle from her nervous fingers, he tucked it into the knot at the nape of her neck. "Gravity doesn't suit you, Miss Cullen. You're fashioned for dancing and good times. Perhaps you'll give me a dance or two soon, eh?"

"Sure, and I will," she said, still distracted by his story of Hunter.

"Good day to you then," he said, giving her a wink. "It was a pleasure seeing you again. And don't be giving your heart away to one of these local fools. I intend to win it for myself now that I'm back."

Tamasin scarcely heard him. She felt sickened. She could think of nothing but Hunter Kinshella, locked up in a dark cell for six months and treated like a beast. She wondered how he had displeased his superiors, then clearly recalled the echo of the groomsman's words, spoken long ago. *Where you're content to do another man's bidding, I am not. And never will be. I'd rather die first.*

With an automatic bend of the knees, Tamasin took up the rope handles of the bucket. How many times had she heard, deep in her heart, those same words, as if over the ten years of his absence, Hunter had repeated them across miles and continents, reminding her of her treachery? God in heaven. She must avoid meeting him again. There would be the devil to pay if he encountered her.

Before she had gotten halfway to the house, a clatter of hooves on the drive set the foxhounds to barking. Glancing up, Tamasin saw a white mare approach the paddock. Attired in a fashionable habit and low-crowned hat, Eushanie Hampton rode, holding the reins in one hand and a black-spotted spaniel in the other. A few paces behind, a liveried groom followed, looking harried, as if his mistress had led him on a merry chase. Catching sight of Tamasin, Eushanie called out, "Is my father up and about yet?"

"Aye, Miss, just this past hour."

Eushanie guided her mount closer, and Tamasin stepped back, studying Avery's sister. She was tall and plain, almost ugly, her jaw too heavy for the rest of her undersized features. Her eyes were the same flat coppery hue as Avery's, but her hair—her best attribute—was as fair in color as the corn tassels at harvest.

"Where can I find Papa?" she asked. "Is he out hunting already?"

"I saw Sir Harry strolling about the grounds a half hour ago, Miss," Tamasin answered.

Eushanie glanced around and, failing to locate her sire, pulled an embroidered handkerchief from her sleeve and dabbed at her brow. "Fetch me a cup of water, will you, Cullen?"

Scarcely able to tear her eyes from the huge gold plume fixed to the lady's hat, Tamasin drew up a fresh bucket of water from the well. Taking the dipper from the hook then, she filled it and offered it to the lady.

Eushanie made a moue of distaste. "Do you expect me to drink from *that? A glass,* if you please."

Mortified over her breach in manners, Tamasin hastened to the kitchen, and, a moment later, as she backed through the door with a brimming crystal goblet, heard a commotion in the yard.

Sir Harry, having removed his circus bear from the malt house, led it down the drive by a chain. The beast ambled along docilely enough, until one of the hounds from the kennel managed to squeeze through the fence and charge at it.

Rearing up on its haunches, the bear threw back its monstrous head and growled.

Eushanie had reined her mount around in order to bid her sire good morning, but as the horse got a whiff of the bear's scent and heard its roar, the mettlesome animal shied to one side with a violent jerk. The lady was thrown so off balance she almost toppled from the sidesaddle, but, frantically grasping the long mane, managed to regain her seat. However, the black and white spaniel she had been protectively clutching took advantage of the chaos to wiggle loose and escape.

In a yapping frenzy the little dog joined the escaped hound and, after circling the bear several times, made a beeline for the stables. In its scramble for cover, the resident cat created a fuzzy gray blur as it scurried through the open double doors.

"Oh! Get him! Go get him!" Eushanie shrieked, still attempting to settle her sidestepping horse. "Go after my dog!"

Tamasin ran to aid the lady, grabbing the bridle reins, but Eushanie shoved her hands aside and demanded that she give chase to the precious pet instead. "He'll be trampled by Papa's stupid thoroughbreds or get fleas from that cat!"

"You can rely on me, Miss," Tamasin said, already running. "I'll bring him back!"

She dashed into the stable after the spaniel, sprinting between the long rows of loose boxes. Tamasin could not see the spaniel, but heard its sharp barks and, following the direction of the noise, veered into the harness room. There, well-oiled saddles gleamed upon wooden trees; bridles hung beneath shelves of grooming tools and hoof picks; the smell of oats, saddle soap, neat's-foot oil and liniment combined to form a pleasant odor. As if someone had been interrupted in the midst of polishing,

a flannel cloth lay draped across the pommel of a saddle. The
lustre on the burnished walnut-colored leather was so beautiful
Tamasin was tempted to stop and stroke it with her fingers.

But the spaniel was snuffling about the dangling stirrups to
pick up the cat's scent. In vain Tamasin tried to snatch him by
the scruff, losing him when the clever feline leapt atop a tall
pile of oat sacks and began to parade back and forth tauntingly.
With a bark the spaniel renewed the pursuit, eluding Tamasin
when she attempted to seize him by the tail.

"Troublesome dog!"

Not to be entrenched with an enemy, the cat wriggled through
the narrow space between the wall and the oat sacks and,
prancing off with his tail held high, left the complaining spaniel
trapped behind.

The dog whined and scratched while Tamasin considered
the height of the mountainous stack of bags, which stood at
least a foot above her head. Lifting her skirts, she managed to
climb them, only to realize that her arms were not long enough
to grab the snarling dog in its corner. She sighed, and still in
her prone position, contemplated the situation. If she were to
remove the oat sacks one by one until the pile was low, she
could reach the dog, but each one surely weighed at least a
hundred pounds, too much for her to maneuver. In frustration,
she cursed the dog.

"Pudding!" Tamasin called, cajoling, wiggling her fingers in the hope that he would jump up and allow her to haul
him out by the collar. "Pudding! Come to me, lad. Jump.
Jump!"

He responded with a savage growl and, growing desperate,
Tamasin slid down further over the sacks. "Pudding . . ." she
wheedled, " 'tis time to go back to your mistress. Perhaps
she'll give you a bone if you're good. Come. Come, you'll not
deny my reward, will you?"

"Still doing favors for the gentry?"

Tamasin froze at the sound of the words. For several seconds
she lay still, draped over the sack, perspiration prickling beneath

her arms and her heart hammering. She wondered over the fact
that, even after the passage of so many years, it was still possible
to remember the tone of a voice so frighteningly well.

She licked her lips in dread, still motionless, wishing she
could slide down and join the dog in its corner. The hardness
of Hunter Kinshella's voice confirmed his knowledge of her
conspiracy to banish him from Ireland ten years ago. *He knew.*
She could not mistake his tone; there had been no amusement,
no friendliness in it, only contempt.

Sainted Mary. Frightened, acutely aware of the ignobility of
her position, Tamasin slid off the stack of oats slowly,
attempting to keep her skirt pushed over the old stockings that
were so patched they puckered in places about her calves. When
her feet touched the planked floor, she took a deep breath and,
knowing she could delay no longer, clenched her fists and
turned around to face her guilt, personified in the form of the
handsome groomsman.

Hunter Kinshella stood just inside the harness room. A brass
blade of light slanted through the window to silhouette his
form. It was a tall form, muscled, thin in a way that suggested
a kind of brittle toughness acquired through hard and continual
labor. Although he wore only the full-sleeved white shirt and
brown breeches of the workingman, his attire was neat and
clean, painfully so, and the boots that had earlier been soiled
with river mud now gleamed with such a high polish that
Tamasin fancied she could see her face reflected in them.

She took another breath, an unsteady one, for despite the
fact that Hunter's countenance was handsome, severely so, it
was a face that looked out upon the world with a sort of sardonic
gravity.

Without consciously realizing it, Tamasin took a step backward. Until now she had never met anyone who had intimidated
her in a way that made her physically afraid. Avery's wealth
and power had always awed her into submission; Father Dinsmore's Old Testament sternness subdued her now and then; but
she had never experienced the strike of respectful fear that she

experienced now in Hunter Kinshella's presence. Long ago, the boy Hunter had possessed a candor that, while brash at times, had at least been familiar and warm. The man standing before her now was wintry in every way.

And yet, inexplicably, his unsmiling mouth, his bleak and long-lashed eyes were so stirring to Tamasin's passionate senses, that her gaze was loath to let the image of them go.

She did not know what to say in answer to Hunter's question, and he did not attempt to relieve her awkwardness with any sociable remark. He merely awaited her reply in the same motionless stance that she had seen him hold yesterday on the drive.

"M-Miss Eushanie's dog . . ." she managed to stammer at last, pointing behind her to the stack of oats. "He's trapped in the corner there—behind the bags."

Hunter did not shift his gaze, but regarded her for another two or three seconds as if he were not finished with his examination and intended to prolong it until a point of satisfaction had been reached. When his eyes finally shifted from her face, he walked to the stack and, taking hold of the topmost bag, hefted it onto his shoulder.

Tamasin could see the muscles in his arms flex as he carried the sack a few paces away and, leaning over, let it slide down to the wooden floor. He repeated the process, shifting another and another of the sacks to the new location, moving rhythmically, saying nothing.

In awkward silence Tamasin continued to watch, and although she fought to keep the vision away, she remembered in a sudden flash the way he had looked, long ago, hefting stones in a glen green with life.

Her eyes fastened upon him again, followed him as he passed back and forth through the sliver of sunlight where dust motes swirled like dizzy fireflies. He labored hard; she heard the scrape of the perfectly polished boots against the wooden floor, heard the occasional hiss of air through his white teeth as the weight of a sack bowed his shoulder. For an instant Tamasin felt as if she and Hunter Kinshella had been hurled backward into time.

Even while she stood mesmerized, the groomsman gave her a sidelong look from beneath black brows. She knew he had read her thoughts, for a gleam of understanding as bright as a drop of quicksilver flashed in his eyes.

He had removed five bags, enough to allow him to lean over and scoop up the spaniel for her. And yet, he did not perform the chore. Instead he jerked his head, and with a disdain that cut through the final layer of Tamasin's composure, said, "Go ahead and do your job, Miss Cullen. I wouldn't dream of stealing the privilege from you."

His words made Tamasin feel indecent in a way that the villagers' snideness had never done. Color swept into her face while her mouth opened to form a retort, then snapped closed. She realized that she had no defense to make for herself.

Stepping in front of Hunter while he stood silently by, she bent over to retrieve the dog. It proved contrary and flattened itself against the floor, snarling when she tried to slip a hand beneath its belly. Acutely aware that Hunter Kinshella was observing her from his pose beside the wall, she ignored the spaniel's warning growl and seized him by the forelegs, smothering an exclamation as his needlelike teeth sank into the soft flesh of her hand.

She gasped with pain, bit down upon a cry, too proud to show distress. Keeping her back to her silent companion for several moments, she settled the squirming dog in the crook of her arm, and, with dismay, noted that blood beaded on her palm and trickled to spatter the striped skirt. Clenching her fist to try and stop the flow, she turned to go, but Hunter had positioned himself in front of the exit, barring the only path.

Tamasin paused, loath to push past and brush against his shoulder, loath to demand that he move over and let her pass.

To her surprise, he reached toward a shelf lined with green glass bottles and, selecting a jar, uncorked it. Then, leaning to clasp her bloodied hand, he splashed a measure of the liquid over the open wound.

While she stood with her teeth gritted, refusing to whimper when the astringent burned, he removed a worn but immaculate handkerchief from his breeches pocket and wound it round her palm, roughly, almost clumsily, as if his hands were unaccustomed to the simple gestures of gentleness.

She kept her fingers splayed stiffly, and he closed them over the folds of the handkerchief, his hands hard and calloused.

The spaniel wriggled in Tamasin's arms, and she tightened her grip upon it. Then, wanting to make it clear to Hunter that the lady's dog had not singled her out as its only enemy, she mumbled, "He bites everybody."

Hunter did not answer, but re-stoppered the bottle and replaced it on the shelf. Then, much to her astonishment, he lifted his clenched left hand and held it out for her inspection.

Tamasin sucked in a breath. A pattern of punctures identical to those she wore marked the hard heel of his palm, beaded it with bright, shining drops of scarlet blood. She stared, then raised her gaze to meet Hunter's eyes. They had not brightened with one pinpoint of light, nor had the wintry gray left their green.

But at the corner of his somber mouth, deepening the shadowed indentation where the deeply carved upper lip joined the lower, a ghost of a smile seemed to hover and disappear, a smile fleetingly familiar. A smile heartbreakingly beautiful.

Chapter Three

Suddenly, a commotion in the stable yard arrested their attention. Hunter pivoted and headed to investigate while Tamasin trailed behind toting her squirming, hard-won prize.

" 'Tis the bear! The bear!" Loftus was shouting in the stable yard. "The beast has gone stark mad, it has! Sir Harry let it inside the lodge, and now the creature has the master and his guests trapped in the dining room like rabbits in a hole!"

The gardeners and the stable lads dropped curry combs and shovels and scurried out to see.

When one of the men made to run inside the house, Loftus barred his way with a beefy arm. "Don't be going in there, you fool! Come with me, round to the front. We'll look through the window."

As a half dozen servants dashed between the privets to follow, Eushanie slid from the white mare and ran after them, tripping over the velvet hem of her riding habit.

Hunter Kinshella strode after them all in his long-legged, unhurried fashion, as if the emergency did not particularly interest him, or if it did, failed to move him to any haste.

Tamasin, on the other hand, jogged in his footsteps holding
the scratching, nipping spaniel, her heart racing with enough
excitement to compensate for the calmness of Hunter's own.

The sight she beheld through the row of leaded dining room
windows astounded her, and although she had never seen a
circus, she guessed that the act taking place in the panelled,
portrait-lined room where Sir Harry hosted his most famous
routs would rival such a show.

The long oak table was overturned, and beside it lay a silver
tea service, a leaking silver coffee urn, and a torn damask
tablecloth littered with assorted pieces of silverware. All around
the room the oil portraits of Hampton ancestors hung askew
or facedown upon the rumpled Turkey carpet.

The gentlemen in the scene of bedlam moved in various
states of undress, some still in yesterday's finery, wrinkled and
wine-stained, others wearing satin dressing gowns and slippers,
a few shaven and bewigged, many in a more natural and less
dignified condition. They each held a dining chair to their chest
to fend off the bear, while Sir Harry stood in the center, hopping
up and down, shouting obscenities at the beast.

Near the doorway, the great bear reared on its haunches,
growling and lashing the air with monstrous paws. The chain
looped about its neck dangled out of reach, and every time Sir
Harry made to creep up and snatch the end, the creature batted
at him with its claws.

"You blasted beast!" the excited master yelled, looking less
than formidable in his yellow satin knee breeches and silver
buckled shoes. "I'll see you returned to the circus where I
found you, and shut up in a cage again. Would you be liking
that? Devil, you are! I'll see your blasted head mounted over
the mantel before the day's out, I will!"

He snatched a butter knife from the rug and pointed it ineffectually at the bear, waving it like a sword while he continued
to issue a series of threats.

All the servants stood with their noses flattened against the glass, while Eushanie screeched at them to stop staring at the helpless men like cowards and go and save her father.

Loftus held an ancient fowling piece snatched from Sir Harry's historic collection. He lifted the weapon, aimed, then lowered it to the ground with a shake of his head and a grave excuse. "I can't be takin' a chance. So many gentlemen shiftin' about the bear makes a difficult target. 'Twould be a gamble to fire into the crowd."

"Sure and it would," agreed a stable lad.

Loftus propped the fowling piece against the stone of the lodge wall and leaned upon it, shaking his head. "Nay. I cannot be riskin' the master's life."

Tamasin glanced at him and, in that moment of confusion, sensed that the footman lied. A malicious gleam lit his gaze as he followed the movements of the maddened bear and the panicked gentlemen. He was hoping that the master and the others would be hurt, she realized in astonishment, perhaps even wishing they would all be killed.

A coldness settled over Tamasin, and for the first time she understood the hatred, ever increasing, that the lower class felt for the upper. It was a hatred gathering strength over the unsettled landscape of Ireland.

She searched all the sneering faces pressed to the glass, looking for Hunter Kinshella, wondering if his eyes, too, would be as full of blood lust as theirs. But Hunter had disappeared, gone off to see to his own interests apparently, disdainful of the excitement.

Inside the dining room, the sweating Sir Harry still stood in the midst of his peers, full of bravado. He wielded his butter knife with a series of flourishes, one hand behind his back in the manner of a fencer preparing to lunge forward.

Irritated by the antics, the bear lumbered forward with a growl, causing the line of guests with their raised chairs to step backward and fall against the velvet draperies. The combined weight of the gentlemen pulled the huge brass rod loose from

its moorings, and the drapes collapsed, shrouding half of the
struggling men in its folds.

Utter pandemonium ensued. The maddened bear, agitated
by their muffled shouting, lunged forward, intent it seemed
upon mauling the struggling men. The faces of the watching
servants pinkened with mirth, their eyes bulging with the same
kind of lust that Tamasin had seen at their Saturday night
bullbaitings.

Hunter suddenly materialized with his army musket in hand,
which he loaded and rammed even as he strode to the window.
After using the walnut butt of it to smash a windowpane, he
lifted the weapon to fire.

"Don't kill it!" Tamasin screamed.

He ignored her, and in one swift move, aimed and fired.

The musket cracked, and with dread Tamasin stared at the
dining room scene. But the weapon had not been fired at the
bear. Instead, the magnificent chandelier, which was constructed of at least a hundred dangling crystals, descended like
a shower of rain, tinkling and shivering before landing square
atop the head of Sir Harry's frenzied pet.

"Good God!" Loftus exclaimed beside her, staring at
Hunter, awed by such a show of marksmanship. "Who would
have thought to stop the bear in such a way as that? And
shooting through a chain on the first shot!"

Stunned and confused by the blow, the bear crouched down
upon the carpet and growled plaintively while the terrorized
gentlemen took the opportunity to flee the dining room, falling
all over each other in their rush to find the door.

Hunter lowered his musket. Keeping his eyes trained upon
the bear, he spoke to Tamasin over a shoulder. "Go to the
kitchen and fetch several pots of jam—or berries if there are
any. Meat will do if you have nothing else. Be quick about
it."

Without argument Tamasin did as he requested, returning in
a matter of minutes dragging a wooden crate of strawberries
Cook had earlier earmarked for the gentlemen's dessert. With-

out a word, Hunter hefted it over his shoulder and carried it toward the house.

She followed as he strode through the front door. He entered the dining room now emptied of gentlemen and, with no hesitation at all, set the berries near the bear.

The wretched animal lay quivering beneath its crown of broken crystal, but at the scent of the strawberries seemed to recover. In a tinkle of sound, it crept across the room, and with one swift swipe of a paw, tipped over the crate and began devouring the fruit.

"Starving," Hunter muttered, securing the animal's chain.

Tamasin crept behind him, watching. "It hasn't been fed for days. Sir Harry never gave orders."

"Does no one move around here unless Sir Harry orders them to?"

"He is the master," she answered simply.

"Whose? The bear's or yours?" he said with scorn.

Loftus ambled up just then, lugging pails of hot water for the gentlemen who milled about upstairs demanding service of the meager and overtaxed staff. Having overhead the conversation, the footman gave Hunter a jaundiced look and said, "You've been gone a long time, Kinshella. Aye, the beast is starvin', indeed. Just like our own Irish brothers. The master feeds it only when it's convenient, or when he stops hunting or drinking long enough to remember that it eats." He shifted the pails, so that steaming water splashed over the hardwood floor. "You should've let the bear have its way with the mad old bugger and his friends—or used your musket on 'em all and had it over with quick and sure."

Hunter made no reply, but his eyes flicked over the footman like the ends of a lash. "If you want to rid Ireland of the gentry, find your own way of doing it. I don't do the dirty work of any man."

Offended by the groomsman's insolence, Loftus glowered. "Watch yourself here, Kinshella. Be remembering where yer loyalties ought to lie."

Hunter pinned him with a stare. "I'll be remembering what I know."

Offended, Loftus stalked away, and Tamasin felt an impulse to applaud Hunter for his brashness. She watched as he eased the chandelier carefully off the bear's neck. In a quiet jingle of multifaceted drops, he then set the priceless fixture on the crumpled carpet.

"Well!" Sir Harry declared, suddenly strolling into the room. Readjusting his skewed wig and maintaining a safe distance from the bear, he affected a calm mien while scanning the scene of disarray with a baleful eye. Addressing Hunter, he said, " 'Twould seem I owe you a few words of gratitude, young man. Quite a marksman, you are—cut the chandelier chain clean through on the first shot. Quick thinking, too. Er— what did you say your name was?"

"Hunter Kinshella."

"Kinshella, Kinshella . . . ah! Seamus's grandson." Sir Harry tapped his forehead, causing a puff of powder to waft from the paste curls of his wig. He frowned with consternation. "But, I thought you were in the army, lad. Aye! Put there for thieving from my young Avery, you were, years ago."

"I was discharged."

At the cooly delivered reply the baronet lifted a brow. "Dishonorably?"

"No. My discharge—and my brother's—were quite honorable, in fact."

"Is that so? Well, I wouldn't ordinarily welcome back a thief under any conditions. Too many of those roaming the countryside as it is, but under the circumstances, I daresay you can be permitted to stay on and help old Seamus. I'll even pay you a bit if you prove useful about the place. Of course," he added with a forefinger pointed in warning, "if anything turns up missing or there's a hint of trouble, I'll haul you before the constable without hesitation. 'Twould be my duty to see you tried regardless of what presence of mind you displayed here

today. Aye, a man in my position has to take his responsibilities
seriously, quite seriously indeed.''

Sir Harry paused as if waiting to hear Hunter declare his
trustworthiness, but the tall groomsman merely observed him,
almost as if he were gazing straight through the baronet's head
at something more significant on the other side.

"Well," Sir Harry cleared his throat, unnerved but loath to
show it. "Lead this creature back to the malt house when it's
finished eating then. And you," he added, turning to Tamasin
and waving an arm, "Tidy up the place, lass. What am I paying
you to do?''

When the baronet had left, Tamasin surveyed the disorder
with a sigh. Then, skirting the bear, she bent to retrieve the
silver tea service she had polished the previous day. With
reverence she repositioned it upon the now scarred sideboard,
moving it an inch to one side until it was precisely centered.
Upon the carpet a pipe lay smoldering. She quickly stamped
out the potential blaze, then stood perusing the broken porcelain
cups, the scarred gilt frames of the Hampton portraits, the
cracked Wedgwood plates. "Such a waste of beautiful things,''
she muttered aloud, shaking her head at the destruction. "If
they were mine—''

She found Hunter looking at her, observing her in that peculiar way of unsettling penetration and, for the second time that
day, colored beneath his wryly silent but still stringent scorn.
She wondered if he hated her, and almost wished he did. His
hatred—which she admittedly deserved—would give her a
reason to hate him in turn, and hatred might help to ease her
nagging conscience.

Pretending to ignore him, she went about setting things
straight, struggling to right the heavy, toppled table alone when
her companion made no offer to lend his strong back to the
effort. Dragging the crumpled velvet drapes away from the
dying embers in the fireplace, she struggled to lift and rehang the
portraits. While she worked, she remembered Loftus's ominous
words; his disquieting behavior continued to plague her. On

impulse, wanting to gauge the attitude of the man who had once been such a faithful friend, she questioned Hunter.

"About Loftus," she whispered, making certain no one in the corridor could overhear. "As he said, he would have liked to see Sir Harry and the other gentlemen killed by the bear today. He hates the gentry—just like all the other servants seem to do. What about you? Do you feel the same?"

The bear had finished its meal; its large flat tongue licked berry juice off the floor with relish, going in and out, curling to get the very last drop. When the creature was pacified, Hunter tugged on its chain and led it toward the door, pausing only long enough to answer, " 'Tis the bear I should have shot."

At his callous reply, Tamasin's chin dropped. She stared at his back, wondering how he could value a beautiful animal so little.

But as Hunter crossed the threshold, as he led Sir Harry's misused pet by the chain, she realized his words had not been cruel at all. They had been a comment on Ireland, on its privileged, well-fed few, and its starving remainder. Hunter Kinshella knew what it was like to be yoked to a way of life, to be denied freedom of decision, to be told what to do and how to do it by a master. He was an Irish peasant, a common laborer with neither wealth nor power nor education. He had only intelligence and a strong back to serve him, and that would buy him little in the country he loved.

Tamasin frowned again, deep in thought, musing as she went about clearing up the mess caused by an eccentric old man born to authority. She wondered why she felt no similar bitterness herself, why the yoke she wore seemed such a light one. Indeed, she wore it gladly, felt privileged to touch beauty, to work among walls packed full of priceless objects. What did she care if she had to bow and scrape, just so long as she received something for her efforts in return?

Suddenly she gasped, remembering the black and white spaniel. Miss Eushanie had grabbed the dog from her arms while they had stood outside looking through the window. Obviously distracted, the young lady had failed to offer Tamasin a reward for finding the pet. There would be no silk scarf today, no embroidered handkerchief.

Glancing at the still sore dog bite on her hand, she shook her head in disappointment and swore.

Mam died the following week, slipped off to heaven or hell or somewhere in between after coughing herself to death on the pallet she had shared, willingly or not, with her husband of nearly thirty years.

Now the middle-aged woman, who had looked eighty, was laid out upon the same scarred table upon which she had set her meager family meals of cabbage and leeks—or on rare and festive occasions, the more tasty colcannon made of milk and potatoes.

Dressed in her Sunday black and covered with a sheet, Dora Cullen, in accordance with custom, lay with a plate of salt atop her chest. The salt represented immortality. But Tamasin knew that once her bent, seamed body was covered with damp Irish soil, nothing about Jamsie Cullen's wife, not even the memory of her, would prove immortal or even of long duration.

The tiny mud cottage was crammed with mourners who had been offered no food and probably had expected none, for it was summer, and now that the peasants had planted their potatoes, sown their corn, and cut their turf, many, like Jamsie, were without work or food. Some would be forced to trudge the roads soon, begging, eating wild mayflowers along the way for lack of anything more nourishing. In an effort to forget, a group of them now swigged mugs of poteen, lingering around the homemade tin still, knowing that the contraption was illegal and would be seized by revenue officials if any happened to ride by and inspect the premises.

Few of the guests spoke to Tamasin, but she found she did not care, wanting to distance herself from them just as much as they wanted to distance themselves from the girl who believed herself above them all.

Although she could scarcely bear to admit it to herself, Tamasin did not mourn her mother's death as she should have done. There had been times when she had even refused to believe she *was* Dora's daughter. It was said that the fairies sometimes maliciously stole babies from parents and dumped them on other doorsteps. As a little girl, Tamasin had believed herself the victim of such a prank, stolen from some lord and lady faraway. She had even given the mythical mother and father faces and names, created a mental picture of the house in which they lived. It was a mansion complete with garlanded ceilings, gilt furniture, tables overburdened with food, and, most wondrously of all, built with marble walls.

Unable to bear the smoky cottage a moment longer, unable to look at the black-clad figures, Tamasin opened the door and slipped out. Outside, a harper played a jig accompanied by a set of bagpipes. The younger mourners danced. They laughed and kissed and made marriage plans, which would likely not be settled until the fertility of the prospective bride was tested. Bundling, it was called, an ancient practice. Although they could scarcely feed themselves, the peasants all yearned for full cradles.

Tamasin avoided the mourners, circling the house to stand upon the rise and breathe the heather scents. She stared at the landscape scattered with the opal glitter of a full moon. On a distant hill, the windows of Hampton Hall reflected the pale shine, winking every now and then like diamonds set in black.

Tamasin felt herself leaning toward the mansion. She wanted to run to it, be welcomed into its beautiful halls. Hunger never called at Hampton Hall, nor did cold or poverty.

She stilled, hearing the voices of several men, including that of her father, as they discussed politics in hushed, angry voices.

"We can't take much more, I tell ye," Jamsie Cullen said. "We can't keep paying tithes to the Protestant church as well as to our own parish priest. And rents are unfairly high—six pounds a year for a cottage and plot. That bastard Sir Harry spends more than that in a day feedin' his bloody hounds!''

Loftus snorted. "Aye. Some of the lads in the secret society are plannin' a raid over in Kildare. They say they'll be killin' a few of the gentry's cattle there.''

"Maybe they'll be gettin' up the nerve to kill a few squires while they're at it."

Tamasin stood listening as Loftus said, "That fellow Hunter Kinshella is a cool one. I don't know what to make of him. Hard sort, he is. Ruthless to the bone, I'd guess. But handy with a musket. We could use a man like that, if he can be persuaded to come round."

"Talk to old Seamus," Jamsie advised. "He'll make him see right. What do ye think about Brendan Kinshella? What sort of man is he?"

"Worthless sort, I expect," Loftus scoffed. "Does little but spend his time playin' cards and drinkin'. Whorin', too—the wenches think he's got a pretty face."

"Then send him up to the Hall to dandle Sir Harry's spoiled young chit," Jamsie laughed. "She'll have him, I'll be bound. Aye, even a stable lad would suit that dog-faced Eushanie— if Brendan could force himself to touch a girl with such an ugly look."

"As for myself," Loftus grunted, "I'd like to set a torch to the whole place, burn the Hall to the ground. I'd not feel an ounce of regret, I tell ye."

Tamasin shuddered at the footman's wickedness. Drawing her shawl about her shoulders, she slipped past the pair of men, but not before her father caught sight of her and snatched her by the sleeve.

"Ye'll be takin' the place of yer mam now, lass," he said, his breath reeking of poteen. "I'll expect ye to cook fer me and keep me company at night. We've even been discussin' who ye might take for a husband. How about young Peader over there, or Sean?"

She stared at the two prospective bridegrooms, both filthy

and shaggy-haired, and imagined a future with one of them in a thatched mud hut full of peat smoke and hungry bairns.

"I've got my work over at the lodge," she said firmly. "I don't need a husband."

Her father laughed. "And where are your wages? The squire doesn't pay his people. Squanders his coin on his own pleasures, he does. Or maybe he's so daft he just forgets to dole out the pennies. You'd be better off marrying, girl."

"Don't be making any marriage plans for me, Da. I'll be making my own plans when I'm ready. Not a day before."

"You'll do what I say, ye little hellion!" he shouted as she jerked free.

Tamasin pushed past the men and ran down the night-black hill. When she had jogged a mile over the open fields and filled her lungs with the sweet Irish air, she plopped down beside a hedge and, having an excellent view, stared at the dark spires and turrets of Hampton Hall. She stared and stared, defiant and resolute, until all the lights twinkling from its windows were snuffed one by one by dutiful servants.

"I'll go there some day, live there in that grand fairy-tale house," she said aloud, making a vow. "I'll not suffer the life Mam did. Never. *I promise myself that.*"

Chapter Four

A few evenings later, one of Sir Harry's guests complained of having such a dreadful toothache that the pain could not be diminished by a full bottle of claret. The baronet's valet, frazzled and overworked as usual, asked Tamasin to journey to the apothecary and request a powder so that the gentleman could sleep.

The hour was quite late and the night dark, lit only by an occasional shaft of milky moonlight flitting through the clouds, and Tamasin drew her shawl close, passing shadowy groves and ghostly glens. Progressing gingerly so as not to stumble into a bog and ruin her precious pair of shoes, she walked quickly toward the village, scattering a flock of Sir Harry's sheep.

She gave wide berth to the circular rath alongside the trail, for it was a ruined fortress of the ancient Celts, sacred to the fairies. The villagers swore that the elf clans lived deep beneath the fort ruins, dwelling in beehive chambers made of unmortared stone.

Tamasin scurried past the eerie place, taking a shortcut to

the village of Wexford, situated on the Irish Channel at the
mouth of the River Slaney. As she reached its outskirts, she
wondered about the original inhabitants of the ancient village,
the fierce Norsemen who had founded the trading port. After
remaining in Ireland nearly three hundred years, they had sailed
away again in their crimson dragon boats bound for an icy
land, leaving many of their sturdy walls and roads intact. The
pearly mist hung heavy with smells of saltwater and wet
wharves, and Tamasin imagined the tall English ships now
moored gracefully in the quay, imagined what it would be like
to board one and sail off to some exotic land.

The town walls came into view, rising up out of the haze
like a line of gray horses, and she hastened through the gate,
following Selskar Street through the narrow, irregularly laid
plat until she came to John's Lane. The shops, built shoulder
to shoulder, were closed, and the crooked stone houses lay unlit
and sleepy beneath their caps of thatch. Only the infrequent
bark of a dog or the laughter from tavern patrons floated over
the air to keep her company, those sounds, and the occasional
grind of a wheel car as it was pulled home over the glistening
cobbles.

The apothecary's sign swung over his bow window, and
Tamasin cupped her hands and pressed her face against the
panes to peer inside, seeing nothing but the dark shapes of
glass bottles on long rows of shelves. Rousing the slumbering
chemist proved no easy task, but after her knuckles were nearly
raw with pounding upon his door, he finally emerged in his
nightcap and, grumbling, thrust a packet of powders at her for
the suffering patient.

Chilled now by the drizzle, she began to hurry, seeing the
ancient steeple of St. Paul Church at the end of the hilly street.
Just then the sound of contentious voices reached her ears,
floating from an alehouse called *The Hound*.

She slowed. Three men scuffled outside on the stoop of the
tavern, their figures backlit by amber light spilling through the

window. One of the fellows stumbled, and with a painful grunt, fell heavily upon the cobbles with his arms outflung.

When Hunter Kinshella emerged from the public house, Tamasin stepped quickly back into the shadows. He bent over the man who had fallen in the street, shook him, and when he failed to rouse, turned back to shout at someone in the tavern. "You should have sent him home, Ira," he barked.

"He wouldn't go. I'm not his keeper, I am? Brendan's a man, and if he wishes to wager every cent he has and drink himself insensible, 'tis his business. Besides, if I sent all the fellows to bed when they were half-foxed, my taproom would be empty by sunset, would it not, Kinshella?"

Tamasin lingered beneath the overhanging story of a confectioner's shop while Hunter hauled his brother to his feet. But the young man only crumpled to the ground again and doubled over, holding his golden head in his hands.

The groomsman swore. "Hell, Brendan, get yourself up. I have better things to do than stand here in the rain with you."

The younger brother wore no shirt and his naked torso gleamed palely in the yellow light of the window. "I'm f-freezing, Hunter," he complained, not unlike a child who had misbehaved and been made to suffer the consequences. "So blasted c-cold. Can't remember where I left my clothes . . ."

Hunter shouted into the tavern again. "Where's my brother's clothes, Ira?"

The huge landlord stepped outside and, wiping his hands upon his apron, snorted. "No doubt the boots are in the wench's room upstairs."

"And the shirt?"

"He wagered it. Likely would've wagered his breeches, too, if anyone had cared to have 'em. Might as well go without them anyway, as much as they're down. Indecent, he is."

In a quick snapping of temper, Hunter made to seize the man by his collar, but the landlord snarled a warning. "You and your brother are too eager to use those fists of yours—just like you always were. Well, they'll be landing you in trouble one of these days, laddie, wait and see if I'm right. Now, go on and take that ne'er-do-well home with you, or I'll call the constable and have you both hauled off to jail—mayhap you'll be sent back to the British army for your trouble.''

Hunter hesitated, struggling to quell his temper. Then, removing his own trusty, the long woolen jacket worn with the rough corduroys and boots of almost every Irish workingman, he draped it over his brother's shivering shoulders while Ira hurled a pair of boots out the door.

''Brendan,'' the elder brother said with no patience, ''make an effort to get yourself up. I've little desire to lug a sixteen-stone man all the way back to the lodge.''

But nothing more than a grunt came from the huddled shape on the street and, realizing that Brendan could never stagger the distance home over the boggy fells, Hunter leaned down to hoist him over a shoulder. Shifting his burden, he started forward, pausing just long enough to jerk his head around and gaze into the darkness.

Although she stood well concealed in the shadows, Hunter's eyes fastened upon Tamasin as if she were illumined by sunlight.

''If you've had you're fill of staring at us, Miss Cullen,'' he said, ''make yourself useful and carry the boots home. And don't creep along behind my back like a coward. You're as bold as they come and twice as greedy, and timidity doesn't suit you.''

The words piqued Tamasin's temper and wounded her pride. She was tempted to refuse, but as she looked at the tall Irishman with his back bent beneath the slumped form of his drunken brother, some prick of sympathy touched her; she stepped forward obediently to retrieve the boots from the puddle for him.

''And don't think you'll be getting a handkerchief for your service, either,'' Hunter added unsparingly. ''I reckon you could stand to do a good turn for nothing, once or twice in your life.''

Arms akimbo, Tamasin countered with a pert retort. ''The

priest keeps tallies of my good deeds, thank you. As well as my bad ones. You needn't do it for him.''

"And which side of the ledger is longer?" he asked with a raised black eyebrow.

"The good side, of course," she countered. "Carrying all those bloody boots for people in the rain, you know."

He laughed in spite of himself, then his voice quietened provocatively. "And what about dragging fox pelts over the fields? Are you still doing that for the inestimatable Master Avery?"

Sensing the danger, Tamasin did not reply. She was afraid; Hunter was hedging too close to the treacherous deed that stood between them, and at the moment she wasn't feeling brave enough to provoke him into airing it. Instead, she simply stared at his tall, well-formed frame for a moment, and against her will felt desire run through her veins.

Hunter seemed to sense it, for she saw an arrogant, purely wicked grin flash briefly across his face.

They trudged over the rough ground together after that, saying no more and, strangely, Tamasin regretted their uncomfortable silence. It could have been companionable once, she thought, long ago, before she had obliterated the trust between them.

She slogged through a puddle, her teeth chattering both with the frost in the air and the remoteness of Hunter Kinshella. To heighten the strain of their togetherness, the landscape seemed inhospitable, bleaker than usual, smelling of water and ancient earth. She thought of the Celts who had roamed the land once, leaving their stone symbols and lingering myths, and wondered if she were treading upon their crumbled graveyards. Nothing was visible in the darkness except Hunter's white shirt, tinted violet-blue by the night, and the garment seemed disembodied, ghostly, as he strode over the tufted grass carrying Brendan's heavy body.

He *is* a ghost, Tamasin thought with unwilling regret, a ghost of the man he had once been. And yet, as she followed his broad back, which was stiff with an anger that was both old and new, she experienced a sort of pity for him. He was chained to his brother, and to the land, and would not set himself free of either because he loved them both too much. She would have liked to have spoken to Hunter about it, expressed her understanding, for she felt a growing, tenuous thread of identity with Hunter Kinshella that she had first felt many years ago beneath a hedgerow. And yet, rather than let the thread strengthen and weave itself into a knot that may complicate her life and the direction of her dreams, she let it remain fragile and frayed. She would not permit herself to be wrenched by Hunter's bitterness, by her own remorse over the years she had stolen from him, and as she watched his back bowed beneath the burden of his brother, she steeled her emotions against any pangs of softness. Hunter Kinshella was no more than she was, after all, no more than a lowborn, penniless peasant burning for more, and she would give nothing of herself to him—not even one secret, silent share of her regret. She could not afford it.

They arrived at the lodge to find the yard behind the house aglow with lanterns, astir with activity. Sir Harry paced up and down the length of it with a pistol in his hand.

"Damned peasant rebels!" he shouted, puffing out his chest and waving his weapon in the manner of a Lilliputian general. "They've been sneaking around here, intent upon mischief, trying to harm my horses. Knocked my fences down in the glen, they did, and would have killed the cattle if the hounds hadn't made a racket. Who's there?" he demanded, squinting at Hunter, pointing the pistol at him. "Ah, 'tis you, Kinshella. Go and get your musket and patrol the stable yard. Kill any blasted rebels you see skulking round my property. And look sharp in the morning. My guests and I are going hunting, and I'll need a strong back to carry the prize home."

He screwed up his eyes and peered at Brendan's limp form. "Sober up that worthless brother of yours, too, and bring him along. If he doesn't make himself useful, I'll not be keeping

him about, you know. He can lie drunk in the road just as
easily as he can lie drunk in my stable yard. I'll cut off his
wages, I will.''

All during Sir Harry's tirade, Hunter had continued walking
as calmly as if the master were not speaking at all, were not
even standing in his path. But at the last words, the groomsman
halted and swung about, his eyes glinting in the lantern light.
''We've not been paid a penny since we started work here.''

Although his tone was not insolent, it bordered dangerously
upon disrespect, and Sir Harry straightened, apparently debating
whether or not to take the groomsman to task.

Perhaps he decided that Kinshella's value outweighed his
insubordination, for after making a blustery sound in his throat,
the baronet snapped, ''You'll be paid on the morrow if you're
useful at the hunt.''

Without answering, Hunter took the boots from Tamasin's
hand and, climbing the narrow stairs that led to his grandfather's
garret, carried his brother to bed.

Tamasin watched in consternation. Hunter made life difficult
for himself, she thought. If he didn't learn to lower those dark,
disdainful eyes, he would be made to suffer for it; he would
come to ruin.

She had no doubt of it.

''Good night to you, Damsel,'' she heard him whisper. The
deliberate intimacy in his voice made her shiver—together with
the endearment. He had remembered it all these years and used
it now, either to taunt her or to thrill her, she wasn't sure which.

The next morning as she sat at the kitchen table taking
breakfast with the other servants, eating eggs and potatoes
roasted over turf ashes—not the smoked herring, peppered
beef, and champagne reserved for the gentry's meal—Tamasin
overheard gossip concerning Avery Hampton. According to the
servants' grapevine, the young master had finally arrived at
Hampton Hall.

"Looking like a man now, he is," Loftus said between mouthfuls. "And actin' like he's the king of England."

A round of laughter followed, but at the mention of Avery's name, Tamasin's heart lurched. She scarcely tasted the hearty fare she had enjoyed a moment before. She had thought endlessly of the baronet's son these past few days, anticipating his return and wondering what her response—and his—would be when they came face-to-face with each other again.

Leaving the table without a word, she went into the study where the six graceful greyhounds dozed by the hearth and, peering into the mirror above the mantel, surveyed herself critically. She knew her mouth was too wide and her face too narrow for classic beauty. But her hair was neat, black as ebony and cleverly coiled at the back of her neck in a twist of thick sleek braids. Last week she had been provided with a new white apron, which, donned over her old black jacket and skirt, appeared crisp and feminine. She was lithe and pretty, she thought, if not flamboyant. Wistfully touching the plain linen apron, she wished it were edged in Holland lace, wished her ruched cap were a gold feathered bonnet. Her expression tightened with resolve, and she murmured, "And they *will* be, one day. Before all is said and done, I'll have plenty of fine things."

The barking of the hounds outside shattered her vision of the future, and she scurried back to the kitchen where feverish arrangements were taking place in preparation for Sir Harry's hunting picnic. It was to be held on the banks of the River Slaney after the gentlemen had exhausted themselves shooting game.

A farm cart was brought round, the picnic items and tapestry rugs packed inside it, and with Tamasin and the long-faced valet walking alongside, driven down to the river's edge.

The water flowed by languorously, edged with umbrellalike rowans and emerald grass, its surface broken now and then by the flash of a silver fin or the bobbing branch of a hawthorn. The late summer morning was cool, still asparkle with dew, and fresh with the scent of yellow gorse; but in the distance, as Sir Harry released his dogs, the tranquil air seemed to shiver while the creatures of the woodlet scurried for cover in a rush to escape the coming danger.

Before long the baronet and his friends breasted the hill like a line of mock-heroic kings, their middle-aged bodies caped in the dashing magenta coats of their hunt club, all of them carrying their muskets like scepters, some stumbling from their night of debauchery. Sir Harry led the regal procession, swaggering, his rotund figure and short legs lending him a childish bearing.

With a few sharp commands he directed his greyhounds toward the woodland, where the eager dogs bounded through the brush searching for the scent of a red deer. Tamasin watched, knowing that before the end of the day, there would be another trophy for the lodge walls, another antlered head to keep company with the others, which she dusted every day.

As she spread a collection of Turkey rugs out upon the grass, their jewel dyes a swirl of color against the green grass, she saw Hunter and Brendan Kinshella strolling down the hill, the former's pace measured and steady, the latter's dragging and slow. Rather than acknowledge them, she turned her back, and out of the corner of one eye saw them walk out upon the river pier, bend down, and untie the boat moored there. As always, Hunter's appearance commanded her attention, despite her unwillingness to give it. How tall he stood and how self-assured. She cocked her head to the side, observing him, and with a peculiar flash of irony thought that *he* should have been the master of Hampton Hall.

A few of the guests joined the brothers and were handed into the little vessel. Others followed Sir Harry into the woods, where the deer would be forced through the trees, into the water, and then shot by the huntsmen aiming from the boat.

Forcing herself to concentrate on the picnic, Tamasin laid out crystal champagne glasses, Meissen china, and Italian silver, and as she folded a napkin into a perfect triangle, heard footsteps behind her. Without much interest she glanced over a shoulder, then froze.

Dressed in a blue silk jacket and a brocade waistcoat, Avery Hampton observed her with amusement. He had changed, lost much of the fat he had carried as a younger man, which had left his body less round, and defined the thin features of his patrician face. His coppery eyes were set close to an arched nose, and he had abandoned his wig, wearing his fair hair scraped back from his forehead and tied in a queue with a black satin ribbon.

As Tamasin stared up at him, speechless and reverent as in the days of girlhood, he suddenly seemed to represent all the grace, all the mystique of the class she so envied, and, as if he were a god instead of a mortal, she curtsied so low that her knee touched the muddy soil.

Avery raised a brow and laughed. " 'Tis my little Tamasin, is it not? Upon my honor, you've grown, become a half-decent-looking female. Which dismays me in one sense, and delights me in another.''

Leaning down, he grabbed an orange from the picnic rug, and with long white fingers began to peel the fruit, sending up wafts of sharp fragrance. Between bites he continued looking at Tamasin, talking to her, his voice lazy with good humor. "I could have used you once or twice. 'Twould have been convenient to have you with me in Florence and Venice—oh, and in Paris when I met a few fellows from my university. But then, you are not as small and unnoticeable as you once were. Are you still as clever?''

He turned about, motioning to a young man who had been hovering behind. "Rafael, this fair damsel is the clever little cottier's maid I told you about. All grown up now, isn't she, eh?'' Reaching out a hand, he pinched Tamasin's chin, and when she winced, laughed at her.

Tamasin colored and turned her eyes to the person called Rafael, who was just as finely dressed as Avery, but very dark and small-featured, almost pretty with his slanted black eyes and tilted nose. He regarded her in a way she did not like. His stare was not lewd, but cool, almost demeaning in its hard assessment.

His fingers sticky with orange juice, Avery insolently touched the tip of Tamasin's nose and stroked it insolently. "Will you still do favors for me if I ask? Ah . . ." he answered for her, grinning with satisfaction as her eyes glanced at the diamond stickpin in his stock. "But of course you will."

A shot pierced the air to interrupt them. It was the first sound other than Avery's voice Tamasin had consciously heard since his arrival, and she looked toward the river, where Sir Harry's guests were standing up in the boat and aiming their muskets at the water. The Kinshella brothers struggled to row them into position.

The sharp bark of the greyhounds blended with the shouts of the excited gentlemen. As he was ordered to do, Hunter put his strength into the oars, maneuvering the craft so that the guests could hit their target, which was a magnificent red stag, panicked and plunging from the green woods into the river. The animal floundered, then began to swim in a wild circle, its great eyes rolling as the sound of musket fire resumed again.

"We shall have venison tonight, Rafael," Avery drawled, waving a hand. "At least, if any of these old fools who are my father's playmates can manage to hit the mark."

One did, and the frantic struggles of the stag abruptly ceased. Its head lolled, its body floated on the surface, and the churned, muddy water turned quickly crimson.

Cries of exultation filled the air, and in his excitement, one of the guests lost his balance in the boat and fell overboard. When the cold water began to envelope him, he cried out, his wig whirling in the current while his velvet-clad arms waved wildly for help.

But none of his fellows proved brave enough to venture into the cold depths; instead, they shouted at him to try and swim ashore. With no hesitation Hunter Kinshella dived in himself, his arms cleanly cleaving the water, his dark head as sleek as an otter's beneath the surface. While he retrieved the drowning man and dragged him ashore, Sir Harry waded out and fetched his antlered prize, towed it with a long crooked pole before leaving it to lie upon the bank, forgotten as quickly as a toy that was no longer new.

Having enjoyed their sport, all the gentlemen crowded about, their boots muddying the picnic rugs laid with platters of fruit, meat, and cheeses. They laughed and bragged of their triumph, then teased their half-drowned fellow as he toddled toward them and shrilly ordered Sir Harry's valet to remove his own dry jacket in exchange for the soaking velvet one.

"Yes," Avery drawled again, "venison tonight, Rafael, with plum sauce, I'll wager."

When Tamasin offered him a tray of cheeses, the baronet's son declined, taking her chin in his hand again and examining her face in the sunlight. "Perhaps it's time for you to leave the lodge and come up to the Hall," he mused. "I shall have to think on it."

It was only when Rafael shifted his feet impatiently and offered his friend a glass of champagne that Avery chuckled and released her.

Flushed from the encounter, Tamasin caught sight of Hunter, dripping wet, kneeling upon the bank beside the slain stag. He cross-tied its delicate, once nimble legs to a long stout pole, and when he had finished, spoke a few low words to Brendan, who helped him hoist the burden.

The two brothers rested the pole atop their shoulders as a way to transport the prize home. Almost staggering beneath its weight, they passed the feasting gentlemen who lay sprawled on their rugs like a group of happy, overdressed children.

Tamasin studied Hunter. What a contrast he was to all the others, his physical superiority obvious. He was sturdier, much more vital than any other on the hill, and his rough Celtic features, now christened by the River Slaney, were stamped with the nobility of the original Irish princes. As they so often did, Hunter's words of long ago echoed in her memory. *I'll not do the bidding of any man . . .*

Well, she thought with rue, he was doing Sir Harry's bidding now, and would likely be doing it the rest of his life. What chance had he to rise above his lot? No more chance than Loftus or Da, of course, and less chance than she, who had always had Avery Hampton's attention, and now . . . his eye.

Oh, yes, Jamsie Cullen's daughter sensed the young master's new, manly interest, and with great excitement, wondered how far that interest would stretch. She had heard tales of maids who had caught the attention of highborn gentlemen and been lavished with gifts, or been set up as courtesans, or even been taken as brides. Such possibilities intrigued Tamasin, and she set her mind to work searching for a course of action, a way to make Da's smoky thatched hut nothing more than an unpleasant memory as soon as possible.

"Hold up there!"

The harsh voice alarmed her, and she glanced round to see Avery step forward and saunter toward Hunter and Brendan, barring their path with his authoritative stance. "By God!" he exclaimed in outrage. "It's the Kinshella brothers, isn't it? The two thieves I had banished from Ireland. Father!"

Sir Harry, looking annoyed by the interruption, excused himself and joined his son, obviously prepared for the confrontation but not anxious to endure it. "Yes, these are the Kinshellas, discharged from the army and here by my leave. What of it?"

"You're letting felons stay on Hampton property, reside here, work here?" Avery phrased the question in amazement and anger, his malicious gaze returning to meet Hunter's.

The groomsman regarded him with wintry eyes, saying nothing.

"They're useful to me presently," the baronet insisted, waving his champagne glass so carelessly that the expensive liquid sloshed out. "At least, the older one is. Good with my horses. Old Seamus is getting too feeble to do a proper job. I've got

races coming up this autumn and need to have a skilled man
to train the thoroughbreds.''

"Then find someone else.''

"I will not. I am still master here, you young pup, whether
you like it or not—and I suspect you don't—and the Kinshellas
will stay as long as I need them to stay.''

As if knowing himself defeated, at least for the time being,
Avery bit off a retort. He turned cruel, calculating eyes upon
Hunter again, looking him up and down. With apparent satisfaction he examined Hunter's dripping shirt and the chilled brown
flesh beneath it, the shoulders that would be bruised tomorrow
from the weight of the rough pole.

Then, in a gesture made solely to provoke, to break the
laborer's temper and cause him to lash out, which would in
turn provide an excuse for a flogging, Avery put a hand upon
the pole and bore down hard upon it.

Although the strain must have been intolerable, Hunter did
not buckle beneath the weight, nor did he groan. But his jaw
clenched in pain, throbbed. And as if murder were in his mind,
his cold green gaze raked the baronet's son with a chilling
contempt.

The minute stretched. Everyone on the hill eagerly awaited
the outcome. The gentlemen hoped for another sporting spectacle, hoped to see the insolence from a Catholic peasant squashed
properly, as it should be, before it got out of hand.

Do nothing. Tamasin concentrated hard upon the thought,
willing Hunter to hear it in his own mind. Her eyes fastened
pleasingly to the dark face flushed with pain. *Do nothing,
Hunter. Avery will have you beaten without a qualm, ruin you,
and you will be helpless against him, for he and his father and
all their kind rule the world and everyone in it.*

Of course, the groomsman could not hear her silent, vehement
words, but Hunter Kinshella did not lack for shrewdness, even
if his temper and pride overrode them both at times. In that
moment of tension, as Tamasin had prayed, he said nothing,
did nothing. And yet, every line of his strong young body

proclaimed his desire to prove his superiority over the baronet's son. He waited until the pressure of Avery's hand had relented, and then said in a very low voice, *"Dia dhuit."*

Color rose to Avery's face. He hesitated. He could not understand a word of Gaelic, but was too proud to admit it and ask for a translation. For several seconds he remained undecided, his fists clenched, his face twitching. Finally, to cover his ignorance of whether or not he had been insulted, he said succinctly, "Bastard." Then he spat at Hunter's feet before guzzling his glass of champagne, swilling it flauntingly, as if it were water.

Without a word Hunter started forward with Sir Harry's deer again, Brendan following to carry the other end of the pole. Tamasin let out a breath of relief. The party continued, picking up its previously merry accord, and with a forced smile she offered pastries to the lounging guests, grateful that Hunter had kept his temper curbed, refused to be goaded, and avoided trouble.

The baronet's son came to stand beside her, and as he bit into a leg of mutton and furiously chewed it, she saw that his eyes followed the muddy path that the groomsman had taken. He couldn't know that Hunter's Gaelic words had not been in the least insulting. The groomsman had simply said, "Good day." Nothing more. And yet, through his cleverness Hunter had managed to gain the upper hand today.

Avery, his whole body taut with concentration, clearly yearned for retaliation. Another day of reckoning, Tamasin thought with trepidation, would surely come.

"God preserve us," she prayed silently as she dutifully arranged another tray of comfits. "And keep Hunter safe." She realized that she had come to care deeply for the groomsman again. Too deeply. Perhaps she had never really stopped.

Chapter Five

During that long and golden-hued summer, filled as it was with champagne picnics, out-of-season hunting, fishing, boating, riding, and all the other self-indulgent pastimes enjoyed by the gentry and smoothly engineered by obedient servants, Tamasin witnessed several subtle and, on the surface, insignificant events that would change not only the face of her world, but the chronicles of Irish history.

One of the most important of those events occurred on a sparkling afternoon. A fresh rain had just rinsed the countryside, and its traces still trembled in the crevices of sun-splashed stones strewn haphazardly across the wild green fields.

With a basket over her arm full of herring purchased from the village market, Tamasin walked barefoot down the lane, her shoes slung over a shoulder by the laces, her nose wrinkling with the smell of peat wafting from the cottages she passed along the way. The cabins possessed neither windows nor chimneys, only holes in the thatched roofs for the spewing of peat smoke. Wandering in and out of them were half-naked children left to entertain themselves while their mothers worked along-side husbands in the fields.

A few paces in front of her, a young man with a bundle on his back trudged, doubtless an out-of-work laborer journeying to Dublin in search of employment.

In the far distance Miss Eushanie galloped astride the milk-white mare that could have made a fitting mate for Pegasus had it sprouted wings. Her groom was nowhere in sight, and Tamasin paused to watch enviously as a girl no older than herself flew over the landscape like a medieval damoiselle— Isolde perhaps, going to find her doomed lover Tristan. But Tamasin speculated that Eushanie would never have a dashing lover. It was a strange, if cruel, kind of justice, she thought, that fate had given the baronet's daughter wealth and plenty, but had deprived her of a pretty face.

The day was so fine, it seemed everyone had come out. Not far away Hunter and Brendan Kinshella strolled across the fields leading a mettlesome thoroughbred stallion toward a roadside forge. Tamasin could hear their laughter, distinguish Hunter's low-timbred voice as he began to sing in Gaelic, joined by his brother, who crowed terribly out of tune.

All of a sudden a fine coach and four appeared on the road at the crest of the hill, barreling down the descent at a breakneck speed. The laborer with the bundle upon his back was tramping in their direction, and the coachman of the glossy, mud-bespat-tered carriage, seeing that the insolent fellow had no intention of clearing the way, lashed out with his carriage whip. His contemptuous gesture was hardly uncommon. Members of the aristocracy felt it their right—and the right of their servants— to flog any peasant who got in their way or who failed to show proper respect.

But the wandering young traveler, perhaps so down on his fortune that he no longer cared to be cautious, put up a fight and swung his unwieldy bundle at the nervous carriage horses. The two leaders staggered on the slippery ground.

Amid the resulting snorting and rearing, the frantic coachman

attempted in vain to bring the team under control. The coach
slithered off the road, and like an unwieldy turtle, teetered and
turned over in a water-filled ditch. At the moment of its toppling,
Eushanie crossed the road, and her mare, startled by the turmoil,
darted to one side, lost her own footing, and fell to her knees.
In a jumble of flying white legs and blue serge skirts, the lady
and her mount jolted to the ground near the toppled carriage.

The hapless coachman, having been thrown from his box
into the ditch water, struggled to stand. His passengers, two
foppish Dublin gentlemen wearing spencer coats and beaver
hats, climbed over the top of each other and thrust their heads
out of the coach window.

"Who the devil's responsible for this!" one bellowed, glancing about. "Who startled the horses?"

Not surprisingly, the laborer had disappeared, melted into
the green and white tapestry of rowans and mayflower hedges
like the infamous *Far Darrig* fairy known for practical jokes.
Wary that she herself might be made the scapegoat and horse-
whipped in the laborer's stead, Tamasin stepped behind a hawthorn tree and watched the proceedings from a safer vantage
point.

Brendan Kinshella ran from his brother's side to aid Miss
Eushanie, pulling her from the ground with a solicitous hand,
his hair shining like a crown in the sun, his cavalier phrases—
pure blarney to Tamasin's experienced ears—charming the
naive young girl.

"Are you hurt, Miss?" he asked with just the right amount
of worry. "Shall I fetch a surgeon? Nay? Then shall I carry
you to the side of the road so you can sit a spell and recover?
Nasty spill, that. What a grand horsewoman you must be to
have broken your fall as you did. I saw you handling the mare
brilliantly as you went down."

Despite her faint protests, the audacious Brendan swept an
arm beneath the lady's knees and, with all the gallantry of Sir
Lancelot, carried her through the ditch water to an outcropping

of rock, where he sat her down as gently as if she were Guinevere reincarnated.

In the meantime the pair of foppish gentlemen had crawled out of their disabled carriage, grimacing as their pointed Moroccan leather shoes squelched in the mud. Both turned their wrath upon the coachman, demanding to know what he proposed to do now he had landed them in such a predicament.

"We must set the carriage aright, milords," the poor fellow offered reasonably, holding the bridles of the trembling horses. "We must pull it out of the ditch."

"*We* must do no such thing," the taller gentleman shot back. With his hands on his hips, he surveyed his surroundings, wincing in pure disgust at the crude mud huts and rooting pigs, the stacks of peat and the giggling, staring children. "You there!" he shouted, spying Brendan standing on the side of the road. "Come here and help my man with the carriage."

With a shrug and an eloquent apology to Eushanie, Brendan complied. The aristocrats had also spotted Hunter, who was still making his way to the forge as if nothing untoward had happened, as if two wealthy young dandies were not standing helpless in the mud, ruining their shoes, delayed upon their country jaunt.

The groomsman strolled past leading the thoroughbred, his eyes scarcely turning their way.

"You, man!" the gentleman bellowed.

Hunter kept walking, his step neither slowing nor faltering, his back arrow-straight.

Incensed at being ignored, the young lord withdrew a dueling pistol, which he aimed and fired not at Hunter, but directly at Brendan's feet. The report echoed so loudly in the tranquil country air that the watching cottier children covered their ears and scurried to safety.

Hunter swung around. Even at a distance, Tamasin could see the quicksilver fierceness in his eyes, that hard, challenging ferocity she feared would eventually—or God forbid, today—lead him into trouble.

"Are you a poor shot, sir?" Hunter shouted loudly, his voice thick with a brash contempt. "Or did you intend to fire a bullet into the mud?"

Provoked, the aristocrat reloaded the pistol and jerked his head in Brendan's direction. "Next time," he declared imperiously, "I shall put a lead ball into your companion's knee. So unless you don't mind carrying him home upon a plank, I suggest you get your impertinent carcass over here and help set the carriage aright."

In deadly earnest then, he pointed the pistol squarely at Brendan, cocked it, and with arrogant anticipation awaited Hunter's response.

Tamasin clutched her hands together and watched anxiously. She suspected that if Hunter himself had been threatened instead of Brendan, the groomsman would have turned about and calmly walked toward the forge again, testing the measure of his luck—or the bravado of the rich young lord.

But with Brendan's well-being at stake, the brother hesitated, weighing the odds, speculating, his keen eyes remaining on the gentleman's white, pinched face.

In the end, he apparently judged the fellow sincere, capable of wounding Brendan. He stepped toward the carriage, and with no haste or lack of composure, tethered the thoroughbred to the hedge. Then, wading through the ditch in his polished boots, he stooped, put his hard-muscled shoulder against the roof of the disabled vehicle, and with tremendous might, began to shove.

On the opposite side of the carriage, the coachman had already anchored a rope to the window frame, and he and Brendan tugged upon the taut line as Hunter employed the sure, steady strength in his back and legs, the brawn of Ireland, to push the carriage square upon its wheels again.

Without so much as a word, the two gentlemen wrenched open the door and climbed inside, and while the driver was busy mounting his perch, Brendan went to stand beside Hunter at the rear wheel, which had been slightly loosened in the

accident. The mischievous younger brother gave a further twist
to the hub nut, loosening it more, so that before too many
miles, the wheel would spin off and leave the carriage stranded
again.

Hunter did nothing to stop his brother's prank, and Eushanie
was too preoccupied with her straggling hair and its
rearrangement to notice any misdeed.

The expensive carriage lurched forward as its team felt the
coachman's lash and, avoiding the spray of mud flung up in
its wake, Brendan sauntered back to Eushanie's side with his
grin in place. Pointing out that the white mare seemed to be
unsettled, he offered to lead the lady home.

While trying to appear dignified enough to remind him of
her station, but not so arrogant to discourage his further compliments, Eushanie nodded graciously and allowed Brendan to
lace his fingers so she could step up onto the mare's back. She
gathered the reins, demurely hooked a knee over the horn of
the sidesaddle, and waited while Brendan took hold of the
bridle and urged the horse forward. Tamasin couldn't help but
grin as Eushanie glanced down and, with a surreptitious gaze,
admired his golden head.

Nearby, Hunter wiped the mud off his hands and went to
untether the thoroughbred. Even though Tamasin was sure he
had noticed her standing in the shadow of the tree by now, he
gave no greeting. Disappointed, she retrieved her basket of fish
and started to walk past, but before she'd gone a step, a flutter
of movement at the side of the road arrested her attention.

There, forgotten beside the ditch, lay Eushanie's glorious,
braid-trimmed, plumed riding hat. How magnificent it was! For
long seconds, Tamasin stood staring at it, admiring it, coveting
it. Several possibilities began to tempt her, and she hastily
considered each one in turn.

Hadn't the lovely hat been abandoned? Eushanie had forgotten it. Since she owned so many hats, would she bother to
return and search for this particular one? Likely not. Therefore,
the hat was simply free for anyone to pick up, wasn't it?

At the mere thought of touching such an expensive confection, stroking it, a thrill chased down Tamasin's spine. Glancing over a shoulder to assure herself that Eushanie was a safe distance away and still absorbed with Brendan's charms, she walked to the ditch and stooped to retrieve the beautiful accessory. She handled it gingerly, as if it were some live bird of exotic plumage moored to a crown of bright gold felt. She ran her fingers over the feather reverently, over the silk lining, over the firm crease of the curly brim, flicking off a spot of soil while feverishly considering her options.

Should she keep the hat for herself, nestle it in her trunk of treasures for a future purpose? Or should she return it to Eushanie and hope for a greater reward?

"Keep it."

Engrossed in her prize, Tamasin had almost forgotten Hunter. He had come to stand behind her, and his voice was both blandly amused and tinged with sarcasm.

Flushing, she whirled around to face him, prepared to defend herself.

"You're wondering if Eushanie Hampton will reward you for its return, aren't you?" he went on, regarding her with mocking, narrowed eyes.

Mortified at being so astutely understood, Tamasin remained mute, her chin high.

"Well," Hunter mused lazily, "I figure you could pawn it for three or four shillings—maybe more, if you're lucky and bargain well. What do you think the young miss will give? Money, or a trinket?"

Nonplussed, angry that Hunter had read the workings of her mind, Tamasin raised her chin another notch and attempted to defend herself. "Of course I intend to return it to Miss Eushanie. She'll be grateful to me. And she's generous. It wouldn't surprised me if she gave me a whole guinea in reward."

Hunter laughed, his teeth white in the bright sunlight. "She'd likely give you nothing and you know it."

Tamasin put her hands on her hips. "Do I?"

"You do. Not only do the gentry like to make us believe they have a code of conduct, they like to make us follow it." Leaning his weight upon one hip, Hunter regarded Tamasin with a kind of taunting, cynical humor. "I believe Father Dinsmore preaches the same sort of code. You may have heard him say something to the effect that—how does it go?—ah, yes, that honesty is reward in itself. It's one of those irritating little points of morality the priests think we need to practice in order to get into heaven. Do you believe in heaven, Miss Cullen?"

Tamasin forced herself to meet the directness of the groomsman's gaze and, because she knew he goaded her, took a turn at taunting him. "Of course I believe in heaven. It sits on top of a hill, over there." She pointed at Hampton Hall. "Avery and Eushanie Hampton live in it."

Hunter laughed again, the humor at last touching his black-lashed eyes, along with a measure of pity she did not like.

"I'm not the fool you think I am, Hunter Kinshella," Tamasin asserted. "At least I'm clever enough to *get* something for my trouble."

She almost regretted her words, for they invited a dangerous retort. Hunter could well ask, "And what did you get for *me*, Miss Cullen? What did you get in exchange for ten years of my young life?"

She waited, scarcely breathing, expecting him to speak the words. But he did not. Hunter Kinshella did not take the opportunity to unleash an anger that had surely seethed all during the time he had fought and sweated and suffered in the tight scarlet tunic she had dressed him in ten years ago.

"Go on," he said instead, using the same tolerant tone he might use with a child. "Take the blasted hat if you want it."

But Tamasin hesitated. For some odd and irritating reason she felt deflated. Had she actually *wished* for Hunter Kinshella's admonishment? In a moment of self-realization, she knew that she had indeed wished for it; as unlikely as it seemed, her conscience needed Hunter's raking-down, his hot contempt.

Perhaps her shoulders need his hard rough hands shaking them as well.

Bewildered by the unsettling thoughts, her voice unsteady, she pressed, "Is that all you have to say to me, Hunter. Just, 'take the hat'? Is there nothing more?"

The groomsman's expression tightened, and he looked away. "Haven't I said it all, Tamasin? I've given you a lesson in morality and then encouraged you to steal at the same time. That's profound enough for one day, don't you think? For now, at least?"

"Hunter—"

He paused at her impulsive cry, one eyebrow cocked in question. "Yes?"

Looking at him as he held the halter of another man's horse, Tamasin searched the muddle of her own feelings. She wondered why Hunter had spared her his condemnation. She wondered why he had come back to Ireland in the first place. Lowborn and Catholic, he was doomed to endure the demands of his betters, to cater to the whims of malicious men like those who had just spun away in an elegant black carriage. "Why did you come back?" she asked suddenly, surprised by her own vehemence, by her burning curiosity. "Why did you come back?"

As if the question angered him, he turned away, his hand clenching the thoroughbred's reins more tightly.

"Why?" Tamasin demanded again, her emotion building. "You could've gone anywhere in the world, for heaven's sake—America or Canada. You could've made a life for yourself there, been *free*. Why didn't you, Hunter? Why did you come back to Ireland?"

He paused just long enough to give her a long look, his beautiful mouth slightly curved, saturnine. When she continued to give him a flushed and serious stare, he smiled suddenly, broadly, then turned and continued to lead Sir Harry's pampered horse down the hill toward the forge, his boots tramping through the grass while a Gaelic melody began to vibrate deep in his throat.

Cradling the plumed hat, vexed with his dispassion, Tamasin followed, wanting an answer, determined to get one even if she had to trail him all the way home and pester him for it. *"Why,* Hunter? Why!?"

At last, with his eyes fastened on the horizon where green met blue, the groomsman halted, his shoulders rigid, the fragrant green breeze ruffling his hair. He spoke through his teeth, curtly, as if she should have known the answer all along, knowing his mind as he knew hers. "Because I belong to Ireland, Tamasin. And because Ireland belongs to me."

Loyal to nothing except her own ambition to climb above squalor, Tamasin could not fathom such faithfulness to a country, and retorted harshly, "You belong to Ireland's masters, you mean! Just the way that all of Ireland belongs to them."

"Is that what you believe?"

"Why shouldn't I believe it? Not ten minutes ago I saw you put your back to use for a spoiled young lord, muddy your boots in ditch water. You do the same in countless other ways every day. Sir Harry, Avery, and all the rest of their kind are your masters, Hunter, just as they are mine and Brendan's and Loftus's." She was breathless, incensed. "And they always will be, until the day you manage to escape them. Or until the day one of them beats you half to death for your insolence."

Hunter gazed down upon her, the anger he had earlier kept smothered now shining clear and brightly hard in his eyes. "They are not the masters of my mind, Tamasin. Not as they are of yours."

Although she knew she should have been offended by the words, Tamasin was not. They were true, after all. And yet, the need to defend herself spurred a sharp retort. "That's because they have what I want. And I'll find a way to get a piece of it, see if I don't! Then I'll be free. You can't fight them, Hunter Kinshella. You can't kill them all and overthrow the government, make masters of peasants and peasants of masters, if that's what you're thinking to do.''

"I've no intention of fighting the gentry in any half-baked rebellion cooked up by the United Irish rebels if that's what you're implying. Loftus and the rest are fools. They'll never defeat the English army. They'll never free Ireland.'' Hunter tightened his grip on the bridle reins and started forward again, his stride so long Tamasin had to trot to keep up with it.

"Then what *will* you do?" she persisted, unsatisfied. "Will you continue to stare at the gentry with that anger in your eyes, nurturing it, letting it hover on the brink of explosion? And it *will* explode one day, you know it as well as I do. What then? What *then?*''

"Don't be concerning yourself with my well-being,'' he snapped. "Not now. 'Twould be better if you simply plopped Miss Eushanie's hat upon your head and trotted back to the lodge. I don't need you looking after me. God help me if I ever do.''

He was walking too fast for her and, unwilling to run after him, Tamasin put her hands on her hips and yelled, "You might need me one day, Hunter Kinshella. You just might!''

"I'd rather be hanged.''

For a moment Tamasin watched his squared, retreating back in exasperation. She wanted to run after him, bar his way, banter with more words until his temper gave way and he laid his hard Irish hands upon her. But then, the breeze blew, and the beauty of the golden plume as it rippled like a wild bird's wing fully claimed her attention.

Unable to resist, she set it at an artful angle atop her hair, and for a few green and windswept miles, pretended she was the highborn lady that destiny had surely meant her to be. A lady at whom Hunter Kinshella would gaze and admire, but be unable to touch.

Chapter Six

Hunter knelt in the straw, his fingers covered with the warm blood of a thoroughbred mare. As she heaved, he thrust his hands inside her, grasping the life there, slowly dragging it forth by one fragile foreleg smaller than his wrist. The foal came slithering out, glistening with its dam's fluid, its coat a matted black, its ears flattened against its small but well-shaped head.

As the odor of birth filled the air, the mare snuffled and lifted her head, turning to look at her offspring where it lay exhausted in the straw. The colt struggled to stand, falling back again, but its instinct was strong, telling it that it would not find nourishment lying down. Again it tried to stand and failed.

Snorting, the mare straightened her forelegs, and with a push of muscled haunches came to her feet, shaking the straw from her hide while her foal renewed its efforts to balance, finally bracing its body on four trembling, pipestem legs.

" 'Twill be a fine, fast one, that," Seamus Kinshella commented, ambling up to rest his forearms across the top of the stall rail.

"Aye," Hunter agreed. "Look at the set of his eyes. At the alertness in them."

"A champion, surely." Hunter's grandfather had the look of an aged Zeus. His white hair was long and silky thin, his eyes still bright, and a vestige of strength yet remained in his knotted, weatherworn hands, which for five decades had held the leading reins of the fastest thoroughbreds in Ireland.

"You'll be the one to see him trained, lad," he said, gazing at the foal with sudden wistfulness. And yet, Seamus was relieved just the same, too tired to carry on much longer, pleased that his grandson would carry on after his death. Seamus fixed shrewd but age-pale blue eyes upon the vital young man before him, and added, "That is, if you stay on here."

Hunter met his grandfather's gaze. "I have no plans to go."

"Things are going to be changin', you know," Seamus predicted. "Men are rising up against their masters. The makings of a rebellion are spreadin' all over the country. After it's over, 'twill be a better life for you than it ever was for me."

Retrieving a pitchfork, Hunter stabbed at the straw soiled by the blood of the mare and tossed it into a wooden barrow. "Everyone is full of such talk, Grandda, but the Irish brotherhood will never succeed."

"The devil you say!" Seamus exclaimed as if hearing a sacrilege. "Why, there's even talk that Napoleon himself will be helping us, that he'll be sailing French troops over here and marching with us to Dublin."

Hunter cast another measure of straw aside, wisps of the coarse chaff dusting the darkness of his hair. "No one will get England out of Ireland, Grandda—at least, not upon any day you or I will ever see."

"You're wrong, lad." Seamus drew himself up, his already gruff voice deepening, his old eyes reflecting the airy hopes and grand illusions shared by many of his poor Catholic countrymen. "I hope to heaven ye'll not be disappointing me with any more of such talk. The men in the Brotherhood have been askin' about ye. They're of the mind ye'd make a fine leader, and I agree, of course. I told them ye'd be taking their secret oath before long.''

Hunter paused, pitchfork suspended, his expression tautening at the words. ''You had no right to speak for me. Those fools will find themselves fighting regiments of His Majesty's redcoats if they're not careful, with nothing but homemade pikes for weapons. Do you think the Good Lord is going to swoop down with His sword and aid them on the battlefield? Short of such a miracle, the Irish peasants will never defeat the government, and I'll not be there to watch them litter the fields with their bodies.'' He tightened his jaw. ''I've seen war, Grandda, watched it and tasted it and smelt it until I'm sick of its stench, and I'll not be a part of the storm brewing here.''

Seamus clenched his fist and slammed it down upon the wooden rail, his old body atremble with conviction. ''The United Irish are yer brothers and Ireland is yer land! Are you a coward who would stand back and watch the others fight?''

Hunter straightened. How could he explain to an old man who had never traveled more than fifty miles from Wexford, who had never fought, who had never seen what the world could be, that the optimism of boyhood was easily diminished? Hunter walked a path alone now, believing in nothing or no one but himself and his own resources. In the army he had been ostracized because he was Irish, but he had never flinched. Instead he learned to use his fists so well no one dared to bother him after the first few months. He thought it odd now, when he believed himself hardened to feeling, that his grandfather's words could still wound him so.

''I haven't spent my life swilling poteen like most of the young men of Wexford, Grandda,'' he said, concealing his hurt with sarcasm. ''I have brains enough to know a lost cause when I see one, Grandda.''

''What has happened to ye, Hunter? You're a stranger to me. You're not the man ye were when ye left here.''

Hunter tossed the pitchfork aside. ''Nay. I'm not. I've learned what's worth dying for and what's not. I had a great deal of time to ponder it, you see, tucked away for six months in a dark hole no bigger than a feed bin. And before that, I saw men dying with tropical diseases and wounds, none of them having a notion as to why they suffered. More than one died asking the question—asking *me* why. I had no answer to give. Call me a coward or a traitor or whatever you will, but to my way of thinking, I've earned the right to a bit of peace.''

His words had been harsh and angry and Seamus answered in kind, pinning him with incredulous eyes. ''Do ye not love Ireland any longer, then?''

''I love the land with my soul. But not its causes, Grandda. Causes are designed by men of politics who never die of anything but old age, yet they fill the heads of young fools with idealism and then consign them to a death on some bloody battlefield nobody's ever heard of.''

''There have been some good causes, Hunter, ones that have changed the course of history, ones that have freed men.''

''Aye, but this one that the United Irish are cooking up will free no one. 'Twill only leave the burial yards full and the chapels overflowing with widows and children.''

Seamus quivered, his feeble constitution scarcely able to weather the force of his emotion. ''Ye have disappointed me, lad. Ye were my hope for the future of this village, this country. I'm beginnin' to believe ye lost something important, something deep in yer vitals while ye were in those foreign lands. Aye, I believe 'twas yer *honor* ye lost. Ye have come home without it.''

After delivering his stinging words, the old man turned and stomped down the aisle of loose boxes, a figure of dignity even with his coat worn through at the elbows and the white cobwebbing of his hair no thicker than the wisps atop a toddler's head.

Hunter watched him go. He rubbed a hand over his brow and looked down at the foal, at its fine downy black hide, at its gangly legs still atremble with the strain of standing, at its vulnerable eyes. He felt no less vulnerable. Suddenly he felt no less vulnerable, as weak from life's struggles as the newborn. Sinking down in the straw with his back against the wall, he pondered the future of the foal in order to force his mind away from the hurt of Seamus's disappointment.

He wanted to train the horse, not for Sir Harry's sake, but for the pleasure of watching it grow. He wanted it to grow beneath the guidance of his hands, to feel its life, to hear its breath, to watch its whirligig legs fly free someday. He realized that he had felt numb for a very long time, numb to every emotion except rage. He yearned to feel alive again, to feel happy. He wanted to honor life, not death. He wondered how his life might have been if it had been spent here in Wexford, insulated from the rest of the world. Then, perhaps, he would have been the first young man to take the secret oath his grandfather so revered and, with a weapon in his hand, go out hunting rich gentlemen wearing velvet coats instead of rabbits.

But for now, at least, he wanted to feel the pulse of the land, taste the rain, watch the river, go in search of himself once more in the woodlets green with life. He wanted no one's interference, no one's commands, no one else's ideas forced upon him. He gazed out at the hills. He would like to feel the body of an Irishwoman beneath him again, he realized, feel his senses reawakened by her warm flesh, even see the fruit of his seed slip from her loins, just as he had seen the colt emerge, so that he might experience the mystery of his own immortality.

Tamasin Cullen's face came to mind treacherously, and he closed his eyes against the image. She was not for him. God, no, she was not. Tamasin would never be happy with any man who could not provide her with the things she believed gave happiness.

But he wanted her, nonetheless, desired her as he had never desired any other.

Putting a firm hand upon the foal's neck and murmuring softly in Gaelic, "*Oiche mhaith.* Good night, little lad. With luck, we shall fly like the wind together one day."

* * *

Unfortunately, the lodge had no quarters for female servants. Each evening, when her long day of labor was complete, Tamasin tramped over the dark hills to Da's cottage, which was more ramshackle than ever now that Mam was gone.

Its maintenance claimed far more of her time than she would have liked. But Tamasin, despite her shortcomings, was faithful to her flesh and blood, and so, pilfering bits of food from behind Cook's back and sneaking it home in her apron, she kept her father fed.

" 'Tis lonely in this place," he grumbled one night, a jug of poteen cradled between his knees as he sat unshaven and unwashed beside the hearth. " 'Tis lonely for a man without a woman at his knee."

The pig, which he was fattening for market, plopped down at his feet with a grunt as if agreeing with the complaint. Tamasin glanced at the pair in disgust and crept to the old trunk placed behind a tattered curtain. She had hidden all her treasures inside it, tucked them beneath folded quilts and yellowed sheets, and sprinkled them with dried wild roses to drive away the cottage smells. It was her habit to open the trunk occasionally and reassure herself they were still safely there. By touching them, she was able to sleep more peacefully. She knelt now and fingered the handkerchiefs, the hairpins, the wondrous plumed hat, and the white silk scarf that had once adorned Avery Hampton's neck. She could scarcely look at it without remembering how she had earned it, and wondering what Hunter would do to her if he knew how little ten years of his life had been worth. She pondered the length of silk, trailed it through her fingers, and became so lost in remorse that she failed to hear her father's footsteps until he had flung the curtain back.

As if protecting a set of beloved children, Tamasin hastily stuffed the scarf and handkerchiefs into the trunk and slammed the lid.

"What are ye hidin' in there, lass?" Jamsie asked suspiciously, reaching out. He reached out to pluck at the leather clasp of the trunk. "Show me."

" 'Tis just some of my things, Da—female things."

"Show me."

"Nay."

"Show me!"

But she refused, slapping his fingers away, throwing her body over the trunk, battling until the two of them were locked in a physical struggle, her strength pitted against his, a daughter's will testing a sire's right to pry and possess anything she had managed to get for herself.

When she clawed at his hands he began to beat her as he had once done his wife, boxing her ears, slapping her cheeks, and then, with one sweep of his wiry arm, knocking her backward so that she lost her balance and fell against the hard clay wall. With a spiraling kind of horror, Tamasin watched him open the lid, watched him violate its contents with his dirty hands, plunder the pureness of a dream that was hers alone and nurtured since the earliest days of childhood. She felt the throbbing of her lip not at all, nor the swelling of her eye, only the pain of a suddenly endangered hope.

Jamsie seized the silk scarf, then the handkerchiefs with their dainty love knots and lace, then the striped cloud of skirt and the comb, gathering them all to his chest while his seamed, crinkled face stretched with a wide smile.

"Ye did not pawn them to the gombeen man, then, lass?" he hissed. "Ye did not trade away these fine, grand things ye got from the Hall?"

When she failed to answer the rhetorical question, Jamsie leaned over and grasped her by the hair, wrenching her to her feet and shaking her until her head lolled back. "Ye didn't pawn them?"

Tamasin merely stared back at him, hating him in that moment, hating the light in his eyes, hating the wide mouth and its long lower lip that resembled her own.

"Yer mother told me ye had pawned them to the gombeen man," he said in confused wonder, his dense brain attempting to function through its alcoholic haze. He released Tamasin's hair, but kept her treasures clutched to his chest. "She told me ye had pawned them to get us through last winter, the lyin' witch."

Her mother had told him that? Lied?

If Dora had been standing in the room at that moment, Tamasin knew Jamsie would have beaten her for her deceit. So why had she risked it? Why had Dora lied for Tamasin and allowed her to keep the handful of fripperies that could have been traded for a few precious shillings? In the end, had she understood her daughter, given her the only gift she had known to give? It would seem so. Even if she had had no dreams herself, Dora Cullen had protected the dreams of her child. Tears came to Tamasin's eyes even while Jamsie laughed in delight. Setting the elegant plumed hat atop his head, he began to dance about the room, his old shoes tapping the dirt floor in a half-drunken jig, his smile so wide, the gaps in his teeth showed. Tamasin sat watching him, knowing that tomorrow the precious castoff odds and ends from Hampton Hall—the things that might eventually have bought her freedom from Da and his cottage—would be traded for a new striped waistcoat, or woolen tam and a few bottles of whiskey.

Eushanie's hat slipped off Jamsie's head, and he caught it by the feather, tearing out a few wisps of gold fluff in the process. Then he wheeled about to face his daughter with a look of speculation in his eye.

"Come here," he commanded. "Put on this grand bonnet. And the skirt and scarf, as well. I'd like to be seein' me girl dressed up like a lady. Aye, I want to see ye all trussed up in silk and feathers. Come here, I said."

Tamasin obeyed, woodenly uncurling her legs and standing up, allowing her father to perch the hat atop her hair and tilt it at a ridiculous angle. She felt sickened as she slipped the striped skirt over her woolen gown, slowly wound the scarf about her neck, tied the ribbon about her loosened hair, and stood for his inspection.

His ogling repulsed her, and she recoiled when he put his fingers alongside her cheek and stroked it.

"Well," he announced in a considering tone, rubbing a hand over his bristly jaw. "Ye're quite a fine one—finer to look at than me old eyes had realized ere now. Come over here, closer to the firelight."

He scurried to pull up a stool for her, kicking the pig out of its warm place, dusting off the seat with the palm of his hand while Tamasin clutched the striped skirt to her waist. She eased down, experiencing the humiliation of being assessed like a piece of livestock for sale.

Jamsie examined her, swilling poteen as he grasped her chin and turned it to catch the most advantageous light. Taking one of the delicate handkerchiefs he clutched, he slowly pushed it inside the neckline of her gown. Tamasin shivered. But she forced herself to endure his scrutiny, to endure his breath, his hands as they tucked the last scented square of lace where the others had gone before it. And then, when he had raised the jug of poteen to his lips again, his eyes closed in the savoring of it, she leapt from the stool and wrenched open the door.

"Hey, girl!" he bellowed, lunging for her as she fled.

But once Tamasin had escaped to the yard and the dark fells spread before her like a familiar plaid blanket, she knew she was safe. Her agile young legs were too fleet for her father's stumbling pace, and she ran on and on, breathless, veering toward the lodge as if it were a haven, her true home. She knew she would have to find a place to hide her treasures, a place where Da would never find them, never threaten again to take away her hopes.

Avoiding the kennels, she rounded the shuttered lodge, creeping along the privet hedge, for if she were caught by one of the servants wearing Miss Eushanie's new hat, questions might be asked.

The shadowy perimeter of the stable provided no hiding

place for her bundle of treasures. The home of Sir Harry's valuable racing horses was more neatly kept than his house, and no tall weeds or heaps of discarded stone provided a concealing niche. Around the shallow paved pool used for washing carriages, the cobbles were clean-swept, and the stone walls did not even offer a crevice large enough to stuff a lady's handkerchief.

Tamasin sighed and glanced around, loath to hide the treasures in a field somewhere. Wandering beggars slept beneath the hedges and along the ditches, and their roaming children might spy the tall gold plume and steal it. She realized ruefully that she would be joining those thieves and beggars tonight, for she could not go back to Da and sleep.

The wind changed direction all at once, and the lion-shaped weathervane atop the stable roof swung around, galloping a new course across the sky. Its creaking caused the pigeons in the neat white dovecote tucked beneath the eaves to awaken and flutter restlessly.

Tamasin glanced up at their aerie, envying their snug, aloof home, wishing she could transform herself into a feathered creature and with her head buried beneath a wing, go to sleep unnoticed.

Scrutinizing the dovecote with a sudden interest and judging it accessible, she hastily leaned to remove her petticoat. After spreading it out, she folded the scarf, handkerchiefs, and skirts inside, and then tied it into a bundle. The hat she crammed securely upon her head.

With difficulty, and with the sharp slate shingles cutting her hands and elbows, she managed to hoist herself to the first elevation of the steep roof. Once she had gained her balance there, she tested the strength of the drainpipe. Climbing was not as easy as it had been in childhood, especially with a bundle tied round her waist, but after several attempts, Tamasin maneuvered close enough to the high eaves to swing her feet over to the dovecote ledge.

At her intrusion the pigeons beat their wings in alarm. She held her breath, fearing the noise would alert a restless stable lad, or worse, the noisy hounds in their kennel. Holding still, she waited, gazing out over the rooftop, suddenly feeling as if she stood on the top of the world, she and the galloping weathervane, with nothing above them but sailing clouds and a cold blue moon. A marvelous feeling, it was, exhilarating and liberating. How eerie the purple scattering of mud huts appeared, and amid them, but not a part of them, the spires of Hampton Hall. Suddenly, she wondered at the capriciousness of fate, which had strewn people over the rough green land and consigned them either to providence or misfortune with a seemingly random hand.

There was a little hinged door at the side of the dovecote, built there so that the nests could be cleaned out, and this she wrenched opened, shutting her eyes when the pigeons dashed about, raising feathers and feather dust. Seeking escape, they finally pushed through their tiny round doorways and flew heavenward in a whisper of frantic wings.

After their departure, the night grew quiet again and, untying the bundle from her waist, Tamasin squatted down and balanced. A sound alerted her. After a moment of listening intently, she realized that she had been discovered.

"Communing with the birds, Miss Cullen?" a familiar voice inquired. "Or are you thinking to get another feather for that hat?"

Her fingers were slipping, losing their grip on the dovecote, and she was hardly reassured to have a musket aimed at her chest. But at least, even if he despised her, Hunter Kinshella would be easier to deal with than Loftus or Sir Harry.

"If you're intending to fire that musket at me," she hissed, shifting, trying to regain her hold, "then Sainted Mary, do it quickly before I fall off the roof."

"Come down," he ordered, grinning at her discomposure. "Come down where I can see you in all your grand finery. Shall I ask you to dance?"

Tamasin decided that even the rudiments of civility had been stripped from Hunter Kinshella's social repertoire. And yet, because she had now reached a point of near desperation, she decided to admit her plight. Even if her honesty did not touch him, perhaps his good nature—if he still possessed any at all—might prevail and let her have her way.

"I meant to hide a few things in the dovecote," she admitted, staring down at his dark, moon-limned face with its lingering smile. "Personal things. It's the only place I know that's safe."

Hunter considered her with his head tilted back and the musket cradled in one arm. For a moment Tamasin believed that he had decided to help, that an ounce or two of sympathy had stirred somewhere in that steel-lined breast of his. But her hope was quickly dispelled.

"You'll not be hiding anything up there. Get down," he ordered again. "And bring those things with you."

"But—"

"*Get down.*"

With a last longing look at the dovecote and the verdigris lion, whose back was now turned against her, Tamasin retied the bundle about her waist and eased her way down the roof line on her stomach, cursing silently all the way. Slipping to the next elevation by way of the drainpipe, she climbed gingerly down to the top paddock rail where Hunter awaited. Her hands were bleeding, cut by the shingles and the seams of the drainpipe, and she was angry enough to spit.

"Why are you stalking around with a musket anyway?" she snapped, covering her disappointment with disdain. "Have you appointed yourself the guardian of Sir Harry's stable?"

The groomsman upended the musket, leaned upon it, and rubbed a smear of mud from its barrel with a long, idle hand. "If I were given to appointing myself to do anything, Miss Cullen, being the guardian of Sir Harry's stable would not be my first choice. But then, I don't always have a say in what happens to me, much to my annoyance. For example, I thought my days of sentry duty were over when I left the army. But," he indicated the musket, "it seems I was mistaken."

"Are you patrolling for peasant rebels?" she asked, incredulous. "Has Sir Harry stationed you to watch for them in case they come here to do mischief?"

"He has. Every night."

"And does he really believe you would kill your own kind in his defense?"

"Apparently he does. And with a great deal of confidence. Wouldn't you kill for your master, Miss Cullen?"

She resented his deliberate sarcasm and countered, "You would have. You saved Sir Harry's life when you caused the chandelier to fall upon the bear."

"So I did. And I was well rewarded for it, too." The remark was cynical, uttered in his clipped Irish brogue. "I was allowed to stay on here and make myself useful to him."

"Then why did you do it? You could have stood by like the rest of the servants and hoped he would be mauled to death."

"Indeed I could."

Tamasin raised an impatient hand, prompting him to go on. "Well, then . . . ?"

"Then Avery Hampton would have been my master, I imagine."

She almost smiled, for a measure of Hunter's careful humor had slipped out past his armor.

She looked at him, at his white shirt, painfully clean, his polished boots, which he surely buffed at the end of every long day, and realized that, while Hunter Kinshella was made of the Irish earth, he was not subservient to it like the others who labored. He had set himself apart somehow, not a master of the land, not a slave to it, but simply *of* it. And again, as she had done more than once before, Tamasin experienced an affinity for the groomsman. Perhaps he had returned to Ireland a harsher man, withdrawn, stripped of emotion, but on the inside, in some deep and secret place, she suspected his spirit still remained intact and perfectly whole.

And because she believed her spirit was well anchored and fierce, too, her dream indestructible, her strong will able to carry her anywhere she wanted to go, Tamasin felt not only a kinship with Hunter Kinshella, but desire. She was ready both emotionally and physically for a man, young enough to feel passion and old enough to understand it, and because this man before her was so attractive in face and form, so alluring in his detachment, she knew she could love him physically. And be loved by him.

He was looking closely at her now, searching her face in the damp, fragrant night, and she realized that he could discern her swelling eye and bleeding lip. Hastily, she lowered her lashes, unwilling to let him see the ugly traces of Da's beating, afraid he might think she had allowed some coarse village swain to do the deed. "Me da had a go at me tonight," she muttered.

Hunter was silent a few seconds. When he finally spoke, his voice was quiet, raspy with an emotion he suppressed out of pride perhaps, or out of fear of what he felt. He covered it with a layer of wryness. "I see. Well, then, give me the bundle and I'll keep it for you, along with that damned nuisance of a hat. Unless, of course, you want to carry it around until someone steals it from you, or accuses you of thievery—a charge, if memory serves, that would be entirely justified."

Hunter put out a hand to take them, and instinctively Tamasin jerked away, childishly clutching her possessions as if he were no less a threat to their security than her father had been.

"Don't you trust me?" he asked. Then, clearly enjoying her dilemma, he gave a short, almost self-deprecating laugh. "You shouldn't, of course."

A shred of alabaster cloud veiled the moon, and unable to see the groomsman's face, Tamasin could only listen to the rhythm of his breathing, smell the neat's-foot oil on his boots, imagine the texture of his rough brown skin. She wondered what sort of life he would have lived had she not betrayed him, how much less suffering he would have endured. Her guilt almost choked her all at once, and in a faint, whispery voice she asked, "Why would you help me? Why would you help me after. . . ." Although the words burned upon her lips, she couldn't finish them.

Her deep contrition seemed to touch Hunter too keenly, and he stiffened. Then, as if annoyed that he was having to explain his tiny act of kindness, Hunter jerked a hand through his hair and said tightly, "Let's say I understand you, and leave it at that."

"But, do you? Do you understand me?"

"Eminently. You've never made a secret of your motives, have you?"

He was flirting softly now with the subject of her past treachery, a treachery that had changed his life—and *him*. And still wanting to hear him plunge into the subject with all the frightening force of his nature, to castigate her, even put his hands on her body and shake her half to death, Tamasin goaded his temper. "You've never been in my circumstances, Hunter," she accused. "I'm a lass born to a half-starved family, to a drunken cottier without an ounce of decency in his body. My mam died from the life she led. My only escape from it is a good marriage, or pandering to a rich man. You've never been desperate like that, with so few choices. If you were, you just might sell your soul to escape—your body and your soul."

Her voice rose, sharpened with a fierce need to break Hunter Kinshella's emotion, unleash it so that it might cleanse her. "You might even sell *me*," she taunted, "if you got the chance. Ask me what I got for you, Hunter Kinshella," she said feverishly, leaning close, close enough so that he could easily seize her if he chose. "Go on, ask me what price Avery Hampton put on your life. Ask me what payment I received!"

She was breathless from emotion, from the strength of her need to hear his terrible anger, to see rage in his eyes, to feel his hands upon her. Nearly gasping, she stood with her fists clenched, staring into his eyes, waiting for his fury.

But he only leaned against the paddock railing without a trace of tension, without any sign of wrath or discomposure, and simply asked in a quiet and rational tone, "Do you intend to give me that bundle of trifles, or don't you?"

Tamasin wondered why Hunter Kinshella was being kind to

her tonight. Did he refuse to give her what she wanted—his blame, his raging anger, in order to punish her in the most painful way he knew?

She thrust the bundle at him violently, and cried, "Take them then! Take them all—all but one."

He looked at her questioningly and she yanked the scrap of silk from the rest and wound it about her neck. "The scarf," she said breathlessly. "You cannot have the scarf." She thought he might ask why, she wanted him to ask, but he only reached out to take the bundle. She watched his fingers close about the pieces of her future, the only things of beauty and grace she owned.

He tucked the bundle under an elbow with no regard for them and, shifting his musket to the other hand, turned to go. With his back to her, he hesitated, then said quietly over a shoulder, "No one would bother you in the dairy if you decided to sleep there tonight. 'Tis dry, at least. And safe."

The doves returned to roost all at once, one by one, and Tamasin glanced to see them duck into their nest for the night. The groomsman went to stand apart in the purple shadows, regarding her from a distance now.

She met his gaze, made certain he watched. Then she walked in the opposite direction of the dairy, heading for the cold open fields, making it obvious that she planned to sleep beneath a hedge rather than accept his second, punishing little kindness that night.

Chapter Seven

Steam from the pudding Tamasin boiled for Sir Harry's foxhounds wafted up from the iron kettle and reddened her cheeks. She flapped her hands to disperse the cloud, closing her eyes to smell the hearty aroma of the oatmeal mixture. She poured cooled broth into the pudding, then a pail of milk, and after she had stirred it with a long wooden paddle, added the pans of raw meat Cook had chopped.

"The blasted creatures around here eat better than we do," the white-aproned woman griped, eyeing the morsels as they disappeared into the mush. "Feedin' good meat to a bear and to dogs! A disgrace. And the amount of corn those horses burn would be keepin' the whole village alive for a year or more, I wager. I'll throw me lot in with the United Irish, I will, pour a few drops of aquafortis into the soup one evening and do away with all the gentlemen carousin' about this house."

Ignoring her empty threats and familiar complaints, caring not a whit about politics and the grievances of those who were not clever enough to better themselves through any means save violence, Tamasin filled two buckets with the oatmeal

concoction and backed out the kitchen door to the yard, glad
of the coolness of the early morning.

As she trudged over the cobbles toward the kennels, her
shoulders bowed with the weight of the buckets, the hounds
began their hoarse barking, hurling themselves at the iron gates,
each attempting to outyelp his fellows in order to gain attention.
She set down the pails, and for a moment observed the frenzied
black and tan bodies, wondering if she dared open the gate and
risk being knocked off her feet in the rush for breakfast.

The kennel keeper, a crusty Galway man nearly as ancient
as Seamus Kinshella, was nowhere to be seen, not waiting
impatiently beside the gate and grunting a greeting as he usually
did each dawn. Instead, out of the freshening darkness Hunter
Kinshella appeared, his white shirt visible where his knee-
length, unbuttoned trusty gaped open, his hair combed back
from his brow and still wet from an early morning washing.

Although Tamasin spied the groomsman working about the
lodge stable every day, the two of them had not exchanged a
word since the night he had taken her bundle of treasures. But
they *looked* at each other. Every day, while drawing water from
the well, Tamasin surreptitiously watched Hunter groom the
horses, watched him put a gloss on a chestnut hide with a
woolen cloth, or comb burrs out of a long coarse tail. Of late
he had been spending much of his time in the paddock with a
black foal, which he always addressed in Gaelic, rubbing his
hands over its body to accustom it to the touch of a man. Other
times, when the dew still sparkled upon the turf, Tamasin would
peer out the kitchen window and see him astride the back of
one of the racing stallions, setting out at a graceful trot toward
the practice course.

His appearance—the texture of his hair, the angles of his
face, the build of his frame—had come to be as intriguing to
her as any of the expensive treasures in the lodge. He stirred
her physically, too, but she attributed that infatuation to the
needs of her inexperienced body, knowing that it was natural
for a lass to ogle a handsome young man. She knew, too, that

although she may be unable to control her wayward thoughts, she would never act upon them. She was too ambitious to risk a dalliance—or a pregnancy—with anyone of her own class. Even the splendid Kinshella.

Tamasin suspected that Hunter, unwillingly or not, enjoyed looking at her as well. On one or two occasions she had found him paused at his labors, observing her, examining her with a contemplative masculine interest. And yet, for all the irrepressible and uneasy looks, there had formed between them a sort of truce, one unspoken but mutually agreed upon the night she had entrusted her hopes to his hand.

Now Hunter stepped forward and unlatched the gate. "Old Donnel is ailing this morning. You can help me feed the hounds."

Not waiting for an answer, assuming compliance, he took the pails from her hands and forged a path through the lively pack of dogs. The feeding space was a small lean-to whose walls were lined with wooden troughs built to hold water and feed. As he poured the oatmeal mush into them, the dogs crowded about his legs in a pushing tide.

One of the hounds, gray-muzzled and slower-footed, was forced out of the huddle by the more aggressive pack members and, hanging back, paced hungrily with saliva dripping from his jowls. Hunter knelt down, tipped over one of the buckets and allowed the elderly dog to lap up the remains.

"Fine old fellow, this," he commented. "He's trained his share of pups, been a grand leader. But likely he's seen his last season."

"He trains the pups?" Tamasin echoed.

"Aye. Puppies in their first season are always tied to an older, experienced dog. If they have any sense at all, they learn from him."

"Learn what?"

"The ways of sport. They learn to ignore hares and deer, to track only foxes, and to bark as soon as they strike the line of scent."

Tamasin studied the groomsman's bent head, the sinewy slope of his shoulders, as he turned the pail again so the old hound could reach the last dollop of feed. It struck her that whenever Hunter tended animals, he lost all traces of his brittleness. He seemed attuned to them.

"I never realized dogs had to be taught to kill foxes," she admitted. "I thought they were simply turned loose and knew what to do on their own."

"Fine instinct makes a fine foxhound. But there's a deal of training to be done as well. And a hound only has a few good seasons—four, maybe five." Hunter rubbed the old dog, his fingers kneading the loose silky hide at its neck. "Sometimes the fox keeps them running twenty or more miles on a morning hunt. 'Tis a grueling test of endurance."

"I thought you knew only about Sir Harry's horses," Tamasin said, leaning to pat the hound's back.

Hunter glanced up at her from his hunkered position beside the dog, and in the first smudge of dawn, Tamasin could see a shaving nick upon his chin. It still bled a little.

"Besides the racing thoroughbreds," he explained, "I tend the hunting horses Sir Harry owns. In order to understand them properly, I make it my business to understand the hounds, even the foxes."

"What does anyone need to know about foxes except that they're sly and quick?" Tamasin asked, yanking a handkerchief from her pocket and offering it. "Your chin . . . it's bleeding."

Hunter ignored the handkerchief and used his thumb to wipe the blood away. "Foxes duel. You've probably heard them at night, making a racket like yowling cats. Sometimes they settle with one mate, which they keep for a lifetime—fourteen or fifteen years." He bent to retrieve the bucket. "Of course, around here, most foxes only live to be three or four before Sir Harry's hounds track them down."

Tamasin shivered, and although she did not think there had been any deliberate gruesomeness in Hunter's comment, only a statement of fact, the old hound suddenly appeared less of a cuddly pet and more an instrument of death.

"Come with me," Hunter said, smiling suddenly at her squeamishness, melting all her own defenses. "Come with me."

Tamasin followed him into an adjoining space that was straw-filled and musty, and exclaimed when she spied a litter of puppies.

"They were whelped in July," he told her, scooping up the runt and depositing it in her hands.

Tamasin had never held a puppy before. Cottiers could not afford to keep any animal save those used for food or for working the fields, and the notion of handling a creature purely for pleasure proved a novel one, especially after the nastiness of Miss Eushanie's pet. A smooth pink tongue licked the spaces between her fingers, finding the pudding there, and she raised the pup to her cheek, feeling the fuzziness of his head.

"He feels like Miss Eushanie's sable cloak," she remarked, delighted. "I was allowed to touch it once when I was called up to the Hall to help the laundry maids. 'Twas soft and warm like this."

"Do you measure everything in your life by what's in Hampton Hall?"

His words were spoken quietly, with the usual sarcasm, but Tamasin answered honestly. "Aye. I suppose I do. But you needn't lecture me. As I've told you before, Father Dinsmore does plenty of that when I give him the chance."

Hunter's lip curled wryly. "I wouldn't dream of trying to discourage you from your course. Truth to tell, I'm curious to see just how far from a cottier's hut your ambition can carry you."

Not answering, Tamasin put the pup down, only to have one of its dew claws snag in her knitted shawl. She frowned, struggling to unhook the squirming dog without unraveling the yarn.

Hunter reached to perform the task himself, and she watched

his fingers, unsurprised to see that they were clean, the nails having no black rims of dirt beneath them, the creases no stains like the hands of other laborers.

When he released the wriggling pup and set it down, Tamasin followed him out, but before they had crossed the kennel yard the little dog chased after them to play, veering in front of Tamasin's feet so that she tripped and lost a shoe. The pup snatched it by the heel and galloped off.

Fearing that the whole litter would descend upon it, chew and mangle the precious leather, Tamasin quickly gave chase and rescued the shoe, then plopped down on the ground and, unhooking the laces, struggled to slide it on again over her stockings. Hunter stood by, and on impulse, she extended her hand, inviting him to help her up.

The groomsman merely observed her for a moment with a rueful expression. Tamasin thought he might refuse. But, finally, he reached to take hold of her fingers, his grasp as hard and firm as it might have been gripping a pair of reins. She clasped his hand with equal firmness, not letting go when she should have done, when it would have been appropriate. She wasn't sure why she held on, except that for weeks she had been imagining what it would be like to be held by Hunter Kinshella. In the pink morning air there lingered a kind of passion, she thought, as well as in the breeze that smelled of gorse, and in the warm tan bodies that brushed against their legs. Most of all, her healthy young body ached with a budding, vital need.

Hunter felt his blood rush, his nerves quicken with the sudden restive urge to touch and be touched. In that moment he forgot everything but a single, simple need—the need to be with a woman. All at once his face twisted with the exquisite imagining of sensation. Since returning home, even before, he had denied himself the gratification of coupling. Having been made to suffer the misery of war and isolation during his time away from Ireland, he had, in a perverse way, wanted to experience denial's deepest depths, its darkest torments, its sacrifices.

But now, all that was past, or nearly so. He wanted to put his mouth on Tamasin Cullen's full red lips, he wanted to touch her breasts, feel the heart that beat beneath. He realized suddenly that he wanted her selfishly. Her own pleasure mattered not at all to him; indeed, if his mouth hurt hers, bruised it, he would not care. He wanted to bring her pain. Her treachery had altered his young life just when his future had hovered like a bright arc upon the horizon. Once, he had owned thirty guineas, coin earned over the course of his life with hard labor and a few fortunate days at Sir Harry's races. It had been money enough to make a start. But it had been taken from him when a stickpin and pocket watch had been tucked among his clothes by a small perfidious hand.

I have hated her, Hunter reminded himself, even as he thought of dipping his head and taking her lips. He imagined the pressure of his mouth, his teeth on hers, imagined her allowing his hands to know her body intimately. Lost in his bright, passionate thoughts, he heard nothing but the roaring of his own blood.

Tamasin leaned closer, raised her face to Hunter's. It seemed natural, she thought, this wanting to tempt him, this wish to be tempted. He was staring at her so oddly, his intent eyes showing no tenderness, no affection, only a raw and terrible yearning.

Hesitating no longer, he bent to press his lips to hers, swiftly, almost awkwardly, his body driven by her offer. He invaded her mouth with his, trailed his lips over her face, then moving with an urgent possessive hand to find her breast. She arched, responding to the prompting of her own desire and, encouraged, he slid his fingers through the hooks at the back of her gown. She knew little of men, but sensed that he had denied himself, and now was overwhelmed, shaking with the force of his own suppressed need. He was lost, physically and sensually, drenched with his desire. He backed her against the stall of the kennel, pressed himself against her, touching her hair, her throat, her breasts. His breaths mingled with hers as he took her lips again and again, and she relinquished herself. She knew he would not stop as long as she allowed him, encouraged him to go on.

"Kinshella!"

Both of them heard clearly the barked word, but only Tamasin jumped and jerked her head around. Hunter stood his ground, his breaths coming hard, his eyes glinting, his hands still upon her body.

Avery Hampton, dressed in hunter's pink, leaned against the fence, watching them. The gazes of the two men immediately locked, communicating a mutual detestation.

"You're not paid to dally with the maids, Kinshella," Avery drawled. "Go and fetch my horse."

The groomsman did not comply. He merely continued to regard Avery with level eyes, his hesitation a deliberate denial of authority.

"I shall have you and your brother and the old man thrown out today," the baronet's son drawled. "Your grandfather would not survive a month on the road."

Tamasin knew that only through a great force of will did Hunter prevent himself from striking Avery Hampton. And yet, when he finally moved, it was as if he deigned to do so by choice and not by order.

As he turned, Hunter looked at Tamasin, noted that she was unnerved—a reaction rare to her nature. How subdued she was, how contrite. With a sudden, rueful realization, he guessed that she was ashamed to have been caught with a groomsman's hands upon her body. She feared that Avery's opinion of her would be diminished, feared Avery would think her sullied now, no longer worthy of his masculine attentions—should he decide to honor her with them one day.

Hunter could almost see the frantic workings of Tamasin's mind as she considered the possible consequences of kissing a groomsman.

Then, confirming Hunter's suspicions, she impulsively drew

her hand across her lips as if to wipe away the moist remains of his kiss.

"Wipe the kiss away as you please, Tamasin," he hissed. "You'll not *forget* it so easily."

Unable to hear the groomsman's words, but sensing undercurrents, Avery tapped the end of his riding crop atop the rail and attempted to provoke his adversary. "Surely you can do better than a penniless stable hand with a hot temper, Tamasin Cullen."

She slanted her eyes at Hunter, formulated a response, then hesitated.

Hunter pinned her with a caustic look and said savagely, "Go ahead. Agree with him. I want to hear you say it."

But she hesitated. She sensed that her future hung in the balance, that its course would be determined by her answer. She needed Avery Hampton to escape Wexford, to escape her mother's life. Hunter Kinshella could offer no escape, except fleeting ones, when he held her in his arms.

Taking a breath, she looked directly at Avery and declared in a quiet, arrogant tone, "Aye, you're right. I can do better than a groomsman." Speaking the words hurt her.

"I beg your pardon?" Avery cupped a hand round his ear, feigning deafness. "I didn't hear you."

Tamasin forced herself to repeat the words, to defy her feelings for Hunter, to wound him yet again. "I can do better than a groomsman."

The tall, dark subject of the conversation smiled unpleasantly. Then, pivoting on a heel, he stalked away.

Waiting until the groomsman had pushed through the gate, Avery entered it, the puppies trotting up to explore his scent. With his toe, the young master nudged them aside and came to stand next to Tamasin. He studied her face, her bruised mouth, and smiled nastily. "Rough, was he? Did you like it that way?" When she made no reply, he asked, "Do you know what I think, Tamasin Cullen? I think you're every bit as insolent as Kinshella. The difference is, you understand your

place. He does not. You know there's more to be gained by
serving the upper class than by opposing it. You're a beautiful
lass. And you're clever. Quite clever, and not a little ambitious.''

"Do you disapprove of that?" she asked baldly, sensing that
her boldness attracted him.

Avery laughed and idly trailed his riding crop through his
gloved fingers, squinting his eyes as if pondering a problem.
"How could I?" he asked, raising a shoulder in an eloquent
shrug. "Especially when I myself have no ambition at all. Very
little anyway. Not enough to move me to any great accomplishments."

"But gentlemen are born for leisure."

"No, they're not. How wrong you are." Avery watched
the pup snuffling about his boots, his eyes half-lidded. "A
gentleman is born to manage his estate. He must keep an alert
eye on every steward, agent, tenant, footman, stable hand, and
maid so that they do not cheat him, bring rack and ruin to his
dynasty—which, by the way, is occurring even now to my
father's holdings, although he is too busy entertaining himself
to notice it. And I, who will inherit whatever is left, might very
well find myself in straitened circumstances by middle age.
Not that the money is lacking now. The gold still flows, but
'twill not last forever."

Avery surveyed the soft blurred landscape stretching toward
the river, the green fields crisscrossed with dark emerald hedges
that formed a woven plaid of fertile earth. "Truthfully, I don't
give a scrap for the estate or for the land. But I care very much
for what it supplies."

"Then why don't you take its management in hand?"

Pushing a lock of yellow hair from his eyes, Avery smiled.
Tamasin recognized a kind of resigned and unembarrassed self-
pity in the expression. "Because," he said, "I have no ambition,
as I told you. I'm indolent. The thought of spending my life
pouring over account books and tenantry records is appalling

to me. Too tedious." The wry smile came again. "I am my father's son, you see."

"Then you should surround yourself by people you can trust."

Avery's smile changed to one of genuine amusement. "And you are going to suggest that I can trust you?"

"I've always done your bidding," she asserted. "Faithfully, haven't I?"

"That you have." He grasped her chin and she looked into his coppery eyes with no abashment, feeling the authority of generations in his grip. And as he held her imprisoned with one squeezing hand, her hopes suddenly soared. She knew that she and this gentleman were playing a sort of game together. It was a more serious game than the one they had played before, one that could lead to grave consequences only for her; for it was quite common, even an accepted practice among the male gentry, to dally with serving girls. Requiring no responsibility whatsoever, nor even any pangs of conscience, dalliances were a cheap, pleasurable pastime for young masters. Most peasant lasses considered it a privilege to be despoiled by a man of position. Daughters were sometimes given away in ritualistic ceremonies by honored cottiers, then borne in a carriage to some ancestral hall, where they stayed one or two nights. Or until the gentleman grew bored with them and sent them home.

Tamasin had pondered such a relationship with Avery Hampton, but had not determined her course of action should the situation arise. Being a party to his misdeeds called for a different level of servitude than the bestowing of her body. She was not certain she wanted to surrender that part of herself, for it was the only thing she had to give away or not if she chose. However, she *did* know that if the young master desired her body, and she decided to relinquish it to him, the price would be very high.

"I shall have to think what to do with you," Avery mused, watching her expression, her clever violet eyes, "before you

fall prey to someone like Kinshella and end up in a mud hut
producing a brat every year, spoiling your looks.''

Tamasin's gaze met his soberly. "I'll not be falling prey to
anyone who'll keep me in a mud hut.''

"Hunting bigger game, are you, eh? Of course, you are.''
Avery released her chin and gave her a speculative examination
before his eyes clouded with some distressing, even urgent
problem. "I wonder ... ?'' He glanced over his shoulder in
the direction of Hampton Hall, and then back at her, murmuring,
"Well, you might indeed catch bigger game. Soon, if you're
clever and fortunate. Yes, you might. That is—'' he pinched
her chin again, hard. "If you can manage to keep yourself
away from the groomsman long enough. I will not have you
after him.''

It was a measure of his anger than the state they had, the
way that could bear to grab his composure, while tearing the
rest of the admonitions in accented one notes again, she said
nothing to dry ask eyebrow time, Remaining no correct bell,
answered, nor even any pinch of censors and continued way
a clever, prudent do practice for young matters. Those pressure
seemed some what mattered for to be intruded by a man of
caution. Daughters were something of less than in original
her comment in her Compassed, then blood to a bride was
some arousing half, where they stayed her two two-pledges till
until the guardians peer halted wash them, and sent there some.

I imagined that conceived such a relationship with Avery would
dial, but that she determined her course of action as ash the
situation arise found a force to the satisfactory action that care.
one level of terrible, than the prostitution or her body. She was
so coming, she worked, to that was first part of the only to a
was, the only, thing she had to give away—or not, if she chose.
However, she did know she'd the would easily claimed her
body, and she continued to refinished it to him, the prices would
be very high.

"I shall have to think what to do with you," Avery mused,
watching her for reaction. Her shrewd widen eyes. "Before you

Chapter Eight

When hunting was the order of the day, it was done with all the pageantry of sight and sound that the gentry loved, complete with silver-laced hats, stirrup cups, curled brass horns, and embroidered saddle cloths.

But the hunting of foxes across the green turf and over thorny hedges and stone walls was not the only sport occurring on Sir Harry's estate one morning. A less obvious one was taking place—in full view if one knew to look—right in the center of his cobbled stable yard.

Eushanie Hampton, not permitted by her father to join the men in their play, had trotted over from the Hall with the excuse of seeing the hunters off, but with the real intention of seeking the company of the charming Brendan Kinshella. Tamasin was certain of it, and with dismay watched the unfolding of what, considering Brendan's rashness and Eushanie's social class, would surely come to no good.

"Good mornin' to you, Miss." Brendan doffed his cap when Eushanie, after having furtively searched for him, reined her mount across his path.

"My mare has been favoring her near hind leg," she said
with her chin raised. Sadly, her hauteur did not match her large,
plain features framed by the fine-spun hair escaping from a
feathered hat. She peered down at Brendan as if to confirm the
fact that her romantic memory had not exaggerated his golden
good looks, and apparently finding that it had not, proceeded.
"Would you take a look at the hoof, please?"

Brendan favored her with his dimpled grin. "Let me just
help you down from the saddle first. There now, careful of
your fine boots, Miss. The ground is a wee bit wet. Just put
your foot here—dainty, it is, if I may be allowed to say so."

Tamasin rolled her eyes and, listening unashamedly from
behind the low wall of the kitchen garden, waited to see just
how far the two of them would go.

"I think 'tis a thorn embedded in the soft part of the hoof,
Miss—the frog we call it," Brendan went on. "Aye, feel the
heat here at the top of the hoof above the corona? Put your
hand where mine is . . . there—such a small hand yours is. Just
let me go and fetch a pair of pliers now, and I'll have the nasty
thing out in no time a'tall."

Tamasin smiled, knowing that the thorn in the mare's hoof
was just as imaginary as the alleged limp. Putting down the
cabbages she had picked, she stood up and peered over the
wall, interested to see Brendan go through the exaggerated
motions of prying out an invisible thorn for a calf-eyed Eushanie.

But at that moment the hunt party returned, arriving home
unexpectedly early in a clattering of hooves, the horses mud-
spattered and lathered, the hounds milling about with hanging
tongues, still excited and loath to be penned in the kennel again.
Sir Harry trotted forward in a streak of magenta and black, his
hat askew and his face red. One of the foxhounds was draped
across the front of his saddle, where its scrabbling claws had
put scratches in the fine shiny leather.

Tamasin glanced at Eushanie and Brendan with dread, fearing that the baronet would notice the flirtation so blatantly

going on beneath his nose. Then she relaxed and almost smiled, reminding herself that Sir Harry never noticed anything unless it either impeded or furthered his own pursuit of play.

"Blasted hound is a babbler!" he growled, referring to the one he held. "Barked his head off, fooling us and the pack into thinking he'd found a scent. Ruined the day, he did! Where is that groomsman Kinshella!"

When Brendan looked up, the baronet waved his hand in impatience and grumbled, "Not you, you ne'er-do-well. Your brother!"

Hunter emerged carrying a handful of mended bridles, his face, in contrast to Brendan's, wintry and closed. Without so much as an "Aye, Sir?" or "How can I please you, Squire?" or even a nod of his head, he waited for instructions from Sir Harry.

"Come here and take this hound," the baronet said. "Worthless bit of cur, he is. Carry him down to the river and drown him, or use your musket on him—it makes no difference to me. I'll not be keeping an ill-bred dog, let him spoil my hunting and ruin the pack."

"Oh, no, Papa!" Eushanie cried, rushing toward him, coming to stand at the head of his horse. "Can you not give the hound to me?" She pushed her straight thin hair under her hat—a new russet one adorned with a pheasant feather—and touched her sire's knee urgently, pleading with him.

"Nay, Eushanie. You've already got one pet you've spoiled 'til it's mean. And these hounds are meant for sport, nothing else." He all but threw the hound—a pup in its first season—at Hunter's chest. Then, with a call to his friends, he apologized for the disappointing day while issuing an invitation to take the chill off the morning with a few glasses of claret, which flowed in endless supply from his cellars.

The disgraced hound whined in Hunter's arms. Tamasin eyed Hunter's face with interest, not envying him his unpleasant task, especially since he was accustomed to caring for animals, not destroying them.

"Avery!" Eushanie called agitatedly, seeking her brother in the huddle of horsemen who were dismounting by the paddock. "Do something! The dog doesn't deserve to be killed."

Avery slid off the saddle, whip in hand, and shook his head. "He's a bad apple, Eushanie. He's not fit to keep around the kennels, and that's the way of it. Whoever or whatever is of no use to Papa he gets rid of, don't you know? Haven't you learned?" His mouth turned up in an ironic tilt. Then, shrugging indifferently, he took his sister's arm and escorted her into the house.

As the stable lads rushed forward to take the bridles of the spent hunters, they eyed Hunter aslant, all of them speculating whether or not he would obey his master's orders. Without a word or a responding glance for any of them, Hunter elbowed past, carrying the dog. He made his way directly toward the river.

Tamasin abandoned her basket of late summer vegetables, and after a moment, skirted the stable and kennels to follow the path he had taken, the one that meandered through the meadow before declining sharply toward the River Slaney.

Ahead, Hunter crossed the mossy turf asparkle with diamond drops of moisture, then descended the sloping ground overgrown with heather and rowan. The dog, as if sensing its disgrace, rested passively in his arms with its tail dangling.

Before long, Tamasin spied a portion of the twisted, foggy river peeking through a stand of hawthorn trees. The trees were so sacred to the fairies that the villagers never dared cross beneath their branches, but after boldly trespassing over the knotted roots, Hunter made for the shore, where he apparently planned to drown the hapless dog.

Tamasin shimmied behind a tangle of blackberries, loath to proceed any further lest Hunter discover her presence. She peeked through the tracery of tangled branches long since stripped of berries by wandering beggars, and saw that Hunter, with the hound in his arms, had gone to crouch close to the burbling river. She could hear the waves lapping and purling, could imagine him holding the hound's head forcibly underwater, resisting its struggles with determined hands until its lungs filled and it ceased to battle. She grimaced slightly, surprised at her own squeamishness, for killing animals was a necessary part of farm life. Since childhood she had helped Mam slaughter pigs and wring the necks of chickens on the rare occasions when Da could afford to buy and butcher them for his family.

But as Hunter set the dog on its feet, he did not grasp its legs and drag it into the water. Instead, he removed a length of lightweight chain from the pocket of his trusty. Kneeling, he fastened it about the pup's neck before securing the other end to one of the sacred trees.

Tamasin smiled. He had no intention of destroying the dog. He was tethering it in a place unvisited by anyone, close enough to the river so that it might drink, close enough to the stable so that he might slip away every evening and keep it fed. Sir Harry would think he had drowned it and cast the carcass into the current. Unless the hound managed to escape and return home, or bayed so persistently that someone grew suspicious and came to investigate—which would seem unlikely given the eerie location—the groomsman's secret, as well as the dog, would be safe.

Abandoning her hiding place, Tamasin went to stand on the edge of the fairies holy ground, the branches of their sacred trees a tattered parasol overhead. In a quiet voice, she addressed Hunter. "There's a woman in Wexford, the stationer's wife from America, who claims to have a special fondness for animals. Sometimes, if she has room, she takes in strays."

Still kneeling, Hunter turned his head to look at her. Flustered by his stare, by his long condemnatory silence born of her action in the kennel, Tamasin stammered, "I-If you take the dog round tonight to her back stoop, after dark, no one will see. She's closemouthed and can be trusted with a secret, I think."

He continued to observe her through narrowed eyes the color

of the grass beneath his feet, and seemed to struggle with some emotion. Gratitude? If so, apparently it did not rest well upon his heart. He sat back on his heels and cocked a cynical brow. "Avery would pay you a pretty price for news of this. I've no doubt that word of my disobedience would be worth a great deal to him. Perhaps a dozen silk handkerchiefs, even a lace shawl or two. Shall I give you a few minutes to mull over the possible gain? I wouldn't want you to suffer regrets tomorrow, on my behalf."

"I'm never impulsive in my dealings," Tamasin answered sharply, stung. "I put a great deal of thought into them."

"No doubt. Why not seize this opportunity?"

She lowered her lashes, thinking of his kindness toward the hound, then met his eyes again. "Maybe for the same reason you didn't drown the dog."

The groomsman gave a short laugh, but his handsome lips failed to form a smile. "What if I told you I'm saving the hound because he's worth something to me? He's purebred, after all. I can trade him to the gombeen man for money. Whether or not he ends up in a cooking pot as a meal for some starving cottier's family is not my concern."

Tamasin glanced at the animal, who had rested its head upon Hunter's thigh to be petted, its brown eyes sad and unsuspecting. "I wouldn't believe you," she said steadily. "I think you could use your hands to kill a man without a qualm—and probably have done on more than one occasion—but I don't believe you could put them around that dog's throat and drown it or sell it for a cooking pot."

His mouth curved. "You have a higher opinion of my good-heartedness than I have of yours. And since I'm not convinced that your offer isn't some momentary whim of mercy—brought on by God knows what motive—I'll not do anything with the hound until tomorrow. I'll leave it tied here. And if you should have any dreams tonight of marble houses, Miss Cullen, you'll still have the chance to go and tell Avery what you've seen.

The evidence will be waiting right here, in plain view, as damning as can be, on the end of this chain.''

Tamasin could scarcely believe that Hunter remembered her dream of marble houses, for she had confided it long ago, before he had been sent away to the army, on the very day she had betrayed him. She stared at his cool, derisive face, and wondered if he recalled everything about that day just as she did. Certainly, neither of them would easily forget the scene in the kennel with Avery Hampton.

"Very well," she said crisply, smothering her thoughts. "Since you seem to find this sort of test appealing, I'll consider it."

"I thought you might."

His expression wry, Hunter tipped his cap in the customary token of respect. But, oddly, the gesture resembled the sort of mocking salute one gives an enemy across a battlefield.

Giving the dog one last pat, he strode away over the twisted roots of the sacred trees, whistling a haunting Gaelic tune that carried over the rough green fields and blent with the wildness of its wind melody.

Tamasin watched his back, the set of his shoulders, as he covered the rocky ground in his steady, long-legged pace. Suddenly, the breeze whipped off the river and chilled the air of the fairy grove, stirred its leaves of citrine, emerald, and jade so they jingled like shiny coins. She shivered, knowing Hunter Kinshella sincerely meant to test the bounds of her ambition, the limits of her trustworthiness. He had placed his future in her hands just now; if Sir Harry were informed that the dog still lived, he would not be lenient with the man who had defied him.

She wondered about Hunter Kinshella. Both he and his brother seemed to dance lightly on the brink of disaster, pushing everyone and everything to a limit. But, where Brendan did the pushing mischievously, Hunter did it intrepidly, with a calm and calculated daring.

Tamasin lifted her shoulders and sighed. His decisions, his

risks, were his own. She could not allow thoughts of him to make her lose sight of her own purpose. She glanced down at the dog, who lay now with its head upon its paws, looking up at her as if in appeal. Running her tongue over her lips, she wondered how much the news of the hound's whereabouts would be worth to Avery Hampton. If she approached him shrewdly enough, as a woman determined to bargain, perhaps he would reward her with a handful of guineas or even a position at the Hall. As a servant there, she would likely have a garret room, whose windows would view the flower gardens and the perfect parkland, the neat stone outbuildings, the brass-accoutered carriages. There would be no mud huts visible from such a vantage point, no dirty children, no wandering beggars, no single reminder that poverty existed only a few short miles away.

She patted the smooth head of the hound. Then, squaring her shoulders, she went back to the lodge to do her work.

Chapter Nine

If Hunter was surprised that Tamasin had no dreams of marble houses that night and therefore did not betray him, he gave no sign of it beyond a brief, rueful lift of his lip the next afternoon as he settled a saddle atop the back of a racing stallion. Perhaps, Tamasin thought, he even despised her for not taking the opportunity to earn herself a valuable reward. She didn't know what he thought. He was becoming increasingly unfathomable to her, a man who was an intriguing monument of complexities.

An hour ago, she had slipped away from her duties long enough to run down to the riverbank and peer through the branches of the fairy grove. The tethered hound had vanished, and she knew that Hunter had found an opportunity to take it to the stationer's wife. Either that, or she had misjudged his character altogether and he had traded the dog to the gombeen man for a coin after all.

Once he had exercised the racing stallion, Hunter was ordered to manage Sir Harry's bear, who, after its atrocious behavior in the dining room, had been confined exclusively to the malt house in disgrace. Now, having been remembered at last by its master, the beast was being consigned to the circus once again.

A pair of oxen had been yoked to a sturdy cart, and while Sir Harry supervised, Hunter fetched the bear and tethered it in the back. A pair of stable lads, none too happy with the task, were to drive the poor animal to Dublin, where it would be delivered to an agent.

The other servants gave the monstrous bear wide berth, the old gardener standing ready with his hoe poised, afraid the creature might escape and go on another rampage. But Hunter led it along with his back turned, and when he climbed into the cart and tugged at the lead, the bear followed him obediently, emitting only one disconsolate grunt as it was tied.

Relieved to be rid of the disappointing pet, Sir Harry dusted his hands, passing Tamasin as she fetched water from the well. Hunter returned to the paddock and took up a rake, which he used to spread straw over the scattered mud puddles, his shoulders swinging rhythmically with the motion of his labor.

Hearing a familiar whistled tune, Tamasin turned her head and saw her father strolling down the drive, his pace jaunty, his old trusty so short in the sleeves that the bones of his wrists poked out. His woolen cap was jammed low over his grindled hair, a wildflower was stuck through a hole in the brim, and his unfastened suspenders dangled halfway to his knees.

Since her violent encounter with him two months ago, Tamasin had not returned to the cottage, sleeping in the dubious shelter of the garden toolshed with a blanket borrowed from the lodge, freezing and damp half the night. And during the interim, without her at home to nag him as Mam had done, Jamsie Cullen had obviously neither washed his clothes nor bathed. Already, even while he remained yards away, Tamasin could smell the sharp odor of his body. He appeared to be in a chipper mood though. With a suspicion acquired through years of living with him, Tamasin wondered at the brightness of his eyes and the happy tilt of his head.

The activity in the yard slowed as the curious laborers

watched the cottier approach, doubtless wondering if the old man had come to drag his daughter home again. They all knew she slept out-of-doors and never went to the cabin. Likely they guessed why. The bruises of Jamsie Cullen's beating had remained upon her tender face for longer than a week.

Perhaps, Tamasin thought, they hoped to see her chastised. She knew they had always disliked her arrogant manner, even while they had looked at her body longingly, more than once, since her fourteenth year.

"Tamasin, girl!" Da yelled, waving an arm when she would have turned her back and slipped inside the kitchen. "I'll have a word with ye!"

His coarse voice carried across the cobbles and echoed off the stone walls of the stable. Although she glanced about in search of a private place to talk, Tamasin knew no secrecy would be afforded her here; ears would listen no matter where she chose to confront her half-drunk and strangely elated sire. The stable lads had always found her high-spiritedness amusing. Later tonight, over ale and cards at *The Hound,* her confrontation with Jamsie, if there was to be one—and it looked as if there were—would be retold again and again for entertainment.

In her usual way, she steeled herself, preparing for their amusement.

"I'll be speakin' with ye, Daughter," Jamsie stated sternly, weaving toward her in his old cracked shoes. "So don't be thinkin' to avoid me. I'll only catch up with ye and give ye a clout or two about the ears for yer trouble. Do ye hear?"

"What is it you're wanting with me, Da?" she hissed when he stumbled close. "I've got my work to do."

He chortled and, seizing her hand, yanked her out into the middle of the stable yard. There, he whirled her around in a merry dance so dizzying that the young colts in the paddock bolted in fright.

"Aye, ye've got yer work to do, begad!" he cackled, dragging her a few more steps. He clenched his clay pipe harder between his teeth and made a loud, if puzzling, announcement. "Ye've got yer work to do up at Hampton Hall, ye do!"

She shoved his hands away, mortified. Every servant in the yard and the stables had now stopped their work and come to gloat over her discomfiture. "What in heaven's name are you raving about, Da?" she demanded.

Jamsie straightened, swayed, then hooked his thumbs beneath his waistband. Flattered that an audience had assembled to listen, he took his time answering, allowing the suspense to stretch. " 'Tis the young Master Avery," he said with satisfaction, holding up a black-nailed finger. "Avery has asked for me own fair Tamasin, he has. Who would have thought old Dora could've whelped a creature that looks like ye? But she managed—with a wee bit of help from me, of course." He winked. "And now the young master up at the Hall wants a piece of it, he does. Asked for ye specially."

"What do you mean, Da? What do you mean, Avery's *asked* for me?"

The wildflower bobbed as Jamsie dipped his head. "Why, I mean he wants to honor ye in the old way. This morning Avery sent—all right and proper like—a messenger who asked that ye come to him. On any night of yer chosing, me lass, he's that much of gentleman, at least. Fancy it."

Tamasin stood frozen, staring at him. Vaguely she was aware of the stable lads lined up along the paddock fence. Surely they found her father's news lewdly amusing, worth a round of shared smirks. They would think it a fitting reward that the uppity Tamasin Cullen had been singled out for deflowering by the baronet's son, whether she wanted it or not. And yet, not one of them sneered or laughed; instead they simply regarded her with faces as unreadable as the stones scattered in the fields. Except for the snuffling of the horses, the hush in Sir Harry's clean-swept yard was complete.

Tamasin glanced at Hunter Kinshella, hoping to glean through his face a hint of the reason for the uncomfortable silence. He stood gripping the rake, his eyes grim, their only animation a gleam which seemed to flicker and hold steady as he, like all the others, awaited her response.

She was not certain what reply she would give, for although she had pondered Avery's possible carnal interest, she had not been able to decide her response to it. She thought of Avery now, pictured his looks: the fine yellow hair, the broad white brow, the large body that was no longer fat, but elegant in its French velvets and brocades, the pale hands with their long delicate fingers. Hadn't she always worshipped him in an idealized way for the symbol he represented?

Then why, now that an opportunity to spend a night in his splendid bedchamber had been presented, did she hesitate? Did she hear, suddenly, in the back of her mind, the dim warnings of her mother, who had told her more than once—when she had taken time to pass on advice—that there was never as much pleasure in receiving a dream as there was in dreaming it? Had Dora once envisioned Jamsie romantically, only to have the vision shattered when she was held for the first time in his brutish arms?

And yet, Tamasin reasoned, to lie with Avery Hampton would not be the crude act that had been Da's way with Mam, but an act performed on fragrant sheets by a refined man accustomed to handling gently-bred ladies. He had been *trained* by his class to treat women properly, he had danced with fragile, silk-spun specimens, chatted with them in ballrooms set in centuries-old mansions. He had revered them, touched them as one would touch an easily shattered piece of porcelain. To Avery, women were not the chattels they were to the lower class. If she were embraced in his arms, Tamasin was certain she would be able to *absorb* the mystery of his grace and wealth, to feel the blood of generations rushing against her breast.

And afterwards, knowing her penchant for pretty objects, Avery would probably offer her a gift. If the present were fine enough, she would be able to buy her freedom from the village, from Da, from her mother's fate.

Suddenly, standing amid the rough-clad members of her own class, men who had no real concept of a gentle life, Tamasin felt privileged. She had been singled out. All at once, in response to the rude stares pinned upon her, she put her hands on her hips defiantly.

Looking hard at her father, her voice no less shrewd than those of the horse traders at the fair, she demanded, "What is Master Avery offering in return?"

Jamsie grinned like a child. "He's offerin' to pay me a guinea, he is. And just think what I can do with a guinea. I can get me a new suit of clothes, to start. And a new hat and pipe, and enough whiskey to—"

"What is he offering *me?*"

"Why . . ." Jamsie hesitated, and then with a rejoinder which he doubtless believed to be amusing, added, "Why, he's offerin' himself, of course. Isn't that enough?"

Tamasin's gaze shifted momentarily to the watching stable lads. Still, inexplicably, none of them grinned. They shifted their feet and fixed their eyes to the ground, stuck their hands in their pockets.

And Hunter's eyes? They had grown darker, green black. Strangely, she fancied she saw a faint, fleeting trace of anxiety flash in their cold bright darkness.

"I'll not go to Master Avery for nothing," she said slowly, clamping her jaw. Now that her decision had been made, she felt relief, and an unexpected sense of power. "Tell him I'll not be coming."

Jamsie glared at her, his bleary eyes incredulous. "What are ye sayin', girl? Are ye a fool to turn down such a chance? Why, 'tis all me and yer mam heard, yer palaver about the Hall, about the grand things they had up there. Ye could stay there a whole night—more if ye're clever enough at pleasurin' the young master. Have ye suddenly gone daft?"

Tamasin wavered only a moment, then said again, "Tell him I'm not coming." Turning away, she crossed the cobbles toward the lodge.

But Jamsie was greedy for the promised guinea and, determined to have it, seized her arm. He bellowed, "Ye *will* go! Ye *will!* Already ye've cheated me out of that bundle of fripperies the young master gave ye, and ye'll not be cheatin' me out of my guinea, too!"

She attempted to wrench free of his hold, but he throttled her, squeezing, grabbing her hair when she struck out to wound his face.

"Let her be."

The words were frighteningly low.

Gasping for breath, Tamasin looked up to see Hunter standing over her father, giving him the knifelike stare that made men pause.

"Let her be," the groomsman said again, daring to interfere where the other lads had not.

"No lackey smellin' of horses is goin' to tell me what to do with me own girl!" Jamsie declared, drawing himself up.

"I'll not stand by and watch the lass abused, Cullen. If you care to have it out, here and now, while I have a minute away from my duties, I'll oblige you."

Jamsie well knew he was no match for the younger man, who was said to be unpredictable, hot-tempered, and deadly with his fists. He straightened his jacket, considered his options and, finding none, gave Tamasin a glare over a wagging finger. "I'm not done with ye yet, lass. Ye and I will be havin' this finished one way or another. See if we don't."

She watched her sire stalk away, his step no longer light, but his rigid bearing and infuriated glance promised future trouble if he could get his hands on her.

She turned to Hunter, her head lowered, her hands fidgeting, wanting to say something in gratitude, but unable. This, she felt, was another of his punishing kindnesses. "I—"

"Don't go to Avery Hampton," he cut in bluntly.

"Why?" she asked, surprised. "Why shouldn't I?"

"Because he's not the gentleman you believe him to be. He's no gentleman at all."

Tamasin sighed, deciding his statement was made out of sourness and nothing else. "I would hardly be trusting your opinion of Avery, Hunter Kinshella, knowing how you hate him. Besides, how would you know whether he's a gentleman or not? How would you know more than I do about him?"

Hunter contemplated her for several seconds. His eyes were so serious and sharp-edged that Tamasin suddenly shuddered beneath their observation.

"Stable lads always know everything about their masters," he said tonelessly, turning on a heel. *"Everything."*

It was a tradition for the stable lads of the lodge to enjoy a sociable round of whiskey and a game of cards at *The Hound* on their Saturday evenings off. Although Hunter felt decidedly unsociable, more inclined to spend his evening alone, he relented beneath Brendan's persistent cajoling and Seamus's quietly delivered invitation.

Over the past days his relationship with his grandfather had deteriorated. The kinship once so easily and naturally shared was eroding slowly beneath Hunter's continual refusal to join the secret society whose cause Seamus held so dear. And Hunter was aggrieved by it, more than he would ever let on, more perhaps than he would even admit to himself.

Now, walking behind Seamus and Brendan, he followed the stony path to Wexford, uncommunicative, watching as the sky darkened to mauve and copper and brass. The shops in the village were not yet closed. Seamus wanted to purchase tobacco, and the three men entered the grocer's, their boots scraping against the stone floors as they bent their heads to enter through the low portal. The dark cramped store was packed with bins and boxes and crates, lined with shelves, well stocked with both necessities and luxuries, redolent with spice.

While Seamus made his purchase and Brendan gazed through the window, Hunter idled, standing with his hands behind his back, scanning the cannisters of tea and sugar, the raisins and figs, the strung beads, the pumice stones, and watercolors. The grocer had lit his candles, and in the flickering half-light, a length of violet ribbon pinned to the plaster wall shimmered brilliantly.

Hunter's gaze fastened upon it, his maleness reacting to its feminine beauty. He wondered how it would look in Tamasin's hair, envisioned it twined in the long black locks as she ran over the fields, dancing and whirling in the way she had done as a child.

Reaching out, he touched the ribbon, and the roughness of his palm snagged upon its smoothness.

"Hunter, are you coming or not?"

Brendan's voice intruded. Hunter let the ribbon slide through his fingers, condemning himself for his foolishness. Why was he determined to have Tamasin Cullen, one way or another? The thought of her and Avery Hampton together had begun to sicken him, enrage him, even though a strong warning instinct told him that intertwining his life with Tamasin's would earn him nothing but disaster, just as it had done before. The ribbon had slipped to the floor and he bent to retrieve it, then paused with his fingers outstretched, allowing it to stay where it lay.

At the tavern, Seamus motioned for the two brothers to follow him into a crudely furnished private room lit by rush-lights, where four other men, including Loftus, sat at a scarred table over cards. A fire snapped in the fireplace behind them, and smoke from their long-stemmed pipes hazed the air.

After the newcomers had been invited to draw up stools, they ordered whiskey, and the talk turned to politics. The cottiers sitting with Loftus made no secret of their sentiments and, after listening only a few moments to the drift of the conversation, Hunter suspected the company had been assembled specifically to persuade him to join the United Irishmen.

"Every blacksmith in the county is makin' pikes," Loftus commented, pouring another round of whiskey. "Our store of arms and ammunition is growin' every day. Word is that the boys in Kildare are plannin' an attack on Dublin."

"Aye," Seamus cut in, his old voice quavery but full of conviction. "We've fine leadership in Dublin, to be sure. Lord Edward Fitzgerald is backin' us, which just goes to show that even the privileged Protestants know our cause is just. There are five Catholics to every Protestant in Ireland, and yet we're allowed to have no seat in government, make no decisions as to our own fate. And even though our young men serve in the army, they cannot ever aim to be officers. All because our religion happens to offend King George and his Protestant puppets in Dublin."

"Napoleon himself will be comin' to our aid," Loftus said with certainty. "He'll liberate us, give us a revolution just like the one in France. And then he'll go on to defeat England."

Unable to resist comment on this noble rhetoric, Hunter tossed down the last of his whiskey and drawled, "Don't think Bonaparte has the least interest in liberating Ireland for any charitable reasons. War is expensive. His troops are expensive. When it comes down to it he'll not risk many men—if any at all—to free Irish peasants. Not when he can attack England with better odds using different strategies."

"What better way to defeat England than through her back door—Ireland?" Loftus demanded.

Hunter was tempted to explain the finer points of military strategy, but knew it would be incomprehensible to them. "It would take not only a vast French army, but a very well-organized Irish movement to make your scheme succeed. And your so-called United brothers are riddled with turncoats and informers, poorly equipped, untrained, with only a half-assed notion of how to raise an army."

Seamus set his glass down with a thump, his faded but still fierce blue eyes flashing. "Our man Wolf Tone is negotiatin' even now with Bonaparte in Paris."

Hunter shrugged. "Negotiating is talk, Grandda."

Seamus scowled, and beside him, Brendan rose from the table. Glass in hand, he moved about the room as if eager to be free, not from English oppression—which did not bother him in the least—but from the discussion that was keeping him from the pleasurable pursuit of the talented maid upstairs.

Smiling, he ambled to Hunter's side and put a hand upon his shoulder to break the tension. "Look, old man," he said lightly, "they only want you to take their secret oath, to hold up your hand and recite a few noble—if exceedingly illegal words. It's quite simple and painless, really. Why don't you just do it and have it over? I have."

No surprise crossed Hunter's face at that piece of news.

"We need ye, son," Seamus implored. His voice was earnest, the intensity of his longing evident. "Ye're experienced, just out of the English army. Ye could be a fine leader for us."

Hunter set his jaw. "You have Brendan."

A silence ensued at the words, and rather than let the thoughts of all in the room go unspoken, Brendan chuckled and raised his glass. "Have you forgotten, brother, if the taverns happen to be open at the onset of the rebellion, I can't be trusted to see a lick of action."

A minute passed. Then, without meeting his grandfather's eyes, Hunter said, "I've done all the soldiering I intend to do."

Loftus leaned forward and, taking his pipe from his teeth, said in a challenging voice. "Ye served in the English army. Now are ye sayin' that ye'll not be servin' yer own countrymen?"

Hunter met his eye, his patience—never plentiful—at last exhausted. "I was forced to serve one army and will not be forced to serve another."

Seamus stood up with such energy that his stool toppled. His body shook and spittle fell from his lips. "Ye disgrace me, Hunter Kinshella. Ye are a traitor to yer own kind. I am no longer proud to call ye me own!"

With that wounding declaration, he stumped out, his frail body a-quiver with heartbreak.

Loftus and his silent companions shuffled out as well, leaving Hunter with hostile stares and half-empty whiskey glasses.

"Well, old man," Brendan sighed, lounging against the fireplace with his ankles crossed. "You've done it now." Seeing the unfinished bottle on the table, he put it to his lips. When he spoke again his voice was deep with the fire of the drink. "But then you've always gone against the grain. Why is that, do you suppose? Why make it difficult on yourself? I confess, I've never been able to fathom it. Where I'm determined to drink and fornicate myself to death, you're determined to get your skull cracked out of sheer, devilish contrariness. Ah, well." Brendan lifted the bottle again, drank, then wiped his mouth and grinned, his blithe good nature, as always, easily back in place. "Know where I'm going? I'm going up to settle myself square between the very accommodating, very soft, if somewhat overfed legs of Bonnie McKey. And what I'll be getting there is surely what you're needing, Hunter, if my advice means anything to you. Why don't you go ahead and bed Tamasin Cullen? It's all you can do to keep yourself from her—'tis plain. But, no doubt you'll just sit here alone and *think*—although what topics you find to ponder with such concentration I'll never know. You're a dark one, brother. Aye, a dark one indeed."

Brendan sauntered toward the door. Then, wanting to dull the pain of Seamus's censure, he squeezed Hunter's shoulder and said quietly, "But I'm fond of you just the same. Even if you are a fool."

The door closed and Hunter sat awhile. Feeling a weariness, a deep sorrow over his break with his grandfather, he heaved himself up from the stool and went out into the night. Alone he journeyed over the dark fields, smelling the sea, feeling needles of cool rain pelt his face. He hunched his shoulders more deeply into his trusty. Vaulting over a stone wall, he avoided patches of bramble and followed a high hedge toward the lodge, thrusting his hands in his pockets to keep them warm.

His path was pocked with swatches of bog, treacherous if one did not know the way, tricky even if one did. Faraway he heard the bleat of sheep and a pair of foxes dueling, fighting over a vixen. And then, a faint rustle in the hedge.

Instantly wary, he paused, focused his eyes in the rainy, deep purple gloom. The foxes yowled again, and for some reason, Hunter recalled Tamasin telling him, a lifetime ago, that she had knitted mittens for the foxes, believing they'd be pleased with her gift and leave her family's chickens alone.

Rubbing a hand over his jaw, he pushed thoughts of her away, scanning the fields again.

Nothing moved except grass raked by the nervous wind. Hunter decided the rustling had been only a little Johnny-of-the-bog fluttering in the hedge, nesting for the night. He started forward, having time only to tense his body in defense as six figures leapt out from the hedge and took him down.

He wasted no time, throwing punches like a madman, managing to shake off two of the assailants, grunting when a fist ground against his jaw and nearly snapped it. With effort he pinned one of the men by the throat, but another hurled his body on top of Hunter's back, cuffing him in the temple.

He was outnumbered, could neither fight them all nor escape their continued assault. When he attempted to lurch to his feet a pair of them pinioned his arms behind his back and held him fast. Another sunk a fist deep into his belly, hard enough to knock the air from his lungs and make him double over.

Forcing him to the ground again, they shoved him facedown into the boggy earth, holding him with the weight of their heavy bodies. One planted a boot on the back of his neck.

"We'll be makin' it hard on ye, Kinshella," an unknown voice growled. The pressure was doubled on his neck. "We'll be makin' it hard on ye until ye decide to do yer duty to Ireland, take the secret oath. Ye don't go against yer own kind, by God, and get away with it. Do ye hear?"

Although the boot pressed unrelentingly, pushed so that mud clogged Hunter's mouth and robbed him of the ability to breathe, he made no response to the threat.

"Answer me, ye stubborn bastard, or I'll drown ye here and now!"

The pressure increased, smothering him as his face was submerged in the watery mire. Battling to stand, to move, he arched his back and tried to pull his knees beneath his hips, but another boot pressed against his spine. His arms were held so high behind his back he thought they would snap from their sockets. His eyes closed. His body stilled, pinioned like one of Sir Harry's stags.

I'll not be letting them break me. I'll not let anyone break me. He repeated the words to himself, over and over, teeth clenched.

Seconds passed.

"Let up," one of the men growled at his fellows at last. "Ye'll kill him, and then what use will he be to us?"

"Aye, man. Let the bugger go. I'm thinkin' we've made our point. He'll come round. Aye, one way or another he'll come round."

The pressure relented.

Instinct made Hunter move his head and open his mouth, gasp until air filled his lungs again.

The sound of retreating footsteps floated dimly to his ears then, like the tramp of marching boots. Rain fell upon his body, ran in rivulets over the nape of his bruised neck and down his shoulders, invading the thinness of his shirt to chill his flesh. He shivered and his teeth began to chatter.

For awhile he merely lay where they had thrown him down, plastered to the soft Irish earth, smelling it, tasting it, his head pillowed on it.

"I told you stubbornness doesn't pay, you stupid lout. Didn't I?"

As if from a very great distance, Hunter heard the drunken voice.

"Good thing I found you," it said. "Tavern wenches have more than one good use. If you'd use them more often you'd know that. They babble everything when they're treated properly, and—if I do say so myself—Bonnie was treated properly tonight. The lass knew enough to send me out here after you."

Brendan leaned down and, hardly steady himself, gave his

brother a hand in rising. "Begad, you're filthy . . . don't be touching my shirt, damn it. You may as well fall into the water trough when we get home. Or I can push you into the river along the way. Your choice."

The two brothers stumbled along, the younger being of service to the elder for once, so pleased with himself over the opportunity that he alternately sang at the top of his lungs and loudly philosophized. "They nearly did you in, didn't they?"

Hunter merely grunted.

"Did you ever think about women and their ways, Hunter?" Brendan said after awhile, his voice slurred.

Limping, Hunter used a sleeve to wipe the mud from his bruised and throbbing face and mumbled uncommunicatively, "Only when I'm forced to, Brendan."

"I mean, did you ever think how it is that a gentlemen, when he decides to marry a lady, expects a dowry? He's *paid* to take her off a father's hands, paid to sleep with her every night, to look at her over breakfast every day. On the other hand, when a gentleman decides to spend an evening with some common woman like Bonnie, he pays *her*. Did that ever strike you as being damned funny? Did you ever ponder it?"

"Obviously not with the concentration you have," Hunter muttered, in no mood to talk. Holding his battered middle, he jerkily steered Brendan's dragging feet away from the edges of a bog, then groaned when he realized his shirt was ripped, irreparably, from collar to waist.

"But I bet there's something else you've pondered with more than a little interest," Brendan went on, his voice slurred and teasing. "Do you think Tamasin Cullen will go to Hampton Hall? I thought she showed a deal of sense today in refusin' Avery, didn't you? I think she'll hold out, tease him a wee bit perhaps, but deny him his little tumble in bed."

Hunter trudged over an expanse of flat stones rimmed with silver dew. His jaw was sore and one of his eyes was swelling shut. The last subject he cared to ponder was the cottier's lass. Tasting the mud in his mouth, feeling grit abrade his eyelids, he distanced himself from his brother by several paces, feeling unsociable. Ill-naturedly, he snapped, ''Don't wager against Tamasin Cullen's ambition, Brendan, not ever. You'll lose if you do. When the price is right, the greedy little opportunist will march straight up to Hampton Hall and into Avery's bed without a qualm.''

''You really think so?'' Brendan sounded disappointed.

''I know so.'' Wanting to be alone, the groomsman went on, leaving his brother to make his own blithe way home as the uncertain orange lights of Hampton lodge appeared, lambently, through the black-green trees.

Chapter Ten

She had been seven years old when she had first heard herself
called ugly, and although the speaker had only been a scullery
maid who had eventually been left in a compromising way by
the butler, Eushanie Hampton had been badly frightened. For
long hours she had scrutinized herself in the looking glass,
removing her pinafore and petticoats, turning her body at all
angles to determine if the maid's opinion were true. As she
matured and her jaw began to resemble her great grandfather's
in his gallery portrait, and as her body showed no signs of the
pink and wispy delicacy so prized by prospective bridegrooms,
she began, finally and with great dismay, to believe in her
ugliness.

She did not examine her shape closely anymore, not after
she had been caught doing it naked once, at age fourteen, by
her governess.

She was nineteen now, and although her father's income was
reported to be respectable if dwindling, no young man had ever
asked for her hand or ever asked to court her. This sad state
of circumstances she attributed entirely to her looks—or lack

of them. To no avail she had employed every cream and beauty aid sold by the traveling Gypsies, just as she had tried the little pots of rouge and powder that Avery—dear Avery who always brought her something pretty when he could manage to remember—had purchased in France. The French paint had only made her appear garish and vulgar, like the gilt chairs with the claw feet and cherub-shaped arms Rafael had brought with him from Italy.

She did not like Rafael. The young Italian encouraged her brother to drink too much, and their wild laughter as they sat together late into the night was crude, disturbing her as she lay in bed reading, which she did constantly, with a compelling need to be absorbed into fantasy. Often she read the same volumes over and over until she could repeat the lines by heart. She loved poetry, especially verses about lovers, and always in her mind she *became* Juliet or Isolde, courted by charming but tragically ill-fated heroes.

Now, like some languid Greek goddess, she lounged in the open octagonal garden house beneath a vaulted ceiling. The cool afternoon breeze fluttered the volume resting in her lap. She had pressed violets between the pages, and the scent of them caused her to close her eyes and escape to an imaginary island where wine flowed from springs and lovers fed each other grapes. So lost was she in her private dream that the footsteps crunching on the path behind the garden gate barely penetrated her consciousness.

Glancing up, vaguely irritated by the interruption, she saw that the intruder was only Tamasin Cullen, the maid from the lodge, the one who had rescued Pudding on the day Papa had nearly been mauled by that wretched bear. Eushanie watched her hurry down the path toward the Hall kitchens, frowning perplexedly when the girl paused and stood staring at the estate's facade with an expression that could only be termed rapturous.

With a growing interest, the lady studied Tamasin, suddenly envious as she realized the maid had the privilege of seeing

the charming Brendan Kinshella every day. When Tamasin
fetched water from the well or crept to the privy, Brendan
would be laboring about the stables. Given the moral laxity of
maids and the virility of stable lads, Eushanie wondered if the
pair had ever flirted, or even kissed. Her imagination could not
wander far from the act of kissing, for what came after was
never detailed in books, and she had learned everything about
life from books, for no one bothered to take the time to speak
to her on any subject more profound than that of the daily
menu. Taking up her parasol of Valenciennes lace, Eushanie
followed Tamasin. She meant to ask her what she was doing
staring so fixedly at the Hall. But as she wound through the
maze of shrubbery after the maid, she lost sight of the black
skirts and fluttering apron strings.

At the other end of the path Tamasin rapped on the kitchen
door. She had been sent by the cook at the lodge to ask for a
bit of ginger root, which would be grated and sprinkled over
Sir Harry's dinner oysters. The Hampton Hall kitchen was a
busy, fragrant place filled with shelves, trestle tables, hanging
copper pots, and drying herbs. Tamasin waited while the cook's
boy dragged out a step stool and fetched the ginger from a jar.

She sniffed. The quality of food here was much better than
that at the lodge, perhaps because Eushanie and Avery were
more particular than Sir Harry, who was usually too inebriated
to know whether or not his beef was well-seasoned.

With a watering mouth, Tamasin stared at the table of cus-
tards, layer cakes, and fruit pies. She eyed the servants' stairs,
knowing it led up into the halls of the mansion, and wished
she could have a leisurely tour, transform herself into a dor-
mouse and creep about unnoticed. Of course, she reminded
herself, if she were to accept Avery's offer, he might escort
her through his mansion and show her everything she asked to
see.

"Ye could've knocked me over with a feather," the cook
said to her now. Biddy spoke with snideness as she arranged
preserved gooseberries in a dish of whipped cream. "The staff

was expectin' ye to pay us a visit through the *front* door,
Tamasin, not through the back. Aye, 'twas a different sort of
visit we were expectin'—one in the evenin' hours. After dark."

Although not failing to understand the remark, since her
mind was running along the same channels, Tamasin stared at
the woman in feigned puzzlement. "Why, whatever do you
mean, Biddy?"

Cinnamon was dashed over the gooseberries, and the gold-
edged porcelain plate set aside. "The footman had it from the
housekeeper who had it from Master Avery's manservant that
ye were *invited* here by the young master," the cook said,
giving Tamasin a sly glance while the two scullery maids sidled
close to hear.

Tamasin took the ginger from the boy and slipped it in
her pocket, answering with the sweet, caustic smile she had
perfected over the years. "And when he learned I wasn't coming, was the young master sorely disappointed? No doubt you
found him crying in his cups."

The cook pursed her lips. "Ye're a brassy one, Tamasin
Cullen. And don't think ye'd be approved of either way. We
don't think ye any purer for not sharing Master Avery's bed.
And if ye did, we'd be callin' ye a harlot."

"Thank you for giving me your opinion, Biddy Blalock,
which isn't worth tuppence to me. The truth of it is—which
I'm certain you're fair dying to know—is that Master Avery
wasn't offering me enough money for my favors. I can't be
selling myself cheap after all, now can I?"

The cook sniffed and the maids opened their mouths in shock.

Tamasin shrugged. "Good day to you then," she said cor-
dially enough. "I'll let you get on with your gossip, which will
surely be burning my ears all night."

Just as she yanked open the door, the sound of shattering
glass and musket shots shuddered the peaceful garden air.

"God bless us and save us!" Biddy exclaimed, dropping
her spoon in terror. "What's happening?"

While the others huddled together, Tamasin ran outside to

investigate. In the twilight, which had brushed the lawn pale blue, she saw shadowy figures skirting the shrubbery. The ragged creatures carried blunderbusses and pikes, shouted obscenities, and hurled stones at the beautiful leaded windows.

When the male servants began pouring out the door, ordered by the butler to stop the destruction, the attackers fled. They veered in all directions, acquiring the uncanny ability of animals to blend with the landscape.

"United Irishmen," Tamasin murmured, watching them escape—watching the servants *allow* them to escape. She recalled the rumors alleging that such attacks on the landowners were frequently happening in other counties. Wexford's turn had come, it seemed.

Suddenly remembering that Miss Eushanie had been sitting alone earlier in the garden house, Tamasin hurried in that direction, wondering if the lady were safe. Amid the eventide's wash the white columns of the delicate, fairy-tale structure seemed to spiral toward heaven, topped by its dome of copper, and Tamasin adjusted her eyes, searching for a figure clad in silk.

After a few seconds she finally spotted Eushanie Hampton, who appeared to be terrified. The lady's arms were upraised in a defensive pose, her mouth slack, while a tattered strip of a man threatened her with a ten-foot pike.

Spurred by concern, Tamasin shimmied warily through the thick shrubbery, hearing the attacker's young, cracking voice, which was hungry, desperate—and strangely—a little apologetic.

"Give me that trinket at yer neck, ye ugly bitch," he demanded. His hands quivered with the weight of the pike, whose tip was aimed at Miss Eushanie's flat, corset-bound middle. "Ye'll be givin' it over right now, or I'll spit ye like a pig!"

While the terrified lady—who had never faced anything more daunting than her pet dog—fumbled with her brooch, Tamasin grabbed a large stone that bordered the flower bed. Posing it threateningly, she jumped out of the lilac bushes not more than five feet from the attacker. "Get on with you, Paddy O'Malley!" she yelled, "or I'll be hurling this stone at your stupid skull."

Startled, the lad spun around. Then, uncertain, he aimed his weapon more menacingly at Eushanie's middle. Tamasin lifted the stone high above her head in warning, fully prepared to throw it at him. "Go on!" she snapped. "Go home to your mam and stop playing silly games with the United Irishmen."

Cowed at last, the lad lowered the pike.

"Wait!" Eushanie cried, fumbling to unclasp her cameo brooch, finally ripping the lace at her throat to free the pin. "Here, give this to him. He looks—" She paused, as if uncertain how to phrase the description delicately, her inbred decorum coming to the fore even in dire circumstances. "He looks peaked." As if unable to bear the thought of risking contact with his horn-nailed hand, Eushanie relinquished her brooch to Tamasin, who tossed it to the lad.

The overgrown urchin gave no thanks, no nod, but seized the little cameo as if it were a diamond—or a loaf of bread—and with all the agility of a rabbit scurried away through a line of thick green yews.

Tamasin watched him run. With a start, she realized she had been willing to bash in the head of the starving lad, her own kind, in order to protect a Hampton.

"Dreadful . . ." Eushanie breathed now, still flustered. She looked as if she didn't know whether she should cry or not. "Was anyone in the Hall harmed?"

"Not that I know of, Miss."

"Why were those men attacking us?"

Because they hate you and despise what you represent.

It was the truth, and yet, considering the sheltered upbringing of the lady, Tamasin watered down her explanation. But only a little. If Eushanie and her family were going to be the targets of rusty iron pikes and ancient blunderbusses during the next turbulent months, they should at least know the reason why.

"Because they don't like the land system, Miss," she answered truthfully.

"Why ever not?"

"Well, for one thing, the peasants are all tenants on your father's estate and they believe his rents are too high. If Sir Harry decides to turn them out and graze cattle instead, he can do it, without notice. The cabins they've built and the crops they've planted are all his. Even if they have a poor harvest, the rent is still due, no matter. 'Tis collected by an agent carrying a whip—which he's not unwilling to use. Between the seven pounds per acre rent and the twelve shillings for tithes, the cottiers can barely live. 'Tis the same all over Ireland, Miss, and the peasants are banding together to make a rebellion."

Eushanie put her hands to her cheeks, distressed. "I didn't know. No one tells me anything, you see. Do you suppose Avery realizes?—no, 'twouldn't matter if he did. Do you suppose my father knows?"

Tamasin smiled and opened her mouth to reply. Then, deciding that it was her duty, as one more worldly, to spare Eushanie a sarcastic reply which might, truthfully, not even be understood, she said, "To be sure, Miss. I'm certain of it." *Whenever he's sober.*

"Well," Eushanie said faintly, fumbling about in the cool purple darkness for her poetry volume and paper. "I'd better go inside. I suppose someone will be worried about me."

No word of gratitude, no offer of a small, heartfelt token was offered to Tamasin. Disappointed that her loyalty had gone unrewarded, she turned away.

"Oh, I almost forgot . . ." Eushanie began.

Tamasin pivoted hopefully.

The lady yanked a page from her notebook and held it out. "Perhaps you'd care to have this. Having such courage, you'll appreciate the sentiment of the verses. Er—you *can* read?"

"Aye, Miss. I can read. The priest teaches us, you know, if we're willing." With no enthusiasm, Tamasin accepted the paper Eushanie offered, its black flourished curlicues barely visible in the darkness.

The young lady smiled brilliantly, as if pleased to bestow the present. Then, obviously uncomfortable making further social conversation with a servant, or not knowing how, she turned away.

Tamasin watched her silk skirts slide over the smooth lawn like a pink silk dragon tail, and when they had been swallowed up by the garden shadows, closed her fingers, crumpling the scented scrap of paper without bothering to read a word of it.

Chapter Eleven

It seemed a portentous day, as if some imp of ill omens soared through the sky, out to cast mischief and spread chills over old bones ready for the boneyard.

"Trouble is, I don't *feel* more than twenty years old, begad," Seamus Kinshella said, sitting on a bench and resewing the loose stitching of a saddle girth. He paused to watch his two grandsons labor in the sun. "I feel like the same lad who earned meself a trial ride upon the old master's best racing stallion sixty years ago. Changed my destiny, it did. I rode that nag like a demon, made it fly. And here I've been ever since, not a single day away from Hampton Lodge except to go to race meetings—or to the alehouse in Wexford, o' course."

Hunter and Brendan moved behind him, unloading sacks of grain from a wheel car. Hunter unloaded two for every one his brother managed. As always, he looked after his irresponsible sibling, did his share of work for him, watched his back, kept him out of trouble whenever it was humanly possible. Although Brendan could brawl with the best of men, Hunter knew that inside, in his heart, he was lacking, weak. Even now he lounged against the wheel car with a straw between his teeth, his head tilted and his eyes half-closed in the sun as he watched a flock of geese wing lazily over.

Seamus pinned surly, speculative eyes on Hunter and said, "By the by, there's a United Irish meeting tonight. But I don't suppose you could be bothered to come."

The words were biting, the first his grandda had spoken to Hunter since the night in the alehouse. And yet, the groomsman knew that if he agreed to join, all would be forgiven; it was a last chance for reconciliation. Nevertheless, not a man to compromise the few, strong beliefs that governed his honor, Hunter shook his head stubbornly, "No," he said.

The old man gave him a long, considering gaze, one full of wrath and sorrow, and Hunter knew Seamus would never raise the subject again.

"Don't you wish you'd traveled the world a bit, Grandda?" Brendan interrupted musingly, breaking the terrible tension.

Seamus shook his head. "Nay. When a man finds his own spot of earth, he's wise to stay there."

"Yet, you were a stubborn old rogue not to go with me and see the sights of Dublin when I asked years ago."

"Aye, perhaps." Seamus gave Brendan a fond, faded smile, and for some reason, the expression wounded Hunter, who happened to glance up and catch it. It shouldn't have affected him, not anymore. Since the days of his boyhood Hunter had tried in his own proud way to win the sort of affection his grandfather gave so freely to Brendan, but long ago, with no bitterness, he had accepted Seamus's inability to give it. He wondered why that inability bothered him today, especially on such a beautiful morning when the sun was breaking free of the clouds and the scarlet smell of autumn hung like cinnamon in the air.

Tamasin came from the kitchen carrying a jug of mead—a beery drink made of honey, ginger, elder flower, and yeast kept stored in a barrel. Hunter observed her as she crossed the yard, scrutinized the neatness of her rich black hair, the rose of her cheeks, her confident, graceful stride. He had been preoccupied with relentless sensual thoughts of the lass since the day he'd kissed her. Often at night, he found himself pondering the color of her eyes, the shape of her figure, the graceful strength of her small thin hands. His dreams of her were plaguesome, driving things that caused him to wake with an obsessive need to see her, a need to create chance encounters, or watch her in a brooding, irritable silence across the lawn.

Suddenly now, with a flounce of black skirts, she darted into the shrubbery in order to dodge Avery and Rafael as they strolled jauntily into the yard. Hunter almost smiled in satisfaction.

Tamasin felt the groomsman's regard but ignored it, too intent upon avoiding a confrontation with Avery Hampton. Now that she had rejected his offer of a dalliance, she wondered how he would react. Would he be angry, cruel, flaunt his authority and demand that she come to the Hall whether she wanted to go or not? Or would he simply shun her?

Perhaps he had only made the offer impulsively on a dull evening when he searched for a diversion, any diversion, to relieve his boredom. Perhaps Tamasin's refusal, because it had meant so little to him, had already been forgotten.

Two stable lads led out a pair of sleek jumpers and, after adjusting the stirrups for Avery and Rafael, stood aside while the gentlemen mounted and made wagers as to which horse would complete the steeplechasing course first.

With a jabbing of spurs, the bright-coated companions cantered recklessly away to compete, laughing as they went.

Her way safe now, Tamasin walked out into the yard carrying her jug of mead and some wooden mugs. She offered refreshment to Brendan and his brother.

"We heard about your brave defense of Eushanie Hampton, Tamasin," Brendan commented as the three of them lingered beneath the eaves of the ivy-hung stable. Humor gleamed in his blue eyes, but its lightness was underlaid with a hint of gravity. "Paddy O'Malley's father came round last night and told us all about it, about the way you threatened to crack his lad's head with a stone. Noble of you, to be sure, defending Eushanie.''

Tamasin could not help but glance at Hunter, whose rueful expression seemed to say "Were you defending her, or only after the reward she might provide?''

''But 'tis unfortunate that you called Paddy by name,'' Brendan remarked, sipping his mead.

''Called Paddy by name . . . ?'' Tamasin echoed with a bewildered frown.

''Aye. Apparently Eushanie heard you mention his name. She later repeated it to her father—under pressure, I think. The lad is to suffer a public flogging on Saturday for joining the United Irish in their raid on Hampton Hall. Fifty stripes for the raid, and fifty for stealing a piece of Eushanie's jewelry.''

Tamasin shook her head and breathed, ''Sainted Mary. I didn't realize I'd said Paddy's name aloud. I was only thinking of Miss Eushanie's safety at the time. And Paddy didn't steal the jewelry, Brendan. Miss Eushanie *gave* it to him.'' Sickened to think of the flogging Paddy must endure because she had unthinkingly betrayed his identity, she leaned her brow against the stable wall, ignoring Hunter's steady stare.

Beside her, Brendan shrugged. ''Eushanie told Sir Harry she had given Paddy the jewel, but it made no difference. He and the other landowners are looking for any excuse to punish peasants who are fighting for the cause. They're thinking that when they lay a few stripes with the cat-o'-nine upon the back of young Paddy O'Malley, the leaders of the United Irish will stop and consider, think twice before raiding another house. Indeed, if Paddy weren't so young, they'd surely be *hanging* him on Saturday instead of using the whip.''

''He shouldn't have been tagging along with those rebel troublemakers,'' Tamasin groused. ''He's not too young to know the risks, is he?''

''To be sure, he's not.'' Loath to place blame, Brendan uttered the words agreeably, then, with mischief in his eyes, pointed to the thoroughbred. "Why don't you take Miss Cullen for a ride, Hunter, like you used to do when she was a wee lass? No one is around to see."

Hunter folded his arms and spoke dryly. "I doubt Miss Cullen has an interest in such things now."

"Of course I've an interest. He's such a fine animal. I'd like to try him out."

Hunter gave his brother a dour look, then strolled to the horse and untied him. With mockery twinkling in his eyes, he bowed as if Tamasin were the grandest lady, and leaned to cup his hands for her to mount.

Playing out the charade with enjoyment, she allowed him to help her into the saddle, then straightened her shoulders regally as the groomsman led her away. Brendan's impish laughter followed.

"What do you call the horse?" Tamasin asked.

Hunter guided the animal over the green hill toward a copse where sunlight sparked off fiery autumn leaves. *"Augh-ishka."*

"Isn't that the name of the fairy horse that lives in the sea?"

"Aye. He's born of the sea, and once in a great while, comes galloping out of the waves to live on land. This one has a colt—the black one you've doubtless seen me curry."

They had come to a flat open field with a fenced course where the throughbreds were exercised, and Hunter, without speaking, led the horse into the enclosure. "Would you like to know how fast *Augh-ishka* can run?" he asked.

At the thought of such speed, of such a free wild flight, Tamasin cried, "Aye! Let him go as fast as he will, Hunter."

"You'll not be afraid?"

"Nay. There's little I fear."

"I can well believe it." Hunter vaulted up behind her and took the reins. "Hold on tight then, Damsel. You'll swear he's sprouted wings."

She gripped the animal's mane as Hunter dug his heels into its sides and let out the reins. They sprang forward, the horse's great muscled haunches propelling them, its long slender legs churning tender sod. Tamasin heard the rush of the autumn wind and the beast's rhythmic breaths. At her spine Hunter's body pressed, and glancing down, she saw his brown arms moving with the cadence of the gallop, his fingers closed confidently over the reins. The earth spun past, the trees multicolored blurs all around, and for a moment she felt indeed as if the horse had grown wings and sent them airborne.

"I'm afraid I might fall after all," she blurted suddenly, her stomach tightening with both excitement and fear of their hurtling pace.

Hunter chuckled and wickedly urged the horse to greater speed. "You'll not fall, Tamasin Cullen. You wouldn't dare let a horse best you."

But despite the groomsman's amusement she began to slip in the saddle so that he had to take hold of her waist with one hand and right her. As they sped along, balanced now, she began to grin, then laugh in abandon until she heard Hunter laughing, too.

At last he reined in the thoroughbred, slowed it to an easy canter, while Tamasin still laughed softly, her hair tumbling down. "How fortunate you are to be able to run like this every day."

He checked the reins until the horse walked. " 'Tis the only thing that makes my servitude tolerable." The humor had evaporated from his voice, leaving it sober and soft.

"What do you dream, Hunter?" Tamasin asked suddenly, staring at his well-shaped hands again, thinking how unjust fate had been to arrange that he be born to serve a master all his life.

"Not of marble houses, I can tell you."

"Of what, then?"

"I keep my dreams to myself. 'Tis better that way."

She detected admonishment in his tone, as if he implied that she should be less blatant in the voicing of her own ambitions. She stiffened. "Very well, then. Keep everything to yourself."

The moments of carefree delight had disappeared, and Hunter

regretted his surliness all at once. Tamasin's hair had come loose and he gazed at it, leaned closer to catch its scent, to study the sheen of the sun in its strands. He had agreed to their outing for no other reason than to be close to the cottier's lass. His eyes traveled over her back, her small waist, her hips beneath her black skirts, and as they entered the copse where leaves seesawed down from trees, he pulled the horse up short.

Tamasin turned her head in question, and he leaned to kiss her mouth. She jerked away but he took her chin in hand and pulled her lips to his again, kissing them until she yielded.

"No . . ." she protested when he grew rough and insistent. She was flushed, afraid of her own impulse to let him slip with her to the earth and continue what he'd begun.

But he did not persist, only swung down from the horse abruptly and regarded her with pinning eyes. "Playing the lady again, Tamasin? Avery Hampton is not here to watch."

"It has nothing to do with Avery, only my own wishes."

"At least you do not deny that I have the ability to tempt you."

"Your abilities have never been in question," she admitted, averting her eyes.

"Nay. Only my fortunes." His voice was hard.

"May we go back? Please, Hunter. Let's not end our time together in anger."

Without speaking again they went on, Hunter leading the horse, Tamasin sitting quietly, reflectively atop the saddle until they reached the stable yard.

The pigeons, which had been perched along the shingled gable, suddenly fluttered their wings and launched into the air. Unsettled, they circled the stable, creating black half-stars against the sky. Other, smaller birds joined in, forming a disordered wheel. Tamasin could feel their beating feathers stir the air, hear their odd, monotonous cries. A chill chased down her spine all at once.

"Brendan," Hunter called tensely. His keen eyes shifted from the birds to the field. "Where's Grandda?"

Brendan lifted a shoulder. "I don't know. I'm thinking he might be down in the glen shoring up that old section of wall that's starting to crumble. Aye, now I think on it, I saw him taking the wheel-car in that direction with a bit of timber stacked in the back."

Tossing the reins to his brother, Hunter pivoted and strode away.

"Wonder what's ailing him?" Brendan murmured curiously.

Tamasin, having caught a pinpoint of anxiety in Hunter's eyes, frowned. Carefully, she watched the pigeons as they continued to arc over her head in disorder, their wings *whooshing* and dropping feathers. A sudden gust of wind stirred an eddy of leaves over the cobbles, and a hound in the kennel howled. It was an eerie sound to match the sudden wild creaking of the verdigris lion in his gallop atop the roof.

"Something's amiss . . ." she muttered. "Something's not right." She crossed herself, studying the gray, boiling sky.

Brendan calmly poured himself another mug of mead. "Is it the fairies again, Tamasin?" he teased. "Are they up to mischief, do you think?"

She didn't answer. Her eyes were following Hunter's tall figure as he descended the hill at a rapid pace. Dismounting, leaving Brendan, she began to trot after Hunter. And when Hunter started to sprint, she sprinted, too, her skirts whipping about her legs, her heart hammering with a dread she couldn't name. After a while she grew breathless. How fast the groomsman ran! She couldn't begin to match his speed, but her own legs were young and nimble, used to miles of walking, and she was able to keep him in sight at least.

A thin fog hovered over the landscape in milky shreds. A hawk soared through it with a predatory cry; a flock of sheep, their white wool blending in with the fingers of mist, bleated for their shepherd.

Down in the glen, Tamasin could see the crumbling wall Brendan had mentioned, and close to it, the pony and wheel-car. Squatting on one side of the wall, in the ditch, Seamus

labored, using pieces of timber to brace the poorly mortared
stones. His movements were slow and stiff, his hands unsteady
at their task, every line of his body old.

On the opposite side of the wall, which was seven-foot high
or so, there stretched a line of birch trees, and through their
clacking autumn branches, the river sparkled with a brief flick
of white sun. Fronting it, tall green reeds and zigzagging hedges
intertwined. It was a tranquil landscape of crisp copper and
bronze, and yet, unsettled somehow. Dangerous.

Tamasin scanned the stand of trees as if to discover the
source of the strange disquiet. Through the leaves she saw a
flash or two of crimson—the bright coats of Avery and Rafael as
the pair dashed along the steeplechasing course at a breakneck
speed. She could catch snatches of their distant voices, their
echoes of shouting and laughter as they raised the stakes of
their jumping contest.

She gasped, realizing, as Hunter surely did, that when the
two gentlemen rounded the trees and approached the wall, they
would be unable to see Seamus working in the ditch on the
other side.

Hunter was running, waving his arms, and at the same time
the powerful horses, bred and trained by Seamus himself,
pounded through the drifts of star-shaped leaves. Their riders
leaned over their manes, intent only upon winning some exorbitant wager. Rafael's black mare, lathered with foam, followed
close upon the flying heels of Avery's bay, who increased his
crashing pace beneath the force of his rider's whip.

Nothing could be done. Fate could not be averted or deterred
any more than the hurtling pace of the horses could be halted.
Tamasin tensed, screamed, prepared for tragedy even as she
watched it unfold amid a swirl of gold, emerald, and terrible
red.

Avery's horse, after a slight falter when it caught the old
man's scent, bunched its haunches and leapt over the crumbling
wall. Just as old Seamus heard its thudding approach and raised
up from his stooping position, the animal sailed over.

Startled in midair by the sight of the man, the steed landed off balance and stumbled. Alarmed, Rafael's mount broke stride and took the wall uncollected. Headfirst, it tumbled into the ditch.

Tamasin saw the tragedy so clearly, with such infinitesimal detail, that later she could recall the glint of a snaffle, the bend of a knee in the stirrup, the flare of a distended pink nostril.

Someone cried out, a male voice, low and furious and piercing. A horse grunted. A hawk screamed.

With a shuddering, heaving effort, Rafael's horse recovered itself and staggered to its feet. Trembling, it faltered forward just as Rafael, who had been thrown to one side, groaned and rolled over on his back. Avery ran to his friend's side to help, and unsteadily, the disoriented pair of gentlemen looked about for the cause of the disaster.

Tamasin sprinted down the hill at such a speed her feet nearly went out from under her. She saw old Seamus sprawled on the ground with Hunter bent over him, and abruptly halted in her tracks, frozen by a spiral of horror.

Dear God.

Seamus lay upon his back in the leaf-strewn ditch, his mouth and eyes wide open, his bloodied head cradled against a rock.

For several seconds Tamasin could not move. Avery had staggered forward to see and, grimacing at the sight, hastily averted his head. "God in heaven—" he gasped, shocked, his face contorting.

Tamasin realized he had no idea what to do. No idea how to behave, what to say. Had it been a gentleman dead on the ground and a gentleman grieving over him, he might have conquered his squeamishness and offered to help lift the body, offered some word of regret. But such was not the case. A laborer lay dead, one from the stable, a Catholic one; and Hunter Kinshella knelt at his side with blood on his hands.

"My leg!" Rafael cried out suddenly, keeping well back. He clutched his left knee and shouted, "I fear I've injured my leg, Avery!"

As if dazed, Avery swung around. Then, seemingly relieved to be distracted from the horror of old Seamus's body, he fetched the quivering horses and helped the Italian to remount.

Tamasin did not hear or see the pair ride away. She saw nothing but the scene in the ditch, one too terrible for such a soft jewel setting.

Hunter could not call the life back into the old man, of course. He could not, with either the force of his own strong hands or with pleas to the Almighty, recall the freed soul to the broken body. But he tried. He tried.

Tamasin watched Hunter kneel in the mud, the front of his shirt soaked red, his grandfather lying in his arms. She heard his low racked voice, and felt as if she herself suffered the anguish that twisted the handsome face and bowed the sturdy back.

For several moments she simply stood and stared. The groomsman pillowed the white head in his lap, lifted the shoulders up as if to ease Seamus's pain. During his years of soldiering he must have seen many dead men, but he behaved as if he had not, as if this were his first sight of death, his first encounter with horror.

When he finally let the body go and turned away, he braced his hands upon the stone wall and leaned against it with his head bowed low, Tamasin walked forward. Her arms went around him. She pressed her cheek against his spine, clasped him tightly, as if to anchor his soaring lament.

Hunter would not turn around in her embrace, but at her touch the hard, stretched muscles of his belly convulsed and his chest heaved with the forcing out of grief. For long minutes, Tamasin held on to the damp curve of his back and, finally, without looking at her, without speaking, Hunter bestirred himself.

With great care he lifted his grandfather, his boots slipping in the mud as he laid the frail body on the planks of the wheelcar. He did not ask for Tamasin's help, but she gave it. She took hold of the pony's halter and began to pull the little animal

with its wheel-car and burden up the hill. Hunter walked a pace
behind, next to the body of Old Seamus.

Halfway up the hill Tamasin halted, stepped back, and
touched Hunter's hand, and the groomsman, bleak-eyed and
remote, grasped it gladly.

Chapter Twelve

Avery Hampton had left the Hall, had literally run away to catch a breath of untainted air, to try and escape Rafael—or his own unsettled self—he was no longer certain which.

He stood at the end of Monk Street on Custom House Quay, still breathing hard after his brisk half-walk, half-run over the fields, his head throbbing from his overindulgence last evening—too much claret and too much lobster in cream sauce with Rafael. The young Italian's influence over him seemed to be increasing, growing tighter, like a net drying in the sun.

The analogy had struck Avery a moment ago as he stared at a fisherman's net draped over the planks of the weathered pier. It was soaking wet, its brown fibers twisted into a mesh so strong that only a well-honed knife could have severed it. Beneath the net a large fish lay helpless, caught, some fisherman's prize with dull eyes and a back beautifully sheened in scales. Every now and then it flopped exhaustedly.

"Wretched creature," Avery murmured. "Stinking creature. Trout, I wonder . . . ? Rafael's favorite."

He had discovered Rafael, an impoverished second son of

a once noble family in Florence, at the Galleria dell' Accademia beside Michelangelo's *David*. The slim young Italian had seemed to resemble the sculpture itself, classical in face and form. Rafael possessed sharp wit and lazy elegance and an aristocratic conceit that simultaneously fascinated and repulsed Avery. He was well educated and worldly, and loved to spend hours philosophizing and quoting literature. There was something enthralling even about Rafael, and Avery was beginning to be afraid of his own affection for him. And because of that affection, he mortally feared that what Sir Harry had been suggesting for years was true.

I question your manhood, my son.

At first such alarming remarks were a comment upon Avery's immaturity, his prank playing, his inability to settle down at his studies, his childish perspective. But now, when his father took time to notice him—which was not too often—the baronet all but threw the malicious accusations at him.

"What in the devil is wrong with you?" he had demanded just last week. "Are you so unmanly that you cannot even rouse yourself to *look* at women?"

The comment had been made after Avery had declined to accompany his father to Dublin where, Sir Harry had declared, a particularly talented courtesan had come on to the market, available for the pleasure of some well-connected young man. With Hampton money, this lady of erotic skill could be established as Avery's mistress. A splendid arrangement, especially since Avery seemed uninterested in putting out any effort to find a wife—not that both varieties of women couldn't be accommodated at once, of course.

"I looked at plenty of women in Europe, Father," Avery had said defensively.

"But brought none of them home, my boy."

Avery had found ample opportunities in the drawing rooms of Europe to choose a bride, but as he had scrutinized their pink faces, yellow curls, and modish necklines, he inwardly recoiled. He feared that if he were to wed one of those spoiled,

glass-fragile darlings and take her to bed, he would prove unable
to do what was necessary to produce an heir. Such a failure
would be the most humiliating consequence any man could
imagine. It was his private, ever humbling nightmare.

So, he had clung to Rafael, and the pair of them had sampled
the wild, money-saturated society of other bored young men
on the Grand Tour. Truthfully, the utter depravity of Europe
had intimidated Avery, though he had never admitted it, of
course. But all the while his secret fear had festered, leaving
him plagued with a restless need to prove himself in some way,
not so much to stop his father's condemnation, but to test his
own dark depths so that the torment of doubt would cease.

On more than one occasion, he had paid women to spend
an evening with him, paid them to keep their mouths shut so
that word of his failed performance would never reach interested
ears. Just last week, in fact, in a back room of *The Hound,* he had
humiliated himself with a common tart, then tossed a handful of
guineaus at her smirking face.

Trembling now, he breathed deeply of the sea air, realizing
that he still wore his evening clothes from last night, that his
face was unshaven, his hair undressed. A fisherman came to
retrieve the netted fish, and after giving Avery's gentlemanly
clothes a hostile look, slung the catch over his shoulder and
turned up Common Quay.

Cold, having failed to snatch a greatcoat when he dashed
out of the Hall like an escaping prisoner, Avery followed,
his hands thrust in his pockets, the salt wind chafing his fair
complexion as he passed the bullring and entered the bustling
corn market. The place was crowded, packed with farmers,
peasants, and merchants' wives. Cottier brats roamed about,
hoping to steal anything edible that might tumble off the back
of a cart.

Through the press Avery glimpsed a smooth dark head and
white apron. He shoved aside a ragged urchin to get a better
look, and was rewarded with the sight of Tamasin Cullen.

She stood at a wooden barrow sorting ears of corn, her nimble fingers peeling back the husks to inspect the golden kernels. She was cleaner than any other woman in the market, he noted, meticulously groomed, even impressive in her efforts to mimic a lady in manner. She was not well bred and would never be, nor was she delicate; but there was a kind of primitive earthiness about her, a fierce tenacity that he had always found attractive.

Tamasin was physically fashioned for the delight of a man's hands, her figure a tantalizing combination of fullness and slenderness, her mouth long and fleshy, her eyes unabashedly direct. She had no doubts as to what *she* wanted out of life. Nor did she have any qualms about how she managed to get it.

Avery watched her a long while. Not for the first time, he felt that if he could only touch her, possess that lithe, strong-willed body, his manhood would no longer be in question. Recently, the notion had been growing, quivering inside him so that he dreamed about it in the hellish nights after he had drunk too much wine with Rafael and lay dizzy in his bed. And yet, illogically, when Tamasin had refused his offer to spend a night in Hampton Hall, Avery had not been angry. He had been relieved that the testing of his manhood, which was becoming of colossal importance to him, had been postponed.

As she continued to sort through the barrows, he elbowed his way through the press of carts, draft horses, and children. Strolling up to Tamasin, he leaned over her shoulder and asked casually, "Do you find the crop good?"

Tamasin started and wheeled about, chagrined to have been caught off guard, especially when she had been so careful to dodge Avery after refusing his offer.

But noting the smile on his face, a genuine one it seemed, she smiled tentatively. Then, mustering confidence, she glanced down at her basket. "Fair. The crop is fair this year."

"Good." Avery's smile widened. "That means my father's tenants will be able to pay their rents on time, which means more money in the family coffers. I could use a new phaeton and a pair of English high-steppers."

The gentry's unfairness to the cottiers did not unduly concern Tamasin, for she had long ago set herself apart from them, emotionally if not quite physically. But that, too, would change in time—*if* she could manage to keep the light in Master Avery's eyes burning as brightly as it was now.

"It must be a thrill to ride in a phaeton. To ride very fast," she said, looking at him through her lashes.

"Would you like a ride?"

"Oh, aye," she said excitedly. "It's something I've always dreamed of doing."

"Have you?" Avery eyed her shrewdly. "Then I hope you've been keeping yourself away from Hunter Kinshella."

It satisfied him to see Tamasin's fingers close reflexively about the ear of corn she held. Her tenseness caused him suspicion, as well. Had she dallied with the groomsman? Avery knew his own desire would evaporate like a burst bubble if she ever did. He despised Kinshella, and the fact that the groomsman seemed to have all the vital, conspicuous *manliness* that he, the baronet's son, lacked, galled Avery even more.

"Hunter's off in Kildare," Tamasin murmured, her eyes lowered. "Racing your father's horses."

She was obviously disconcerted, and Avery grinned. He liked to distress her, for it made him feel effectual, reinforced his notion about the two of them together. Purposefully, he had offered Tamasin no money for her favors, no enticing trinkets, for she would have come eagerly to him for payment. He did not want her under those circumstances. The occasion would be spoiled if money were involved. He desired to have the cottier's daughter on a level of passion, even if the passion were not lustful, but some other violent emotion that would make her wild with life. He did not want her to be like one of the common doxies a man could find anywhere, one of the docile, blowsy women who would make him feel inadequate and then smirk behind his back. He wanted, needed, Tamasin Cullen to provide something more.

He drawled, "So Kinshella is away? Ah, yes, I seem to recall my father talking about the races. I suppose Hunter must take up the slack now that old Seamus is gone.'' Avery didn't care to think about the old man; the sight of his body on that dreadful day of steeplechasing had sickened him. He glanced at Tamasin's smooth skin and cool violet eyes to dispel the image.

She hesitated a moment, then with a guileless, very appealing modesty, asked outright, ''You're not angry with me because I . . . refused you?''

Avery thought it better not to chastise her, not to increase the tension between them and make her skittish. He shrugged as if the matter were of little importance. '' 'Twas just a whim I had one evening. I thought you'd make a lively companion for a bored young gentleman, such as I was.'' He managed to make it sound as if he'd almost forgotten the incident, and remembering it, was a trifle wounded. ''I recall being surprised when you refused, however. I thought you'd be pleased with the chance to come up to the Hall.''

Tamasin met his eyes, vaguely taken aback by his reaction. She had expected him to be angry, retaliatory. Instead, he seemed wounded, truly disappointed. She must handle him carefully so as not to offend him and change his mood.

Her eyes roved over his fine clothes: the green spencer coat with the stand-fall collar, the brown nankeen breeches, the ruffled, white linen shirt. He looked the worse for wear with his eyes puffy and his mouth pinched with cold, but still, he was a gentleman. The sort of gentleman she wanted for herself, on her own terms.

The crush of the market goers as they threaded their way through the narrow streets closed in around them. Tamasin, shopping for the lodge larder, slid a last ear of corn in her basket, delaying a moment to gather her thoughts. She must be clever, bold. She threw her head back, knowing her pride always appealed to Avery, even stirred him. ''I'm a young lass, Avery. Surely you don't fault me for valuing my virtue.''

His eyes fastened on her strong thin hands, then upon her

intelligent eyes. He smiled broadly. "On the contrary. I know very well that you've never done anything without payment. Why should I expect you to change now?"

He had altered his tone slightly, hardened it. Negotiations for her favors would now begin. They both expected it, even looked forward to it. "Actually," he said with a lift of his shoulder, "I thought your overnight stay in the Hall, with all its comforts, would have been a sort of payment to you. Not to mention the . . . honor of my company, if I may be so bold to suggest it." He spoke with a flippancy that was both arrogant and serious.

"But those are not—" Tamasin hesitated, sensing that she must be careful. "Those aren't things that I can *keep*. I can't take them away from the Hall with me when . . . when you decide it's time for me to leave again."

"Ah." Avery nodded as if understanding perfectly. "I should have realized, of course."

The wind skimmed over the quay, ruffling the brown iridescent feathers of the butcher's pheasants hanging on hooks above their heads. Avery rubbed his arms. He looked cold, Tamasin thought, his body unaccustomed to walking in misty Irish mornings without a velvet-lined surtout, kid gloves, and beaver hat. Odd that *she* didn't feel the chill weather beneath the meager covering of her shawl.

My blood is different. The thought came to Tamasin suddenly, unpleasantly. Avery's blood was thin, patrician, where hers was thick and warm with peasant breeding. Could it change? If she were allowed to sit long enough beside blazing coal fires clad in velvet, sipping cups of chocolate, her stomach full of rich food, would her blood dilute? Could it become pure, like bog water forced through a sieve?

"Where have you gone?" Avery asked curiously, for he recognized the look of musing on her face. "Not too far away, I hope."

Tamasin released a breath and looked at him directly. She decided that honesty was the best tactic, for she wanted Avery

Hampton to know exactly what he would have to do to please
her. Her eyes turned a hard brilliant violet, and she said, "I've
just been to Hampton Hall, that's where. I've been imagining
myself sitting beside the hearth in the library. Picturing myself
dressed in the most sumptuous clothes money can buy, with a
pot of hot chocolate and a box of comfits at my side."

Avery raised a brow and, unable to help himself, laughed
out loud. "Indeed? Have you really? Well, I think we'll find
a way to come to terms, Tamasin. Eventually. 'Tis only a matter
of time."

She regarded him solemnly. "I agree." And she did. It came
to her that Avery's desire for her had not been such a whimsical
idea, after all. A few weeks ago, he had wanted her badly when
he had sent the offer; he wanted her badly now, for whatever
reason. The game went on. There was one characteristic she
knew well about the gentry: the more expensive and unattain-
able a thing, the more they wanted to possess it, at any price.

Avery expected to have her. Sooner or later, right or wrong,
Tamasin knew she would overcome her hesitancy and give
herself to him.

But it would not be for a striped silk skirt or a hat or for a
whole barrow full of lace handkerchiefs embroidered with love
knots. The baronet's son would be made to compensate her
dearly, although at this point, she had not settled upon anything
specific. The bargain would require a great deal of keen and
careful thought. But ultimately, it must be a bargain that would
put her as far beyond mud huts and hunger as possible.

She met Avery's eyes again, noting that his hair had come
loose from its black ribbon to lay lankly against his cheeks.
His light complexion was chapped, his nose red, and his teeth
clenched against the cold. "As you said," she answered, touching his hand so lightly, so fleetingly, that he scarcely had
time to feel its warmth, "we'll find a way to come to terms.
Eventually."

Avery regarded her a moment, a man of twenty-eight who
suddenly felt barely sixteen. If he didn't master his sudden

DAMSEL   179

pang of desire, he knew his need for her would show too clearly.
Then the game would be lost, his bargaining power weakened.
Giving her the heavy-lidded stare reserved for her breed, he
said curtly, "You'll hear from me. When it's convenient."

Tamasin watched him hasten through the throng of shopping
villagers, his coat tails flapping above his chamois-lined boots.
"Yes," she murmured determinedly. "I'll go to you, Avery.
But not too soon."

An image of Hunter rose to haunt her, but she pushed it
away.

Chapter Thirteen

It was said that on All Hallows Eve the fairies clambered out of their raths and, with a mischievous wave to the mortals who were chained to their barren plots of land, moved off to winter quarters, dancing jigs all the way. Ghosts returned from otherworldly climes, floating over the fields to re-inhabit earthly homes. Doors were left open for them, and inside they found tobacco and bowls of steaming *sowan* set on a stool beside a fire. Fairies must be humored and accommodated, or else they might put a pox on the family or dry up the family cow.

The holiday was a festive time, a favorite of the peasants; it provided an excellent excuse to drink and dance and play games. And oddly enough, perhaps because it was such a mysterious night, one so danger-fraught with roaming fairies and gliding specters, Tamasin wanted to return to her own people and participate in their half-pagan rite. It was one of the rare times she cared to be among them, allowed herself to be reminded that she was one of them—whether they welcomed her back into their ranks or not.

She stood back from the circle of the celebration, listening with closed eyes to the music of the fiddles, uilleann pipes, and harps as they blended together in song. Drums pounded and seemed to call up the old, still revered Celtic spirits from the moon-frosted fells. Even the cattle stood as if enchanted, and Tamasin, as she hovered on the fringes of the huge shadow-circle of peasants, felt the flesh on her arms rise in answer to the eerie atmosphere.

She breathed excitedly, glancing at the crowd that wreathed the roaring bonfire; their faces flickered with orange and scarlet, and their bare feet tapped as children zigzagged through their circle. Work-swollen hands clapped as each cottier walked around the fire thrice to insure a year without sickness. Poteen flowed freely from illegal stills. Lovers kissed, and unless their parents remained vigilant, stole away to find a lonely trysting place. The air was cool and crisp, prompting Tamasin to edge nearer the fire, smell its warm peaty odor mingled with the sweat of bodies and the sweet fragrance of heather and bruised grass.

The musicians struck up a jig and couples began to pair, laughing, lifting their feet, their striped waistcoats and dyed petticoats flashing color as the fire reflected it. They were fun-loving people, and possessed a kind of natural grace which made their feet skillful even at dainty dances.

At first, none of the lads, not even the boldest, invited Tamasin to jig, but after the jugs of poteen had been passed round several times, one young man, the most brash in the village, made a show of presenting himself to her as if she were a princess. Putting one black-nailed hand across his waist and the other behind his back, he bowed.

The crowd laughed uproariously at his posturing while the piper struck a low sarcastic note. Peasant girls tossed braided flowers at Tamasin.

But, with an arrogant toss of her head, she declined the boy, knowing that he mocked her, that they all mocked her. She knew, too, that they were remembering vividly Paddy O'Malley's flogging. They blamed her for his beating, believed her a traitor to her own kind. To them, that was a greater sin than murder.

Brendan Kinshella, full of liquor but still nimble on his feet, stepped out in the midst of the crowd to jig. Despite the fact that he dallied with their daughters, owed them gambling money, and woke them when he staggered through the streets singing ditties on the nights when he didn't have to be carried home on his brother's shoulder, Brendan was a favorite of the villagers. He winked at Tamasin, and she knew that he meant to distract them from carrying their taunting game to crueler lengths.

Managing a respectable performance, he was admired by every female eye. Especially a pair of dreamy, pale blue ones gazing at him from a distance.

Tamasin saw the feminine figure standing near a cottage, unnoticed by anyone else. She sucked in a wondering breath, scarcely believing Eushanie Hampton had dared venture so close to the celebration. With peasant spirits and tempers running high, and with the seeds of rebellion germinating in the hearts of almost every man present, Miss Eushanie's daring was ill advised.

How ironic, Tamasin thought, that the baronet's daughter fancied herself in love with a common laborer—even if he was a charming specimen—when any number of titled men of wealth were probably prepared to take her dowry and resign themselves to finding a less than ornamental wife facing them over breakfast every morning. Eushanie should have been sitting in her drawing room entertaining a bevy of gentlemen tonight, instead of standing alone in the shadows making calf eyes at a man she could never have. Tamasin noted Eushanie's heavy fur-lined pelisse, which was probably worth more than Brendan could save in a lifetime.

In contrast to the lady, how poor the cottiers looked! And yet, some spiritual flame, feeble but bright, gleamed in their eyes like a reflection borrowed from the topaz fire. No wonder so many poets emerged from their ranks, Tamasin thought with an unexpected surge of pride. Throughout the centuries, the Irish had been blessed with an unquenchable imagination.

As Tamasin scanned the crowd, she saw a figure materialize out of blackness, his face limned in fire colors. He stood back, apart from all the rest, one foot propped on an overturned plow, a bottle in his hand. His bearing was one of detached interest, as if he were content to observe the merrymaking, but had no desire to join it.

She was surprised he had come at all, and wondered why he had, unless it was to be on hand to lend his back to Brendan when the young rogue could no longer stand. She had not seen Hunter Kinshella since old Seamus's death, had avoided him in fact. And he seemed to avoid her, retreating into his private, hard-working world while leaving her to her dreams of Hampton Hall.

But he was looking at her now, so dark and satyr-eyed that she fancied him a member of the spirit world all at once, one of the fairies. Weren't they all fallen angels, after all, moving around on some nebulous plain, hovering between heaven and hell, too unworthy to be saved, but not wicked enough to be lost?

As Tamasin held his gaze across the space, as the strum of the harps and the cry of pipes crescendoed on the air, she felt herself mesmerized all at once. As the drums beat, the earth trembled beneath her bare soles. She smelled the pungent odors of the fire.

A persistent village lad detached himself from the press and approached her suddenly, doffing his cap, bowing low at her feet, inviting *Lady* Tamasin to dance. Cackling laughter followed when, as expected, she shook her head and refused to accept his outstretched hand. Again and again, in like manner, she rejected every contestant who approached.

For several minutes the lads continued to entertain the gathering in such a way, purely at Tamasin's expense, while she continued to disdain them all. She flushed beneath their mock-

ery but stood her ground with the stiff-backed haughtiness she
had learned to use over the years.

When the last man stepped forth—taller than any other, older
and more forbidding than the rest—it caused the noisy throng
to fall silent, the musicians to soften their lilting melody.

Tamasin did not move, but her senses began to stretch with
anticipation. Here was a man just as rebellious as she, a man
who did not bow like the others, the only man who had ever
stirred her passions.

Slowly, Hunter Kinshella extended his hand, daring her to
have the courage to clasp it.

She stared at the hard brown fingers, wondering why he had
chosen to make the offer. Had he been pricked by some whim
to dance? Had he decided to lay aside his brittle shield for a
few minutes and enjoy himself, even while his mouth remained
unsmiling? Or did he imagine himself doing her a favor, offering one of his punishing little kindnesses?

She found she didn't care to know his motivation. She would
dance with him. And because he was strong, and she needed
to feel strength at the moment, she reached out.

His was the firmest hand she had ever held, its grip inescapable. It sent a current to her feet and made them light. She
yearned to be a part of the music through this man, to capture
a measure of the mystery of the spirit-filled night, to know its
secrets, its *meaning,* if she could.

Amid the high-pitched sound of ribald laughter Hunter drew
her forward. The drums increased their pounding and the fiddles
whined. A jig was struck, and without hesitation the groomsman
began to dance.

Tamasin stared at him in smiling awe, for lately Hunter's
nature seemed devoid of gaiety. Then she remembered, poignantly and with a slicing sense of shame, that once, long ago,
he had moved like a dream with her wrapped in his arms,
showing a barefoot lass the way to dance beside a hedgerow.

Now, just as he had then, Hunter danced with narrow-hipped
agility, precisely in time; and across from him, so did Tamasin.

With their arms folded over their chests they performed the jig together, Tamasin's skirts churning above her calves, her eyes alight, her breath fast while wildness bubbled up from her soul. The flames leapt higher and she grew as carefree as the air and the earth, gloried in being at one with the elements, a child of the fells devoid of ambition, of yearning, innocent of all except the moment.

And as she danced opposite the groomsman, struggled to match his endurance with her hair tumbling down, he watched, and Tamasin saw the fierceness of desire in his eyes. Then, his mouth slowly curved into a smile. It was a slash of white that carried her swiftly, piercingly, back in time to the days before she had turned his world upside down. It was striking in its rarity, a quicksilver thing enduring only a second or two.

The jig ended in a flurry of steps, accompanied by a prolonged frenzy of clapping. A group of laughing children formed a circle around Tamasin and Hunter, then pulled the pair away from the firelight and into the darkness, where they were conspiratorily abandoned.

Tamasin struggled to catch her breath, holding her sides and drawing in gulps of air sweetened by drifts of autumn leaves and wet grass. Frost settled itself atop the landscape, gathering in crevices and making the air brittle and thin. A silence fell between Tamasin and Hunter, one filled with the high eerie notes from the uilleann pipes. Her young body still tingled from her dance beside the fire, and her senses were vitally aware of the tall form standing near. She searched for something to say to break the spell.

"You dance well," she whispered.

"And you."

Conversation stopped again. Awkwardly, Tamasin asked, "You've been away at the races?"

"Aye, I have, indeed."

"I suppose you won a great deal of money for Sir Harry. The stable lads say his horses are the swiftest, the best trained.

They say you're as skilled with the beasts as your grandda was.''

"Sir Harry's horse ran well and won a heavy purse,'' Hunter answered, amused, his eyes flickering ruefully over her face in the darkness. ''If money's what you're interested in.''

Tamasin did not rise to the taunt. Airily, she said, ''Sir Harry was pleased with you, no doubt.''

"I suppose so. He gave me a new woolen cathamore for my trouble.''

"A cathamore? Why?''

He made a derisive sound. ''Probably so I wouldn't inconvenience him by freezing to death this winter.''

"No matter the reason, you got a fine new coat. Won't you be the envy of the stable. Watch yourself, Hunter Kinshella, or you'll be getting the same treatment from the villagers that I do.''

Hunter shrugged, an eloquent gesture of wide shoulders that was truly indifferent. ''And I would handle it with even more unconcern than you, Miss Cullen. What any of the villagers thinks of me doesn't matter. It did once, as I recall. But my perspective has changed.''

"Mine has not,'' she said, stroking the fringe of her shawl.

His lips curved wryly. ''I know. Your viewpoint of life and its important aspects has always remained steadfastly fixed as that moon up there, so far as I can tell.''

"Do you condemn me?''

"If I did, would you care?''

She glanced up at his shadowed face, at the hard planes lit by a ray of scarlet firelight that managed to escape the circle of peasants on the hill. ''Nay,'' she answered with false flippancy.

He laughed and shook his head. ''Sometimes, Tamasin, your honesty is endearing.''

The celebration quieted as the musicians paused to enjoy a round of poteen. A few yards away, the low sound of voices arrested Tamasin and Hunter, and they glanced toward the dark, humped rows of mud cabins.

In the open, lit by moonlight, Brendan and Eushanie stood together, the lady nervous and excited, her hands thrust in the pockets of her pelisse, while the fair Mr. Kinshella laughed engagingly and touched a forefinger to her nose.

"What are those two about?" Tamasin whispered.

"They're tasting the forbidden, I should imagine."

Brendan leaned closer to Eushanie and, with the smoothness of a seasoned lover, set his mouth upon the lady's untouched lips.

"Aren't you going to stop them?" Tamasin asked Hunter.

"I make it a policy never to interfere with my brother's conquests, especially one that he expects to be lucrative."

Tamasin sighed in disgust. "He's a fool and so is she."

"She?" Hunter inquired, a black brow raised.

"Aye. Eushanie will let Brendan dally with her, ruin her. And then when some suitable young earl comes along with a marriage offer, what a row there'll be when he discovers he's not the first. Being the innocent she is, no doubt Eushanie will tell the gentleman exactly who came before him."

"She simply wants something she shouldn't have," Hunter replied with a shrug. He turned his eyes back to Tamasin and studied her face in the darkness. "No different than you, when it comes down to it."

Tamasin was offended by his comment. A little sulkily, she argued, "My reasons for wanting what I want are more complicated than that."

Looking off into the distance, toward Hampton Hall, Hunter mused, "I suspect you want something you can't even name, Tamasin. You think it's very near because you can see other people enjoying it. You believe all you have to do is find a way to reach your hand over the high wall of your own gray world and into the gold of someone else's, then grab with all your might." Stooping, he picked up a pebble and cast it high into the sky, toward the stars. A few seconds later it pinged against the earth. "It doesn't work that way."

Tamasin stared at him, disturbed, hurt. He implied that her

dream was not only foolish, but unrealizable. Caustically, she asked, "If what you say is true," she demanded, "then why is Eushanie Hampton—who lives in the 'gold' world—muddying her fine kid slippers in order to kiss your silly brother?"

"Because there's no one like Brendan in her world," the groomsman shot back, "or at least, if there is, she hasn't found him yet. My brother isn't tied to anything, not to a title or land, to wealth, or even to honor."

"More's the pity."

"My brother is reckless and romantic. He enjoys the sort of freedom Eushanie would doubtless like to have herself. Aye, he's indolent, but he's not corrupt, unlike—" Hunter's gaze raked her. "Unlike your delicate-fingered Englishman, Avery, and his friends."

"He's not *my* Avery," she snapped.

"But he would like to be—for three quarters of an hour or so, at least."

"You're coarse!"

The groomsman moved to stand before her, so close Tamasin could feel his breath stir her hair. "Coarse? But how would you expect an Irish laborer to be?

His silkily uttered words in no way appeased her and she attempted to wound him. Words rose easily to her lips, words to put him in his place. "Just as you are! Bitter. Crude. Dishing out blarney about gray and gold worlds as if you were one of those tinkers-turned-poets who trundle about in painted green wagons."

Hunter regarded her in the contemplative, knife-blade way of his that never failed to cleave her composure in half. Unnerved, her blood high, Tamasin complained, "Why do you always look at me that way? As if you're trying to get inside my head."

His stare did not diminish one degree, and his voice was chilling, dangerous. "Because I am, I suppose. The workings of it fascinate me. Although, generally, I understand them very well."

Gooseflesh rose along Tamasin's arms. His tone and manner had suddenly grown provocative, heated. He seemed just on the verge of seizing her arms, dominating her in the same way he had on a day when a litter of hounds had circled their feet. Astoundingly, she *wanted* him to seize her, crush her in his arms. Her eyes locked with his, flirting, daring his emotion to snap. "That isn't a very flattering thing to say to a woman who has just given you a dance," she whispered huskily.

Hunter smiled, reading her well. He knew that she still wanted the lash of his anger as an assuagement to her long-held guilt. He knew, too, that her young body throbbed for something only he could give her, something she desired desperately. Her needs and his had become entangled with each other like strong wild vines. It galled him that his own body demanded that he satisfy it. He leaned close and whispered, "Did you expect flattery as well as the dance then, Tamasin? I wonder, why did you dance with me at all?"

"Because you asked."

"But the others asked, too." His voice had lowered, and he found himself bending his head toward hers.

"So they did . . ."

"And you refused them all."

Tamasin could smell the earthy odor of Hunter's flesh, sense its warmth. The wind ruffled his homespun shirt, and she could see the strong bones and sinew that tied together beneath his neck. She raised her chin so that her mouth met his. "The others mocked me. You did not."

"Do you think me honorable, then?"

"No."

His lips parted and came to rest against her own. Her jacket was laced across the front and he hooked his forefinger into the frayed, crisscrossed ribbons. "How do you know I'm not mocking you now?"

Uncaring, she closed her eyes and gripped his hand, sliding it slowly past the laces.

He accepted what she offered, invading her jacket with his calloused hands while she leaned into their pressure.

"You told me that I'm bitter," he whispered, his mouth brushing the corner of her own. "Do you think you caused me to be that way?" His tongue traced her lips and he breathed, "Just a little, Damsel?"

Her head tilted, her eyes closed, and her nerves felt nothing but his fingers and lips, which were forceful now, exactly the way she needed them to be. "Aye . . ." she mouthed, thinking of the stickpin and watch, of the manacles and bright dreams of scarlet coats and muskets. She spoke dreamily as he touched her now bared breasts and kissed her throat. "I made you that way . . ."

"I shall punish you for it, you know."

She allowed his hand to stray down to her skirts, below the waistband, where his fingers pressed.

"How?" She barely spoke the word.

He drew back so that the chill air of night replaced the dry heat of his hands, leaving her to stand half-naked in the spirit-filled night, staring up at him.

With a dark, retaliatory lift of his brow, he said, "That's how I'll leave you. To yearn for something other than marble houses for a change."

He had spurned her, hurt her, and she shivered. But she did not reach out to draw him back.

Hunter turned to leave, and over a shoulder he said obliquely, "By the way, that little bundle of nonsense you value so much is stuffed under my bed. Remember it tomorrow."

Angry at his treatment, bereft, Tamasin echoed, "Tomorrow . . . ?"

"Aye. Before breakfast, I would guess."

"What are you talking about? What do you mean?" she demanded in confusion.

"Simply that you might find yourself in need of money soon."

"Hunter!" she called after him. "What do you mean? *Hunter!*"

But he strolled maddeningly on, thrusting his hands in his pockets and whistling, refusing to heed her repeated calls. In seconds the black fairy night had swallowed up his form.

"To the devil with you then!" Tamasin yelled at his back. "To the devil with you, Hunter Kinshella!"

Chapter Fourteen

She hadn't long to ponder Hunter Kinshella's disturbing words; before the next morning had quite dawned, the grooms-man's prediction had proved devastatingly accurate. She was never able to fathom how Hunter had known what was to happen.

Sir Harry and his guests, grown bored with country diversions, had piled into their coaches and rumbled merrily toward Dublin to sample the pastimes there, leaving the overworked lodge staff behind to stuff themselves with forbidden delicacies and breathe a sigh of relief.

While Cook slid golden loaves of bread from the oven, Tamasin stirred oatmeal for the servants' breakfast and gazed through the window, noticing a pony cart as it turned down the drive. At first, in the mist of early morning she could not discern the identity of the caller, but as his formidable starched shirt front invaded the tranquility of Cook's domain, she recognized Thackary, the English butler who ruled below stairs at Hampton Hall.

He swept into the room. Automatically, his exacting gaze

took in the order of things, searched for waste, for dirt, for disarray as if he were the master himself—and indeed he was— over every domestic servant employed by the baronet.

"Cullen," he said without preamble. His pale eyes swept beyond Cook to Tamasin, who stood with her oatmeal spoon poised over the steaming pot. "You *are* Cullen, aren't you?"

"Aye." Not to be intimidated by his withering tone, or by a sudden shiver of forebodement, Tamasin kept her voice light and her smile engaging. "What brings you out into the morning dampness, Thackary?"

"Business, miss," he stated, not charmed. "As a matter of fact, you may put on your shawl and go. Sir Harry won't be needing you. He'll not be in residence again till spring. The cook and footman will have to make do alone here."

Tamasin stared at the man, sure that she had misheard his words. "Leave?" she managed to stammer at last. "But the place is understaffed now. Ridiculously understaffed. There should be at least a dozen of us when Sir Harry's about, not less than six when he's away. Isn't that so, Cook?" She glanced at the other woman in appeal.

"No one's asking for your advice on running an establishment, Cullen," Thackary replied cooly, his practiced air of superiority erasing all expression from his features. Long ago, his heart had hardened to the sometimes harsh but necessary duties of a butler. "The decision has already been made. Go now. You're finished here."

Tamasin continued to stare at him. All at once, instead of seeing his pudding-colored countenance and berry nose, she saw the warm coal fires of the lodge hearths, the Turkey rugs, the gleaming crystal, the wood-panelled rooms, the three filling meals a day. If his orders were obeyed, every cherished inch of comfort would be gone, out of her reach. No longer would she be able to touch the silver, handle the collection of porcelain on the mantelshelf, polish the ancestral armor standing in the vestibule.

Da's mud cabin loomed in her imagination like a decrepit

dragon, crude and stinking, a grave for the living, the symbol of a struggle for survival. There would be pigs beside the peat fire and skinny chickens in the best of times, anxiety when the rent came due, fretting when the tiny plot of land did not produce enough to keep body and soul together after the major portion had been handed over to church and landowner. In a sudden chilling wave, all the cares, the hardships, and the fears of every peasant born to depend upon the land and its lords swept over her.

Hunter Kinshella's cryptic words of the previous night haunted her suddenly, and, pinning suspicious eyes on the butler, she demanded, "Who gave you these orders?"

Thackary drew himself up, bristling. " 'Tis not your place to know or to—"

"Sir Harry did not give the order to let me go, did he? 'Twas Master Avery, wasn't it?"

Rankled to have his authority questioned, the butler declared, "The orders have come down, and I'll not discuss the matter. Now get yourself out of here, Cullen. Arguing serves no purpose but to goad my temper more."

Tamasin hid her dismay, frightened over the loss of the bright future she'd dreamed for herself, which—until it had been extinguished in one fell swoop by Thackary's order—had seemed like a small but reachable star.

She understood suddenly that Avery Hampton meant to force her hand in this game they played. By stripping her of her position, he had undermined her power to bargain. He would have her come to him out of desperation, knowing she had no alternative but starvation, knowing the glitter and bountiful tables of Hampton Hall would call to her like a siren song.

Eventually.

She had wanted to squeeze out of Avery every farthing and favor possible in the deal. She had wanted to go to him with her pride intact, knowing she was worth something, even if her value were measured in coin or in a secure staff position at the Hall. Now, if her life with Da in the cabin proved unbearable, she would have to give herself away. She would likely receive nothing in exchange except one dreamlike night between his embroidered sheets, before being cast out on the fells again like a stray kitten who had lost its novelty. She had no illusions that Avery's life was made up of a never-ending stream of quickly fading diversions.

"Your wages will be sent to you," Thackary said stiffly.

"In a pig's eye," Tamasin laughed scornfully. She had not been paid in months, for Sir Harry seemed to hold the opinion that providing employment to a cottier's lass was largesse enough. And indeed it was these days. With bitterness Tamasin thought of Hunter Kinshella and his new cathamore coat. Doubtless *he* had received *his* wages from the baronet.

Throwing the wooden spoon aside, she snatched her shawl from the peg by the door and marched past Cook and the butler, putting on a facade of bravado, breathing hard with both fury and fear. "Good day to you, then."

Outside, the morning sky was brightening to pink. Tamasin shivered in the new sunshine, dragging her shawl close as her feet skimmed over the dewy turf. She paused only once, just long enough to pull off her shoes and stockings. They might be her last for a very long time.

All at once she was anxious to see the cabin, to see if, by some miracle, Da had stored enough potatoes for the winter, repaired the deteriorating roof, swept away the filth, hoarded a few coins for necessities. She wanted to find that the smoky hut was not really as wretched as she remembered it to be, that it was adequate if not comfortable, livable if not welcoming— *bearable.*

She climbed the hill breathlessly, then sighed with relief. Jamsie had at least cut enough peat to last the winter. The large stack resembling an upended pine cone stood beside the west cabin wall. She told herself determinedly that she could endure a cottier's life again. She could endure it until spring, when Sir Harry returned and was persuaded by her humble, pretty smile to reestablish her position at the lodge.

Wrenching open the flimsy cabin door, Tamasin entered, surveying the space, gasping at the odor. She found her father curled up like a heap of rags on the floor, snoring on what had once been her pallet, wrapped in what had once been her blanket. The bedding was filthy now. The pig was gone, likely traded in the village for ale.

Kicking aside an overturned stool, Tamasin checked the cellar, finding only enough potatoes to feed two hungry people through a month, maybe a month and a week if she were frugal. Blast Da for having accumulated so little, for having failed to plan. This year he obviously had not worked the plot of land to its full potential, or had bartered away most of its meager crop for drink. Having believed herself to be secure in her position at the lodge, Tamasin had washed her hands of him, left him to his own squalor, instead of browbeating him to work as Mam had always done.

Tamasin leaned to throw more peat on the fire. Since Mam's death she had rarely helped her father or even thought of him. Occasionally she had left a basket of food pilfered from the lodge beside the cabin door before hastening off again. But there would be no more food from that source now.

Once again, she stood in the center of the place she had tried to escape. Devastated, she sank down and, reaching inside her jacket, pulled out the white silk scarf. She held it up, turned it this way and that so that its delicate weave glowed with the sunlight pouring through the window.

After a few moments, she tucked it safely into her jacket again. Then, with vehemence, she cursed Avery Hampton with every vile word she knew.

In the days of that early winter, the wind whined around the cabin walls like a wolf on the prowl, ferreting out every chink in the wattle, every hole above the bogwood rafters. Tamasin had repaired the thatch with handfuls of potato stalks and clay, asking no one for help. She would not give her neighbors the satisfaction of turning down her plea for help.

Day in and day out the peat fire smoked, giving adequate warmth at night if she huddled around the hearth with a shawl over her head and her bare feet thrust into the warm gray ashes.

Hunger began to gnaw as persistently as the cold. Tamasin had rationed the potatoes, hoarded them diligently, even knowing that they would never stretch through the long winter months. One by one, every pot and pan, and then every piece of earthenware went to the gombeen man in exchange for milk and meat. The old deal table followed all the rest; Tamasin had haggled over its scarred surface with all the stubbornness of a fishwife, determined to get no less than seven fat potatoes for it.

Da grumbled incessantly, often stalking off to beg an ale from one of his cronies at The Hound. Tamasin sighed with relief whenever he quitted the cabin. The stare of his bleary eyes grated on her nerves, and she was ever dreading his drunken tirades, which were often accompanied by the throwing of anything he could get his hands on, including the black iron kettle that hung over the hearth.

More than once Jamsie had cursed Tamasin for a fool. One night he had even attempted to drag her by the hair up the hill to Hampton Hall, where he intended to throw her across Avery's threshold with a demand for the promised guinea. She had battled him like a wild animal, coming away bruised but free of his hands, running off to spend the night beneath the hedgerows.

Jamsie Cullen had left her alone after that, perhaps realizing that his life was more comfortable with his daughter around, for she at least put a hot if unsatisfying meal before his nose every morning and kept his bedding clean.

But in spite of her care, Tamasin began to realize that Jamsie Cullen suffered from a wasting disease that seemed to gnaw at his stomach.

One afternoon, trudging home half-frozen and empty-handed from the river, where she had been fishing all day hoping to catch anything edible, Tamasin came upon Father Dinsmore. He was heading toward her cabin, a snowy-haired Moses in flapping garments and worn leather shoes. As he walked, he stabbed the turf with his cane, his fine-veined nose reddened with cold, but his voice gruffly warm as usual.

"Good day to you, Tamasin Cullen!"

Cold herself, half-famished and discouraged, she fell in beside him, suddenly craving a kind word. How long had it been since anyone had spoken to her, really spoken to her? Had it been weeks? Months?

Once she had passed Brendan Kinshella in Wexford and spoken to him briefly, but since Paddy O'Malley's flogging, no one else in the village had given her more than the barest nod of acknowledgement. Even Hunter Kinshella, who wouldn't have cared enough to shun her over the issue of her values, and who would have spoken to her, even tried to kiss her, was away at a horse auction in Dublin.

"Good day, Father Dinsmore," she murmured. Her head was lowered against the wind, her shawl scanty protection. Noting that the priest's clothing was scarcely more adequate, she invited him inside the cabin.

When he refused to sit down on the comfortable *suggaun* chair made of twisted straw ropes—the last piece of Mam's once proud collection of furniture—she smiled wanly and accepted the seat herself. Father Dinsmore was truly a servant even to the lowliest, she thought. He gave away almost all he owned to his flock of sick and poor, which not even a hundred generous priests could entirely rescue.

"How is your Da, lass?" he asked when she had offered him a cup of water. "Is he up and about?"

Tamasin threw more peat on the fire. "Aye. He's gone off to the village. But likely he'll be wandering back soon. He scarcely has any strength left these days and often stays abed. His health is gone."

The priest shook his head, extending his hands in their frayed knitted mittens toward the fire. "What will you do when he's gone? Have you thought of it?"

Tamasin shrugged. "Precisely what I'm doing now. His dying will hardly make a difference in my circumstances."

"Oh, but it will, Tamasin. You cannot do the work of a man come springtime. You cannot put in the crop and manage to pay the agent. Sir Harry will have you turned out."

It was growing dark, and Tamasin went to light a rushlight. "I know," she admitted quietly.

Father Dinsmore cleared his throat and set both hands atop his cane, pinning her with his gargoylish gaze. "You were wise to resist the temptation Master Avery cast your way several months ago. Oh, aye, I heard all about it. Before the day was out, your da had spread the tale all over the village. He condemned you for refusing Avery, of course, but I set him straight. I told him, and anybody else who cared to listen, that you were a good lass at heart, that you knew sinning with a gentleman would get you nowhere."

Tamasin looked away from the priest's probing gaze to the earthen floor. With a quietly spoken but caustic maturity, she said, "Don't think to be saving my soul, Father. I'm afraid it has been lost a very long time. And what's left of it I would sell this very moment to the devil himself—or to Avery Hampton—if he offered me a half-dozen guineas for it."

The priest straightened and leaned toward her, placing his palms upon his black-covered thighs. "You don't know what it is you're saying, lass—"

"I know precisely what it is I'm saying!" she cried, coming to her feet. "It takes either a saint or a fool to sit here day after day, cold and hungry, coughing with smoke. 'Tis the life of an animal, or a savage, Father. And I'll not be suffering it. Not like me Mam. Why should I not be able to sit beside a coal fire in warm clothes with a cup of chocolate by my side? Why should I live *this* life when—if I could find a way—I might go to Hampton Hall and be well fed? Would God be blaming me for that, Father? Would he be blaming me for taking a bit of comfort and happiness from life? Is it written somewhere that only those born with a title and blue blood are allowed to have good food?''

The priest came slowly to his feet. His emotion seemed to match hers. With worldly, sympathetic hands that had tended the dead, brought forth babies, and wiped fevered brows, he grasped her shoulders. "Now you listen to me, Tamasin Cullen. Their bellies might be full up yonder in the Hall, but their hearts are not. They're a diseased lot with not a thought for anyone else but themselves. They use up whatever comes falling into their hands and then discard it when they're done with it. Don't be thinking you'd be any different in Master Avery's hands, because you would not be.''

"You can't be certain of that!" she cried.

"Yes, I can. The only thing you own in this world is your soul, 'tis the only thing you'll be taking with you when you leave the earth, and the only thing worth making a sacrifice for. 'Tis not a thing to be treated lightly, nor to be bartering for coal fires and chocolate.''

His lack of sympathy inflamed Tamasin. She exclaimed, "Preach that to the rest of your flock. I've knocked upon every door in the village asking for work, asking for a bit of meat and buttermilk for Da since he's been ailing. Would you care to be guessing how many answered their doors? Well, I'll tell you. Not a one. Not *one!*''

"Ah, Tamasin," the priest sighed. He released her shoulders and shook his head, his white hair radiant with the firelight filtering through it. "You've turned them all against you, put yourself beyond the pale. Where do you belong, lass, where do you fit in? Neither here nor there, I fear.''

" 'Tis not belonging I care about, Father," she retorted, her expression intent. " 'Tis *having.*''

Father Dinsmore's face softened, his knowing eyes as blue as the spring iris that grew on the fringes of his church yard. " 'Tis a man you're needing, girl. One to keep your head out of the clouds and your feet upon the ground." He paused, rubbed his chin, uttering his words with care. "Hunter Kinshella would do."

Tamasin stared at the priest, then laughed aloud. She laughed so heartily that she had to put her hands over her mouth to smother the high-pitched sound of it. "Hunter Kinshella would die before he took a wife," she said when she had regained herself. "I know him well enough to assure you of that."

"Nay. You're wrong. He'll want a woman one day, mark my words. The two of you could get ahead together if you put your minds to it, for both of you are ambitious and unafraid of hard work. Aye, you'd do well together, I think."

"Don't start with your matchmaking, Father," Tamasin warned. "If I take any man a'tall, 'twill not be of Hunter Kinshella's class. 'Twill be a gentleman."

"Fie!" Father Dinsmore scorned the notion of her gaining a marriage proposal from a man above her status. "Get that sort of foolishness out of your head, lass. 'Tis folly. When it comes to marriage, like should wed like. I've told ye that many times before."

He grabbed his cane and stumped out of the cabin then, ignoring Tamasin's unhappy glare, pausing in the yard to stare up at the unsettled clouds as they rolled like a cavalry across the sky. "We'll have a storm today," he predicted, his old frame so buffeted by the wind that his garments snapped.

When Tamasin made no reply, he shrugged and ambled on down the rough green hill, doubtless going off to deliver more advice to the souls of the tempted.

Tamasin watched him until he had disappeared. The cold air snatched at her clothes and made her shiver. She felt disquieted, wished that the priest had not come to call. How ironic, how fitting, that Avery Hampton, at that moment, should be cantering across the fields toward her cabin.

Suddenly calm, she turned to await him.

A moment later he drew rein, his chestnut mount's warm hard breaths frosting the air. She could smell the liniment on its pampered legs, the oil on its bridle, and the purebred heat of its sweaty hide.

With a sudden hunger for the fine things she had missed since leaving the lodge, Tamasin's eyes consumed every detail of Avery Hampton's attire: the ruffled cuffs, the beautifully tailored surtout, the perfectly creased beaver hat, and gray suede gloves.

Every article was worth a fortune, worth *food,* a great deal of it. Enough to keep a family fed a year or more, she guessed. She looked hard at Avery's face. It seemed almost handsome, healthy with the glow of exercise and excellent wine. His cheeks were full, and his eyes bright and clear.

"You look a bit out of sorts, Tamasin," he observed, amused, crossing his hands over the pommel. "Was the priest giving you a lecture?"

Disinclined to talk about the priest, she only murmured, "In a manner of speaking."

"Ah. And did the good man strike close to home?"

"He seems to believe that we all should be content with our lot in life. I don't agree. That's all."

Avery considered, tasted the words. "To be content with our lot in life. Well, 'tis an interesting notion, at any rate." He fiddled with the reins in his hands, then eyed her with humor. "Do you believe that I'm happy with my lot in life, Tamasin?"

"I believe you should be."

He laughed. "Perhaps you're right."

The horse stamped and mouthed its bit, causing the snaffle rings to jingle. Muscle rippled beneath the chestnut hide and the long brushed tail flicked the air. Tamasin recalled that, when Hunter was at home, he curried and exercised the animal.

Avery leaned down from the saddle, one gloved hand reaching out to touch her cheek. His voice was sober. "My offer still stands, you know."

Tamasin had expected him to address the topic, but not so early in the conversation. She looked at the gray suede glove on her cheek, at the raindrop that suddenly fell from the swollen sky to stain it. As she had told Father Dinsmore, she felt prepared to barter her soul for every penny of its worth. Taking a deep breath, she stated bluntly, "I'll come to you, Avery. But only in exchange for a position at the Hall. A good one, one that's permanent."

He said nothing. He merely regarded her from his elevated position in the saddle and, removing his hand from her cheek, slowly shook his head in denial of her offer.

Growing desperate, Tamasin bit her lip and looked away. The mud cabin seemed to wink at her through its single window. Knowing that she degraded herself, she said quietly, "Very well. I'll come to you for six guineas then."

Avery grinned broadly. "I'm surprised you didn't ask for twenty."

"Should I have?"

"You wouldn't have gotten it."

The chestnut pawed the earth, one delicate, oiled hoof scraping the tender grass, and Avery checked the reins with a jerk. "The original offer stands, Tamasin. You'll get one night in the Hall. There'll be plenty to eat—all the venison and gravy you want. And your pick of a dessert smothered in plenty of fresh cream. As much wine as you want."

At the imagined taste of every food he mentioned, Tamasin's mouth watered. But she was not yet desperate enough to relinquish herself for something so common as food. No, not yet. Her eyes locked with his. "I'll not be coming for wine and venison. There'll have to be more."

Pointedly, Avery let his eyes survey her frayed shawl, her pinched face, the hair she no longer bothered to pin, but braided with worsted tassels like the other cottier girls. Finally, he regarded the blue whorl of smoke puffing from the crude earth cabin.

"I don't feel moved to offer anything more," he said, stroking the chestnut's silky mane. "Not at the moment anyway. But my whims change, my appetites alter. We'll see, Tamasin Cullen."

"You don't believe I can outlast you, do you?" she asked in a fierce voice, stopping him as he reined the horse around.

His coppery eyes regarded Tamasin's speculatively. Something unnameable flashed within their violet depths, something discerning, far too knowing. With no relish he admitted, "Yes, I believe you can outlast me. But I don't believe you can outlast your ambition. 'Tis stronger than your pride. You'll come to me one of these days, and scheming, too, sure that you can find a way to get more out of me than what I've already offered."

Tamasin disliked hearing the hardness of her nature uttered so baldly. It was one thing to harbor such feelings in her heart where she could justify them to herself, another altogether to have them exposed by someone else.

"Perhaps I'll surprise you," she said.

"No." Avery shook his head. "I think not. I've known you too long, remember? Perhaps I've even helped to make you who you are." He tipped the shiny beaver hat and touched his heels to the horse. "Good day, Miss Cullen."

Chapter Fifteen

Jamsie Cullen relinquished his ghost, dying conveniently in bed, his passage to the underworld scarcely mourned by his daughter. Because of her apparent indifference, she suspected Father Dinsmore prayed tirelessly for her soul.

She was alone. The allotted time in her hourglass seemed to be shifting through its narrow neck with unrelenting speed. She waited for something momentous to happen so she would have to react, to make a decision, to *do* something. As it was, she simply survived. Every morning, in place of a warm jacket, she drew a cloak of tenacity around her shoulders, arising from a lumpy pallet placed so close to the hearth it was a wonder the straw sacking did not catch fire.

Loneliness, cold, and hunger were her unflagging companions during that winter of howling laughs and frosty fingers, a winter which seemed to ask in mocking whispers where all her grand plans had gone.

Father Dinsmore visited regularly, his feet numb from the tramp over the wind-gashed fields, a precious oatcake from his own Spartan table tucked in his pocket. Always he brought spiritual encouragement. Tamasin began to liken him to a self-appointed guardian angel, who, knowing temptation to be greatest when the spirit was low and the belly hungry, constantly implored her to persevere. He had grown adept at lavishing encouragement; he had doled it out to hundreds of fevered, starving, out-of-work cottiers, who—unlike Tamasin—probably likened him to a saint.

Tamasin's greatest concern was not her soul, but the few remaining potatoes in the cellar, which she counted as if they were gold pieces in a pirate's hoard. Yet no matter how often she counted them, no matter how often she made do with just a half ration, she knew they would not last.

She had developed a cough, a nagging condition that, combined with her ill-nourishment, left her with a lethargy that sapped her strength and made her yearn to lie abed too much. She dreamt of milk and white bread, the plain fare she used to take for granted at the lodge.

One afternoon, frightened by her own decline and aloneness, she forced herself to get up, feeling as if she were an old woman. Although the effort of standing and moving her arms was exhausting, she tidied her hair. She had no mirror, and the thought of how dreadful she must look with the pall of poverty pinching her features made her shudder. Perhaps she already looked like Mam.

The possibility made her panic. If she lost her looks, what would she have left of any marketable value? Even the *suggaun* chair was gone now, the last and most valuable household item traded for bacon before Da's death.

She set off toward the village, climbing the hills of cold damp green, passing the pitiable dwelling places of the spalpeens. They were wandering laborers who simply stopped anywhere and constructed a shelter of branches and clay against a bank. She skirted a row of the wretched creatures along the road, irritated at them for squatting so close to her cabin. She knew they were not above thievery.

As she passed she saw one of the desperate fellows hunkered

down in his strange little stick nest, bearded and tattered, staring out at her. In her old, superior way she drew aside her skirts and swept on, out of breath, tired, her hands icy and her cough starting up again.

It was market day, and as Tamasin neared the gray walls of Wexford, she could smell the fish and the spitted meat the butcher roasted outdoors. Her mouth watered and she quickened her pace, prepared to beg if necessary. Or steal. God would forgive her for it. In her halfhearted, dimly formed prayers last night she had told Him that He should.

She eyed the sacks of oatmeal piled in the back of a farmer's cart, then the bags of flour and the loaves of bread resting so temptingly in a basket outside the bakery. From the confectioner's window, boxes of French chocolate winked at her, nestled in fragile paper beside a loaf of sugar on a silver platter. The goods were all guarded well by vigilant eyes trained to spot light-fingered customers. As Tamasin scrutinized the faces of the people she had known all her life, she found she could not ask any of them for help. She could not beg. Stealing would be preferable. And she *would* steal, she told herself, if only one of the merchants relaxed his alertness long enough for her narrow hands to plunder a basket and conceal the prize beneath her shawl.

Noreen Fitzdenning, the butcher's daughter, spotted Tamasin and strolled over, her plump body sporting a new gown and quilted petticoat. With satisfaction, she smiled at Tamasin's unprepossessing appearance. "You'd be better off going up to the Hall for leftovers, Cullen," she taunted. "Don't think you'll be getting charity here."

Tamasin didn't answer. She turned her back and began to tramp homeward, angry with herself for having gone to the village in the first place. She wanted nothing so much as to lie down. With a vague unconcern she realized that her hunger had vanished at sight of the food. What had been so tempting about fresh milk and white bread anyway?

Rain began to fall, sharp needles of ice, and she bowed her

head against it, trotting faster, her feet heavy, her lungs aching. She passed the spalpeens' dens and began to count her own dragging steps, calculating the distance home.

By the time she spotted the blurred shape of the cabin she was soaked to the bone, gasping, and her shoes—precious shoes—were caked with mud. She saw that the clay she had packed in the window in order to plug it up and keep the wind out was melting with the rain.

Mindlessly, she bent to grab handfuls of earth, trying to repack the aperture, fighting to keep her little abode safe from the malicious paws of cold, which had come to be her most forceful enemy. Her head was so muddled and the rain coming down so fast she could scarcely see. But she kept packing and patting and stooping as the clay slipped frustratingly through her hands.

Suddenly, another pair of hands were there beside them, clean and hard, taking over the task with the same efficiency they used on every job.

At first Tamasin believed they were illusions, ghostly things conjured up by her imagination. She paused, staring at them bemusedly, at the dark earth that stained them and ran through the fingers.

And then she looked over her shoulder. How grand he looked. How good. Infinitely better than fresh milk and white bread. Better than anything she could imagine, standing in his gray wool cathamore and dripping black bicorne. He was so sturdy and undaunted; she so weary, so defeated.

"Go inside," he ordered. "I'll finish this."

Even though it seemed to Tamasin that there was not an ounce of kindness in his voice, she obeyed gladly, gratefully.

She knew a moment of shame when Hunter ducked his head and came through the door, when his eyes swept a room devoid of every stick of furniture, every pot and pan, save one, which she kept to boil her few remaining potatoes. She could not even invite him to sit down. So, dripping water, fighting to stay on her feet, Tamasin simply *beheld* him, having no notion why the sight of his dark, grim face touched her, made her want to sink down at his well-kept boots and weep.

He removed his hat, tucked it beneath his arm, and stood observing her in turn, his eyes penetrating too deeply, too knowingly. Had she ever noticed how green they were, how the corners of his mouth turned up slightly at the corners? The shadow beneath his lower lip was long and deep, his jaw wide. He looked fit, very fit, not as Avery had—how many weeks ago?—with wine and sporting exercise, but with honest labor. He was a man of solid bone and muscle, born to carry burdens, to walk with his feet firmly planted on the ground.

Tamasin put a hand to her wet hair, the hasty motion purely feminine, a great effort.

"You seem to have exhausted your resources, Tamasin." Hunter stated the words simply.

"Have you come to gloat?"

"Perhaps."

"Get out then."

But Hunter quirked his mouth and went to the hearth where a few slabs of peat were stacked. After tossing one or two on the dying fire, he asked, "Haven't your friends been round to leave you baskets of cheese and trifles? I'm surprised Miss Eushanie hasn't left off a hat or two. Surely she remembers how you defended her from the vicious Paddy O'Malley."

"Did you walk all the way here in the rain just to taunt me?"

Hunter pulled loose a weed that had grown through the thatch and tossed it into the fire, avoiding her question. "I've been away. I just arrived back at the lodge yesterday."

"And couldn't wait to come calling, to see the unfortunate cottier's lass? Well, you can leave the way you came."

Tamasin's tone had been as bitter and sharp as a fishwife's, and she regretted it immediately. Her asperity might cause Hunter to go away, and she realized with a terrible desperation that she didn't want him to go away. She had only spoken acidly to keep herself from being overcome by gratitude that he had bothered to come at all—no matter the reason—when no one else had. She had used bitterness because, as weak and tired as she felt, to say anything heart-felt would have dissolved her into a well of tears.

"Have you heard when Sir Harry will be coming back?" she asked, steadying her voice but failing to keep the desperation out of it. "Will it be soon, do you think?"

"I don't know." Hunter's eyes swept the length of her body, then fastened upon her face again. "I haven't heard anyone say."

Disappointed, she moved toward the fire, shivering, her knees wobbling, and leaned down to drag the blanket from her pallet. She threw it over her shoulders, but it did nothing to warm her, nothing to stop her teeth from chattering. She wondered if Hunter Kinshella enjoyed seeing her this way, humbled and unkempt. She straightened herself, put iron in her backbone. She could not let him see how tired she was, how ill and defeated.

"What's the news of the United Irish and their rebellion?" she asked. "I rarely get any word."

Hunter roamed about the room, his fine, soft cathamore steaming in the warmth. "The rebels are murdering government magistrates all over the country. In Cork one was hacked to pieces by a peasant with a rusty scythe, and his host and hostess thrown over a balcony. Estates are being robbed and burned. The United Irish are walking onto gentlemen's lawns and cutting down their ash trees in broad daylight to make pike handles. Wexford has remained one of the more peaceful counties. But here, as everywhere, beggars are still dying in ditches."

"What's the government doing?"

"Nothing about the beggars. They figure Ireland can afford to lose a great deal of those. And they can, can't they? As to the United Irish, the viceroy had sixteen of their rebel leaders arrested in Dublin recently. But the biggest catch, Lord Edward Fitzgerald, escaped. 'Tis rumored that he sailed off to France

with his French wife. Everyone seems to think that Napoleon
and his troops are going to land here in Wexford any day.''

"Do you believe it?''

Hunter shook his head. "I'd chose another port. Wexford's
is too shallow.''

"Have you taken the secret oath?''

A sound issued from Hunter's throat, a mockery of a laugh.
He looked at her as if surprised that she had wasted the breath
to ask it. "No.''

"Why? I should think you'd enjoy sneaking about with the
United Irishmen at night, terrorizing gentlemen. After all, you
might get the opportunity to run Avery Hampton through with
a pike.''

Hunter's mouth tilted ruefully. "I admit 'twould give me
pleasure. But afterward I should only be arrested and hanged.
I'm not willing to give my life for Avery Hampton's death.''

"No?'' The word was scarcely a croak. Rain dripped through
the thatch, collected the soot on the bogwood rafters and fell
to the floor, where it made odd-shaped splotches of black.
Tamasin asked softly, "What *are* you willing to give your life
for, Hunter?''

He seemed to have no need to consider. "Not much. Very
little on earth moves me to sacrifice myself for it. Except
perhaps Ireland, and my right to stay here.''

Was he chastising her indirectly, letting her know that by
causing his exile she had done the worst to him? Stripped him
of noble causes? Perhaps not. Perhaps she was too suspicious,
overridden with guilt, too bedazed. She eyed his dark face, so
handsome, so remote, and couldn't read it. But she knew he
often made a game of words.

Tamasin pulled off her boots, her movements very slow and
labored. When she had set them aside, she saw the mud drying
on the leather, cracking it, and wished she possessed the energy
to clean it off.

Hunter settled his hat atop his hair. The thick locks were
curling slightly at the neck, damp, very black. His eyes were

dark and deep. She could tell by the expression on his face that he struggled with some emotion. He strolled the few feet to the door, then paused, his hand on the leather latch. Without turning to look at her again, he said quietly, "I'll bring your bundle of fripperies so you can trade them to the next gombeen man who happens along. It seems to me that a bite of food would be more useful in your present circumstances than a striped silk skirt and feathered hat."

"No!" Tamasin shouted the word at him harshly, almost frantically. "Don't bring them here, Hunter!"

How often she had thought of her treasures. Countless times she had handled them mentally one by one, calculated their value, dreamed of the bacon and sugar and tea they would buy. During freezing nights her hunger had goaded her, told her to the penny what each handkerchief, each comb, each small pin would fetch. But she had resisted.

She would not trade her treasures, her *hope,* for food. After it was eaten, what then? Her circumstances would not be changed, only the inevitable postponed. The bundle beneath Hunter Kinshella's bed was a symbol that sustained her more heartily than food.

Having grown excited, she began to cough. She put her hands to her mouth, attempting to stifle the sound, finally giving in to the hard dry paroxysms.

Hunter turned his head to scrutinize her, chagrined. He had never seen Tamasin Cullen vulnerable or weak. His belly twisted and he stepped forward, wanting to take her in his arms, to hold her, to make her feel spirited again. "Can I do anything for you, Tamasin?" he asked softly. "Get you anything?" He realized immediately that he had made a mistake asking; he should have simply enfolded her in his arms and said nothing at all.

Tamasin sensed that he was uncomfortable, ill-at-ease. *Ah, Hunter. I have made you feel deeply, and the feeling has nothing to do with desire. You don't like it, do you? It discomfits you to feel such emotion for me.* "Nay," she murmured to him, discomfitted, too, "I don't need anything from you."

But he thrust a hand into his breeches pocket and drew out a coin, then held it out to her.

Tamasin stared at the guinea in his hand, then stared at the hand itself, the one that had repaired her cabin, held her own in a dance, caressed her passionately on more than one occasion. The coin represented a fortune to her, a fortune to him, more than enough to see her fed through the remainder of the winter and beyond. Wonderingly she glanced up at the dark face made darker by the smoky gloom, and in a fraction of an unguarded second, read clearly what the groomsman felt for her. He felt pity. She realized how he must see her: a lass with tangled hair and a wan face, ugly like her mam had been, like any cottier's wife. Suddenly she could not bear to see the pity in his eyes.

Seizing the coin she flung it at him. "Take it!" she cried. "I don't want it. I'll take nothing from you while you feel sorry for me!"

It rankled Hunter's pride that she had refused him with such contempt. Wryly, his lip curved and he asked in a taunting voice, "Is it not enough then? Perhaps not, now I think on it. 'Twas the same amount Avery Hampton offered, wasn't it? The same amount you turned down."

On her hands and knees, Tamasin scrambled to grab the coin from the floor. Seizing it, she threw it at him again, at his face this time.

Her aim was poor and the coin only struck the thin wooden plank, spinning off and landing on the floor with a tiny thud. He turned to go, giving her one last angry glance as he shut the door.

Feeling dizzy, sick, Tamasin plopped down on her stomach, staring at the coin as it gleamed temptingly only a few feet away from her hands.

She put an arm over her eyes and groaned. She would never touch it. She swore she would not.

Chapter Sixteen

The next day Brendan Kinshella turned up at her doorstep. Tamasin was ill, more lethargic than ever, scarcely able to rouse herself enough to keep peat on the fire. She simply lay huddled next to it, hour after hour, staring dully into the embers.

When Brendan identified himself she called for him to enter. Forcing herself to stand, she greeted him. She was too proud, too stubborn to permit his pity, too.

Despite the snow outside, Brendan was golden sunshine, his hair bright, his grin in place, his nature always impervious to anything too serious or too grave. Where his brother was hard and solid, Brendan was of scant substance, moving through life skirting its demands, an evader of responsibility, an amiable, beguiling chaser of cheer.

He carried a covered basket. When he whisked the cover off, Tamasin saw a loaf of bread, a hunk of pale cheese, and a jug of milk.

" 'Tis a feast I'm bringing you, Lady Tamasin," he announced merrily. "One that will be putting those fair roses back into your cheeks again."

Tamasin wanted to fall upon the contents of that basket and consume them greedily, noisily, in seconds. But she held herself in check. She leaned against the wall to keep from sinking down, stood as rigidly as possible so Brendan could not see the quivering of her legs. Giving him a shrewd, level look, she said, "Hunter stole them from the cook at the lodge, didn't he?"

"Stole them ... ?" he echoed, feigning bewilderment. "Nay. I'm thinking not, Tamasin. Not that Hunter wouldn't steal food if he needed to. But my brother has quite a charm of his own, he does, when he choses to use it—which, I'll be the first to admit, isn't as often as it should be. I expect Cook was so taken aback by his devilish smile she couldn't resist giving him whatever he asked for."

Tamasin hesitated, her will battling the needs of her body. The watering of her mouth and the cramping of her belly were becoming almost impossible to ignore. "Take it back, Brendan," she said firmly, holding her middle. "Tell your brother I'll not be accepting his charity. He'll know why."

In the face of her obstinacy, Brendan employed his charm; He'd been forewarned of her stubborness, and had been instructed to persevere. "But I've walked up here through the snow and cold to deliver it to you, Tamasin," he argued with his hands stretched out. "Consider it a gift from me, if you must. Friend helping friend. You'd do the same for me, to be sure. Come now, play the hostess and I'll share a bite with you."

"Nay, Brendan. Return it now, please. I'm weary and in no mood to be arguing with you. And don't think to leave it outside the door, for I swear I'll only carry it down to one of those wretched spalpeens and give it to him."

"You're a stubborn lass, Tamasin. I can see that my brother will have to deal with you himself."

Looking disappointed, he opened the door, which allowed a few tiny snowflakes to dance in and invade Tamasin's flimsy fortress.

"And, Brendan—"

"Yes, lass?" he asked hopefully, ready to hand her the basket.

"Take that guinea with you." She forced out the words, surprised that her pride was greater than her good sense. "There, by your right boot. Hunter left it. Give it back and tell him 'tis not enough. He'll know what I mean. And tell him his condemnation doesn't wound me in the least. Nor does his pity soften me. Just tell him that. All of it. Every word."

Brendan grinned, a flurry of capricious snowflakes whirling about his head. " 'Twill be my pleasure to tell him, Tamasin. Indeed it will."

She cursed herself for her foolishness many times during the following hours—or was it days, weeks? Why hadn't she taken Hunter's guinea? It was unlike her not to grab anything that was offered.

Too late now.

She grew unsure of time, merely existing like the rest of the starving Irish population, falling into a dream world of imagination, determined to survive, to outlast the circumstances which, like everything else in life, would pass if she could just manage to keep breathing one more day.

Something would happen, something would change her situation.

As she lay beside the hearth, conserving energy with her eyes closed and her body still except for its occasional dry cough, Tamasin held on to the dream of Hampton Hall. She saw herself there in various elaborate gowns, and in her weaker moments, was tempted to get up and trudge to its gates, fall across Avery Hampton's threshold and beg for the promised night. How glorious it would be up there, how warm, how luxurious! She would gorge herself, grow drunk on red wine, fall back into a fire-warmed bed.

But it would not be enough. Not enough. Some irritating,

too brave voice always whispered the words to her. *Wait, wait,* it said when the needs of her body harrowed.

And so she did.

She had plenty of water, and still hung on to a last potato, the only one remaining in the hoard, which she had saved with a single-minded determination. She had placed it at the end of her pallet, at her feet where she could not easily see it and be tempted to eat before absolutely necessary. She thought, in fact, that she might never eat that last potato, but save it as a reminder of the winter, as a trophy of her perseverance.

She had folded the white silk scarf close to her head. It became a talisman that hardened her resolve, saw her through the coughing spells, the worse days. Lying upon her back and staring up at the dripping thatch, she often contemplated her childhood, searched her mind for some memory which would soothe her, a vision of being held in Mam's arms or sitting upon Da's knee. But she could conjure up no such comforts.

Often she dreamed of Hunter Kinshella. Strangely, his tall figure always stood upon the steps of Hampton Hall, barring her entry when she would walk up the drive.

While she dreamed fitfully, her skin damp and cold, she heard not only the whimpering of the wind outside, but a strange rattle. At first, she thought it was the scratching of a rat. But, no, it came from the other side of the door, which had opened a crack.

The infiltrating light hurt her eyes and the cold air invaded the cabin. She groaned, thinking the wind had blown open the door and she would have to get up and barricade it again.

She raised her head, then froze. A figure was coming through the door, crouched low, moving stealthily forward.

Shifting on her pallet, Tamasin focused her eyes upon the tattered shape; it was both pathetic and terrifying, little more than a wild animal in rags with an odor no less strong. Its sharp eyes quickly discovered her huddled on the pallet.

Warily, struggling against exhaustion, she drew up her legs and tried to regain her wits.

The creature was surely one of the spalpeens from the ditch. He had not come to beg, she feared, but to steal.

Furtively, her gaze shifted to the potato at her feet, then to the white silk scarf folded beside her hand. They were the only two objects of value left in the cabin, and the desperate eyes of the man did not miss them.

In a frenzy she reached out and seized both, hugged them to her breast, daring him to try and snatch them away.

The man shuffled forward, undeterred by her fierce expression and her hoarsely shouted curses. He bent down and reached out. Doubling over, Tamasin coiled into a tight ball to shelter her treasures between her knees and chest. But his frozen, filthy hands thrust and insinuated determinedly. They were strong and, despite her vicious clawing, pried her fingers apart. In moments the potato and scarf were his.

When he dashed for the door Tamasin summoned every bit of strength she owned and struggled to her feet. That such a pathetic scrap of humanity would dare steal the very last of her possessions enraged and energized her.

She staggered across the snowy field after him, stumbling, following his unsteady amble, which was almost as feeble as her own. Once or twice she fell, but struggled to her feet in a blind need to pursue the fellow and claw his eyes out for daring to rob her.

At last, she was in reach of his coat tails. Lunging, she grabbed for his scarecrow frame, managing to get a stranglehold.

Off balanced by her weight, the spalpeen tumbled to the ground while Tamasin savagely grappled for the treasures in his hands.

The fellow attempted to wrench free of her fingers, snarling viciously when she managed to seize the scarf. She kept it wadded in her hand while she fought for the potato. As she kicked and pummelled ineffectually with her fists, the absurdity of such a life-and-death struggle for a bite of food occurred to her, but did not decrease her efforts.

In the end, the spalpeen proved stronger. He deflected Tamasin's furious assault to escape with the food and, clutching the potato beneath what was left of his ragged coat, staggered off to his makeshift shelter.

Tamasin lay motionless in the snow, spent, her lungs airless and aching. Never had she felt so utterly defeated. Coughing, she clutched the scarf, which she could not eat and would not pawn. Icy flakes kissed her exposed cheek; snow melted beneath her breast and soaked her jacket; but she simply lay still, thinking of food.

Would Avery Hampton discover her curled up here in a ball, frozen? She hoped he would. She wanted him to see that she had managed to outlast him after all, kept him from getting what he had hoped to have for nothing.

But it was not the baronet's son who found her. When the snow had covered her body with a gauzy sheet and made lacy patterns in her hair, a pair of worn but polished boots crunched over the hill.

"For God's sake!"

As if from a great distance Tamasin heard the words—tightly uttered, as harsh as the brittle white air.

She coiled herself up even more tightly, wanting to be left alone, willing him to go away. Perversely, her indignity at being discovered in such a state was greater than her desire for help.

Hunter Kinshella did not oblige and leave.

Despite the fact that she recoiled and told him with her body—since she was beyond speech—that she did not want him to touch her, she heard the rasp of his boots as he knelt down in the snow. He put an arm behind her shoulders and an arm beneath her knees, lifted her as carefully he had once lifted his grandfather, as he had once lifted Sir Harry's disgraced hound.

Tamasin's eyes were closed, but she felt her cheek pressed against the coarse weave of the cathamore Sir Harry had given him for his good service. Feeling the prickle of its warmth, knew she was alive at least. And with that knowledge came the strength to struggle. She did not want to be weak in Hunter Kinshella's arms; she did not want him to see her humbled and helpless, brought low by life when she had always been the one to take boldly from it.

Tamasin managed to shift and pull one leg free, but the groomsman only stopped in his tracks and pinioned her again, treating her no more personally than one of the grain sacks he hefted in the stable.

"You've made a game of this," she heard him say, the words a rumble against her ear. "So we'll play it out."

He ducked into the cabin, shut the door with a kick of his foot, then deposited her on the pallet before bending to throw peat upon the fire. His movements seemed urgent, and after a moment Tamasin smelled food, a broth of some sort steaming on the air, peppery and thick.

Instead of making her salivate, it brought her nausea.

But Hunter Kinshella seemed undeterred by her apathy, by her unresponsiveness, by her motionless body as she lay facing away from him. He grabbed her arms and hauled her limp form upright. Then, sitting down, he positioned her between his knees, and propped her up so that her back leaned against his chest.

Tamasin's eyes were half-open. She saw the hazy shape of a spoon dripping brown both poised at her lips, but had no desire to eat. Hunger had left her days ago, and eating, digesting, now seemed too great an effort for her strength. Sleep was what she wanted. She turned her head to the side, avoiding the spoon, avoiding him.

"Eat."

No. Had she said the word aloud?

"I'll force it down your throat if I must."

Tamasin felt his fingers on her jaws, and at the same time, experienced a strange, perverse sense of triumph. She had made the groomsman touch her, hold her, care for her.

But then, he had touched and held Sir Harry's hound, hadn't

he? He'd saved it, hidden it, kept it alive? Did he care for her just because he pitied her?

She clamped her jaw and bowed her head with a jerk. Broth spilled down his wrist. But he soon had the spoon full again. Forcing her head up, he pried open her jaws until warm liquid slid over her tongue and trickled down her throat.

She gagged violently and sputtered. But her body had been jolted into remembering the goodness of food, and her stomach growled, ravenous.

Nevertheless, Tamasin resisted. Scrabbling to find Hunter's hand, she pressed the length of wadded silk scarf into his palm and closed his fingers. "Take it . . ." she babbled fiercely. "Take it . . . as payment for the food. I won't eat . . . if you don't take it."

Seconds passed. Then, in a low, very quiet voice, Hunter asked, "Was this the price of my exile from Ireland all those years ago?"

There, Tamasin thought with magnificent relief. The words, at last, had been said, uttered. Aired. As if the scrap of silk itself, through his touching it, had communicated with him. Hunter Kinshella now *knew*. Dry-mouthed, Tamasin nodded, swallowed, expecting at any second to feel the piece of silk slipped around her neck and twisted into a noose. "Aye . . ." she breathed, relieved to finally utter the words aloud. "The scarf, nothing more. 'Twas the price of your exile."

The spoon was put again to her lips. *"Eat."*

And Tamasin did, allowing the groomsman to feed her like a baby, since he seemed so intent upon keeping her alive. She swallowed every bite. And afterward she slumped to one side so that Hunter would have to keep holding her in his arms.

And he did hold her, tenderly, possessively. His arms, Tamasin thought, were made for embracing a woman and keeping her safe. His body was fit and in its prime; it needed intimacy and release even while the armor of his self-sufficiency resisted it.

The two of us are a fine pair, she mused fuzzily: Hunter

Kinshella bitter over his lost youth and lost chances; herself nearly starved to death because of a stubborn will.

Yet already she was feeling heartened with her belly full. It gratified her to force the groomsman to hold her up, gratified her to feel the support of his arms. When she neared the fringes of sleep, lulled by the hiss of the peat fire and the rhythm of his breathing, he lifted a hand and with the utmost gentleness began to stroke her hair.

A wan smile touched Tamasin's lips. "You like me a little, don't you, Hunter . . . ?" she asked drowsily with her eyes closed. "You don't *want* to like me, not this way, not tenderly. But I think—"

"You'd do better not to think."

He had silenced her. Even so, she felt his hand stroke, once more, the dull, tumbled tangle of her hair, before he kissed her to sleep.

Chapter Seventeen

Ireland was in a state of rebellion, or so the Viceroy, Earl Camden, and his advisors decided after hundreds of United Irishmen near Dublin organized and began robbing the estates of gentlemen. The brigands seized arms and money, and even more outrageously, terrorized gently-bred ladies while invading homes and destroying centuries-old heirlooms. The gentry were dumfounded as well as enraged. Didn't the stupid louts know that when they damaged ancestry tomes and marble busts of English generals, they damaged Irish history? Of course they didn't; they were too coarse, too uncivilized, too *uneducated* to understand.

And if these outrages were not enough to boil the blood of any decent man, the government had uncovered a heinous rebel plot. The United Irishmen were actually encouraging good Dublin servants to *poison* their masters, an abomination that left every sensible lord eyeing his valet with panicked suspicion. What an inconvenience, they all grumbled, not to be able to trust one's own manservant to bring coffee when one's head was a trifle sore from too much claret. What sort of a world had it become, for heaven's sake, to so disturb the natural order of things? And that one's wife and daughters had to avoid their own windows for fear of seeing some ragged peasant pop out of the hedge with a stone in his hand was an intolerable state of affairs.

Finally, but not the least disturbing, was the shocking rumor that every Protestant would be murdered in his bed when French troops landed upon Irish soil—and the United Irishmen swore that Napoleon would send his men before a year was out.

The madness must be stopped, the rabble dispersed, the leaders hanged, so that gentlemen were safe once again to junket about the countryside and hunt foxes without being molested by roaming scarecrows.

Viceroy Camden agreed, and on March 30 signed a proclamation declaring martial law throughout the land.

" 'Twill really only affect the most troublesome counties around Dublin," Brendan commented to Tamasin one morning. He had brought her a sack of oatmeal—one more gift in a regular supply of food—from Hunter. Since the groomsman had been compensated with the white silk scarf, Tamasin accepted the arrangement.

"What does the proclamation really mean, Brendan?" she asked.

The two of them stood outside her cabin in the sun, whose pale rays glazed a landscape beginning to bloom again. The raw winter had melted away with spring, the sharp edge of its lingering barrenness alleviated in the same manner as the edge of Tamasin's hunger had been dulled by Hunter's regular presents of plain but nourishing food. She had not seen him after that strange snowy day when he had fed her broth and she had told him the price of his exile. She wasn't certain she wanted to see him again. Thinking of him interfered with her thoughts of Hampton Hall, even disturbed her usually pure dreams of the house with marble walls.

Brendan crossed his legs at the ankles and leaned against the mud wall to soak up the sun, his mellow voice interrupting her musings. "Martial law means that dragoons will be sent out to try and gather up all the arms and ammunition the rebels have managed to steal or manufacture. After that, if things still don't settle down, the soldiers will be quartered in country homes to keep an eye on things. And of course," he drawled ruefully, "examples will have to be made—public floggings, hangings, and the like. The army has a penchant for making examples."

"Fools," Tamasin pronounced, peeling the outer layers off the rushes she had laid out to dry, which would later be dipped in fat and used for rushlights. "The rebels should have known government troops would be called out."

"They did know. But to a man with a weapon in his hand and blood in his eye, the idea of war is as exciting as a game of hurley."

"Fools," she said again, still peeling.

Brendan agreed with her sentiment. "To tell the truth, I enjoy a good game of hurley myself, or even a friendly brawl now and then, but when a contest calls for musket balls and pike ends, count me out. Too messy."

He reached down and, picking up one of the long graceful rushes, idly swished it back and forth over the tops of his boots. "You know, the gentry really do live in clover. They'll be blaming this whole rebellion on the starving peasants, make themselves out to be the wronged party while they scurry to Dublin for safety and gorge themselves there on lobster and wine. When the storm dies down and the dragoons have mown down hundreds of disobedient cottiers,the gentry will trot back to their country estates as if nothing untoward had happened."

Tamasin made no comment and Brendan eyed her concernedly, his tone softening. "By the way, I'm sorry to tell you Sir Harry will be staying in Dublin until the rebellion is over. Avery happened to mention it at the stable yesterday. But he says *he'll* not be run off by the rabble like his father. He'll stay on here and weather the storm."

Although she was chagrined that Sir Harry would not soon

return so that she could petition him for her old position, Tamasin held back her disappointment. She shrugged and commented, "Avery was never one to be cowed by his lessers."

"Do you believe we're his lessers?" Brendan's blue eyes, so well suited for contemplating rainbows and beautiful women, twinkled with the question.

"I used to think we were, but not anymore. In fact, sometimes I believe the brains have been bred right out of the gentry. And yet," she reflected, smoothing her old patched skirts, "there's still a grace about them, a sort of mystery to their wealth and power, don't you think?"

Brendan smiled, then cocked his sun-warmed head and arranged his face into what passed for a grave expression. "When do you expect Avery will have his agent turn you out of the cabin? The rent has come due, hasn't it?"

"Aye. But . . . Avery and I are playing a game of sorts."

"That's no secret to anyone, lass. I have a little wager on it myself, as a matter of fact. So does my brother."

Tamasin leaned to gather up the peeled rushes. "Does he now?"

"He's betting that you'll be giving in to Avery. Of course, the truth of it is, I think he's *hoping* that you won't." He watched closely for her reaction.

Tamasin glanced at him, wondering if he were delivering his usual brand of blarney, or if he were trying to tell her subtly, without being disloyal to his brother, that Hunter cared a deal more than he wanted to admit.

But Brendan only grinned and leaned to capture the black beetle crawling over the cuff of his boot.

"Where does Hunter get his money?" Tamasin asked, curious. "A few weeks ago he offered me a guinea like it was no more than tuppence."

"I can assure you he doesn't have enough money to treat it quite so casually. 'Tis just his surly way. But Hunter wagers now and then on the horses—far more cleverly than I, unfortunately." The beetle crept over Brendan's forefinger and he squinted, idly admiring its iridescent design of spots. "Especially of late."

Tamasin put her hands on her hips and looked at him with exasperated fondness. "Brendan Kinshella, have you been running up a gambling debt?"

He grinned, his face lighting with a beguiling mixture of boyish sheepishness and eloquent nonchalance. "Aye. A very grand debt, colleen. Losing money is one of my more refined talents."

"One of many, I'm thinking." Tamasin gave him a significant glance, one that told him she knew of his romantic exploits with Eushanie, the young woman who was forbidden to him and whose reputation he risked, along with his own life, by his reckless flirtation.

"Oh, that," he answered, the impish glimmer returning to his eyes. " 'Tis a wee bit like gambling, Miss Cullen, gambling for very high stakes. I find that I cannot quite resist the lure."

A fortnight later Tamasin was to remember those words, along with the carefree shrug of Brendan's slender, sunshine-splashed shoulders as he had so lightly uttered them.

One fine morning when the sun broke through a dawn mist and made prisms of the tiny water beads, she learned through Father Dinsmore that the younger Kinshella brother had been arrested for unpaid debts reportedly accumulated at *The Hound* over a period of several weeks. Brendan owed the landlord an exorbitant sum, the priest explained as he strolled with Tamasin toward the village.

Both were sickened at the thought of Brendan's punishment. Within the hour, as was the custom, the cavalier young debtor would be tied to the tailgate of a farm cart and, while being pulled through the village streets, publicly flogged with a cat-o'-nine-tails.

"What I cannot understand," Father Dinsmore lamented, huffing a little as they climbed the steep rock-strewn hill toward the Wexford gates, "is where on earth the young rogue got hold of such an amount of coin to wager in the first place."

Tamasin's skirts brushed the tips of the tufted emerald grass, catching dew. Her returning health and the brisk pace had put roses in her cheeks and mischief in her eyes, and she needled the priest a bit. "I'm surprised you don't know, Father. Don't you keep an account of everyone's sins, write them down in ledgers opposite the good deeds? Between his gambling and his latest romance. I suspected Brendan would have a volume almost as thick as mine."

The priest raised a brow at her, his voice still hale and full of sharpness. "Is it disrespect I'm hearing from your tongue now, Tamasin Cullen?"

"Nay, Father, 'tis just the truth," she said more meekly, not out of contrition, but out of a desire to avoid his lecture.

"Then out with it. Who is Brendan dallying with now?"

She hesitated, not prone to gossip, but sincerely concerned over the possible consequences to Brendan should his flirtation be discovered. Below them, the river sparkled, sending out tiny stars of light through the lingering haze. A flock of fat sheep parted and skittered out of their path, leaving the way clear. Tamasin sighed. "Brendan has been seeing Eushanie Hampton, Father. She's quite taken with him. In love with him, perhaps."

Father Dinsmore frowned, his white brows forming a line across the bridge of his high-arched nose. "You're certain of what you're saying, lass?

"Aye."

"Ah. A fine kettle of fish this is then. No doubt the young fool is charming the lady even while he holds out his palm for her money. Wasting himself, he is. Deliberately courting trouble when he has the brains to know better."

Father Dinsmore increased his pace, stabbing his cane into the mossy earth with vigor, craning his neck to see the goings-on now that he and Tamasin had entered the narrow village streets.

"Look at them," he grumbled, using his staff to point at the knots of milling townspeople. "All turned out for the spectacle of Brendan's whipping, laying down their plows and butter-dashers to watch. You'd think 'twas a bullbaiting or a cockfight instead of a man's misfortune."

Standing on tiptoe, Tamasin peered through the throng hoping for a glimpse of the hapless Brendan. An air of expectancy hung over the streets, a fair-like excitement scented with dust and ginger beer. Shabbily dressed clerks emerged from their shop doors, housewives poked capped heads from second-story windows, boys in knee breeches bought penny peppermint sticks from corner vendors, while coaches and wheel-cars cleared the cobbled road. Lining the way, weathered fishermen idled with merchants, who stood in their black broadcloth and hose occasionally checking silver pocket watches.

When a clattering of hooves echoed off the stone walls of the cooper's shop, Tamasin looked to see a showy sorrel thoroughbred canter up the steep ascent. The breeding of the horse and the cut of the rider's bottle-green jacket set the pair apart from everyone else.

Avery Hampton drew rein, the hooves of his mount slithering over the cobbles and causing sparks to fly. When he had settled the snorting animal, the baronet's son adjusted his bicorne and folded his hands across the pommel, taking up a relaxed position while he surveyed the crowd through heavy-lidded eyes.

His manner, Tamasin thought, was one of a casually curious spectator who found the simple delights of the lower order interesting in their very novelty, a contrast to the diversions provided by his own elevated life.

She observed Avery as he waited for the flogging to begin, fancying that she could smell the cleanness of his soap-washed clothes and the scent of his hair pomade across the press of unwashed farmers. Then he began to fidget with the reins, run a finger around his tight stock, displaying a nervous energy to match his thoroughbred's mettle.

She wondered what caused him to be suddenly so agitated. What was there to fear in the world except hunger and cold, which Avery's wealth and the solid oak door of Hampton Hall kept securely at bay?

As she pondered him across the sea of capped and bonneted heads, his coppery gaze locked with hers and held. Tamasin raised her chin archly to remind him that she still held her own in their contest of wills. He smiled in response, his teeth white if not perfect, his lips deep-colored and flat.

Rafael had come to join him astride a chestnut gelding, overdressed in the spring warmth but still appearing chilled, his fine-drawn face displaying no more expression than a classical carving. Tamasin wondered what connection the Italian maintained with Avery Hampton, wondered why he didn't return to his country, his family, instead of idling about the Irish countryside dogging the footsteps of the bored and restive baronet's son.

"Ah, there's Brendan," Father Dinsmore remarked, still standing close. His demeanor was somber, and Tamasin followed the direction of his nod.

Escorted by two jailers, white-faced but docile, Brendan proceeded toward the high-wheeled donkey cart to which he would be manacled. A black-garbed official followed carrying a long slender whip and, as he passed, a few villagers tossed shillings at his feet.

"Why are they throwing money at his feet?" Tamasin asked.

Father Dinsmore scowled. "As an incentive to the flogger not to shirk his duty and go too lightly with the stripes."

"Sainted Mary," Tamasin breathed. "Poor Brendan."

Hunter materialized beside the cart suddenly, a tall dark paladin, his brother's keeper. He was obviously willing to stand in Brendan's place and allow the lashes to fall on his own sturdy back. But regardless of his wishes he could do nothing more than watch the punishment, walk beside the cart and, when the flogging had stopped, be there once more to carry home a brother who seemed fated to find trouble.

Tamasin saw the grave concern on Hunter's face. More disturbingly, she saw the anger, the vengeful, black variety of wrath that coiled the sinews of his arms and darkened his eyes as they scanned the length of the excited, jeering crowd. He seemed to be hunting something, or someone.

A frisson of dread shivered through her, an arrow of unclear but harrowing premonition. "Father," she said anxiously, plucking at the priest's rusty black sleeve. "I'm concerned about Hunter—"

But the old man was pushing his way toward Brendan, who had been ordered to remove his shirt before being bound to the farm cart.

"Worried about Hunter, you say?" Father Dinsmore snorted as she trailed after him. "*That* dark scoundrel can take care of himself. 'Tis Brendan I'm concerned about."

The crowd had stepped back to clear the way for the procession. But before the whip could be raised to lay the first stripe, a young woman darted out of the knot of spectators, screamed, and waved her arms in a dramatic display before throwing herself over the back of the astonished prisoner.

Eushanie Hampton, her pale hair straggling out of its knot and spilling over her shoulders, clung to her Lancelot as if to defend him with her life. For several seconds she lay with her arms crossed over his chest and her head bowed, creating a picture of doomed idyllic love.

Brendan seemed reluctant to react, as if uncertain whether his response to the display would further injure Eushanie's reputation or excuse it. He remained passive beneath her smothering grasp, his hands still tethered to the cart tail, his mouth lifting just a trace when Avery Hampton's indignant voice rang out.

"Eushanie!"

In a storm of anger the baronet's son spurred the thoroughbred through the midst of the villagers, who hastily parted to avoid a trampling by the steed's pounding hooves. Wide-eyed, they watched Avery leap from the saddle and seize his sister by the arm.

"You have disgraced yourself!" His furious fingers ripped the fine white lawn of her sleeve. "Return home at once."

But the girl struggled with him. However unobtrusively she moved through the halls of her father's estate, Eushanie had spent her life immersed in tales of Isolde and Helen of Troy, and knew what it was to be courageous. Having found the chance now, she followed the example of her heroines.

Jerking a purse from her pocket even as Avery dragged her toward his horse, she flung it down at the feet of the landlord of *The Hound*. Its contents spilled through the drawstring opening and coins danced in every direction over the cobbles.

"That is the payment of Brendan Kinshella's debt!" she cried, her face splotched with high emotion. "Go on, you greedy pig, pick it up! The debt is cancelled here and now in front of all these witnesses!"

Ira O'Day, the proprietor of *The Hound*, stood clenching and unclenching his freckled hands, eyeing the scattered pieces of silver with guilty confusion.

His hesitation intrigued Tamasin. She frowned, staring at him. A hazy but provoking notion suddenly began to grow into a suspicion that was too monstrous to be true. Was Avery somehow involved in Brendan's punishment?

Tamasin rubbed her temples, frantically thinking. No one knew the baronet's son and his clever schemes better than she, who had often engineered them herself with a quiet and inconspicuous finesse. She knew he was capable of anything devious.

"Don't touch the money!" Avery ordered, moving so that his body barred the cottier children, whose skinny fingers itched to snatch up a loose coin or two. "My sister will not pay the gambling debt of a drunken stable hand. His own irresponsibility has caused him to be sentenced. He should accept his punishment like a man. Get on with what you were about," he told the official, jerking his head in Brendan's direction. "My sister won't be allowed to interfere again."

But Tamasin suspected that Eushanie had already been

allowed to interfere. Avery had known all along that his sister
was meeting the stable hand, had known that she was creating
rendezvous to satisfy her romantic longings, while her pocket
money satisfied Brendan's need to gamble. Had Avery kept
track of the sum? Had he asked the landlord to keep him
informed of the losses at *The Hound,* and when the time was
right, encouraged Ira to call in the debt and press charges
without leniency?

Tamasin glanced at Hunter, whose eyes, always percipient,
were fastened hawklike upon Avery's face. His mind had followed the same course as her own, she suspected, and arrived
at a similar conclusion.

Before she could further ponder the situation, Avery forcefully removed Eushanie from the site. Now free to do his duty,
the official prodded the cart donkey forward.

Tamasin tensed, imagined the sting of a lash upon the length
of a naked back, the effort it would take not to cry out and to
beg for mercy.

The motion of the cart yanked Brendan forward by his fettered wrists. A cry of anticipation went up from the crowd.
When the first stripe was laid upon his smooth narrow back,
he quivered, then relaxed. It had not been too vicious, just
heavy enough to draw a fine red line to the surface.

Tamasin grimaced at the sight and doggedly followed the
crowd, pushing through aproned housewives and skipping children in order to keep the groomsman's tall, tense figure in
view. Creating a disturbance of his own, Hunter had already
shoved several men aside, knocked down one who had thrown
a piece of rotten fruit at Brendan. As his anger grew, a peculiar
breathless anxiety constricted the muscles in Tamasin's throat.

Brendan was managing to stay on his feet, stumble along
with his eyes closed and his teeth gritted. When the lash fell
again, then again, he emitted scarcely a cry. Indeed, as the
procession neared the end of the route, Tamasin began to think,
to hope, he would come through the ordeal without losing
consciousness.

But all at once, inexplicably, the official's hand grew heavier, his wielding of the whip more rapid, more punishing, until Hunter shouted out in protest. Stepping forward, the groomsman seized the donkey's bridle and halted the progress of the cart.

Immediately the two jailers rushed forward to stay the groomsman's interference. He resisted. Then, as the wicked thongs snapped once again across Brendan's slumped back, Hunter took matters into his own hands.

Tamasin knew he would stop the unfair punishment at any cost. He would use his fists to disable the flogger or knock him unconscious or—Dear God—kill him if necessary.

The crowd shouted, but Tamasin scarcely heard them. She hurled herself through sweating bodies and screamed at Hunter not to act. How many times had she experienced this smothering premonition, willed him to do nothing? Even as she recalled past incidents, she knew *this* scheme had been too perfectly engineered, too well planned; Hunter's unpredictable temper had been assessed. The course of events could not now be altered.

With a terrible dismay, Tamasin suddenly suspected that *she* was the cause—or if not the cause—the *reason* for Brendan Kinshella's flogging. One by one, all the pieces began to fall into a picture. Avery knew the groomsman had helped her through a hard, starving winter that was to have sent her stumbling over the windswept fields to Hampton Hall, where the young master would have been waiting to welcome her for the night. Avery was his father's son, after all, as he had made a point to tell her once before, bred to idleness, bred to sport, which in all its varied forms was the only thing that gave purpose to his life.

And Hunter Kinshella had interfered with that purpose, had meddled with the rules of the game. And so Avery had devised a way to change the rules and raise the stakes.

It seemed she had been running for miles through the crowd. Now, Tamasin stood only a few feet from Hunter. Hurtling through the melee, she seized his strong, straining arm, felt its vengeful heat. Intuitively, in that suspended moment, she realized that she was holding on to his very life. Amid the confusion and clamor she screamed at him, hearing as one deafening roar the snap of the whip, the voices of many people, Hunter's own hoarse curses.

He broke away from her grip, broke away from all the other hands that fought to restrain him, and lunged forward, seizing the whip arm of the official—an official who had been bribed with Avery Hampton's money.

The official swung about to strike the groomsman with the whip, but Hunter ducked, balled his hands, and struck.

Tamasin knew that, unlike the others of his class, he rarely brawled, nor did he spar for wagers despite constant encouragement. Only moods of anger tempted him to clench his fists and use them, with purpose, with a blind determination to defend a principle. Or now, his brother's life.

She saw that dreadful determination, saw it pump through the corded veins of his neck. He had no control over it. He had gone beyond reason; only instinct ruled him. How many times had he defended his brother when they were children in the village streets? How many times had he defended him in hot, foreign places amid a pack of idle soldiers? Probably too many times to count.

With the sight of Brendan's bloody back filling his eyes, he landed a brutal blow, then another. It took only two blows to end the official's life, to send him sprawling on the cobbles with a scarlet stream pouring from his ear.

A hush fell as the crowd stared aghast at his body. For several moments no one moved. Even the little donkey stood motionless in its traces.

"Hunter!" Tamasin cried, trying to grab his sleeve as the crowd began to mobilize again. *"Hunter!"*

"Tend my brother!" he shouted at her, still swinging, battling the men who intended to manacle him.

With horror and a terrible sense of a scene repeating itself, she watched as he was overpowered, cudgeled with the butt of a musket. His hands were bound and he was led away, still resisting. Tamasin tried to get close to him, but was shoved, pushed back until she fell.

The sharp shapes and dizzying colors of the scene surrounding the wooden farm cart whirled before her eyes. She raised them, focused upon the spot where Avery Hampton had earlier sat astride his showy horse.

She was not surprised to find him gone.

After all, he had had no need to stay and watch the spectacle. He had been certain of the outcome this morning, before he'd even arisen from bed to sip his cup of tea.

Chapter Eighteen

Knowing well that Avery Hampton wasted little time in matters of importance to him, Tamasin slept poorly that night and the night following, her mind in turmoil.

She asked herself repeatedly why Hunter had lost control of himself and—inadvertently or not—killed the official. Brendan would not have *died* from his flogging; death had not been a part of his sentence. Or had it?

Perhaps Avery Hampton had guaranteed the official's immunity even if his hand grew too heavy and accidently killed Brendan Kinshella. After all, everyone had always known the young ne'er-do-well would come to a bad end eventually. The community would not long mourn his death. As for his brother, who would be surprised if the short fuse of Hunter's temper ignited? It had happened before, and would cause little comment, arouse no suspicion.

Tamasin despaired. Avery, as always, had planned well. And now the groomsman had committed murder, an offense punishable by hanging.

Needing to channel her fevered energies, Tamasin snatched

up a shovel and hastened to the large bog at the bottom of the
fells where the light sphagnum peat used for summer burning
abounded. Out of long habit, she began to cut and stack the
turf just as she had done since childhood, the new spring sun
warming her until she perspired.

As she worked she thought of Hunter, of his hands as they
had packed clay in her window to keep the cabin warm, as
they had fed her broth, as they had stroked her hair in the
tender beginnings of a gentle exploration. Those same hands
had killed a man, and then been bound together with iron.

What was he doing now? Was he pacing his cell, restively
walking from one end to another? No, Tamasin decided, he
would be sitting still, very still, as he had doubtless learned to
do in his scarlet uniform, staring at the walls that held him,
but not seeing them at all, not even knowing what color they
were or whether they were built of stone or wood. What *did*
he see? The open fields sprinkled with gorse, perhaps, or the
little black colt he had been training at the lodge?

Or was he, just possibly, seeing her face?

She gazed out over the sheep-dotted hills quilted with gorse
and tried to understand what Hunter loved about them, why
the green undulating landscape and misty air meant so much
to him. *She* would rather contemplate grand furnishings, touch
porcelain instead of rock, taste French chocolates instead of
blackberries plucked half-ripe from the hedges. The only advantage the earth enjoyed, that she could see, was timelessness. It
would always remain just as it was, unconcerned with the
dilemmas going on atop it, indifferent to human outcomes even
while lending to troubled hearts, at no charge, its enduring
shapes and tranquil voices.

Such thoughts crossed and recrossed her mind now as she
toiled in the bog, and each thought was overlaid with the loom-
ing shadow of Avery Hampton.

Therefore, she was not surprised to see a meticulously liveried footman slipping and sliding down the muddy hill in her
direction. She had expected him.

The English servant said nothing, merely came to stand before her in his blue wool and silver lace, sweating. The fellow looked incongruous in the wild setting, his polished shoes already covered with sphagnum, his face carefully blank as he handed her the missive from his master. "I'm to get an answer, Miss."

The paper carried a scent, a blend of tobacco and the woodsy odor of the desk drawer from which it had likely been withdrawn. Tamasin tore it open carefully, almost gingerly, as if it might conceal a scorpion poised to strike.

In a flourished copperplate learned in childhood, it read: *"Would you now be interested in spending an evening with me at Hampton Hall? In exchange, shall we say, for your groomsman's life . . . ?"*

Tamasin turned away so that the servant could not see her expression. Her stomach knotted. She would have to go, of course. Ah, yes, Avery had planned it all very well.

And afterward? After her night with Avery Hampton—when she had done for him whatever it was he thought he wanted her to do—what would happen? Would she be given some small gift to carry away?

Tamasin doubted it. The baronet's son, no matter how she strove to please him, would likely discard her after one night, set her in the fields again and care not where she went off to beg.

How strangely interwoven were their three lives, she mused. How ironic that Avery was coercing her to redeem Hunter's life when, a decade ago, she had been the one to make such a wreckage of it.

But recalling the strange, eager light in Avery's eye the day in the marketplace, she wondered. Did he desire her more passionately than he would have her know?

"Is there a reply, Miss?" the footman asked, clearing his throat.

"Tell Master Avery that he may expect me tonight."

The man focused his eyes on some polite point just above

her head and nodded. "Very well, miss. I'll relay the message. Good day to you, miss."

Tamasin watched him walk toward the road. Soon she would be following the same path. With luck, she might be allowed to stay longer than one night, allowed to enjoy the luxury of the mansion indefinitely. She knew the key lay in pleasing Avery. She must find a way to make herself indispensable.

Just after twilight had stolen the last of the light from the land and left it a haunted shade of deepest purple, a jailer came to release Hunter Kinshella from his cell. No explanation for the boon was given.

But the groomsman guessed the reason, and seconds after the door had swung closed behind him he was running, making for the squat little cabin in the fells. As he'd half expected, he found nothing there but an abandoned den awaiting its next tenant.

Turning away, he headed for the lodge, and a few minutes later, vaulted up the steep wooden stairs to the room above the stable he shared with Brendan.

His brother rested on a pallet, arms outflung so that his healing back lay exposed to the air. A bottle of whiskey was positioned close to Brendan's hand, and at the furious sound of Hunter's entry, he started so violently the bottle toppled to the floor and shattered.

"Begad, Hunter! What in the devil are you about?"

"Where's Tamasin?"

"Ah, Tamasin . . ." Still prone, Brendan made a halfhearted attempt to lift his shoulders in a shrug. "How should I know? I expect she's up at Hampton Hall by now. Why do you think you're walking about a free man, for God's sake? Bloody shame, all of it. My fault, of course. Fine lass, Tamasin is, really. Pity to be spoiled by Avery Hampton. You've heard what they say about him, I suppose . . . ?"

Hunter remained silent and Brendan shifted, turning his head to face the wall. He murmured against the pillow. "Of course, some of this trouble is your fault, dear brother. The official— that damned blighter who put the pretty red ribbons on my back—was a United Irishman. The rebels haven't taken kindly to your refusal to join them." Brendan awaited a response and, hearing none, turned his head. "Hunter? Hunter, where the devil are you?"

The groomsman set out toward the moors. Darkness had fallen, but he ran headlong, his sense of direction unerring. He splashed through bogs and leapt over hedges, his breaths coming hard after a quarter hour or so. He passed the fairy rath, pounded over its sacred mound in his muddy boots, then startled a flock of sheep whose bleating seemed the only sound in the world save the lonely cry of a night bird.

In the distance he could make out the vague outline of Hampton Hall enthroned upon its hill. The points of its chimneys created a crownlike roof, and its serpentine drive, through some trick of light, seemed to spiral straight to heaven. They would all be seated at the dining table now, he thought, sipping wine, the man at the head of the company waiting confidently for the arrival of a violet-eyed guest.

Was he too late?

Hunter increased his pace as he slogged across a stream, wended through an orchard, then scaled a high stone wall.

He spotted Tamasin near the wrought-iron gates, a small obscure figure, but regal somehow with her straight determined shoulders.

"Tamasin! Tamasin Cullen!"

Ahead, Tamasin heard his harsh voice, the steady thudding of his feet as he veered onto the lane. Alarmed, she walked more quickly, not giving an answer. He would try to stop her, interfere, and now that her decision had been made, she had no intention of having it weakened, questioned, or stayed.

For a few minutes she was able to elude him like a panicked hare. She cut through a hedge, splashed through a stream, and ran so fast she nearly stumbled in the mud and rolled down a hill. When he caught up with her, she swung around and tried to fend off his hands, slapping, shoving, hissing at him to leave her alone.

Hunter's fingers clamped over her arms, and when she tried to strike him, he lifted her off the ground.

She heard his labored breaths and realized how far he must have run, how fast, to cover so many miles and catch up.

He spoke to her, his voice low, throaty, and raggedly commanding. *"Don't go."*

That was all, nothing more. Just two simple, ineloquent words that explained everything, that explained nothing.

Tamasin could scarcely see his face against the backdrop of night, but she remembered well its rough-cast features, its ordered symmetry, its absence of humor. And he seemed so large, so substantial. Or was it only that she felt insignificant tonight, so pathetically frail?

Across the inches that separated them she could feel the heat radiating from his body, the heat of his blood, of his anger, of his offended sense of honor. And something more, some not-quite-fathomable motive for chasing after her.

"I've given my word to Avery," she breathed finally, desperately.

"Then bloody break it!" He snapped the answer viciously through his teeth, and his fingers bruised her arm. "I won't allow you or anyone else to bargain for my life. I killed a man and I'll go to the gallows for it. No cottier lass is going to serve herself up to some rutting whoreson of a baronet, lie in his bed with her legs spread, and sacrifice herself for me."

She struck him, struck him twice. "You should be satisfied, you witless Irish lout! You should be thanking me on your knees for getting you out of jail!"

"Avery Hampton *used* me to win his game with you, Tamasin, by God, and I'll not allow it. I'll not have my conscience muddied—"

"You have no choice! The say is mine. *Mine!*" She shoved at his chest. "So run back over those fields you love so much,

Hunter Kinshella. Go on. Get back to your horses and your stable muck. I've got a better place to go. One that's full of the best of things in life, one that all the dim-witted clods around here think to be getting for themselves by fighting instead of by using their brains—''

"Or their bodies?'' Hunter barked.

She lifted her arm to strike him again.

He seized her wrists and pinioned them behind her back.

Maddened by his hard handling, wanting to goad him, Tamasin hissed, "There's nothing you can do to stop my going to Avery Hampton. I want to go, do you hear? I *want* to give myself to him!''

Hunter leaned close, his hands bruising her wrists as he waited for the moment to calm. He struggled with the mastery of his own emotion. When he spoke, his voice was low, meaningful. "Are you sure, Tamasin? Are you sure Hampton Hall is really what you want?''

She understood the underlying question in his deeply uttered words, knew he spoke to her as man to woman. She felt the pull of his mystery suddenly, the allure of the raw emotion he had just revealed in the quietness of his voice. " 'Tis meant to be, Hunter!'' she cried in sudden plaintiveness. "What's between Avery and me is meant to be. It always has been. You must know that.''

Hunter answered urgently, "I'll not let you do it to save me. 'Tis not worth it, Tamasin. 'Tis not worth the cost you'll pay. I'm asking you, once more, not to go to Hampton Hall.''

She was astonished to hear the entreaty in his voice: unwilling, but detectable. There had been a trace of gentleness in it, too. Had she ever heard such a degree of gentleness forced from the carefully guarded inner self of this man?

All at once she felt as if the hopeful young lad of long ago had returned from whatever dark region had been keeping him, that he was a tentative, hovering spirit who was asking for something. If she were only to agree to it, she could bring him back. She could redeem Hunter Kinshella from the past.

"Don't do this, Hunter," she begged, disquieted. She pulled away. "Don't try to keep me from what you know has to be done."

He took hold of her arm again. "Not until after we've finished what we've begun."

"What we've begun—"

His mouth came down on hers for answer.

Tamasin parted her lips, accepting, wanting the groomsman. She threw her arms around his neck, and they kissed in hunger for each other, lips and tongue together.

Their bodies strained, grew eager, breathless.

"Let Avery Hampton go to hell without you," Hunter whispered against her mouth.

"Hunter—"

"No." He squeezed her arms. "Stay with me tonight, Tamasin. Here. Now."

In a thrilling, frightening wonder she watched him slide his arms out of the fine woolen cathamore and toss it on the ground, then stand by. Unspeaking, he waited, the wind ruffling his damp black hair.

Tamasin stared at him, then at the pool of wool upon the grass. Yes, to lie down with him was what she wanted! How wondrous it would be to allow nature its course, to sink down on the mossy ground with Hunter Kinshella and experience what she had longed to experience since his return to Ireland. There would be a purity in the act, she thought, an honesty she would never find with any other man, certainly not with Avery Hampton.

She sensed that Hunter yearned for the honest passion, too. He leaned toward her, rubbed his hand gently over her sleeve, drew her close again.

"No, Hunter . . ." she protested, even while he kissed her. " 'Tis madness to do this . . ."

"Aye. Madness, indeed . . ." He touched her face, the rise of her brow, seeing the color of the moon reflected in her eyes. His hand trailed down the length of her throat, over its soft white arch, and he bent to fasten his mouth upon her lips again. She opened them, welcomed the invasion, ran her hands over the planes of his back, then trailed them through his hair. She clenched him tightly to her, felt him pull her down, and glanced to see the cathamore, soft dark wool, awaiting the pressure of their bodies.

Seconds later she lay beneath the groomsman, captive but free, her eyes fixed upon the few bright stars overhead as his mouth found, just below her jawline, a pulse beat. His fingers had already loosened the lacings of her gown, and lost inside herself, she aided him with trembling hands. Scarcely thinking, only yearning, *wanting,* she invited him to lower his head and find her breast.

Driven, Hunter assured her of her beauty in low Gaelic words, closed his eyes when her hands slid beneath his shirt. Fearing that she would stop him, he abandoned leisure and lifted her skirts, compelled to make her his quickly, sensing that once they were joined, he could keep her at his side.

He found the place where no other man had been, touched her there, and made her ready.

The breeze cavorted, scattered flower scents of the garden of Hampton Hall across the rough wild hills. Rose scents. Honeysuckle. Carnation. Tamasin recognized them, and the fragrances startled her, acted as strongly as hartshorn to bring her to her senses.

"No, Hunter . . . No!"

"Be still, my sweet—"

"Stop, we mustn't!"

He was beyond his own restraint, agonized to continue.

She shoved at him, pushed at her skirts, struggled to stand. Eluding Hunter's hands, she drew her gown together and cried hotly, "What if I *were* to lie down with you tonight? *Think!* What would happen to us tomorrow, Hunter? Avery's bargain would be broken. You, with your stupid brand of honor, would walk straight back to jail. And what of me? What do you think would happen to me?" She gave him no chance to answer.

"I'll tell you what would happen. Avery would put me out of the cabin tomorrow. After that, I'd have ditches for beds and mayflowers for breakfast. That would be the price I'd pay for lying on the ground with you instead of walking up to Hampton Hall."

Gripping her shoulders in a fierce effort to hold her until she resisted no more, Hunter argued, "But you'd survive it, Tamasin, you'd find a way."

"Would I? Have you forgotten? I tried once to outlast Avery Hampton and nearly starved for it. And now it has brought us to this pass." She threw off his hands, battling him, and wheeled about to face the Hall.

Its distant lights winked at her, reminded her that a night spent with its young master was the last and only hope, not only for her, but for the groomsman. The road leading up to it was the only way to break the destructive circle of their lives.

As she stared at its grand silhouette, she willed the flame of her ambition to rekindle itself. She concentrated upon her resolution to lie first with a man who had softer hands, a paler scented skin, a true gentleman who would murmur pretty words in her ear and keep her safe from hunger.

Across from Tamasin, Hunter sensed the rapid, frantic workings of her mind. As the wind swept the earth and blew breaths of cloud over the moon's white surface, he moved close, looked down into her face. "Don't go, Tamasin," he asked. "Please, don't go."

Like a snow crest collapsing beneath its own weight, she felt her resolve weaken. But she must not, *could* not, give in. Hunter's life was at stake. Her dream was at stake. *Think. Think.*

She gazed with longing at the groomsman, fought her own desire for him. When his dark green gaze continued to stay locked with hers, she forced herself to utter a few irretrievable words she knew would always stand between them. "I'm not going to Hampton Hall for you, Hunter. I'm not going in order to save you. I'm going for twenty guineas." She spoke the

words clearly, slowly. "Avery promised me twenty guineas if
I'd come to him for the night."

The lie had come with ease; hurting the groomsman had
been as difficult as inflicting the wound upon herself. But it
was best to hurt him, Tamasin told herself with fierce resolve.
It was the only way to keep him safe.

He made no response, simply contemplated her with an
intensely silent stare.

" 'Tis what I feel I'm worth," she continued in her ruthless
way. "Don't you? 'Tis more than you have, more than you'll
ever have. A stable lad till the day you die, Hunter Kinshella,
that's what you'll be. Nothing more than that. Ever!"

His eyes did not flicker. "Likely so."

"*Surely* so!"

Unable to look at him any longer, to see how true her arrow
had flown, Tamasin pivoted. She was afraid he might strike
her for her impertinence. She almost hoped he would, for physical pain would take the sudden numbness away.

But when she stepped forward and began to climb the dark
road toward the fairy lights of Hampton Hall, Hunter followed.
He grabbed her, held her, shouted, "I'll not let you go."

"Yes! Yes, you will," she counted, her face close to his,
her ears hearing the harshness of his breaths. "You'll let me
go because I've made my choice. Must I say the words again?
Aye, I see that I must, so you'll not forget them." She steeled
herself, even as tears started in her eyes. "I can do better than
a groomsman."

She saw him stiffen, and knew that had she thrust a dagger
at his chest his pain would have been less than this. His hand
loosened upon her arm.

She could not bear to look longer upon his face. Turning,
she fled. She ran to the top of the hill where, aggrieved, unable
to resist, she paused and swung around for one last look. She
wanted to savor the picture of the groomsman standing where
he should be, amid his wild fields. The sleeves of his shirt
rippled in the wind, and his boots still glistened with water

from the brook. The earth was all about him. He belonged to it. It would comfort him where she could not.

Tamasin put a hand to her throat. Her feet felt heavy, as if she were about to walk through hell instead of through the gates of an earthly heaven.

Hunter's voice rang out, echoed low over the black night space between them. His tone was knowing. Wounded. Harsh. "What you want is not there, Tamasin. 'Tis not there. Damn you. Damn you!"

Chapter Nineteen

Did the reality meet the expectation of the dream?

Tamasin asked herself the question as she stood in the center of a vast chamber of rich brown wood, its windows embraced with amethyst drapes, its walls traced with fleur-de-lis wallpaper above oak panelling, its hardwood softened with jewel-hued carpets. Contained in this lavish space, packed into its every niche and corner, were treasures to delight a guest and give her comfort: perfume to scent the body, clothes to cover it, a fire to warm it, and food—rich, delicious, *abundant* food—to feed it.

There were glossy paintings in gilt frames, silver vases of potpourri, silver boxes of bonbons, and silver caskets that, when opened, delivered beautiful music. Inlaid furniture gleamed with wax; tapestry pillows reposed invitingly upon every chair. And in bright haste, without a thought for economy, two dozen candles consumed themselves on cherrywood sideboards. A bed plumped with the feathers of a hundred geese awaited some weary frame, canopied by more amethyst velvet and fringe.

Creature comforts all; luxuries to be enjoyed for a night; seductive indulgences to be touched, eaten, or simply contemplated.

For the first time, Tamasin's entire body was enveloped in silk, her skin scrubbed, her hair smoothed by a silver-backed brush, and her stomach completely satisfied.

She was overwhelmed by the myriad sensations of luxury, and realized with a sudden fierceness that she never wanted to be without it again, now she had managed to grab it. She wanted to hold on to its feel, its beauty, experience both for as long as possible, no matter what efforts, what promises, what sacrifices had to be made. She had slipped from the gray world into the gold.

As for the price, its collector would be entering soon to demand payment. She had not seen Avery. Earlier, she had been received at the front door—refusing stubbornly to use the back—by a footman who, being the same servant who had delivered the message to her, was prepared for her arrival. Discreetly, he had ushered her up the stairs to the chamber she now occupied.

There had been a maid to assist her—or to make her presentable, she supposed—one very young and English who hid her astonishment over Tamasin's frayed gown and patched stockings, performed her duties efficiently if not cheerfully, and kept her mouth shut. In this well-oiled establishment, so different from Sir Harry's rustic male sanctuary at the lodge, a footman promptly arrived carrying a silver tray of refreshment, and with the utmost politeness, set the food down and unobtrusively departed again with little more than "Can I bring you anything else, Miss? Very well, then. Master Avery will join you in an hour. Good evening, Miss."

And so Tamasin waited, glad of the respite. Anticipating what was shortly to come and recalling what had just passed on the hillside, she could not enjoy the luxuries as completely as she might have done under different circumstances. Hunter had altered her forever somehow, imprinted himself upon her body and her mind. She felt shaken now and incomplete. It

had been folly to come from the groomsman directly to Avery.
How difficult the night would be! Feverishly she paced the
room. She must put thoughts of Hunter out of mind, focus on
the future, the sort of future the groomsman could never provide.

When the heavy panelled door finally swung open and the
baronet's son crossed the threshold, she realized she could
never have prepared herself adequately for the confrontation.
She could not have mentally readied herself for the culmination
of an act that, for whatever complicated reasons, had to be.

Much to her chagrin, she did not *feel* like a lady when Avery
looked at her as she had hoped. Even garbed so finely, she felt
like nothing more than a cottier's lass, gauche and common.

Moreover, to her dismay, Avery didn't appear in the guise
of a dashing Romeo. He looked quite ordinary, or at least
ordinary in the way of Sir Harry and his guests when they
toddled about mornings at the lodge. He wore slippers and a
plum-colored dressing gown with gold trim. His hair was
smoothly tied back in a queue brushed with pomade. He held
a bottle of claret and two thin-stemmed crystal glasses, which
he carried to a table beside the bed. His face was pleasantly
arranged, surprisingly devoid of smugness; indeed, Tamasin
thought with vague amazement, he seemed more ill at ease
than she, and yet at the same time, very eager. His eyes glittered
beneath their half-lowered lids.

"Good evening," he said, his gaze sweeping her silk-clad
figure. He smiled, noting that she stood with her hands clasped
in a gesture of girlish nervousness. "Awkward, isn't it?" he
asked quietly, his tone almost kind. "But natural under the
circumstances, one would suppose."

"Aye," she answered, attempting to smile but managing
nothing more than a stiff sort of grimace. "It is."

"Then before we proceed, let us ease the situation, shall we,
or try, at least? Come and drink with me."

While Avery poured the claret, Tamasin stepped close, dry-
mouthed and dry-eyed, and accepted the glass from his hand.
She felt his soft fingers brush against hers, and caught the

expensive scent of his pomade. Her eyes fastened on the fine braid that edged the brocade of his dressing gown.

She told herself that she had wanted this to happen all her life. She had wanted to be touched by a man such as Avery Hampton, a man bred to dance, to master, and to treat a woman with sensitivity and reverence. Through this man, through his touching her, and his breathing with her in the darkness, Tamasin could surely experience what it was to be a lady, what it was to be wellborn.

As she glanced about the chamber again with the taste of wine upon her lips, the presence of the young master began to thrill her body. The papered walls seemed to shimmer, and she experienced a sensation of privilege. For a moment at least, she was able to shut out the memory of another presence, one rough and very real, and his fine woolen cathamore pooled upon the ground.

Avery was staring at her fixedly, with such concentration that the vein throbbed in the center of his forehead. He leaned toward her excitedly, then pulled back as if to delay the moment. Oddly, Tamasin was reminded of a little boy who, after much wheedling, had received his first pony, only to find himself frightened of trying it out lest he be thrown off and humiliated.

Well, as for herself, she would just as soon get it over with. She knew very well what it was gentlemen wanted most from women, and felt physically capable of providing it, even though honor, pleasure, and sin were battling with each other in her conscience. Which one of the three had sent her here to Hampton Hall? Which one kept her here?

Honor? Was she here on behalf of Hunter Kinshella? Tamasin allowed herself to think of him, and knew, without doubt, that he was the best part of the reason. But as she brought the wine to her lips and let it slide like an expensive fire down her throat, she knew she was in Hampton Hall to satisfy—more than anyone else—a cottier's girl who had known too much hunger in too many forms.

Avery seemed to sense that the groomsman had crossed her

mind. Setting down his glass, he strolled unhurriedly to the window, where he fingered the long gold fringe on the drapes. "So, Kinshella is a free man now," he commented. "Have you seen him, assured yourself that I have upheld my end of the bargain?"

His question was phrased casually, but Tamasin sensed the reply was of great importance to him. Finding no reason to lie, she nodded. "Aye. I've seen him. Briefly." She said no more.

"So I managed to find your price, at last," Avery mused with a smile. "Curious. I didn't have to offer you a single penny. Not even a silk scarf." Clicking his tongue, he parted the drapes slightly and pondered the blackness of the garden. "Kinshella must mean something to you then. A great deal, in fact. For I have known you all your life, Tamasin Cullen, and never before seen you hold scruples above gain."

"It was Hunter's *life* at stake," she countered without hesitation, offended that Avery would believe her capable of allowing a man to hang for the sake of a game.

Avery turned, his brows raised, his attitude one of feigned amazement. "But it was his *life* before, wasn't it, Tamasin? Ten years ago?"

The old guilt pricked her as keenly as ever. "I was a child. I couldn't have been expected to realize—"

"But you do now?"

"I don't see—"

"You *do now?*" Avery repeated firmly.

Tamasin lowered her eyes and nodded. "Aye. I do now."

Stepping nearer, Avery reached out to take her chin in his hand. He tilted her face, scrutinized the lines of her mouth, the texture of her black hair, the heather color of her eyes. "I arranged it," he told her bluntly. There was no smugness in his tone, just the bland utterance of fact. "I arranged all of it."

His face was so close Tamasin could see the slight furrows at the corners of his mouth, the white roundness of his chin. She asked quietly, "Would you have had Brendan flogged to death, if necessary?"

A faint smile touched his lips. "Let us just say it was a calculated risk."

Tamasin stared at him, but she was born of a world too hard to be surprised by the heartlessness of his confession. She asked herself if she liked Avery Hampton. *No.* She never had liked him, not really. But she had liked the life he represented very much.

"I doubt Kinshella appreciates what you're doing for him," Avery remarked, still gripping her chin. "Did he tell you so? Did he try to prevent your coming here to me?"

Tamasin did not want to speak of Hunter. She did not want to be reminded of those last excruciatingly tender, then darkly tempting moments on the road, moments to which Avery could not have been privy, of course, but which he had obviously managed to conjecture.

"I've nothing to say about Hunter Kinshella," she snapped, her confused emotion making her head throb and her belly knot. She felt ill suddenly, so sick that the food she had earlier eaten seemed to sour in her stomach.

"Are you angry with me for goading you?" Avery inquired in a whisper. "Ah . . . I can see that you are. Good. Let us get on with it then."

And they did. Or he did. In a way that Tamasin had not expected.

There was not even the barest pretense of gentleness in his handling of her. There were no preliminaries, no pretty words or the slow snuffing of candles as there should have been, as Tamasin's imagination had demanded there to be, as there had been with Hunter. Instead, Avery shoved her on to the bed, and undressing neither himself nor her except for what was functionally necessary, proceeded to try—without a kiss or any other show of tenderness or regard—to prove himself upon her.

After a few agonizing moments she realized that there was no point in refusing, no point in allowing cowardice to win.

And so, she let Avery carry on with it, let him shatter into a thousand tiny shards the illusion of a long-held dream.

She should not have been shocked by his way. After all, it was a familiar ritual. She had unwillingly witnessed it, heard it, reviled it countless times before in the smoky darkness of a cottier's cabin. With her hands over her ears and her teeth gritted, she tried to shut out the sound of her father's coarse mating with her mother, who, like some dumb animal, had never bothered to resist. Indeed, there came a point when Tamasin closed her mind to what was about to happen to her— just like Mam, she supposed. She simply decided to endure, gripped the sheet in her hands, and tried to concentrate upon anything but Avery Hampton. In mental agony, she thought of Hunter.

She almost pushed Avery's heavy body aside and scrambled up; and for a few almost unendurable seconds she thought that she *would* fight him, kick him, kill him in order to escape. All the treasures in the room could not hold her.

But what of Hunter then?

As if whispered faintly by one of the embroidered angels on the canopy above her head, the question stayed her, calmed her.

What of Hunter? He was *free* because of her act of sacrifice.

Closing her eyes, their lashes dry no longer, Tamasin endured further, forced herself to be as resigned as her mother had always been. Was this, then, the lot of women?

And when the baronet's son was finished and had rolled aside, she knew that, despite the fact that he had taken all the time he had wanted to take, or been able to take, her body had failed to satisfy him.

She knew it unquestionably when great sobs began to shake his shoulders. His cries were wrenching, horrible sounds that filled the room. As she lay rigid and wide-eyed listening, they gradually diminished to convulsive whimperings, pale, childish mumblings accompanied by silent tears.

How astonishing, she thought. How sad. So sad, in fact, that the edge of her own misery began to thaw just a little, melt into pity.

But not entirely. She found herself shuddering in the great canopied bed, afraid to move. She was even afraid to reach down and retrieve the sheet and draw it over her freezing limbs.

How long did she lie there, scarcely able to bear the closeness of Avery's body as he wept? A few minutes? An hour?

Teeth a-chatter, she finally stirred, crept out of the cold rumpled bed where the baronet's son lay curled on his side with his back turned.

Tiptoeing to the dressing room, Tamasin closed the door and huddled in a dark corner, her knees to her chest, her head bowed. A feeble little sound quivered off her lips. It was the name of another man.

"Hunter . . ."

He did not hear his name breathed, of course, but outside the gates of Hampton Hall, Hunter Kinshella waited. He had refused to allow the cottier's daughter to suffer the price of his freedom alone. For hours he had paced in the cold fine drizzle, bareheaded and restless. Often he paused and stared up at the candlelit window and imagined what was taking place inside, fearing it, loathing it. He knew it would not be the act Tamasin had expected.

Hunter felt a sickening, blinding rage born of love and jealousy. Tamasin belonged to him, and yet she was lying in another man's arms. When he saw the candlelight snuffed from the room upstairs, he pounded a fist upon the iron gatepost and groaned aloud before raising his head up to cry a protest to the heavens.

When Avery Hampton had done with Tamasin and sent her packing, when she came trudging through the huge iron gates at dawn, Hunter determined that he would be waiting to pick up the pieces.

It was not the future he had envisioned for himself, nor,

obviously, the future Tamasin had wanted. But Hunter had learned long ago that visions were for dreamers and poets. The worn fabric of his nature no longer held any golden threads of idealism; his heart had been stripped of everything except what was hard and real.

And yet, he and Tamasin would manage fine together, he reckoned, somehow. There were worse existences, God knew. Far worse.

He glanced up again at the windows of Hampton Hall.

Avery sat in the library. His chair faced the series of vertical windows providing a view of the rain-drenched garden. Since the hour was still early, the sky was only one shade lighter than night.

A cup of tea in eggshell porcelain cooled near his hand, but he did not pick it up; he had forgotten its existence. His mind was working, racing up and down several different avenues, trying to decide which would take him to the most desirable destination with the least amount of delay. He was shaking. His hands gripped the arms of the chair to keep still, and he sweated from the fire some fool had laid despite the seasonable spring weather.

The thought of what had passed a few hours ago sickened him, made him squirm, so that he became disgusted with his own company. If it had been possible, he would have fled the house and all those in it, ordered a horse saddled and ridden off as if the devil himself were snapping at his coat tails.

What should he do?

The cottier's lass had disappointed him. His desperate hopes had been shattered. Tamasin's earthy, ripe young body had failed to rescue his manhood.

He slammed a fist down upon the chair arm. *No. He had failed himself.*

"What's the matter with me?" he growled savagely beneath his breath. "Why haven't I already thrown the girl out the door, saved myself the torment of being reminded of my failure? The sight of her, her presence in this house should repulse me, even enrage me.''

But strangely, it did not. Tamasin had been quiet, unresisting during the whole ordeal. She had been patient when Avery had expected her to scream and curse, or laugh at him. Even while he had sobbed aloud amid the wreckage of his own inadequacy, she hadn't made a sound.

For awhile, she had left him in the bed to suffer alone, before creeping quietly back to his side. Then, after a few moments of awkwardness, she had led him to grasp her by the waist and lay his head upon her breast. Neither of them had moved or spoken a word, but Avery had experienced an unexpected, wondrous sense of comfort. She had soothed him. And he had fallen peacefully asleep in her arms. He had never been held in such a manner.

His mother, at his birth, had declared herself too delicately nerved to endure a squalling infant. With no regret whatsoever she had passed him on to a series of wet nurses and nannies, scarcely remembering his existence. And finally, in a grim irony that confirmed her long-held opinion that she was unfit for motherhood, she had borne Eushanie and died from it.

Avery watched the dripping garden now. He knew that, at all costs, he must keep Tamasin at Hampton Hall. He did not want her to carry tales; rumors already abounded concerning his shameful inadequacy.

All of Wexford now knew that Tamasin Cullen had come to Hampton Hall, given herself to Avery in exchange for the groomsman's release. Every ear would be attuned to details. Even if he were to bribe Tamasin not to speak, she might, eventually. Then, Avery's tenants, servants, his *father,* would know the truth about him.

He couldn't endure the shame. Most of all, he knew how brutal Sir Harry's accusations would be. Rafael would be thrown out, blamed somehow for Avery's failing to meet the gentry's code, which demanded that a gentleman ride with the best, drink with the best, and above all, establish a reputation for virility, beginning with impregnating several scullery maids before producing legitimate heirs.

He surmised that if Tamasin were kept at Hampton Hall her loyalty could be easily won, for he knew that she had always considered herself above her own kind. But in what capacity could she serve—dairymaid, parlor maid, laundress? No, he thought, nervously tapping his teeth, it must be a more elevated position, a position that would give her a higher opinion of herself, ensure her complete separation from those of the village. Most of all, it must make her agreeable to his occasional nighttime visits—not that he intended to risk a repeat performance of last night's failure any time soon. He shuddered at the thought.

But perhaps, in the quiet way she had last night, she would allow him to lay his head against her, so that he could find an island of security again.

The bellpull dangled only a few feet away, but Avery was too impatient to get up and yank it. "Fetch Tamasin Cullen from her room and send her to me at once!" he bellowed, addressing a passing servant.

A few minutes later Tamasin hurried down the grand, graceful staircase, only dimly realizing the dreamlike quality of such a descent. She was drained, exhausted, still grappling with the enormity of her experience last night. Her stomach rebelled against the rich cream pastry she had eated for breakfast. What could Avery have to say to her under the circumstances? Was she to be dismissed, threatened, reviled?

After hesitating on the threshold, she tentatively entered the hushed library, where leather-bound books marched from floor to ceiling on three sides of the room, packed into dark bookshelves beside leather chairs and tables with gilded leather tops. The marble fireplace blazed, and the room smelled of paper and rich wood mingled with the wet scent of the garden spilling in through open French doors.

Avery was dressed in a tweed jacket and waistcoat. His

ruffled cuffs and stock were immaculate, and his hair neatly groomed. He was the picture of a gentleman, a young master in control, a prince of his surroundings. His chair was positioned in such a way that only allowed Tamasin a view of his profile; his eyes seemed to be fixed on a puddle sparkling on the flagstones outside.

"Cullen," he said. His voice, the same one that had whimpered last night, was perfectly controlled now, haughty again. "I've decided that you shall stay on here. Be a companion of sorts to my sister Eushanie."

"A-a companion?"

"Yes." He affected a casual tone, sipping his cold tea. "With the country so unsettled, 'tis likely the rabble will try to harass us here at Hampton Hall as they've been doing elsewhere. Eushanie will need a sensible woman at her side, one who understands, one who can keep her calm. She's of a rather nervous disposition, you see. Prone to fancies."

Tamasin could scarcely contain her astonishment over this turn of events, and along with it, a sense of triumph.

"One might even call her unstable," Avery went on, still staring out at the garden whose shrubs were slightly windblown, like well-groomed children caught in a storm without their bonnets.

"Of course, I will expect you to . . ." He paused, his voice clipped. "Accommodate me from time to time. As I require."

A hush fell, wove itself around them, settled heavily on the air.

When Tamasin said nothing, Avery continued. "As a result, there will be rumors about us. People will whisper that you're not really a companion to Eushanie, but a mistress to me. But gossip doesn't bother you, does it?" He raised his eyes and gave her a pointed look. "From a moral standpoint? After all, every gentleman makes free with female servants. It's expected."

Tamasin stared at him. His nerves seemed to be stretched like bowstrings as he awaited her reply, waited to see if she would comply, or laugh. She knew well that Avery did not need her to stay here for the sake of his sister; he needed her here for himself.

And yet, just as Avery had discovered an unexpected need in those dark, strange hours, Tamasin had discovered one of her own. As she had listened to Avery whimpering, no less vulnerable than a boy wandering lost upon a moor, and later, as she had let him press his wet cheek against her bosom, she had known that he needed her strength. She thought of Hunter. He was strong and whole; he did not really need her. He needed no one, nothing but Ireland.

Avery awaited her answer, his fingers gripping the chair arm so fiercely the leather puckered beneath them. As she had done last night, she allayed his misery quickly, saying, "I'll stay, Avery."

His fingers stilled. "And do what I . . . require?"

"Yes."

Outside the gates of Hampton Hall, dawn arrived softly, a smudge of gray, a streak of apricot, a wash of pink watered down with pearl.

Wet and hungry, Hunter stood with his hands shoved in his pockets and stared through the iron gate, watching the house, the column-flanked front door, and the path leading up from the servants' entrance.

The night had left rain scattered over every surface, and it shimmered, dripped melodiously into rivulets. Birds sang and fluttered down to sip from puddles. Hunter paced.

Finally, he spied a female figure zigzagging through the yews. He straightened, thinking his vigil over at last, only to realize the girl was a young maid in a ruffled cap with a basket over her arm, likely on her way to shop in the village.

The maid gasped, surprised to see a roughly dressed person loitering at the gate. As if he might be a United Irishman come to do mischief, she eyed him with suspicion.

"I'm here to collect Tamasin Cullen," he said. "Would you fetch her, please."

"Tamasin Cullen . . . ?" she repeated, approaching slowly, warily. "You're here for Tamasin Cullen?"

"That's what I said. You must know she came up here last night."

At his manner, so chillingly anxious, the maid took a step backward. She knew him now, recognized the swarthy, lean face of the handsome groomsman. Intrigued by him in the way of most women, she stammered, "Tamasin Cullen will not be coming down."

"What?"

"Aye. Indeed, the house is all at sixes and sevens this morning. Master Avery barked at us to ready a room for her, then ordered the housekeeper to find her proper clothes and shoes. We were *that* surprised, we were, and didn't quite know what to make of it. But, after all, 'tis not our place to question the young master and his doings. We—"

The maid stopped speaking, for in the midst of her explanation, quite rudely and without a word, the groomsman had turned on his heel and strode away, leaving deep muddy tracks behind him in the road.

She put her hands on her hips and huffed. "What's got into him?"

Chapter Twenty

It seemed that all of Ireland was rapidly going mad, and that everyone, except those who were the most mad of all, existed in a suspended state of terror.

The Irish Militia, the Ancient Britons, and the Yeomanry were dispatched by the troubled government to crack down, viciously if necessary, on the rebellious countries where United Irishmen continued to wreak havoc on Protestant landholders. The landowners, the rebels insisted, were a breed of wastrels who, for centuries, had made the existence of the peasants miserable.

Like a rapidly spreading fire, the madness swept into Wexford, fanned by a cavalry of Yeomanry who claimed to be searching for pikes and weapons, but who were really out to crush the spirit of the United Irish. They gave the villagers fourteen days to surrender arms, to take an oath of loyalty to the government, and receive in exchange a paper promising protection from any acts of violence. Considering the reputation of the army, which had already swooped through other countries burning, raping, and murdering anyone suspected on the merest pretense of conspiracy, most Wexford Catholics clamored to turn in their pikes.

But the fourteen days had not passed when, breaking their word, the cavalry went on a rampage of destruction, committing outrages throughout the countryside, murdering cottiers as they plowed fields or stacked turf, arresting blacksmiths—all assumed to have forged pikes—and flogging them to extract secrets.

Women, for no greater crime than wearing green, the color of the United Irish, were seized in the streets by soldiers, stripped of their clothes with sword tips, and raped. Cabins were looted and burned, the smoke from their thatched roofs hovering continuously over the fair blue skies of May. Catholic rebels who were not already in jail were in hiding.

The gentry, terrified of retaliation by the rebel army—which had by no means been idle—barricaded themselves in their treasure-filled fortresses and prayed.

Often the patrolling cavalry stopped at Hampton Hall to demand refreshment, and on one such day Tamasin and Eushanie, standing behind a trestle table set up in the garden, served punch to a group of soldiers in scarlet tunics. The men strolled about carelessly squashing daffodils with their spurred boots, relieving themselves in the sculptured shrubbery, letting their horses roam in the budding rose beds. The spring breeze, which should have smelled fresh blowing over the meadow, was tainted by smoke. Even the social pleasantries exchanged between the officers and the two women were underlaid with tension. Tamasin and Eushanie could not help but notice the splatters of blood on the soldiers' white breeches.

"We'll put down the disturbance soon, ladies," one lieutenant assured them. Unlike others of his troop, he was a pleasant young officer, one Eushanie particularly favored since his hair was the color of Brendan's.

"They've captured Lord Edward Fitzgerald in Dublin," he commented. "Without his brains and money, the rebel cause will be severely crippled."

"Oh, the poor dear," Eushanie murmured. Then, in case the officer should think her disloyal, she stammered, "I—I mean, Lord Fitzgerald is misguided in his politics, of course, but so handsome. Or so they say."

"And not quite as clever as he believed himself to be. He was hiding in a lodging house and set his boots outside the door to be polished, forgetting that his name was tooled inside them. After his arrest the dragoons paraded him around Dublin Castle, waving his fancy green uniform, firing at the mob who tried to rescue him. Dublin is in chaos, ladies, dark as pitch at night. All the lamplighters—rebels every one—refuse to light the street lamps. The government is cracking down. Every day there are countless floggings. And hangings." Under his breath the lieutenant added, "What we're doing in Dublin—and *here*—is an outrage."

"You're surely the only one of your army who feels that way," Tamasin muttered.

"It would seem so."

Eushanie, touching her straggling hair in a gesture of nervous vanity, asked, "How is Brendan Kinshella, Lieutenant? Have you played cards with him in the village of late?"

The officer grinned. "Last night, as a matter of fact, Miss Hampton. He lost to me again. Good fellow." He glanced at Eushanie and added suspiciously, "Not a United Irishman, is he?"

The army routinely questioned residents in such a way, hoping to discover the names of rebel leaders. Eushanie blanched in fear. Brendan had never discussed politics with her, only poetry and sunsets. He had kissed her, too, of course, more than once, transforming her into a Juliette, a beautiful, desirable woman. The thought that he might be suspected of rebel involvement and transported to Dublin for trial terrified her.

"Good heavens, no!" she cried, defending her romantic hero. "Brendan was honorably discharged from the English army."

The lieutenant scoffed. "That means nothing where loyalty is concerned, Miss Hampton. Not these days. If we catch him—"

"Lieutenant," Tamasin interrupted smoothly, "may I serve you more punch?"

Flattered by her smile, the officer grinned and began to speak of more pleasant things.

After the troops had remounted and ridden away, churning up the lawn, Eushanie ran to the edge of the garden. Its lingering odor of saddle leather mingled with the bruised blossom scents and the acrid smoke that still drifted hazily from nearby cabins. Anxiously the girl looked toward the lodge, as if just by staring at its distant chimneys she might know whether or not Brendan was safe there.

Tamasin joined her, still relishing the feel of her new stiff petticoats laundered in real soap, the fit of her gray gown with its plain but good linen collar, and the comfort of her new shoes and beribboned straw bonnet.

How easily, how naturally she had fallen into life at Hampton Hall, as if she were born to it. She awoke every morning to a breakfast shared with Eushanie, the silver tray sometimes laden with poached eggs or currant muffins, or, because the young miss was partial to them, custard-filled pastries topped with sugared strawberries. Tea was served in early afternoon with plenty of orange butter and scones, then dinner at four, and supper at nine. Even if she were dining with Avery and Rafael, Eushanie always insisted that a tray be carried up to Tamasin, who never ate in the kitchen with the other servants—having a more elevated, if questionable, position than the rest.

The comforts of the house were a continual delight to Tamasin, and her determination to stay at Hampton Hall had hardened. It was not enough to be companion to a young lady of uncertain disposition and at the whim of a gentleman of even more uncertain motives. Now that she was ensconced between such beautiful walls, Tamasin could not bear the thought of returning to the fields to eat potatoes and leeks— or nothing at all. More obsessively than ever, she began to

imagine herself *belonging* to Hampton Hall. She knew that the
key to winning a permanent place lay not in pleasing Eushanie,
but in pleasing Avery. She must become indispensable to that
inward, tormented little boy who wandered lost and alone upon
his spiritual moor.

"Do you think Brendan's at the lodge, Tamasin?" Eushanie
asked now.

"I don't know, Miss. Your brother says all the servants have
bolted, run away until the country is at peace again. If they
stayed on, the rebels might accuse them of being loyal to the
gentry. The lodge has already been looted, you know. Your
father will be fortunate if it's not burned to the ground before
the rebellion is over. Empty it is, and unprotected, for the troops
cannot keep watch over it all the time."

"Yes. They say the enemy is out every night."

Tamasin looked out over the soft brilliant hills with their
variegated ribbons of green, their aquamarine pools, their ominous blue curls of smoke. Who was the enemy? Brendan?
Hunter? She wondered. In the last week, the men of the village
had had to choose one side or the other; neutrality was impossible. She felt certain Brendan would have joined the United
Irishmen by now, believing it easier to sign up than to resist.
But Hunter?

Like a remote but inescapable memory, the groomsman
seemed to always hover close. Sometimes she fancied she saw
him standing in the tree shadows, or caught his scent in the
fresh heather bundles the servants carried in for centerpieces.

Occasionally, she imagined she heard his voice when Eushanie plucked the strings of her gilded harp.

Perhaps, she thought, Hunter would always be with her,
mixed up in her conscience, in her roots. And within one
wayward piece of her heart. She missed him, missed him
unbearably.

Now Eushanie began to fuss with her hair, and as if Brendan
could see her dishevelment across the miles, turned to Tamasin

in exasperation. "Will you tuck this loose strand back inside its knot, please? I can't seem to manage."

While Tamasin performed the requested chore of vanity— one of many asked every day—she thought it odd that Eushanie, who had nothing at all to be vain about, was the most vain person she had ever known. Surprisingly, this fault touched her deeply. Tamasin sensed that, before her own arrival at Hampton Hall, Eushanie had been lonely.

With her eyes still fixed upon the mist-cloaked chimneys of the lodge, Eushanie mused, "Brendan promised me once that, when the time was right, he would ride up here to the garden and steal me away. He said he'd take me to a seashore where we could be alone and watch the sun rise and set. He said we'd be together always."

It was all Tamasin could do not to scoff and declare Brendan Kinshella full of blarney; of course, Eushanie would never believe anything spurious about her romantic ideal. Indeed, sometimes Tamasin wondered if the girl possessed the ability to distinguish the difference between fantasy and reality. She always carried a book tucked in her pocket, usually the much-thumbed version of Tristan and Isolde, which she often quoted as if it were a guide to life.

"If he promised, I'm sure he'll be riding up the lane for you someday," Tamasin reassured automatically. "Come now," she said, taking Eushanie's arm. "Twilight is falling. It's dangerous standing here in the open where a rebel's musket ball could find us."

Later, after Eushanie had shared her pot of raspberry tea with Tamasin and read aloud from a new shipment of books sent from London, Tamasin snuffed the candles, tidied the silver-backed brushes on the vanity, and watched the young lady climb beneath the lavender-scented sheets of the canopied bed. Free to go to her own adjoining chamber, she bade Eushanie good night and walked down the corridor.

Tamasin's room was not a room of grand proportions, but was filled with a framed mirror, a fire screen woven in delicate muted colors, and plenty of cherrywood furniture. Moonlight made a pool of silver on the floor and she hastened to shut the draperies.

The furniture had been moved well away from the windows, for when the bands of rebels were able to elude the patrols, they often made targets of the leaden panes of Hampton Hall. Indeed, last week a musket ball had come within an inch of the parlor maid's head while she went about snuffing candles at bedtime; consequently the whole staff ducked down whenever they dusted the windowsills or cleaned the glass.

Tamasin closed her eyes as her weary body sank down into the feather tick. She stretched as sensually as a cat before burrowing beneath the soft, scented quilt, so unlike the scratchy pallet at the cabin. The events of the day—the soldiers and their shining sabers, the frightening rumors, the brooding thoughts of Hunter—all whirled together in her head. She pulled the sheets over her eyes and shut them out, finally hovering on the outer fringes of sleep until Avery quietly entered the room.

In the fortnight she had been at Hampton Hall, the baronet's son had come to her almost a dozen times. Tonight, as usual, he had spent the evening closeted with Rafael and was half-drunk.

The ritual was the same every visit. She could hear the swish of fabric as he loosened his stock and removed his satin waistcoat. Wordlessly, he crossed the room, peering through the darkness at her face. Then, easing himself onto the bed still clothed, Avery pushed the covers aside and lay down beside her.

Tamasin put her arms about him. With a sigh he clasped her waist and relaxed. Finally, with his cheek pressed against her breast, his breathing grew rhythmic and sleep claimed him.

She eased his head onto the pillow and, free now to sleep herself, turned her back. She knew he would awake before dawn and, after waiting until the maid clattered upstairs with the coal buckets, amble out through her door in his rumpled evening clothes while loudly demanding a bath. Tamasin knew why he timed his departure as he did, knew what gossip filtered down to the kitchens and into the village streets. She knew, too, why the baronet's son wanted everyone to believe he kept a mistress.

Always when her arms grew weary from holding him, she thought of Hunter. The groomsman would never need to lean upon any woman's softer, frailer form out of fear or inadequacy. His feet were planted firmly upon the ground. And his soul, in order to allow it no erratic flights of fancy, was ruthlessly tethered to the iron of his own will.

Did Hunter dream?

She suspected he didn't. Not anymore.

Now, in the darkness, she heard Avery babble drunkenly, restlessly. "The rebels will come. They'll come. Soon, I fear. They'll . . . they'll try to take Hampton Hall away from me . . . won't they? Destroy it."

"Nay, Avery," she whispered, automatically reaching out a hand to stroke his head, soothe him. "The cavalry will keep them away."

"They can't, aren't enough of them. That . . . that damned groomsman of yours will be leadin' the savages. Bloody bastard . . ."

She waited patiently, until Avery grew still, then whispered, "No, Avery. No, he won't. Even if Hunter joins the rebels, he won't let them hurt us." After he had fallen asleep again, to reassure herself, she breathed, *"Hunter won't let them hurt us, because I am here."*

Even while the cottier's lass thought of him that night, Hunter Kinshella stood in the shabby back room of *The Hound,* his eyes focused not upon the surrounding weather-creased faces, but upon the dark landscape outside, which was framed in the bubbled tavern window.

"Raise your right hand," a gravelly voice ordered him.

He obeyed.

"Recite after me."

And he heard his own voice, uncoerced and deliberate, speaking the will of his own mind. "I believe in the Irish Union, in the supreme majesty of the people, in the equality of man, in the lawfulness of insurrection, and of resistance to oppression. I believe in a revolution founded on the rights of man, in the natural and imprescriptible right of *all* the Irish citizens to all the land . . . In this faith I mean to live, or bravely die."

Chapter Twenty-One

The Hamptons invited a party of friends to dine and dance, and despite the unsettled countryside and its roving bands of rebels, the guests ventured out, their thirst for entertainment greater than their fear.

Tamasin watched wide-eyed as the servants readied the Hall, lighting dozens of candles, setting out bowls of fresh flowers, and festooning the dining room with beribboned garlands of green. Aromas of roasted beef, delicately spiced sauces, and liqueur-filled desserts drifted up the stairs as she assisted Eushanie's maid with the final touches of her mistress's toilette. Although Eushanie wore a confection of satin and lace accented with yellow embroidered slippers, she seemed uninterested in her appearance or upon the guest list, which included several unmarried gentlemen. Earlier Tamasin had seen her sitting at her vanity table, dreamy-eyed, quill in hand, penning Brendan's name over and over again in lovely flourished letters.

The guests arrived from nearby estates in a perfumed and powdered stream, the ladies in silk and velvet, their hair ringetted and threaded with pale lengths of ribbon. The gentlemen wore black or plum or deep green, their eyes shining with the adventure of having traveled the dangerous roads. Of course all brought a bevy of armed footmen, and all sported a pistol or two beneath their brocaded waistcoats.

Tamasin watched from the landing, poised in shadow, gazing as candlelight glanced off bare white shoulders, golden bracelets, and the folds of crisp white linen. She imagined herself wearing such finery, could almost feel the draped texture of velvet against her skin and the cool feel of pearls looped about her throat.

As long as Eushanie stayed occupied with her guests, Tamasin was free to linger and absorb the sights and sounds of the genteel merriment, watch the subtle flirtations behind white-feathered fans and the posturing of wealthy gentlemen. It was only when a flustered maid ran up from the kitchen that Tamasin's fascinating pastime came to an end.

"We need help in the kitchen," the girl said breathlessly, grabbing Tamasin's arm and pulling her in that direction. "Maureen took sick and is lying down with a fever, and Cook is all in a dither. Quit your gawking and come with me."

Tamasin hastened with no complaint to help whip a meringue, stir a thickening gravy over the stove, and slice cheeses. Finally, after dinner had been served and the ladies and gentlemen were at last ensconced in the drawing room listening to Eushanie play the harp, Tamasin stepped outside for air. The windows were open and she could hear the music clearly, as it blended with the sounds of the wind in the crooked oaks. She closed her eyes for a moment, breathing sweet garden air, catching snippets of laughter and the distant clink of crystal glasses. Eushanie's fingers coaxed from the harp strings a soft and rhythmic melody, and Tamasin moved her feet, danced a few small dreamy steps, imagining herself swaying in a man's arms amongst all the laughing ladies and gentlemen upstairs.

Footsteps other than her own rapped upon the flagstones and she opened her eyes, focused them in the dark night upon the face and form of the groomsman. She stopped. Her pulse increased, and the lurching of her stomach caused her to realize how forcefully Hunter still affected her. She had not seen him since the night they had lain together upon the hillside, the night she had given herself to Avery in trade for Hunter's life, but he had never left her thoughts.

For several seconds he regarded her without speaking, studying her, his eyes moving from her head to her toes and back again as if the sight of her affected him with no less strength. At last, in a low tone he asked, "Haven't you a dancing partner tonight?"

Tamasin was too self-possessed to be embarrassed. Ordinarily she would have countered with some quip, but found herself too overwhelmed by the sight of him to offer banter.

How good he looked! So tall and solid and real, no less enduring than the fields and the sky. For a few moments she felt compelled to run to him and be held, receive the comfort and safety of his body. Yet she did not. He would shove her away in disgust, consider her beneath his attentions and his touch now that she had become Avery Hampton's woman. He'd surely heard the rumors, even if they weren't precisely true. She felt a sharp pang of regret and sorrow all at once, a heartbreak that she had lost his respect.

Unable to think of anything significant to say, scarcely able to trust her own voice, she faltered, "Why are you here?"

"A boy from the Hall brought me a message a while ago. He said they needed a crate of claret carried here from the lodge cellar." Hunter glanced up at the open casement window with its spill of amber candlelight and added, "The gentlemen have already drunk Hampton Hall dry, it seems."

Humor played in his voice and Tamasin couldn't suppress the tug of a smile. She struggled to find conversation, afraid the groomsman would think she cared not to converse with him, dismiss her and go. Hastily, lamely, she blurted, "Have you been well these last weeks, Hunter?"

"Well enough." He paused. "And you?"

"I'm well, of course." And she believed the words as she

uttered them, ignoring the tiny niggling doubt, the remembrance of a pooled cathamore against sweet night grass, the remembrance of the handsome groomsman and what he had offered her.

"Are you?" The words brimmed with skepticism.

"I am. After all, I have just about all I've ever wanted, don't I?" Tamasin spoke with her chin tilted up, and added a few last words to remind him that she had not forgotten her ambition. "For now, at least."

Hunter's anger, brooding just beneath the hard shell of his pride, surfaced quickly at her reminder. It galled him that he had been cast off so easily for someone else—a rival that he considered despicable and less than a man. Being near Tamasin again brought him a rush of yearning, a tightening of the heart, a need he had tried and failed to fulfil with other women. Although he knew torment doing so, he allowed his gaze to sweep Tamasin's soft black hair, then her trim figure in its neat well-fitting gown, then her young pale face so full of the glow of triumph. He did not begrudge her the good and plentiful food, the rich-panelled rooms, the clothes that Hampton Hall provided. He only resented her happiness with its master.

Suddenly an instinct to spoil that happiness snapped with him. He clenched his jaw to try and suppress it, but the instinct overrode even his great pride, and he smiled a twisted half smile. He would deliver to Tamasin his own reminder of the bond between them, make her feel the same eradicable ache as he. Reaching out to take hold of her arm, speaking in a silky voice, he said, "A damsel should not dance alone."

She resisted at first, tried to elude him, but his fingers closed about her elbow, pulled her close. His other arm encircled her waist. Hunter suffered the mad urge to carry her away, force her from Hampton Hall, ride with her to some place or land where she would forget, at least for a night or two, everything in her mind but him. He yearned for her devotion, knowing that she could love fiercely if she chose, knowing that her heart held the same dark wildness as his. Closing his eyes, he felt his face twist with longing as Tamasin ceased to resist and moved with him to the faint strum of Eushanie's harp strings.

Their movements melted together, and Tamasin recalled their jig beside a bonfire, that wild lively dance so different from this slow, floating sway, but a dance no less thrilling. Now Hunter created steps of his own that matched the time of the music, that allowed her to follow him with natural ease. As her body felt the heat of his, the strength of it, she experienced one of the rare, ungraspable moments of completeness that she found only with him. If only the groomsman could transformed himself in that moment, she thought, crystallize into a gentleman who could keep her safe from poverty, from the peat-filled cabins down the road. The thought, unbidden but strong, brought her guilt.

In his uncanny way Hunter seemed to sense what had passed through her mind, for his hand squeezed hers as if to force her from the clouds, as if to remind her who he was. The groomsman, he was, and no one else.

Tamasin faltered and would have pulled away, but he would not allow her distance and drew her back again, lowering his lips to hers before she could protest, kissing them as he said, "I'll spoil you for him. When he touches you, you'll remember me . . . "

And he held her so that she could not go away, kissed her deeply, thoroughly, with a rough demanding intimacy whose meaning she could neither resist nor deny. She kissed him in kind, as wild as he, breathless and young and unsated.

It was Hunter who forced the embrace to end at last, putting her away from him, staring at her in the darkness with his brows drawn together. "You love me, lass. Aye, you do. You both love and despise what I am."

Her eyes locked with his, and her lips, still bruised from his, parted, but no words came forth.

"Ah, I pity us both, Tamasin," Hunter finished with a harsh release of breath. Bitterness edged his tone as he turned to go. "But I pity you more."

Tamasin stood staring after the groomsman, watching him walk away, suffering an abysmal loneliness as his words continued to echo in her ears. They had been sincere words, true.

The cry of a night bird recalled her to time and place, and she shivered, then shook herself and wandered slowly back inside the Hall. The guests had all gone, and through the dining room doors she could see Eushanie moving about the room while Avery and Rafael idled over an assortment of half-empty crystal decanters. Avery's face was flushed, his stock askew, his brocade jacket and waistcoat tossed on the back of his chair. The Italian was more sober, his smooth brown cheeks only slightly ruddy.

Tamasin had had little contact with the Italian, only passing him occasionally in the corridors, but she had come to realize that in the world of gently-bred people, he was of a distinct and probably not too rare breed. Refined and well-traveled, he, like Avery and Sir Harry, seemed to believe there could be no other reason for life except the pursuit of ease. She suspected he had no money of his own, and therefore found it necessary to enjoy Avery's. He jealously guarded the baronet's son, hovering close, giving Eushanie impatient stares when she dared to interrupt their male solitude, positively glaring at Tamasin if she ventured too close during their drunken routs.

Truthfully, sadly, Tamasin could not condemn him for it; she supposed Rafael was not so different from herself. Perhaps the impoverished aristocrat's alternative to Hampton Hall was a wandering road, too; but one of art galleries and damask-hung salons where another rich patron would have to be found in order to save him the hardship of living a shabby life.

And yet, the Italian's presence troubled Tamasin, for Avery seemed to fear him in some unpleasant way she had yet to put a finger on.

Eushanie had sat down at the harp again and begun another haunting song, and Tamasin loitered in the corridor to listen, too restless to go to her room and rest. She listened almost a quarter-hour as Eushanie's soft square hands plucked the taut strings, thinking of Hunter even while she gazed at Avery. She fell so deep into thought that she jumped as a musket cracked outside.

Eushanie rose to her feet in alarm.

Simultaneously, the heavily draped window across the room shattered just as the great barred front door collapsed beneath a ramming, shuddering force.

"God in heaven!" Eushanie screamed.

"Come with me!" Tamasin gripped her hand to yank the girl forward, but the women hadn't time enough to take two steps before a band of ragged, fierce-eyed men clambered into the house. Whooping a spine-tingling cry, the brigands rushed inside brandishing every sort of weapon imaginable. The servants screamed and fled in all directions. Eushanie and Tamasin crouched in a corner, and in horror watched the invaders. Using ten-foot pikes they scarred wainscoting and ripped the Chinese wallpaper. Their rusty swords cut swaths through the fragile salon furniture. Even amid the nerve-shattering chaos Tamasin recognized the weathered faces, and at first could not bring herself to fear her former neighbors, the cottiers, coopers, glazers, and cabinet makers. All about her, filthy hands slipped silver candlesticks into trusty pockets, muddy boots soiled carpets, pikes gouged the scrolled plasterwork and the damask upholstery and the glossy oil paintings. She cried out in protest when the blacksmith began to rip a plank of hardwood off the floor with no more than a broken knife and his black-nailed hands.

"Leave it be!" she ordered, grabbing a fire tool from beside the hearth to threaten him.

He laughed, lunging to grab her skirts, but she eluded him, frantically searching for Eushanie.

The girl darted through the vestibule and screeched hysterically for her brother. Nearby, Rafael disappeared through the dining room door with the ease of a fox, leaving the drunken Avery to stagger to his feet and bellow inanely, "Where's the damn patrol . . . ?"

Resembling an army of ants invading a honeycomb, the rebels swept through the house. Bent upon destruction and thievery they ravaged every item in sight, taking revenge upon a way of life they believed responsible for generations of hunger and poverty. One brute cut the strings of Eushanie's harp. Another—Loftus, the footman from the lodge—smashed all the crystal decanters on the dining room table with one vicious swipe of his arm. Other scavengers slid porcelain plates in their waistbands or made targets of the dining room portraits. The sound of splintering glass, thudding feet, and crashing furniture created a terrifying roar.

The servants scurried about like mice in a roomful of hungry cats, scrambling for hiding places, crying out when the bravest among them, an under-footman, died at the hands of a pike-wielding ironsmith.

Tamasin could think of nothing but the pair of pistols in the library, lying primed and loaded in a cherrywood box upon Avery's desk. Frenziedly she searched for Eushanie in the melee, finally finding her tripping over her skirts in an effort to climb the grand curving staircase. A cottier with rabid eyes and a knife in his hand pursued the young girl, reaching out to seize a handful of her flying silk skirts.

Tamasin sprinted after them, wielding her fire tool. She knew that if Sir Harry's daughter were caught by the rebels, she might be abducted and forced into marriage, then raped and abandoned in disgrace. It was an outrage that had been repeated many times in other counties.

Just as the savage cottier caught hold of Eushanie's ankle, Tamasin hurled the fire tool at his head. He reeled beneath the blow, stunned, then tumbled down the stairs. Breathlessly, Tamasin clasped Eushanie hand and dragged her toward the library, which was as yet undiscovered by the rampaging marauders.

Her large slippered feet unaccustomed to quickness, Eushanie stumbled along, then crouched behind the massive library desk while Tamasin, with cool practical fingers, unlocked the

cherrywood box and removed one of the silver-chased pistols.
When menacing footsteps breached the threshold, the cottier's
lass wheeled about, and with both hands on the heavy dueling
weapon, squeezed the trigger.

The intruder gasped, fell, then made a huddled pool of rags
upon the carpet, where his blood created a stain as bright as
the ruby wool weave.

"You've killed him, Tamasin!" Eushanie quavered excitedly, her eyes fastened on the body. "You've killed him!"

Ignoring her, Tamasin took up the other loaded pistol and
aimed it at the door, prepared for the next intruder.

But a sudden hoarse shout echoed through the corridor, warning the rebel band. "The patrol, ye fools! The Yeomanry troops
are comin' up the road! Get out while ye can!"

Two dozen pairs of worn boots began to pound a retreat
through the Hall. On the way out, the brutes crammed countless
small treasures into their already bulging pockets and smashed
any object too large to steal. A few raided the sideboard in the
dining room, stuffing handfuls of strawberries and cheese into
their mouths or devouring sweetmeats.

"Avery!" Eushanie cried in alarm. "Where is my brother?"

Tamasin pushed past and ran toward the dining room, discovering the horrendous ruin there, the smashed vases, the
drooping wallpaper, the sliced portraits of Hampton ancestors.
Avery was not in evidence. Even his discarded jacket and
waistcoat, which she had last seen hanging on the back of his
chair, had been purloined.

White-faced servants, like terrified dormice, began to creep
out of hidey-holes. Upon orders from Thackary the butler, they
started a halfhearted search for their missing young master.

"Avery!" Tamasin called, rushing from ravaged room to
ravaged room, pushing aside the debris to look in vain for
him. Finally, she ran headlong into Rafael, who materialized
suddenly from behind a plum velvet portiere.

"They carried him out," he announced as if the baronet's

son had been a marble bust or a piece of furniture. "I saw the damned rebels dragging him across the yard toward the road."

Tamasin put her hands to her face in dread and breathed, "His life will be worth nothing to them."

Thackary sent a group of reluctant male servants outside to search. The Yeomanry troops belatedly arrived, their horses' hooves clattering raucously on the gravel drive. Informed of the raid, the soldiers poked through the garden shrubbery, searched the road, and galloped around the park in the quest. But after an hour of desperate hunting, there was no sign at all of Hampton Hall's young master.

Fearing that he had been murdered, a tearful Eushanie was dosed with herbal tea and finally coaxed to lie down in bed. Downstairs, the polite young cavalry lieutenant spoke with Rafael in low tones, assuring him that the search would resume at first light.

Tamasin slowly proceeded to her own chamber. She, too, feared the worse. The rebels often tortured their victims before killing them, and Avery had always been despised by his father's tenants.

As she washed her hands in the basin, Tamasin felt a sudden quivering in her limbs, a nervous reaction to the horrible night. A vision of the man she had shot to death flashed behind her reddened eyes; she could see vividly his ragged clothes, seamed face, and staring eyes. Sainted Mary. She had murdered a man, one with a family no doubt. He had probably been half-starved, as well, and inflamed by the lofty promises of the United Irishmen. How cool her hands had been upon the pistol. She wondered if men felt such composure in war, such an absence of conscience when they killed.

She had not yet undressed when the boy from the kitchen scratched on her door and, with no explanation, handed her a tattered old copy of the *Wexford Chronicle*. Nonplussed, she stared at it, then noticed a message scrawled in the margins.

I'll be at the lodge gate in an hour if you care to meet me.

*I might know where to find Avery Hampton. If so, I suspect
he'll need a change of clothes.*

Tamasin had never seen a sample of his handwriting before,
but had no doubt that this open, careless scrawl—nearly as
illegible as the groomsman's own nature—belonged to Hunter
Kinshella.

Not wanting to alert anyone in the house, she crept about in
order to gather a bundle of Avery's clothing. The other servants
were occupied with the task of salvaging what they could of
the house, ordered by Thackary to forego a night's sleep and
wield scrub brushes and brooms to eradicate the mud, blood,
and scattered debris of porcelain and glass.

The Yeomanry patrol had dispersed in their search for Avery,
and only a pair of guards now lounged about the iron gates,
inattentive and sleepy, not expecting the rebels to return twice
in one night. Slipping out of the house, Tamasin struck for the
lodge, flitting through the damp mossy shadows so that the
moonlight would not illumine her hastening figure and catch
the attention of some nervous cavalryman with a cocked and
loaded pistol.

Nighttime in the fells frightened her. The wind whirred eerily
over the hills, underground channels burbled, and pagan spirits
seemed to hover about the jumbled ruins of long-ago temples,
joining forces with the hungry, roving rebels and the ruthless
patrols. Before long the hem of her gown grew sodden and her
shoes muddy. Her eyes burned with the effort of finding her
way through the maze of hedges and ditches, any of which
could conceal desperate men. She clambered over an earthen
hedge rather than trespass across the barren fairy rath, then
discerned the black iron gates of the lodge, their spiked tops
brushed with lavender moonlight.

Suddenly a hand clamped over her mouth and the hard form
of a man pressed against her spine. A scream rose in her throat,
dying as she recognized the familiar heat, the familiar scent of
the groomsman.

"Softly," Hunter warned in a whisper. "There's a soldier

stationed very near—over there by the stand of oaks beside
the road.''

He released her, and Tamasin turned to face him. How tall
and dark and vital he appeared against the night sky! But despite
his appearance of indomitability, she knew Hunter was in danger. Roughly dressed and commonly spoken, he would surely
be suspected of the looting of Hampton Hall if he were discovered in the fields. Therefore, when he wordlessly motioned for
her to follow, she obeyed as quietly as possible, trailing his
noiseless step, struggling to keep up with his long-legged stride.

The groomsman traversed the wet rough paths with his musket in hand, his eyes scanning the black landscape vigilantly.
Tamasin jogged behind him as quietly as possible, panting and
stumbling, relieved when he at last slowed his merciless pace.

Out of breath and cold with fear, she asked, ''Where are we
going, Hunter?''

His eyes swept the darkness and he would say nothing more
than, ''You'll know when we get there.''

Tamasin shifted the heavy bundle of clothes she had been
carrying under one arm and studied Hunter's grim, watchful
face with sudden surprise. ''You knew about the attack on
Hampton Hall, didn't you?''

His gaze continued to sweep the sapphire hills, the distant
road, and the nearby river, which winked with stray bars of
moonlight. The lowing of cattle floated on the chill air, and
the wind snaked through the grasses to send an eddy of withered
whirling.

''I knew,'' he said simply, tersely.

''Did you know about the raid in advance?'' she demanded,
accusation in her tone.

''Perhaps.''

At his deliberate evasion Tamasin clenched her fists and
censured him. ''You *did* know. You knew they were coming
to ravage the Hall. God in heaven!'' she cried, both incredulous
and outraged. ''Why did you not warn us, Hunter? Do you
condone murder of innocent people?''

At last, the groomsman swung to face her, and even in darkness she could see the fierceness of his eyes. "Innocent people? Do you think my loyalty lies with Hampton Hall?" he hissed. "Do you believe that just because you suffer no qualms about toadying to the gentry that the rest of us have no pride as well?"

"No, but—" She broke off, almost saying, "But what about me? *I* was inside Hampton Hall when the devils came! Do you not care about me?" A few moments of telling silence passed before Tamasin finished lamely, " 'Twas savage what the rebels did there."

Hunter looked away, fixed his eyes upon a distant hill and spoke low. "It might have been worse, I assure you. Much worse."

Frustrated by his maddening obliqueness, she glanced at him and asked sharply, "What do you mean?"

But the groomsman did not reply. He began his relentless pace again, his stride long and agile as he covered the precarious ground with noiseless speed.

Hefting the bundle of clothes, Tamasin followed in exasperation, running in order to catch up. "Has Avery been harmed?" she demanded in a whisper, plucking at his sleeve.

He neither stopped nor missed a step. "I would expect so."

"Have you seen him?"

"No."

Despite her continued questioning, Tamasin's escort would offer nothing more in explanation; instead he increased his pace yet again, the May night-breeze ruffling his black hair, his back a broad hostile wedge in front of her eyes.

Before long, they came upon a churchyard mottled with moonlight and mist, its lichen-brushed headstones limned in radiance and casting steely shadows. The church slept. Its square Roman tower rose toward a remote heaven, and its yard gate hung askew, set within crumbling walls that had seen so many seasons that the stains of time streaked the mellow-colored stones.

Bewildered, frightened, Tamasin followed Hunter through and, glancing about, felt the chill of death settle in her bones. Bunches of pallid flowers, left by grieving widows, draped rows of fresh, still mounded graves. The deceased were the victims of rebellion, she realized, most of them Catholic poor felled by government swords.

Hunter stopped and stood without speaking. Tamasin saw what he had brought her to the churchyard to see. The sight of it, so unreal, so unnatural and gruesomely unexpected, left her paralyzed for several moments.

Ten feet away, wedged between the rows of tilted black crosses, a disembodied head hovered above the ground.

Tamasin put her hands over her mouth to smother a scream.

" 'Tis your lover," Hunter said shortly.

His callousness helped Tamasin to muster the courage to inch forward. As she neared, she realized that Avery Hampton had been buried to the neck. She had heard tales of such atrocities, knew that more than one gang of rebel peasants had buried an abducted gentleman alive, just as they felt they themselves had been buried for generations beneath a system of unjust rule.

Tamasin ran forward, knelt down upon the mound of earth, touched the fair, matted hair, the still warm head. "Avery . . . ?" she breathed.

A sound issued from his bruised white lips, a faint whimpering sigh, but Avery's eyes remained closed, and his head lolled at a peculiar angle.

Tamasin began to dig, clawing the earth with her hands, wondering in fear how battered the body was beneath the soil.

Hunter had disappeared round the corner of the church, and at first, with alarm, she thought he meant to leave her. But a moment later he came striding up with a shovel in hand, and without a word, stabbed at the earth, systemically exhuming the baronet's son from the rebels' hole.

Staggering to her feet, Tamasin stood back, leaving him to the grim task, watching him thrust and throw the dirt aside as she mouthed a prayer for Avery. In dreams she would feel again the peculiar chill of the churchyard, the icy May mist; she would hear again the hard scrape of the shovel and Hunter's even breaths.

But most of all she would remember the groomsman as he threw aside the shovel, leaned down, and placed his hands beneath the arms of Avery Hampton. She would remember him as he dragged the baronet's son out, left Avery's naked body lying on the dark wet grass.

For a few seconds Tamasin remained rooted in place. Then, realizing Hunter would not do it for her, she yanked Avery's clothes from the bag and awkwardly covered his nakedness.

"The Hall . . . " Avery mumbled through cut and bleeding lips, his eyes still closed. "Did they burn . . . the Hall?"

"Nay," Tamasin assured him gently. " 'Tis still standing. And Eushanie is unharmed."

Hunter stood motionlessly by during the exchange. His long straight black shadow cast itself over Tamasin's trembling hands, and although he said nothing, he watched her so intently that she felt the coldness of his eyes.

"Avery's wrists—they're bound," she murmured.

The groomsman produced a knife from his belt, and tossed it down a few inches from Avery's head.

Tamasin stared at its quivering wooden hilt, then at the groomsman's wintry eyes, realizing that Hunter refused to do the task himself. She wrenched the knife from the ground and, bending over Avery's hands, began to saw at the thongs. Clumsily, she hacked away, feeling inept, knowing Hunter's strong sure hands could have accomplished the chore in one swift slice.

When the last shred of leather fell away and Avery's wrists parted, she tossed the knife aside. Knowing he needed warmth, she grabbed a jacket from the bundle of clothing and slid it over the length of his torso.

Hunter's gaze remained fastened unwaveringly upon her hands as she tended the baronet's son. Tamasin could feel his eyes, the sharp contempt in them, the heat in them. Her fingers quivered. Unable to help herself, she glanced up again.

In that moment she felt as if she herself were naked. As she stared into the groomsman's eyes, her hands stilled upon Avery's ruffled shirtfront, and she knew precisely what was passing through Hunter's mind.

He was envisioning her and the baronet's son together.

His fists were balled at his thighs and his jaw throbbed, but he did not look away from the two of them. Instead, as he held her eyes, Hunter seemed to concentrate more intently than ever upon the carnal vision he imagined taking place repeatedly on the scented sheets of a grand feathered bed. Did he see her limbs entwined with those of the baronet's son? Tamasin wondered with a sudden sharp pain.

She swallowed, mesmerized, agonized, suddenly knowing that Hunter forced himself to envision her in Avery's embrace. He was destroying—or trying to destroy—the remaining vestiges of whatever it was he felt for her. He was attempting to murder the last lingering proof of his feelings.

All at once, beneath Tamasin's hands, Avery began to rouse. Managing to brace himself on his elbows, he coughed convulsively and emitted a feeble moan. Putting an arm about him, Tamasin murmured words she did not hear, her eyes still riveted to Hunter's hard, dark face. She knew he was about to pivot and stalk away, file through the headstones and out through the gaping churchyard gate. She did not want him to go. Grabbing his knife from the ground, she held it up to him in offer. Her eyes pleaded for one parting word from him, one soft farewell, an acknowledgement that he cared at least enough to say goodbye.

He stretched out a hand and, taking hold of the sharp blade rather than allow his fingers to touch hers upon the hilt, slid the weapon into his coat.

"Hunter!" Tamasin spoke instinctively, with a frantic concern. She feared for him on this eve of rebellion, wondered when—wondered *if*—she would see him again, and where, under what circumstances. Would he fight with the rebels? Next time, when a raiding party invaded Hampton Hall, would he be one of their wild and pillaging ranks?

He turned to leave.

"Hunter—" she appealed again, helplessly. She wanted to keep him a moment longer, to impart something of her feelings. Self-consciously she removed her hands from Avery's chest and clenched them in her lap. Then, she stood up and, holding Hunter's icy stare, faltered, "I-I'm grateful. You performed an act of mercy tonight. You risked yourself, acted decently. I suspect—" she stammered, trailed the words, then took a breath and finished. "I suspect you did it for me—"

"Don't say anything more," the groomsman cut in harshly, pivoting. His voice was low and full and his back rigid. "Don't say anything at all, Tamasin. You have what you want, what you've always wanted. Keep yourself safe with it. If you can."

Chapter Twenty-Two

How quickly the country of craggy bays and emerald dales turned topsy-turvy, became a battlefield of scarlet wool against brown corduroy.

Before the month of May had entered its last quarter, the United Irish army had gained control of not only the county of Kildare bordering Dublin, but had won command of the strategic roads leading south toward Cork and Limerick. In their need to protect the capital against siege, the government could spare to dispatch only minimal troops to the ever-spreading sites of rebellion. Consequently, the rebels were able to accomplish several important victories.

Only a few miles north of Wexford, after a horrific battle, the village of Enniscorthy had been captured by United Irishmen. Refugees—landed families who had only a few days earlier enjoyed all the genteel comforts of privilege—began straggling stunned and possessionless toward the port city, leaving their homes and town burning behind them. At Wexford they begged the fishermen to give them passage anywhere. Having little sympathy but a quick eye for opportunity, the Catholic boat owners charged an exorbitant twelve guineas a head for a one-way trip to Wales. Not all the unfortunates were able to secure a space in the crowded holds, and so, while the government troops barricaded the ancient town gates and handed out muskets to the gentlemen, hoards of gently-bred women and children, in a turnabout of fortune, wandered the streets begging shelter and food.

Short of manpower, the government army did nothing to help them. The troops were too busy preparing for a rebel attack, stripping the town roofs of thatch in case the savages should torch it.

At Hampton Hall the inhabitants lived in dread, expecting an attack at any moment. They were afraid to sleep at night, avoided windows, moved through the corridors in a hushed and fine-strung alertness, while feeling like trapped rabbits awaiting a hunter's return. Escape was impossible, for the roads were fraught with danger, and traveling by coach was tantamount to waving a red flag at any marauding band of United Irishmen one happened to pass. Horses were commandeered by either army, just as, weeks earlier, the lodge thoroughbreds had been pressed into government service, probably never to be seen again.

Recuperating from his ordeal, Avery limped about the scarred and half-patched halls of his elegant fortress, pistol at his side, both his eyes still showing signs of their blackening at the hands of the rebels, every line of his well-fleshed body coiled with the need for revenge.

"Nothing but barbarians overrunning Ireland," he growled often, speaking to Tamasin when Eushanie nervously hid her face in a book or when Rafael wandered off to shoot billiards alone. "They're rising in the north now. The news from Dublin confirms that the French are preparing to land in Ireland to aid the rebel cause. Damn Napoleon!"

"But didn't the French plan to land in Ireland once before and fail?" Tamasin asked.

"Yes. Two years ago at Bantry Bay. They intended to sweep

through our country and liberate it—as they termed it—before marching down to London to conquer the king. But a blizzard kept them from landing their ships, and the plot was foiled."

"And you honestly believe they'll be sailing here again, at any time, to aid the rebels?"

"I fear so."

During their talks of insurrection, Avery made no mention of his capture at the hands of the United Irishmen, or of the weirdly terrifying night he had spent in a cemetery, or of Hunter Kinshella's rescue. It was if those events had never occurred, even though they had left their mark in the form of a bruised face and broken ribs. The slight unsteadiness of Avery's hands, his endless, jerky pacing about the house with a loaded pistol in hand showed his nervousness, too.

He seemed to find solace only in Tamasin's arms, which he began to seek almost every night. He confided in her, murmured tales of his lonely childhood, spoke as one might to a friend. She always listened patiently, saying nothing, doing nothing except stroking his head with a soothing hand. And strangely, Tamasin knew that Avery might have cared for her, might even have voiced his fondness, if it had ever occurred to him that his affection for a cottier's lass was possible.

On a late day in May, when the primroses spread themselves like a blanket across the turf and foxgloves spiralled like miniature fairy towers around the bogs, when their scent and the amber sunshine proved too great a lure to resist, Tamasin and Eushanie crept outside the protective walls of Hampton Hall to idle in the now-abandoned garden.

There, the daffodil petals quivered in the moorland breeze while tansy and fern and queen's wort sprouted in the untended beds. The sun warmed the earth, making it difficult to believe anything was amiss anywhere in the world, impossible to accept that an army of peasants amassed nearby to overturn a centuries-old way of life and declare it their turn to be master.

The two women sat on a stone bench. They leaned back and closed their eyes to absorb the sun, and with it, an illusory sense of wellbeing after days of strain. Tamasin was the first to hear the faint, alarming rustle of leaves.

Straightening, she turned warily, astounded to see a familiar golden head pop up out of the rhododendrons behind them. "Brendan!" she exclaimed.

Eushanie leapt from her seat and, with no abashment, hurled herself into his waiting arms. With the natural ease of a practiced lover, Brendan's hands encircled her corsetted, muslin-covered waist. His grin was wide and puckish as he winked over her shoulder at Tamasin.

"Are you insane, Brendan?" Tamasin hissed, glancing round apprehensively toward the house. "If Avery catches you, he'll be emptying his pistol into your foolish hide."

"I've no doubt of it," he returned with a cavalier shrug, refusing to be drawn into the discussion of a serious topic. "But it's been weeks since I've had the pleasure of seeing you ladies, and being in the neighborhood, I could not resist a call."

"Where have you been all this time?" Eushanie fretted, putting her hands on either side of his face, searching it for signs of harm. "Have you been off fighting?"

"Aye. Hunter and I fought at Enniscorthy two days ago. There's quite a celebration going on there now, a fair amount of drinking, flag raising, and dancing in the streets—or what's left of them."

As he elaborated on his war exploits, Eushanie's complexion came as close as it ever could to radiance, even if she guessed— which she probably did not—that half his tales of swordplay and heroism were exaggerated. Raising a hand to her hair in one of her unconscious gestures of vanity, she asked him worriedly, "You're certain you're not injured, Brendan . . . "

"I have a talent for keeping myself out of harm's way, my darlin'. Quite the opposite of my brother, of course, who must ever get himself into the thick of things. Always brash, Hunter is, fighting at the fore, devilishly good at leading the men. That band of ragtags have made him a major. And you may call me Lieutenant Kinshella."

"A lieutenant!" Eushanie exclaimed in rapture.

"What will happen here, Brendan?" Tamasin cut in tensely. "Is a rebel force on its way?"

He lifted a shoulder. "Who knows what that lot of croppies will decide to be doing. But, Eushanie, my love," he said, turning to the moonstruck lady and changing the subject with one of his disarming grins, "have you got a bit of the ready you could loan a poor soldier? Not government pound notes—they're being used as musket wadding. I need coin."

"Musket wadding . . . ?" Tamasin echoed.

"Aye. The rebels are so confident of overthrowing Dublin, they believe paper currency is already worthless."

"I haven't got any coins," Eushanie said, stricken at her inability to help. "Avery has cut me off. But here—" she began to fumble with the pin fastened at her lace collar, a bird-shaped piece encrusted with pearls and set in gold.

When she pressed it into his hand, Brendan rewarded her with a kiss, not a chaste one, but one meant to excite, to make a woman feel possessed, to insure that a virgin with dreamy eyes would remember him and be eagerly awaiting his call, should he ever chose to make one again. "Thank you, my love," he whispered. "I'm forever indebted to you. Now look at what I've done—put tears in your pretty eyes . . . "

A few minutes later, Brendan left Eusanie in a torrent of tears. He winked at Tamasin, who ran a few steps after him and tugged at his sleeve. To make certain they could not be seen from the windows of the house, she pulled him beneath the shade of a beech tree and asked, "Brendan, where's Hunter?"

For a few seconds he scrutinized her face, wariness flashing in his light blue eyes. After a moment of consideration he said, "Sometimes he can be found at the lodge at night, lass. Inside the house. He's hidden a horse there."

"Could I find him tonight, do you think?"

"If he wants to be found. And in this case," Brendan touched the tip of her nose and grinned, "I suspect that he does."

Tamasin took his thin, warm hands, wondering if this farewell would be their last. "God be with you, Brendan," she whispered, moisture in her eyes.

He smiled, a creature fashioned of little more than blue skies and golden air, and gave her a gentleman's deep bow. "And with you, milady Tamasin."

The journey to the lodge, made in darkness when two opposing armies camped nearby, was a venture of madness. Tamasin carried a pistol, one Avery had given her in case she should need to defend Eushanie again. Even after days of practice, his poor nearsighted sister still could not hit a target placed two feet in front of her eyes.

Tamasin carried it cocked and hidden in her skirt pocket as she hastened over the fields, but encountered nothing more threatening than a young fox darting through a hedgerow. And yet, when she arrived safely at the familiar back stoop of the lodge kitchen, where thistle now grew in the neglected herb garden, her heart did not slow its uneven hammering.

Cautiously she pushed open the stout door, its latch broken by the butt of some rebel's musket, then stepped inside the dark kitchen. The smell of hay and horse greeted her nostrils. A shadowy shape, the steed itself—Sir Harry's greatest racer—sidled nervously toward the stone sink, its iron-shod hooves chipping the flagstone of the empty kitchen. As it blew in and out to catch her scent, its breaths sounded unnervingly loud.

"Hunter . . . ?" Tamasin called in a soft, tentative voice. Hearing no reply, she moved through the dusty passageway, a black corridor that led her to an eerily familiar place. Once comfortably filled with old, lovely things, the great trophy room was now as cavernous as an abandoned tomb.

A single sputtering candle lit the place where gentlemen had once drunk claret, played billiards, and wagered. The thin yellow light revealed walls stripped of their panelling, mantelpieces pried from hearths, floorboards gone, not a single item of any value left. Only Sir Harry's hunting trophies—a line of antlered heads accompanied by flying pheasants and stuffed trout—remained mounted upon the gouged walls, oddly gruesome remnants of a sporting way of life now either vanished or temporarily interrupted according to history's coming tide.

The hunting prizes and the guttering candle were the only occupants of the room, save one. A man sat on an overturned crate, a pistol in hand and a sheaf of papers at his feet. His hair was rumpled, his face dark with a day's growth of beard, and his jaw marred by a thin slash—from battle no doubt.

Without surprise, Hunter Kinshella regarded Tamasin as she stood uncertainly upon the threshold, and she sensed that he had known she would come. Intimidated, uneasy, she kept her distance, saying nothing at first. Hunter neither rose to his feet nor offered her a greeting.

"Sir Harry's horse . . . " she ventured at last, just to speak, delaying what she had come to say. She could not voice her request just yet, baldly and without preamble.

"What would you like to know about the horse?" he asked cooly, cocking a brow. "Whether I've stolen it or not?"

"I simply wondered—"

"My grandfather trained the stallion himself," Hunter cut in, leaning to pick up the papers at his feet and perusing them while he continued in a terse tone. "Rather than see some heavy-handed cavalry officer run the horse into the ground, I've taken him for my own use. As you might imagine, he causes rather a lot of envy in that camp of beggars that call themselves an army. I hide him when I can, to save myself the trouble of killing anyone who would like to to steal him out from under me."

"The way you stole him from Sir Harry?" Tamasin could not resist the barb.

Hunter glanced up, his green eyes glinting at her accusation. "Suddenly scrupulous, are you, my dear Tamasin? I thought surely you would have managed to rid yourself of your conscience by now." He made a business of laying his pistol aside.

"But just to satisfy you, when Sir Harry returns—if he ever does—I'll return the stallion to him."

"I see." Tamasin turned her eyes away from his long-legged, well-put-together figure in its circle of candlelight, away from the body whose nearness caused her an unwilling ache. For a moment she could not look at the man who, for whatever reasons, had pulled Avery Hampton from a grave when he surely would have preferred to leave him there.

"I didn't come to talk about the horse," she confessed, faltering a bit. She had come to ask a favor, but considering Hunter's black mood, decided to delay asking it, and for the time being dissemble instead. "I came to thank—"

"I prefer not to suffer your gratitude again, if you don't mind," he interrupted with a cynical lift of his brow. "Even though I suspect that's not really what brought you here." After giving her a raking scrutiny, he began to study the papers again as if to dismiss her. The muscles in his neck tensed with the effort not to feel softened by Tamasin. He did not intend to be softened by her, to touch her and endure the punishment that touch would bring. He wanted her—aye, he wanted her—but knew well that she would not stay with him tonight longer than it would take to secure from him whatever favor she had come to beg. She would leave here and return to Avery Hampton's bed. The thought caused fury to course through Hunter's veins and his fingers crumpled the paper he held.

Tamasin did not intend to be ignored. "Why did you join the rebel army, Hunter?" she demanded, stepping near. "You said you never would. You said their cause would never win."

For a moment more, Hunter's gaze remained fixed upon the papers, his face angled so that his disordered hair concealed the expression in his eyes. Slowly, he raised his lashes again and looked at her. "There are only two sides in Ireland just now, Tamasin. Nothing in between. It's just as easy to be shot down for being neutral—or in my case, for being utterly apathetic—as it is for being zealous."

"So you chose the rebel side."

"I did. You see, I find it easier to fire at well-fed gentlemen than at starving beggars."

Tamasin stepped ever closer, neither intimidated by his flippant attitude, nor trusting its sincerity. "Avery Hampton could have been the first well-fed gentleman for your musket," she remarked in a quiet, provoking tone. "Why wasn't he?"

Casting aside the papers, exasperated both by her probing and by her proximity, Hunter rose and moved out of the circle of candlelight. Taking up a stance beside one of the casement windows stripped of its drapes, he drew in a breath, then released it gustily, tiredly. "God knows," he admitted in a moment of brutal honesty. He shook his head. "God knows why I spared him. I hate him as I've hated no man."

Tamasin regarded him several seconds, hoping he would say more, wanting him to say more. But Hunter remained silent. "The rebel army will come to Hampton Hall, won't it?" she asked, walking forward to join him, standing close enough to study his handsome face. "The savages will come again, and be less merciful to us than before."

Hunter's words were quiet, measured. "Likely so. After the treatment they've received from government troops, rebel brutality knows no bounds these days."

"Then there's no safe place for us, is there?" Tamasin said, numbed. "They'll burn the house and murder us all. The roads are impossible to travel and the river is hardly safer, for the fishermen are Catholic and would gladly drown the Hamptons and all their breed." She clenched Hunter's sleeve, poured out her fear at last, asked what she had come to ask him. "Can't you do anything to help keep us safe, Hunter? We all live in terror at the Hall. Every day we're afraid for our lives, cowering in corners, boarding up windows, shoving furniture against doors, starting at our shadows. You can't imagine how dreadful it is."

"I can do nothing." He stared at her over a shoulder, his eyes narrow, his well-formed mouth thin and wry. "But just out of curiosity, why do you think I would *want* to do anything to save Hampton Hall?''

Because I am there. Tamasin didn't speak the words, but hurt must have shown clearly in her eyes; for even though Hunter gave a short, brittle laugh, his next words were less harsh, pityingly soft even. ''I'm afraid you overestimate my influence.''

Exasperated, Tamasin threw up her hands. ''But you must have *some* authority. Brendan said the rebels had made you a major.''

Hunter made a contemptuous sound in his throat. ''They'd make anyone a major who has a musket and knows how to hit something with it. No one has authority over the rebel army. Most of them don't even know who leads the United Irish organization in Dublin, nor do they care. Some are led into battle by their priests, for God's sake. They're just desperate men—fathers who want a way to feed their children. And they haven't a chance in hell. Eventually the English will get annoyed with their disobedience and send over an army far stronger than that bungling group of Irish militiamen you see galloping about now.''

''Then what should we do up at the Hall?'' Tamasin persisted anxiously, realizing that she trusted Hunter Kinshella's judgement above that of any man.

He turned his back on her and unable to resist sarcasm born of the rage he felt for Tamasin's lover, spat, ''Has Avery finally come to the realization that his arrogance won't be enough to turn the rebels aside? Did his tutors and Grand Tour and blue blood fail to equip him to deal with maddened beggars?''

In the face of the groomsman's sarcasm, Tamasin remained silent, wishing he would look at her, feeling chilled by the hard, formidable expanse of his back. She stared at it, at the bulge of the strong wide shoulders beneath the thin fabric of his shirt. She was close enough to reach out a hand and touch him, feel the power in his body, the vitality of it. ''I have no answer for that,'' she murmured.

After a moment, regretting his callousness perhaps, or knowing it served no purpose under the circumstances, Hunter
advised quietly, "Go into Wexford village, Tamasin. The government cavalry has secured the town the best they can against
a rebel attack."

"Will they be able to hold it?"

"Not for long. Not if reinforcements don't arrive soon. And
I seriously doubt Dublin has them to spare."

"You're giving me no comfort."

Hunter swung around, his face grim. "That's because I have
none to give, damn it! I can't keep you and your friends safe,
if that's what you're asking of me. I can't possibly command
hundreds of fanatical peasants with blood lust in their eyes to
spare Avery Hampton and—" He quirked his mouth. "His
entourage. But knowing your gift for survival, Tamasin, I imagine you'll find some way to save yourself. You always do."

Surprisingly, his tone had been almost charitable. Tamasin
wondered if he had even given her a rueful sort of compliment.
On impulse, she reached out. Her fingers closed over his sleeve,
and although Hunter's arm tautened in a physical shrinking
from her, she did not let go.

"You rescued Avery Hampton because of me," she said in
a soft breath. "You did. I know you did. I thank you for it,
whether you want my gratitude or not."

He gave her a wry look. "I prefer your heartlessness to your
humility."

"Why? Because my humility cracks that arrogant armor of
yours?"

"Are we going to spend the whole evening sparring with
each other or are you going to let me get some badly needed
sleep? Battle tends to wear me out."

"Oh, Hunter," she cried, all her annoyance draining away.
"We may not survive the week—any of us. I never meant to
spend the evening arguing. What's the point in parting with
harsh feelings?"

He rested a boot on the scarred windowsill and propped an

elbow on his thigh, looking out the window as if he could see every detail of the dark landscape. Distantly, from the kitchen, the restless hooves of the tethered stallion clacked on the flagstones. Somewhere a hound bayed, perhaps one of the dozens the rebels had loosed from Sir Harry's kennels.

When Hunter spoke his voice held a deep soberness. "I'm not sure we're able to have any sort of feelings other than harsh ones for each other, Tamasin."

Hurt by the statement, Tamasin pivoted and roamed to the other end of the dusty room, touched the mouldering black nose of a once magnificent stag. Restive, she circled the cavernous room, then returned to Hunter's side. "Sometimes," she told him pensively, "I wish we could go back."

"Back where?"

"To our youth. Remember when you came to my da's cabin with peat for the fire and I offered you oatcakes and milk? I always liked you to come to the cabin, liked to hear you speak about Sir Harry's horses." Her hand slipped down to find his.

Hunter stood in tense silence, as if her touch aggravated him, as if it pained him to endure it and not throw off her hands in a rejection of her tenderness. But she continued to hold on, to stroke the knuckles of his hand, the bones of his wrist, the hard, closed fingers.

"How can you care for him, Tamasin?" Hunter demanded all at once, his teeth clenched on the words, his voice cracking. He jerked his hand away from hers. "How can you care for that bastard Avery Hampton?"

Taken aback by his shouting, by his intensity, Tamasin labored to keep her answer composed. "He-he's only a man like any other, Hunter. He has his frailties, his strengths—"

"What strengths? His title, his money?" The words were rapped out through the thin, sharp edge of anger.

"Hunter—"

"He lacks something, doesn't he, Tamasin?" Hunter persisted with a savage expression. "Something you want, something you're *greedy* to have." Raising a forefinger, he trailed

it across her lips in a meaningful gesture, one light and sensual.
"He can't provide *that,* can he?" he asked in a low, silky
voice. "Not in the way you'd like, not in the way you think I
can . . . "

"Don't, Hunter," she cried, turning her head away. "Don't
be bitter, speak about things that—"

"Why not? Why shouldn't you want to talk of it, when it's
what you came here to get?"

"Came here to get—"

"Yes. Admit it. You want a man and Avery is no man.
Should I throw down my cathamore again?"

"Why do you speak to me so cruelly?"

"Cruelty is easier than kindness where you and I are concerned," he shot back with equal emphasis, his feelings finally
giving way, breaking, allowing him to clasp her face between
his hands.

His breaths were coming fast, as if he'd just run a race, and
Tamasin knew his ardor had been roused by something more
than simple lust. Desperation fueled him, that and the remembrance that there were many more dangerous battles to fight.
When he put his mouth on hers, she groaned and threw her
arms about his neck, pulling him nearer, accepting everything
he gave while giving back as much.

"I *damn* him," Hunter said against her lips. "I damn him
every day."

She knew what it must have taken for the groomsman to
voice the words. She knew that those few ragged syllables
might be the closest he would ever come to saying, "I have
let myself care for you too much. I regret that I have, but it
has happened. God help me, but I envy the man who possesses
you."

The groomsman kissed her more determinedly then, his
hands in her hair while Tamasin clutched the length of his
muscled back in a way that half-caressed, half-clawed. Roughly
invasive, his mouth parted hers and his hands grasped her hips.
She knew by the sudden forceful and eager straining of his

body, by the wildness of his kissing, that he was on the verge of dragging her to the floor and concluding their intimacy in the manner taken by many soldiers on the eve of revolution.

Tamasin yielded, making it known that she would give herself. And yet, strangely, her surrender seemed to anger Hunter, inflame him in another way.

Lifting his mouth from hers, he cursed, then snarled, "No, by God! I'll not be drawn into this again. This is one thing I won't give you now, Tamasin Cullen. Not while you're up there lying with *him*. There was a time when I asked you, when I almost begged you—"

"Hunter—"

"No." Hunter jerked away, eluding her outstretched hands, refusing to heed her protests. Striding across the room, he leaned to snatch one of the papers on the floor and then thrust it at her hand half-crumpled. "Here," he snapped, grabbing her fingers, closing them around the paper. "Take it. It's the most I can do to keep you safe."

Breathless and confused, her young body impassioned for his, Tamasin scarcely spared a glance for the scrap. Her head spun and her heart felt torn, and she could at first make no sense of what Hunter said. "What is it? I—"

" 'Tis the creed of the United Irishmen. Learn it. Memorize it until you can say every word in your sleep."

"Memorize it—why?"

"You'll know when the time comes."

He turned on his heel, put his back to her again, began to gather up his few belongings. His sudden coldness robbed Tamasin of speech. For several seconds, heartsick and bereft, she simply stood staring at him. "Hunter, you're frightening me. Please—"

Hunter ran a hand through his hair in a way that revealed his own frustration. He turned to face her, and she noted the deep lines of concern stamped upon his face. When he spoke again, his voice was hoarse from emotional weariness and from days without rest. "Convince Avery to leave with you at dawn and seek shelter in the village," he told her. "He should take his English servants with him. If worse comes to worse, and the United Irish army captures Wexford, remind the rebels that you're Catholic—and keep on reminding them. Repeat their creed. If you know it by heart, they'll be more likely to believe your loyalty to them and the rebel cause."

"The rebel leaders will be questioning *everyone?*" Tamasin asked. "One by one?"

"They've been known to stage mock trials. To save yourself you must swear allegiance to them." At last he touched her again, clutching her arms, his hands hard and bruising and full of his fear for her, his voice coming through his teeth. "Above all, you must show no loyalty to the Hamptons."

"Abandon them, you mean?"

"Hell, yes." His mouth lifted in a brutal way that shattered the hopeful fragility of earlier moments. "Unless, of course, you feel them worth dying for—and, God help you, I suspect that you do."

"I'll die for them if I must." She squared her shoulders, her pride stung.

With a curse Hunter gathered his papers and pistol, and offered her nothing more than a bitter smile and one last comment. "I've no doubt you will, Tamasin. No doubt at all." His voice carried to her clearly and, after snuffing the candle, he strolled to the door and left her in darkness.

Chapter Twenty-Three

The following day, most of the Hampton household took shelter at *The Hound* as Hunter had advised, grateful for the sense of safety—false or not—that the crowded inn provided. Before they had scarcely had time to settle, news came that a column of government soldiers had marched outside the village gates to meet relief troops from Dublin, only to be massacred by rebels.

A full-scale United Irish attack upon Wexford was now imminent. Feeling like penned lambs awaiting slaughter, the remaining government soldiers threatened mutiny until their officers—none too anxious to be spitted by rusty pikes themselves—ordered a complete retreat out of town. The people who had sought safety within the old Norse walls were left to fend for themselves.

Knowing now that they would find no resistance, an enormous, undisciplined peasant army, nearly fifteen thousand strong, soon flooded in through the ancient gates. Sweeping away barricades, they set fire to the bridge across the Slaney, then fought for space in the narrow streets. They owned no

uniforms, only their ragged trustys and corduroys; the green
cockades on their hats were the only emblems distinguishing
them as members of any group. During their march south they
had robbed the landowners' homes, and some, in an audacious
fashion, sported the assorted bonnets and feathers and under-
wear pilfered from ladies' wardrobes. Their peasant women,
wearing green hair ribbons, tramped behind the men brandishing pitchforks. Bringing up the rear, a disreputable band
of musicians jigged along, playing military tunes on battered
harps and fiddles.

"Erin go bragh!" they all screamed as the green United
Irish flag was hoisted on the pole at Customs Quay. "Ireland
for Ever!"

"Savages!" Avery spat. From the inn room, he gazed down
with contempt at the carousing, leaderless rabble who were
hunting whiskey and entertainment in the streets like scavenging dogs. "They have no notion of how to organize themselves,
much less organize this Utopia they're stupid enough to believe
they can make. Brainless as jackasses, all of them. There's talk
that they're even asking a sympathetic Protestant to be their
commander-in-chief—that weak, shilly-shallying Bagenal Harvey—because not one of them has wits enough take over leadership. What a farce!"

In disgust Avery turned away from the window of *The
Hound,* which, like all the other windows in town, had been
decorated with tree boughs and green flags overnight. His weapons, those he either carried openly or had hidden inside the
household trunks, had all been confiscated the previous day by
so-called rebel officials. The motley group had burst into their
cramped room with pistols trained, demanding arms and ammunition, throwing open the heavy leather trunks and stealing
every item out of them before divesting the gentlemen of pocket
watches and stickpins. Eushanie had been wearing a gold heart-
shaped pin, which one filthy-handed rebel ripped from her
bodice.

Avery had been enraged, but had not resisted. Only a fool

would have tempted men who were waiting for any excuse to murder a gentleman.

The nerves of all in the room were stretched now, their apprehension palpable. Eushanie sat reading in a corner, a frown furrowing her pallid, perspiration-beaded brow as she attempted to force her imagination to some faraway island—a place where Brendan doubtless awaited her. Rafael played solitaire endlessly, his thin hands with their dusting of black hair restless upon the cards, his impatience scarcely controlled. "Avery," he said now for the second time that day, his voice tense, "let us go down to the quay and bribe one of the opportunistic fishermen for passage to Wales. From there, we can catch a ship to Italy. Remember the pink stucco house on the Mediterranean, the one with the view of the pier? We can rent it again, return to a civilized life. Get away from all this damned Irish madness."

His smooth voice seemed to have an effect on Avery. Moving behind the Italian, the baronet's son placed a king atop a queen in the card game. "Only a madman would go out in these streets, Raf. I've told you, we'll have to wait until someone has got the rebels under control. Don't you think it irks me to be confined here in this shabby place, to listen to former coachmen and footmen yelling up that they are my masters now? But one has to use sense, outreason them—which, heaven knows, isn't too difficult to do."

"I wonder what they've done to the Hall," Eushanie fretted, emerging from her daydream long enough to voice anxiety. "I wonder what they've done to my books."

Avery snorted. "You can be sure they won't be bothering *those.*"

" 'Tis obvious you don't care," she replied in a huff.

He turned upon his sister, his already exhausted temper snapping. "For God's sake, Eushanie, they've stolen the silver, the furniture, the weapons, the horses—everything. I'm hardly concerned with a collection of silly tales."

"You're insulting what is important to me!"

"Then perhaps it would be a blessing to have the blasted books stolen. Maybe then you could pull your head out of the clouds long enough to find yourself a husband."

Eushanie was not without her own venom when the occasion called for it, and her voice was waspish and to the point. "I am not the one who must provide an heir."

"You'll watch your tongue!"

Their tempers were high and Tamasin had no wish to interfere. She hovered close to the window, watching the scavenging, whooping rebels, the drunken women enjoying themselves as if on holiday, the leather-hard faces of the more sober men who were dreaming of the next battle, the next hanging of a magistrate, which would take them closer, they believed, to a new Ireland.

And Tamasin never failed to search the swarming streets for a familiar figure—a tall figure holding himself aloof from the merrymaking, disdaining it, thinking it premature or, more likely, simply foolish. But she never caught a glimpse of Hunter Kinshella.

The next day the Protestant landowner, Bagenal Harvey, agreed reluctantly to take command of the directionless army, hoping that his leadership would prevent chaos, if nothing more. For a few days, peace held. The indiscriminate looting ceased and food supplies were regulated. While the rebel army paraded every day at Customs Quay, blacksmiths fashioned weapons, working alongside carpenters in a makeshift, open-air factory in the bullring at the center of town. The racket of their mallets and anvils echoed day and night. Coins were hoarded. "Liberty" placards were nailed to almost every door. Women dyed their handkerchiefs green and waved them at the drilling peasant soldiers.

Although the gentry had so far gone unharmed, most of the rebels craved revenge. In order to pacify them and prevent the outbreak of a massacre, Bagenal Harvey allowed a few gentlemen to be arrested and locked in jail. Yet, witnessing the ugly mood of the men who still roamed the streets like a huge pack of hungry strays, Tamasin feared it was only a matter of time before the tide could no longer be restrained; eventually every last Protestant would be rounded up and imprisoned—or worse. Many Protestants, encouraged by Catholic friends, declared publicly that they had converted their faith and flustered parish priests rechristened them without delay.

Father Dinsmore, looking old and exhausted, laboriously climbed the crabbed stairs to the Hampton rooms. Although given a cold reception by Avery, he invited anyone so inclined to convert.

"I'll not allow a man to be piked because he's failed to be christened by a priest," he said, pinning Avery with his formidable stare. "Now, is there anybody here who'd like to tell me he's decided to become a Catholic?"

Avery made a disdainful sound and turned his back.

Rafael, who in all likelihood was already a Roman Catholic, if anything at all, continued to play cards, laying out yet another hand of solitaire.

Eushanie, thinking perhaps to be practical for once in her life, took a bold step forward, only to be stayed by her brother's angry hand.

"You'll not become a Catholic just because a bunch of ignorant beggars has managed to take the town," he announced with all the loftiness he had been bred to feel. "We are Hamptons, for God's sake, not milksops, and we'll not sacrifice our beliefs to cowardice. Leave us, if you please, Father, and go find converts somewhere else."

The priest, undaunted, looked hard at Tamasin. His eyes communicated clearly what his tongue had always said about her association with Avery. "Do you have a need to confess, lass?"

For a moment she could not meet his eyes. *Confess what?* That she had sinned with the young master? She hadn't, not really, not even on that first miserable night. And since then, she had done nothing but hold Avery in her arms giving comfort. For better or worse, she had cast her lot with the Hamptons, embraced their way of life. Admittedly, she relished the rich food, the soft beds, and warm fires—sinfully relished them perhaps. Once the madness that had befallen Ireland was past, she would do whatever necessary to keep the place she had earned. Yes, *earned.* And if Avery Hampton continued to require her body for a place to lay his head, she supposed she would endure that price, too.

"Nay, Father," she stated with remarkable steadiness, pushing away thoughts of another man, one with hard green eyes. "I have nothing to confess to you."

A few days later the inevitable occurred. The bored rebels, simmering with a need for revenge and light-headed from their taste of power, demanded that Bagenal Harvey round up all Protestants and have them jailed. Resignedly, knowing his resistance to their demands would be useless, the beleaguered leader agreed.

Panic resulted. Some gentry ran into the streets in an attempt to escape, only to be piked on the spot or hauled to a makeshift cell. The town jail was already packed; during the rebel capture, the blacksmiths and cottiers had been gleefully liberated and replaced by furious gentlemen stripped of their fine clothes.

Knowing the arrest of the Hampton household to be at hand, watching the brutality on the street with a thundering heart, Tamasin slid the paper Hunter had given her from her pocket. She knew Avery would never condone treachery from his sister, even if it could save her life, so she pulled Eushanie aside, and in an urgent whisper said, "If the rebels ask you what you have in your hand, Eushanie, tell them you hold a green bough. Do you hear—*a green bough.*"

"What are you talking about, Tamasin?" she quavered, confused and terrified. "I've nothing in my hand."

" 'Tis the United Irish password, Eushanie. A part of their creed. Just say you have a green bough in your hand. And if they ask you where it first grew, tell them in America. It first budded in France, and you shall plant it in the crown of Great Britain. Can you remember?"

Wringing her frozen hands, Eushanie shook her head, trying to muster control. "No, Tamasin. Avery wouldn't like it. I must stand up for our family name. I mustn't be a coward, a traitor."

Tamasin knew a moment of envy; in the direst straits, it seemed that the fine-bred blood of generations kept a baronet's daughter dignified, if not protected.

"What is that paper you have there, Miss Cullen?" Rafael asked suddenly.

Tamasin realized that the Italian had been watching and when ominous footsteps pounded up the creaking inn stairs, he yanked the paper from her hand and quickly scanned it. "The United Irish creed?" he muttered. Before Rafael had scarcely got the words out, a dozen rough-clad men burst through the flimsy door, their eyes bright with the kind of radiance only blood lust sparks. All of them were armed with pistols and stolen swords. Their leader, the former town shoeblack, sported a dashing hat with a bedraggled green feather.

"All of ye are under arrest here!" he barked, excited to lord it over his previous superiors. "Get yerselves out, single file, down the stairs!"

"Look here, now—" Avery began, quickly silenced when one of the brutes raised a sword and put it to his throat.

The shoeblack showed his yellowed smile. "Anyone else care to argue?"

"What about those of us who are United Irishmen?" Rafael inquired with devious innocence, calmly holding up the paper in his hand. "I have our creed right here. And I'm a Roman Catholic, lately of Rome, where I once had the privilege of meeting the Pope himself. Being a foreigner, I had no way of knowing my host's sins against the Brotherhood. I hope I'll be pardoned for my ignorance . . . ?"

Astonished and disappointed, Avery stared at him. He had

obviously held his friend in high esteem, and believed their months of sport and confidences worth some show of loyalty.

Cowards and turncoats came in all classes, Tamasin realized. The Italian intended to bow out, save himself in order to find a way back to the grand salons and sumptuous bedrooms of Europe.

"Rafael!" Avery snapped as the Italian filed, unmolested, past the huddle of rebels.

The young aristocrat merely smiled and sketched a bow that expressed a not-too-humble gratitude for months of free living at Hampton Hall.

"Rafael!" Avery shouted again.

"Sorry, old man," came the bland reply.

In a rustle of mauve skirts Eushanie stepped forward, showing bravery amid the leering rebels even while her pampered hands quivered. She pointed to Tamasin and announced in a firm voice, "This is my servant. She's Catholic. The priest Father Dinsmore will attest to it."

The shoeblack eyed Tamasin with suspicion. Next to him, hands bound now, Avery's eyes locked with Tamasin's; surprisingly, they were not fierce, did not demand her loyalty. But in them, Tamasin clearly read his need. In some way he had needed Rafael, too, and now that the Italian had abandoned him, Avery was wondering in desperation what she would do. Would she return to her roots rather than suffer for the taste of luxury she had enjoyed at Hampton Hall?

Tamasin stood frozen in indecision. If she declared herself a Catholic and recited the United Irish creed, what next? The rebels would escort her out. Would she then take up the life of a camp follower? Or follow the beggar's road? Tamasin was no idealist; even if the rebel army managed to win the rebellion, she knew the existence of most commoners would be little changed. Didn't she owe Avery Hampton a show of loyalty? What had she told Hunter Kinshella? *I will die with them if I must.*

Tamasin took a breath, lifted her chin, and gravely, quietly, stated, "I am loyal to the Hampton family." When the shoe-black spat upon her, she scarcely flinched, and allowed herself, with as much dignity as possible, to be arrested.

A distance from the village there lay a piece of property called Scullabogue whose house and barn had been converted into a jail for Protestants. It was to this place that Avery, Eushanie, and Tamasin were directly brought.

The barn was small, thirty-four feet long and fifteen feet wide, topped by a thickly thatched roof. Inside, nearly two hundred people were crammed, a small portion of them women and children. Most were Protestant gentlemen; a few were Catholics who had in some way offended the rebel leaders.

Space was so meager Tamasin could not sit for fear of being trampled. She stood with all the others, perspiring, nearly suffocating with the lack of ventilation. The stench of unwashed bodies almost overpowered her, and there was no privy. Breathing was difficult. The stays beneath her gown squeezed her ribs so tightly that she found herself taking short, shallow gulps of air like the poor bedazed Eushanie. Attempting to hold hysteria at bay, she wondered, like all the rest, what unpleasant fate would befall the three of them. She wiped the perspiration from her eyes, stood on tiptoe, and looked around.

The gently-bred children, some still in finely embroidered dresses, wailed shrilly with beet-red faces. Their mothers held them and wept. The gentlemen, pounding furiously on the barred double doors, hoarsely demanded water.

Avery shifted beside her. His jacket and waistcoat had been stolen by the rebels. Yanking off his stock, he used it to dab his brow, then leaned against the mud wall beside Eushanie, who was so befuddled with fear she could scarcely speak.

"Why didn't you save yourself?" Avery asked Tamasin quietly, his body pressed against hers in the odiferous, swelter-ing crowd. "You might have had a chance if you'd declared yourself a Catholic. God knows, I wouldn't have asked you to suffer this."

Tamasin met his eyes. "You might not have asked, Avery. But you would have expected it."

He observed her, a man grappling to hold on to the polished hauteur his breeding had taught him to maintain under all circumstances, even when his heart lacked the self-belief to fortify it. "Yes, I believe you're right," he admitted after a moment of introspection. "I daresay I would have."

"You've always expected loyalty from me."

"And you've not been averse to giving it for gain. Most Hampton staff and tenants get nothing for their faithfulness except the privilege of using the land or working on the estate. 'Tis the order of things. There must always be those in privileged positions who decide for the rest. Without it, society falls apart." Avery made a sour expression and looked around. "As it is doing now."

"There are those out there who would not agree with you," Tamasin said, nodding toward the rebel guards, who, through a chink in the wall, could be seen patrolling up and down.

"They're ignorant, hardly above animals."

"Do you think they will kill us?"

Avery's nostrils distended as a current of fear coursed through his vitals. Without conviction he shrugged, "I don't believe they would dare."

Tamasin watched through the peephole. A messenger galloped down the drive astride a lathered horse. Dismounting before the steed had slid to a complete halt, he addressed the guards, his furious voice carrying even above the anxious keening of the imprisoned women.

"There's a battle being fought over at New Ross!" he yelled. "The King's soldiers are murdering Catholic families, giving quarter to none—not even to wee children. An unholy sight it is, cottiers begging for their lives, for their babies' lives, and the dragoons just hacking them down! Hundreds of 'em dead already!"

A wave of outrage rolled through the rebel army, bringing curses and cries and vows of retribution.

"You are ordered to take revenge on the gentry," the messenger declared. "Show the bloody government there'll be a price for their atrocities against us, against the people who *are* Ireland!"

Fear squeezed Tamasin's chest. Wide-eyed, she glanced at Avery, who had also heard the message. His composure abandoned him. He pivoted wildly as if to search for a way of escape. His hair, like everyone else's in the hellish heat, lay plastered against his head, and his cheeks were red, giving him a defenseless appearance. He began to breathe erratically, then wheeze, shoving at all the people around him. Panic rippled through the crowd, until everyone was jabbing and elbowing, crying out, beating vainly upon the walls.

Tamasin fought to take Avery's hand. She clasped it hard enough to hurt, and after a moment or two he regained himself, managed to squelch the spiral of hysteria. As his fingers, so damp and cold, tightened about hers to absorb and drain her strength, she could not help but remember the other hand she had recently clasped, one dark and rough. She wished she could clasp it now.

She continued to watch through the chink, struggling to stay composed, to breathe, her chest constricting when she saw a line of gentlemen prisoners led out of the nearby house. The rebel guards, waving their pistols, demanded that the men remove their jackets. When they had done so, the first four gentlemen in line were commanded to kneel and pray. They realized, as Tamasin did, that their execution was imminent.

A moment later, four shots rang out. A shout of triumph followed, and peasant women from the crowd on the yard dashed forward and began to rob the bodies. Then more aristocratic victims were paraded out of the house.

The captives inside the packed barn, almost fainting with heat and terror, heard the ominous shots. Simultaneously, reason fled and pandemonium reigned.

"God in heaven!" Avery exclaimed, knowing now that his fate was sealed. Like a maddened animal he elbowed his way through the hysterical press to join the gentlemen at the double doors, hurling himself against the wooden planks, pounding, shouting, and snarling, while Eushanie, her gown sweat-soaked and her lips blue, clutched at Tamasin's arm.

"Juliet died," she mumbled inanely. "But she died for her lover Romeo, of course . . . and 'twas surely not a painful death, just tranquil and slow . . ."

Beneath the weight of the desperate gentlemen who pushed against them, the barred barn doors finally began to groan, but as the men stretched their hands through the opening, the rebel guards stationed outside gored their fingers with pikes. Some of the rebels called for torches, declaring that they would set the whole structure afire and be done with two hundred gentlemen at once.

Tamasin had never imagined such terror, such a tangle of wild men and women, all crushing her on every side. The high-pitched shrill of children pierced the smothering air and Tamasin would never forget their scarlet faces. Flattened against the wall, almost fainting with the compression and the lack of air, she knew of nothing else to do but grip Eushanie's cold hands, anchor them, and pray. Surely there was a God; there *must* be a God to listen, to lend courage to die, if nothing else.

She heard shouting outside, loud, contentious voices. Through the roar of chaos, through the dim reasoning of her half-numbed mind, one blessed voice penetrated all the rest, one authoritative and sharp. *Hunter.* She closed her eyes, trying to hear it once more, desperate to catch it. The voice came to her again, called her name, and she shrieked in reply, then began to shove and claw her way toward the door. She was literally lifted off her feet by the maddened press.

The door was opened slightly, unbarred, and when the crazed captives attempted to squeeze through en masse, they were forced back by a dozen poised and jabbing pikes.

"Tamasin Cullen!"

She heard him call out for her again and, raising her hands in the shifting crowd, gasped out an answer. Miraculously, she was yanked out of the screaming, pushing throng, hauled out by her arms, and thrown roughly down on the long green grass.

With the air knocked from her lungs and her eyes blurred by sweat, she was only vaguely aware of the horse's hooves shifting just a few inches from her outflung hands. Raising her head, she saw Sir Harry's black racer prancing nervously in place. Atop him, a grim-faced Hunter Kinshella sat with a green cockade pinned to his bicorne.

Tamasin screamed his name, or thought she did. Perhaps the words had only been hoarse croaks, for Hunter did not respond. All his attention was focused upon the rebel guards who were arguing with him, disgruntled at his presence.

Hunter leaned down in the stirrups, so that Tamasin could hear, and hissed, "Say nothing, Tamasin. Get behind me on the saddle. Quickly."

Slow to obey, she raised up. Her stinging eyes fastened, mesmerized, upon the bodies in the yard. Her ears pounded with the horrible screams of the people trapped in the straining barn, whose thatched roof smoldered now from a rebel's hurled torch.

"Avery and Eushanie!" she managed to stammer, grabbing Hunter's knee, beseeching him. "Avery and Eushanie are inside there!"

But the groomsman only gestured fiercely for her to mount behind him, refusing her request to help the Hamptons, not out of malice perhaps, but because circumstances were against him. "Please, Hunter!" she cried again, reaching up to frantically clench his sleeve. "They'll burn to death in there!"

He hesitated, his eyes scanning the now-flaming roof, the excited rebel soldiers, the bulging barn doors through which the piercing cries of two hundred people could be heard.

With a jab of his heels, he reined his horse forward. "The

Hamptons!" he shouted harshly at one of the guards. "Release them—*now,* damn you! Before they suffocate with the rest."

A pompous, self-appointed sergeant stepped up to argue vehemently. "Bloody hell, Major! The Hamptons are the most despised landowners in Wexford. They've been oppressing the Brotherhood—"

"I don't give a damn what they've done. Release them!" Hunter cut in, producing his pistol and targeting the fellow's chest.

For a moment it seemed the sergeant would not obey. His eyes shifted to the other undisciplined rebel soldiers, who were gleefully distracted, watching the barn as it began to burn in earnest. Finally, eyeing Hunter's pistol and deciding that the odds were against him, the fellow shrugged and did as Hunter bade.

A stream of screaming, coughing captives poured out when the door was unbarred for the Hamptons, only a few escaping the cruel rebel pikes in the smoky confusion. White with fear, Eushanie and Avery stumbled forward, dazed and wheezing. Spurring his thoroughbred close, Hunter bellowed instructions to them. "Both of you run down to the road with Tamasin. Wait for me there."

After they obeyed, he remained on the drive with his pistol cocked. Slowly then, he backed his horse, watching the frenzied activity and the disgrunted rebel guards. When he had determined that the guards were too preoccupied with the fire to bother shooting him in the back, he wheeled his mount around. A few moments later, as he caught up with the harried, bedraggled trio on the road, Hunter reined the lathered horse to a stop.

"God bless you, Hunter Kinshella!" Eushanie cried, moving to touch his hand, to show the depth of her gratitude. Her whole body quivered violently in reaction to the horror. "Bless you for your rescue of us! It was dreadful, so unspeakably dreadful! All those people dying in there. Look at the flames. God in heaven, I can hear the screaming still." Clapping her hands to her ears, she shuddered, then stammered in anxiety, "And Brendan—do you know where Brendan is? Is he safe?"

Hunter merely nodded, preoccupied with watching the activity at Scullabogue himself. He noted the smoke as it began to spiral toward the sky in tremendous black clouds and, addressing the three he had rescued, said, "You'll have to take your chances and try walking on to Dublin."

"Do you mean you're *leaving* us here?" Avery inquired incredulously, contemptuously. "You're leaving us in the midst of the barbarous rebel army, with no weapons and no escort? You must be mad." Despite his dishevelment, he spoke with unsparing scorn, his old manner toward Hunter virulently in place.

For answer Hunter merely touched the brim of his cockaded hat. "I suspect I *am* mad—mad for saving you at all."

His hatred for the groomsman strong, Avery snorted. "Do you have a pistol to spare, at least? After all, I have to have some way to defend the women from your barbarous comrades." His face was pinched and white from his ordeal, and his mouth puckered as if soured by having to request anything of the groomsman.

Hunter regarded Avery through cutting, narrowed eyes, his lips curving slightly at the corners. "You'll have to manage on your own for once—if you can. If a rebel accosts you, why don't you try reminding him that you're his superior."

Avery lunged as if to strike him, but Tamasin barred his way, clenching his shirt and shouting, "The groomsman has already spared our lives, for God's sake, Avery! Do you find that not enough?"

With rage tautening every line of his body, Avery hesitated, then threw off her hands and pivoted on his heel. He snapped his fingers at his sister and barked, "Let us go, Eushanie."

Like a child, Eushanie trailed behind him, her long pale hair tangled down her back, her skirts dirty and torn, her slippered feet stumbling over the rough and dangerous road to Dublin. Avery glanced over a shoulder at Tamasin, who still stood beside Hunter's horse. After raising a brow, he turned his back and went on, confident that she, as dutifully as Eushanie, would eventually follow him.

Tamasin lifted her eyes to regard Hunter, studying his set profile, the spill of black hair over his brow, the weary but proud line of his mouth. In a rush of feeling she reached to grab his hand where it rested atop the saddle pommel. Opening it, she pressed her dry lips feverishly to the calloused palm. "I don't know what to say to you," she breathed. For a moment she laid her brow against his knee, just above the dusty cuff of his boot, feeling the texture of his rough corduroy breeches, the hard bone and sinew that tensed beneath them. The saddle leather, the horse's hot hide, and the warm crushed grass came to her nostrils suddenly: strong, vital smells reminding her of past days with Hunter, better days. With an anguished shake of her head, she repeated in desolation, "I don't know what to say . . ."

"Then say nothing at all," Hunter responded, his own voice betraying no emotion.

Tamasin could not bear to look up, to meet his direct, green stare. She knew he had come to Scullabogue specially to rescue her. No doubt he would have taken her away with him, managed to keep her safe somehow. But she had not allowed him to do that. Instead, she had begged him to risk his command and his life to save a gentleman he hated and despised, a man who, both politically and emotionally, was his most bitter enemy. She experienced a sudden, harrowing ache of unworthiness, realizing that she had forced Hunter to misuse his own sense of honor.

"I have no need of your shame either, Tamasin," Hunter told her suddenly, reading her mind. His voice sounded tired and distant for all its quick harshness. "Nor of your tears. It would be easier for me to see you tagging along after Avery Hampton, hanging on to his coat tails there on the road, than have you sniveling here with me. If you think I pity you for

your pang of guilt, I don't. You deserve to feel it. And I, by
God, deserve to get satisfaction from it.''

"Then tell me what I am!" she cried in a burst of emotion.
"Say it! You've always wanted to. Every time you see me
with Avery you want to censure me. Tell me what I am, so
that you can feel satisfied and I can feel chastised. And then
maybe we'll both be able to walk away from here with our
hearts hardened against the other, wishing never to meet again.
No more guilt for me, no more trouble for you!''

Hunter remained silent for a moment, allowed Tamasin to
catch her breath after the furious spate of words. And then he
asked quietly, pointedly, with no mercy, "Then, shall I tell you
that you're a Jezebel?''

The word, his hard utterance of it, cut her to the quick. But
rather than suffer a loss of spirit, Tamasin experienced a return
of anger. And the anger served to strengthen her as Hunter
perhaps had meant it to. Perhaps Hunter had known that it
would.

Her violet eyes brimming, she threw back her head and
with bitter but accepting self-condemnation, said, "Yes. I'm a
Jezebel. A wicked, painted whore. A traitoress for money.
That's what I am. That's what I've always been, isn't it,
Hunter?''

Silence again then. And after that, astonishingly, the touch
of his hand upon her hair. In a soft, distant voice the groomsman
lamented, "Nay. I suppose you're just a lass who, after getting
one silk handkerchief and finding it nice, wanted another.''

And his tone, which was very quiet, with no more of the
condemnation she had wanted, *needed* in order to release the
guilt she had suffered since trading his youth for Avery's scarf,
caused something in Tamasin's heart to give way.

Her face twisted and she pressed her cheek against the point
of Hunter's knee, reaching up to take both his hands in hers,
holding them tightly, knowing it would be the last time she
would be able to do so for many months. Perhaps forever.

Her eyes closed so that she could better feel the stroking of his hand on her hair. She wanted to freeze the fleeting seconds, which were suddenly one of the rare frames of life where the pain of love was utterly perfect. She and the groomsman were connected in that moment; the blood coursing through their veins was the same blood, their understanding of heartbreak was simultaneous.

The horse shifted, shattering the fragile sphere, setting the pendulum of time a-swing again. Looking up into Hunter's face, Tamasin whispered, " 'Tis time for you to go, isn't it?"

"I fear so."

"Stay safe, then. Will you promise me that?"

He took his hands away, grasped the reins, and looked down at her with the green of his eyes bright. In deference then, he tipped his hat, the hat with the green cockade. "Aye. And you, Lady Tamasin, keep yourself safe."

The words were said with no mockery, and with them he offered his rare wide smile—beautiful and sad.

And the smile, as horse and rider cantered away, caused Tamasin to press her fingers against her eyelids to stop the tears.

But her whispering of his name, a thin desolate cry trembling through dry red lips, could not be smothered.

Chapter Twenty-Four

At Crow Street Theatre, in a box draped with white satin and attended by liveried footmen, Tamasin sat breathless with awe beside Avery Hampton. Below her ranged a sea of feathered and boutonniered patrons, and before them, a painted curtain hung. The pack of rowdy university students in the gallery hurled bottles at it while calling for the act to open.

"Oh, look, Avery!" Tamasin exclaimed when the curtain rose and an actress entered adorned in powdered curls and a shimmering hooped skirt. "Her gown looks to be sewn with diamonds."

"So it does," Avery drawled, folding his arms and leaning back against the crimson velvet chair. "So it does."

Tamasin glanced askance at him. He was unmoved by her childish wonder, his initial amusement over her lack of sophistication turning to aggravation, and since it was always in her best interest to allow him to be the center of attention, Tamasin curbed her effusiveness. But the theatre could have been a dream, she thought, remote from the harshly real world outside which a pair of enameled front doors and a half-dozen footmen kept at bay downstairs.

"I assure you," Avery commented lazily, "if you were to see the actors close up in the green-room, as I have done, you would find everything about them imitation. Nothing is as it seems from this distance. Even their makeup is grotesquely exaggerated. They're in the business of creating illusions, you know."

"Then I wouldn't want to study them close up," Tamasin said, breathing shallowly in her whalebone stays, "for then it all should be spoiled."

Even as she spoke she found herself leaning closer, using an opera glass to inspect the too vivid faces and overly ornate costumes, until she remembered that, even at Hampton Hall, there had been slight imperfections to mar the beauty of almost every treasured object.

Little by little, she was discovering more cracks in the glass dome of privilege. Tonight, for example, even though she wore satin and powder and sat beside a gentleman, she could not quite make herself feel a part of this world of chandeliers and champagne, only an imitation of the breed who belonged to it. For one thing, she was sitting in a theatre box costing five English shillings per performance as Avery's mistress, or—things being what they were—as an illusion of his mistress. He was showing her off because it pleased his father. He was showing her off because it made him feel like a man to escort a pretty female, who, being of the lower class, could serve no other purpose in the eyes of his friends than that of a doxy.

"You really are lovely," he told her now, as he had done more than once tonight, perhaps to reassure his own vanity. "Beautiful, as I have said before, and you do claim a certain sparkle."

"Thank you," she murmured.

"We're happy, aren't we?" he asked. "Getting on well together?"

"Yes. Of course, Avery."

"Do you like being shown off?"

"What woman wouldn't?"

They had been in Dublin at Sir Harry's fashionable Mountjoy address for a fortnight, having survived the harrowing journey from Wexford when a regiment of dragoons had happened upon them and offered an escort to the city. Once there, bathed, fed, and able to reestablish a semblance of his old routine, Avery had regained a measure of his confidence. Wanting to impress his father without delay, he made his nightly visits to Tamasin's chamber so blatant that the entire household could not fail to notice them within twenty-four hours.

"About time," Sir Harry had commented, chuckling with relief. "I was beginning to fear I had whelped an unnatural son. Your tastes run different than mine, that's all, for I prefer more refined women experienced in the art of pleasure. But there is something to be said for simple maids with coarse appetites, and that black-haired one you picked *is* comely. Flaunt her, my son, if you like. Have fun, amuse yourself. And in a few years, when you choose a wife, you can set up the country lass in a discreet little house, have her accommodate you whenever it suits."

He could not know, of course, would never have guessed, what tame, even pathetic events went on in Tamasin's bed at night. Sir Harry would probably have been appalled not only by the lack of sexual activity, but by the fact that his son had fallen in love with a cottier's lass. Tamasin did not believe Avery loved her in the usual sense, of course, for he didn't really know her or make any effort to probe the workings of her heart as a man who cared would do. But he was *in* love with some of her qualities, she thought: her staunchness, and most probably, her thick black hair and full-blown Celtic features. She knew that he still yearned to possess her in order to prove himself a man. But he had not yet brought himself to try again.

Tamasin provided Avery the pair of tender arms he had never managed to find before; she accepted his shortcomings and inadequacies. His love was selfish. He cared little for her deeper needs, but he did provide her with gowns and trinkets. And perhaps, she reminded herself wryly, giving him the benefit of the doubt, those were the only things he believed she really wanted.

Those things had been enough, once. But now, after clawing her way up out of the peat bogs past the smoky mud cabins, she found life with Avery Hampton a little tarnished, unexpectedly hollow. She had gained privilege, but not honor. If she allowed herself to dwell upon that suddenly important consideration too long, she decided she might well become jaded.

"This will be the last performance for a while," Avery told her now. "The theatres will be closed tomorrow, damn it, for martial law has declared an evening curfew of eight o'clock. We shall all have to stay at home and twiddle our thumbs. Inconvenient, but Cornwallis will put things right with the country soon, I have no doubt."

"Is he the same Cornwallis who fought in America?"

"Yes. The king made him the new viceroy and told him to take the rebels in hand. By the way, those contemptible savages who seized Wexford have been routed, did you know?"

She stiffened thinking of it. "No, I didn't know."

"Yes. The British army was sent in, two hundred of them armed to the teeth. The rebels were literally trampling each other to get out of Wexford in time, tossing off their green cockades and leaving their pikes behind. So much for their grand notion of a Republic of Wexford."

Tamasin's hands slowly tightened around the delicate lace fan in her lap. "What has become of them?"

Avery glanced at her, reading her concern and knowing the reason for it, but above mentioning Hunter Kinshella by name. "Some fled to hide in the Wicklow Mountains. It's rumored they hope to link with the Kildare rebel army, which, God help us, is still on the loose. If they surrender their arms and swear loyalty to the crown, Cornwallis has offered amnesty to all the rebels—except their officers," he added with casual emphasis. "Not many are accepting the offer."

"Really? Why not?"

"They still believe they can win. Stupid louts. My father,

and many like him, want to exterminate the whole blasted
Catholic population. He says it's the only way to stop the
burning and looting that's still occurring randomly all over the
country.''

"And you?" Tamasin asked, her voice constrained. "What
do you want?"

Avery's copper eyes narrowed, and she knew he was remembering the burning barn at Scullabogue and those who died
in it. Doubtless he was recalling the living grave in Selskar
churchyard, too. And what about the man who had saved him
in both circumstances? Did Avery think of Hunter Kinshella?

She suspected he did. She suspected, too, that he would not
bemoan Hunter's death if the groomsman were hanged as a
rebel officer.

A muscle twitched in Avery's pale, smoothly shaven cheek.
"I agree with my father. Ireland would be much better off
without the Catholics.'' He patted her hand where it clenched
the fan. "Except for you, of course, my dear.''

Tamasin regarded him through eyes that viewed the world
differently than they had a year ago. She saw a man with
patrician features and a fleshly underchin, a man of his class
who would never see another viewpoint, and, who, without
wealth and a pair of nurturing arms, would be utterly adrift.
She understood Avery, pitied him, and at times even felt
affection for him. But that was all. No wild, kindred swell ever
stirred her breast when he entered a room or when he crawled
into her bed smelling of claret, and then slept, curled and
damply warm, beside her.

But she had what she had always wanted, didn't she? Eventually Avery would do as his father suggested and establish her
in a house where her anchoring arms would belong only to
him, permanently and reliably. Yes, the baronet's son would
keep her even if he married some dowered lady—which he
would not do, Tamasin judged, until he had conquered his
inadequacy.

Avery squeezed her hand now. "Shall we go home?" he asked, and only then did Tamasin realize the play was over.

"Yes," she said, rarely using the less refined "Aye" any more. She schooled her language just as she masked her unworldliness, so as not to offend Avery. And she was still pleasure-loving enough to relish the ride to Mountjoy ensconced in burgundy leather with a tall-hatted gentleman at her side and white satin slippers on her feet.

Nevertheless, as she felt Avery's hand grip hers, she could not help but wonder if Hunter Kinshella—wherever he happened to be—was warm, and had shoes and food. She prayed that he did, repeating the prayer over and over to the rhythm of hooves on rain-slick cobbles. She pleaded to the Almighty that Hunter would not be caught and tried. It was important to her peace of mind that the groomsman remained free. She no longer had a need to ask herself why. Months ago, as she had lain her face against Hunter's knee and felt his hand stroke her head before their final parting, she had admitted to herself that she loved him. If she must suffer that love in the gilded cage Avery had provided her—the two of them obliging each other in different ways inside it—then she would do so, glad of the pain it gave her. The pain made her feel alive, stretched her heartstrings to the point of agony, whereas the silks and sorbets in Avery's world only plucked them into slightly discordant notes.

The house in Mountjoy was, although smaller, as grand as Hampton Hall had been before its ravagement. Its whole interior—plaster, wood, and marble—was elaborately carved or molded. Many of its furnishings were either gilded or uphol-stered with gold damask; the lock plates and door handles were silver; Etruscan vases, porcelain figurines, and countless mirrors adorned the silk-hung walls and mahogany pier tables.

The dining room table with its tapestry runner was no less grand, always laden with salmon, leveret, crab, mushrooms, fillet veal, blancmange, and rich sweetmeats. And Tamasin, who had always had an eye for beauty, an appreciation for the most subtle flavorings, still retained an urge to taste everything, to touch everything, to embrace the texture and smell of prosperity with an endless and eager wonder.

Eushanie, when she was not immersed in a book or scrutinizing her reflection in the mirror, prattled about life in Dublin before the rebellion and the curfew; then, the theatre and the opera, the masked balls, assemblies, and suppers had been nightly pleasures. Since one could still only travel freely by day, the two women spent their time exploring the cathedrals, the dressmakers, the milliners, the confectioners, the Wedgwood showroom in College Green, the races at Phoenix Park, Carlisle Bridge with its excellent view, and of course, every last bookseller in town—at least, until Sir Harry put a stop to it.

Waylaying Avery one morning on the stair while Eushanie and Tamasin pulled on lace gloves in the vestibule, he said quite loudly, "I noticed that you've made public your liaison with that little black-haired maid, son. Not that I'm condemning you," he added in a rush. "A young man must have his pleasures, after all. But we cannot have Eushanie associating with your light o'love, can we? Especially in public, for there's your sister's reputation to consider. Not that she couldn't use a bit of mystery, a hint of scandal to call attention to herself. But a woman usually needs to be beautiful to be forgiven such things—and Eushanie—well—we had best be cautious with her reputation."

"I'll speak to Tamasin," Avery replied, taking another step down the curving stair. "She won't be seen with Eushanie again."

Sir Harry adjusted the pearl stickpin in his carefully arranged stock. "Very good, lad. Just as soon as Cornwallis resettles things and life returns to normal, you must get your fancy piece out of this house and into a discreet establishment of your own. Eushanie," he went on testily, "will be twenty next November—or is it December?—I can never recall, and still she has no prospects. Will she ever marry?"

"She seems to have no inclination toward it," Avery said. "Has her nose in a book half the time."

"Just as well. Heaven knows, she's plain—ugly one might even be forced to say." Sir Harry pursed his lips. "But surely *some* man would be willing to take her for a considerable settlement. Spread the word, will you, my boy? See if there are any takers, so I'll be spared the encumbrance of having a daughter at home for the rest of my life. I'm not particular as long as the fellow is sporting, and of impeccable breeding. If he's a fortune hunter, so be it. 'Tis likely the sacrifice I'll have to make in order to get rid of the girl."

At her father's unkind words Eushanie stiffened with mortification.

Tamasin moved to put a consoling hand on her arm, but the young lady's pale blue eyes were staring fixedly out the window. She had retreated, as she always did when real life became too taxing, into some dreamworld. Tamasin sighed, feeling pity for the girl. She guessed that Eushanie's mind was clouded with dreams of Brendan, whom she probably wished would come, knightlike, to her rescue.

Unfortunately, it was not Brendan who appeared on the doorstep that evening, but Rafael.

Rain-soaked and barely making the city's curfew, but still wearing his usual urbane expression, the young man strolled casually into the vestibule as if it were his habit to do so every evening. Wherever he had been, the Italian had apparently decided that he enjoyed Hampton hospitality, Hampton money, and had come back for more.

At his entrance Sir Harry and his son were sitting over cigars and brandy in the dining room. Tamasin, who had come down to retrieve Eushanie's book, happened to catch Avery's reaction from the corridor.

At sight of Rafael, his face drained of color, and a quiver of fear seemed to follow an insuppressible shudder of nervous delight.

"Surprised to find me here, Avery, old man?" Rafael

inquired, tossing his gloves and hat at a footman. His smile was broad, his accent charmingly thick. "It seems a man cannot escape Ireland at the moment. I managed to get a boat as far as Waterford, but found no one there willing to take me on to England. Thank God a country squire came to my rescue. He offered the use of his damp but well-staffed home while he located a fisherman willing to transport me to Dublin." The Italian affected a disarmingly shameful expression. "You're not incensed with me, Avery, for bowing out during that distasteful charade at *The Hound?*"

Avery smiled and shook his head.

Sir Harry, who had never paid much attention to the Italian, took notice now. Playing the jovial host, he invited Rafael to sit down and enjoy a glass of brandy. Avery—anxious for his father's approval—took the opportunity to extoll Rafael's thoroughbred lineage, his royal ancestry which could be traced directly to the Medicis. Impressed, the old man straightened and leaned forward eagerly in his chair.

Crestfallen over Rafael's appearance and reception, Tamasin crept away. She was unable to sleep that night awaiting the sound of Avery's hand on her door. She kept hearing his high laughter, mingled with Rafael's, floating from the salon. Then, for nearly an hour, she heard nothing at all.

At last he came stumbling in, drunk and disheveled, his hair loose from its queue, his body heavy as it fell against her own. He seemed to cling to her more fretfully than ever.

"What is it, Avery?" she whispered, supporting him, soothing him with a hand. "What's the matter?"

He nestled his cheek against the curve of her neck, his face contorted, his fingers fearfully clawing the fabric of her gown. "Help me, Tamasin, he hissed, as if stalked by a predator who might at any moment pounce. "Help me! I want to die, you see, *should* die ... might die ..."

And then he proceeded with a drunken and inexpert ferocity to test himself again, to hold her in his arms and kiss her. But, more miserably than ever before, his manliness failed him. After only moments of pitiable attempts, he accepted its defeat.

Later, as he had done on their initial night together, he howled forlornly in Tamasin's arms. And then, for the first time, he whimpered that he loved her.

Unfortunately, her heart could not reciprocate.

Nevertheless, a bond of sorts was formed between them. It was the sort of bond that Tamasin knew she could never break, not as long as Avery suffered and begged for her solace. If she were to abandon him when he needed her most, she feared that her conscience, so burdened, so nagging, the last year, would leave her no peace for a lifetime.

Was it honor that made her feel this sort of tender, almost self-sacrificing loyalty toward Avery? Had Father Dinsmore, poor tired soul, accomplished something in his work with her after all? Or had Hunter Kinshella been the one to give her a sense of honor through his own enduring example?

Tamasin sighed and shifted beneath Avery's heavy weight, wondering why the groomsman always seemed to drift in and out of the forefront of her mind. There were times when she grew desperate to know where he was, how he fared. There were times, more frequent, more harrowing, when she thought she would go mad wanting him. She had begun to believe she would do anything to see him again. *Anything.*

Suddenly anxious, she began to stroke Avery's hot, bowed head where it dampened the silk of her nightgown. She forced herself to think of the lovely breakfast she would eat tomorrow, of the expensive clothes in her wardrobe, of the ornate sunlit bedchamber she enjoyed each morning. She tried to hold on to the last shreds of the fierce ambition that had brought her to Avery Hampton. Only then could she stop thinking of Hunter. Only then could she stop wondering if luxury was worth the price she had decided to pay.

Ambition was unfeeling and unsentimental, after all; a much easier companion than honor. Easier, certainly, than love.

Chapter Twenty-Five

Although the government won several large victories against the rebels, killing two thousand near Kilcock, the insurrection was still so widespread that the King's troops were compared to a young dog in a rabbit warren, flying from spot to spot catching little or nothing.

Rebels were surrendering and accepting amnesty in some parts, tired of fighting and fleeing for their lives. Nonetheless, many gentry took the law in their own hands. They tortured and executed any rebels they could flush out of hiding, made examples so the peasants would think twice before speaking of equal rights again.

In Dublin the gallows were busy places. Treason trials were in session, and many rebel plotters were obliged to put their heads in nooses before cheering crowds.

"Surely," Dubliners said, "after three months of war and twenty-five thousand dead, the rebellion is over. Surely things will return to normal soon."

Only one perplexing mystery remained unsolved. *What had happened to Napoleon's French army?*

Tamasin cared little about the French. She was haunted by her own question. *What had happened to Hunter Kinshella?*

One evening during the dinner hour, when the staff was preoccupied with presenting the beefsteaks and terrene peas, the Dutch cheeses, almond creams and chocolate rum torte without a flaw in service, a rap sounded at the tradesmen's door. A distracted scullery maid answered, and found on the other side of the threshold a most charming fellow. Tipping his battered bicorne, he asked with gallant politeness to see Tamasin Cullen.

"Be discreet, if you please, colleen," he told the maid. "There are those in the house who might not be delighted by my presence."

Tamasin had been downstairs in the laundry, where she had taken Eushanie's favorite shawl to see if a wine spot could be scrubbed out. When she heard Brendan's voice she rushed forward, nearly colliding with a footman who was barreling out of the pastry room with a tray of tarts in his hand.

Finding Brendan at the door, she took hold of his arm and yanked him out of the kitchen light, then into the garden. She feared someone in the house might take too close a look at his face and report his presence to Avery.

"Good evening to you, lass," he said, amused by her hasty handling. "Did I interrupt your dinner? You're looking well, I must say. Is that silk you're wearing?"

"Oh for heaven's sake, Brendan, don't be talking about my clothes when I haven't seen you in weeks—dangerous weeks—and have been worrying myself sick over you and your brother."

"Fine, I am, as you can see, if a wee bit the worse for wear."

She could see. The ragged gold hair, the frayed clothes, and the haggard, attenuated look of his face and body told the story of days of running and hiding and fighting. "You're not ill, Brendan?"

"Nay. Just tired of tramping about with the army, which we'll be rejoining tomorrow, Hunter and I. We just came into the city to see a certain pair of ladies, and now that I've assured myself that one is fit and lovely, may I inquire as to the health of the other?"

"She's fine, Brendan. Are you hungry? Do you need anything?"

He grinned, his face momentarily regaining its characteristic sunshine. "I'm usually needing something, as you know, much to my discredit. But I'll be letting Miss Eushanie provide it, if you don't mind fetching her for me."

"Of course not. But Brendan—"

"He's down by the River Liffey, lass," he interrupted, knowing what she would ask. "On Whitworth Bridge. Waiting impatiently, too, I might add. I'd be hurrying along, if I were you. Be careful of the curfew patrols. Take Church Street—the sentries there were quite heavily into a game of cards when I passed them, and won't be noticing a lass who keeps to the shadows."

"Bless you, Brendan."

A half hour later, she found Hunter standing upon the bridge. Although she was unable to distinguish a single feature of his face in the darkness, she recognized the arrow straightness of his body, the tenseness in his spine as he waited. Was he tense because he wondered whether she would come to him or not?

As she approached, the mossy odor of the river filled her nostrils, reminding her poignantly of the Wexford hills, of the lodge, of the rainy day on the drive when Hunter had come home. Breathlessly, she approached, overwhelmed by relief to find him in one piece again.

He did not speak. He simply scrutinized her, consumingly, from head to toe.

Tamasin regretted wearing her fine blue flowered gown, her voluminous hooded cloak with its edging of indigo satin, her kid shoes with silk rosettes. She could smell the scent of her own perfume, evocatively sweet, as it drifted in a cloud to meet the earthy odors of grass and soil. Her finery, her scented skin, seemed to separate her from the groomsman.

As if distancing himself farther, Hunter braced his elbows against the bridge rail and leaned forward. He gazed out over the river, which was sliding swiftly past in a wide gray silver band flecked with amethyst and sapphire. The night sounds seemed loud: the lapping waves, the wind beneath the bridge, a cooing bird.

At first Tamasin could scarcely believe Hunter stood so near; she had dreamed it so often. She took a place beside him, and just to speak, to stop the ache in her throat, murmured, *"Dubh linn . . .* Eushanie says they call the River Liffey the Dark Pool because it's the color of peat."

Hunter turned his eyes away from the river to the ghosts of the buildings that lined it, all of them topped with sooty slate roofs glazed with damp and age. "I see that you are well," he observed, his voice carefully neutral.

She wasn't certain how to answer. Inadequately, she murmured, "Yes. I'm well."

Another silence fell while she examined the groomsman askance. She studied the pared-down leanness of his body, then his profile, which was still handsome, but heartbreakingly wan and drawn. Softly, with a wrenching concern, she said, "But *you've* not fared so well, have you, Hunter? You've been ill."

He lifted a shoulder. "A fever common to soldiers, a hazard of war."

"Where have you been living?"

"In the mountains of Wicklow. In a cave, as a matter of fact. Dining on nettles and an occasional berry or two. Not the most hospitable quarters, as you might imagine."

The thought of it grieved Tamasin, especially when she recalled the abundance she had enjoyed these last months. She said, "And now you are here, in Dublin, the least hospitable of all places for a rebel officer."

"The very least," he admitted, not bothering, as she did, to glance about the shadows of the bridge searching for dragoons.

"What will you do?" she asked in a low voice, steeling herself against the answer. Her stomach knotted with both the painful elation and harrowing anxiety that Hunter's presence brought. The sudden thought of losing him again—perhaps a final time—caused her hands to clench. "Will you return to the rebel army tonight?"

"Within the hour."

"And then, on to a battlefield, I suppose?"

"I'll see this madness through to the end."

"And afterwards . . . ?"

He shrugged, rubbed his broad, hard palm across the wood railing, which was weathered and still saturated from an earlier rain. "Perhaps fate will be deciding that for me."

"You'll not let yourself be captured," Tamasin stated swiftly, as if voicing the words could keep him safe. She knew his chances of escaping the noose were appalling slim. Sooner or later the rebel army would be defeated, and there would be no hiding place for officers. Hunter had known it all along, and yet had joined them anyway, led them. And now he was doomed, his end determined.

His lean, powerful hands, which had been dangling over the rail, formed a steeple, then closed tightly in upon themselves. "I'd put a pistol to my head before I'd suffer that again."

"Good God, Hunter." Tamasin thrust her hands into the pockets of her cloak rather than reach out and grab hold of his sleeve, as she wanted to do. "Don't be talking about death. You'll find a way to survive. You always do."

"I said the same to you once."

"I remember."

As soft as her voice, the river swished against its banks, where long black green grass was plastered like strands of hair to the sand. For a moment, as they watched the motion of the current slide beneath their feet, it seemed that the two of them were moving, gliding gently toward the sea. Tamasin wished fervently that they were.

Wanting to grasp at hope, to be reassured, she said, "A long time ago Brendan told me that you had cleverly managed to get yourself out of the British army. He said that I should ask you about your act of heroism—the act that caused you and him to be released from service so that you could return to Ireland. Will you . . . will you tell me about it now?"

Hunter turned his head to look at her. "Sure. I'll tell you about it. I slept with a general's wife."

She raised her eyes to stare at him, saying nothing.

He shrugged, and even the shadows did not hide the lines of cynicism on his face. "I had to give my all. Anything to survive, just as you said."

The image of Hunter Kinshella's perfect body entangled with another woman's, his handsome mouth and hands pleasuring her fully and creatively so that he might curry favor and win his freedom, repulsed Tamasin. She averted her eyes.

"If you'd seen the lady," Hunter went on in an easy, insolent voice, "you'd understand why Brendan—scoundrel that he is—termed it an act of heroism. Really, though, he exaggerates."

"I don't believe you," Tamasin cried, cutting into his flippant sarcasm, holding so tightly to the rail that the wet splinters dug into her palms. "That is something Brendan would do. But not you. It's too underhanded, too subtle."

Hunter smiled, perfectly collected, his voice lowering to a regretful undertone. "You've always held an opinion of my integrity that's a trifle too high, you know, Tamasin. You were bound to be disappointed in the end."

"But I'm not disappointed," she exclaimed, distraught suddenly. "You only made up the story about the general's wife so I would think less of you, so I would dislike you. God knows why you want to make it more difficult for me tonight than it already is."

"I thought to make it easier."

For several minutes the gentle words hung suspended between them. A sudden sharp, chill wind blew off the river, hurled from the sea with a tang of salt and tar. Tamasin drew her cloak close. Next to her, Hunter shuddered reflexively. He wore no fine cathamore, this man who liked to keep himself immaculate, only an old white shirt, now shabby and torn. It disconcerted Tamasin to see him so inadequately dressed, hurt her to see him vulnerable to the elements. It caused her to fully realize his mortality.

Tamasin closed her eyes, not wanting to see the groomsman as he was, not wanting to remember the sights she had seen in Dublin of late: rebel officers practically torn limb from limb by loyalist mobs, then mocked and hanged.

"Your cathamore," she managed to say in a strangled voice. "Where's your cathamore, Hunter? I was envious of you over it for a while, you know, jealous that you had found Sir Harry's favor when I had been let go from the lodge." She was speaking inanely, she knew, meaninglessly, when there was so much more to say. But she couldn't help herself. "I grew used to seeing you wear it."

Hunter had grown very still. He gazed at the distant cathedral tower etched against an inky sky while the wind tumbled the hair across his brow. "I traded it," he said, his demeanor guarded. "On a whim, one night."

"Traded your fine cathamore? Not for food, Hunter—"

"No. Not for food." He ran his fingers through his hair, winnowing it in an indecisive, delaying gesture rare to his nature, which told Tamasin he was contemplating whether or not to confide in her. He was not looking at her face, but down at the stripe of living river, his eyes fixed hard upon its motion.

"I waited for you, Tamasin," he said finally, his voice as low as the water's passage. "When you went to Avery the first night, I waited for you outside the gates."

Her heart pounded peculiarly. "You waited . . . ?"

"I knew about Avery, knew what he was. I didn't want you to buy my freedom from him. It galled me in a way that wounds me still. But when you made up your mind to do it, I stayed near so you weren't . . . weren't alone.''

''You were there? You were at Hampton Hall throughout the night?'' She said the words sharply, despairingly, remembering how she had held on to thoughts of Hunter during the ordeal of Avery's hurting her. She remembered crying for the groomsman. Had she known of Hunter's patient, guarding presence, would she have cried more sorrowfully still?

Beside her now, Hunter released a breath. ''I thought you'd come walking out the next morning the worse for it, needing someone to help you pick up the pieces. Needing a man.'' He gave a short, self-deprecating laugh. ''A maid assured me you were well taken care of.''

''And the cathamore . . . ?'' Tamasin prompted, feeling a sudden, inexplicable burden of sorrow.

Hunter looked up at the low, starless sky. ''During the course of that night, I found myself pounding on the goldsmith's door. He wasn't pleased to be pulled from his bed, but he made a fair trade with me. He was happy enough to accept the cathamore. For this . . .''

Reaching deep into his breeches pocket, Hunter slowly removed a small round object.

It was so indistinct Tamasin could not discern its shape at first, until he held it up between his rough brown fingers, turned it so that the dullest glint of moonlight made it glow.

The groomsman held a plain gold ring in his hand.

A sharp knife blade of remorse slashed itself through Tamasin's heart.

''You're thinking me a fool, aren't you, Tamasin?'' he said in a soft tone. ''Well, I am, I suppose. But I thought we might have managed well enough together. Of course, I couldn't have offered you a life much better than the one you'd had in the cabin. There would have been no silk gowns, no feathered bonnets, no kid slippers. But I would have kept you fed and safe.''

Dear God. . . . Had she spoken aloud?

"You needn't pray for me, you know." Hunter suddenly smiled, and it was the genuine, heartstopping smile he rarely gave. "It's all worked out for the best now in the end, hasn't it? You've got silk gowns, meals rich enough for a queen, an easy life. No. It wouldn't suit you to be tied to a rebel officer on the run. To be—"

"Don't say anything more!" she cried, putting her face in her hands. "I can't bear for you to say anything more. Not just now." She knew he had told her of the ring only because he would be leaving shortly, because he knew he would likely meet his death before summer's end. His pride wound't matter then, not anymore. She realized what Hunter Kinshella must have felt for her to have waited by the gates of Hampton Hall, ready to accept a woman sullied by the man he loathed.

How many other times had Hunter been waiting, staying close, looking out for her back when she did not have the sense to do it herself?

Too many times. *Too many times to count.*

His offer, and the sight of the plain gold ring which he had traded for the only warm garment he owned, slowly tore her heart in two.

For whom had *she* traded *him?* She had traded him for a man who cried upon her breast in the dark of night, who tossed trinkets in her lap whenever he happened to remember. She was no more to Avery Hampton than a nursemaid dressed as a courtesan. On the other hand, Hunter *knew* her, had always intimately understood her past, her ambitions. And yet, he still had found something in her character worth caring for, worth salvaging.

Now that he had bared himself, the groomsman apparently saw no reason not to finish the confession, not to have everything said and stripped between them. "Are you happy then, Tamasin?" he asked, his eyes resting in tenderness upon her face.

Their penetration was so deep she felt inwardly wounded. And the quiet way in which he had asked the question made her lower lip quiver. In his need to know about her life, he had momentarily abandoned his own resentment, his pride, and his jealousy.

"Happy . . . ?" she echoed hollowly, smelling the green of the brambles alongside the river. "I haven't thought much about happiness. Not lately. Just about being fed and clothed. Too much about being fed and clothed . . ." she mumbled, taking a breath.

Hunter braced his weight upon one elbow. His tone was suddenly fond and pensive. "You vowed you'd be going to Dublin one day. Remember? You said you'd be happy here. As I recall, you were standing in a ditch alongside a hedge when you made your declaration. And your feet were muddy."

He was teasing, and Tamasin smiled. And yet it was not a smile of humor, but one of wonder that he had remembered her childish words at all, much less the time and place where they had been spoken. "Aye. So I did."

"Is he good to you, Tamasin?"

She could scarcely stand the concern in his voice, the searching green eyes, the gentleness in the question. He was a hard man, not supposed to let down his armor to ask such things. His tenderness hurt her far more than his brittleness, for she was used to that, could respond to it. "Yes," she breathed, clutching the damp rail. "Yes, Avery's good to me. In his way."

"I'm glad then."

Hunter had been holding the ring between his fingers, his elbows still propped on the rail so his hands were hanging relaxed over the water. Now he turned the circle once more, pondering it as if it were a puzzle, or held some answer.

Tamasin wanted to take it from him, or better yet, wanted him to slide it over her finger. She wanted the world to be different.

"You were right about me, you know," he said at last, his voice odd, excruciatingly honest. "When you said that I'm a stable lad and nothing more, will never be—"

"Oh, Hunter—"

"Except perhaps a stable lad with a noose already halfway round his neck."

The words were not said bitterly or with any shame, but as a statement of fact. It was as if he were dredging up old arguments just to smooth them over, just to put everything in order, once and for all, before he left.

"I never meant . . ." she faltered, searching for words. "I know you've always done your best in your own circumstances—"

"My best as a groomsman, do you mean, Tamasin?"

"I-I would never phrase it like that—"

"But you would think it. *Do* think it."

She lowered her head, looking at the bridge beneath her feet, black glass where the moonlight reflected off the sheen of moisture. Quietly, she asked, "May I tell you what I've learned from the Hamptons, Hunter? May I tell you what Avery's taught me?"

He did not answer, and by the slight hunching of his shoulders, she could see he had donned his armor again.

"Living with Avery," she pressed on, "has taught me that a groomsman is more honorable than any man of title."

At her words, Hunter turned his head, and the faint light revealed the naked plane of one firm cheek, one edge of an angled jaw. "But how much is honor worth, Tamasin?" he asked. "It doesn't buy silks or champagne, does it?"

She met his eyes. "No. But sometimes it buys a gold ring."

He looked down at the circle in his hand. "Which isn't always needed, after all . . ."

He let the ring drop, permitted it to descend to the water, create its own tiny splash, and disappear.

With it, Tamasin's heart plunged. She suffered an impulse to run down to the bank and dive into the water, flounder about in her cloak and gown and search the muddy bottom. Or simply be pulled down into the current and drowned.

But it was too late even for that.

A distant clop of hooves, the horse of a patrolling dragoon, interrupted the turmoil of her mind, served to remind them both of the need to carry on.

Hunter's eyes scanned the dark city. "I should be on my way." Reaching down, he retrieved a bundle at his feet and placed it in her hands.

Tamasin only vaguely clasped it, not caring to look, not even curious as to what it contained.

"Your treasures," he explained. "Remember? I thought it time you had them back. I can't be trusted with their safety much longer, I'm afraid. I've managed to keep the hat in reasonably good shape. Look."

He loosened the bundle and withdrew Eushanie's magnificent gold riding hat, which Tamasin had once so slyly confiscated. Somehow, it seemed less grand than it had when she had seen it lying in the ditch.

"The feather's even here," Hunter went on, as if oblivious to her wretchedness. "I wrapped it in sheets of paper—copies of the United Irish oath, as a matter of fact—which isn't good for much else these days."

Numbly Tamasin watched while he unrolled the gold plume, shook out its downy wisps, and reinserted the quill into the braided hatband. A lump formed in her throat, seemed to grow hot and almost choke her. With effort she managed to swallow.

"Here. Look up," he ordered. And for the first time that night he touched her, reached to draw the hood back from her hair, and in its place, settle the grand hat. "There now." He angled it to his satisfaction while she stood with rigid limbs and a melting soul. "Pretty. But then—" His voice changed, gentled, paused. "I always thought you were."

Tamasin flung herself against him, buried her cheek against the dark hollow of his neck, and let her tears go. She begged him to put his arms around her.

And he obliged. His own heart beat fast, she noted with joy, his own lungs drew in labored breaths while his body enveloped hers; she could feel the hard spareness of his frame against her

breasts. He put his mouth on hers, parted it, punished it for the
pain she had caused him, for the feelings she had forced him
to feel.

He led her off the bridge, pulled her to a patch of cool moss
surrounded by bramble where the green scents reminded them
of open Irish fields. She did not resist him. Nor did she resist
his urgency. She, in fact, denied him nothing.

The sound of the sleeping city went unheard. There was only
the Irish soil, the lichen, the stones, the water—the elements
of which the two of them had been born. They blended with
the earth as they sank down upon it; she cared not that grass
stained lace and silk. She cared only about the warm weight
of Hunter Kinshella's body as he lowered his length over hers
and pressed himself into its softness.

He kissed her, tore at the hindrance of the cloak, wanting to
accomplish his possession before something could prevent it.
He unfastened silk frogs while Tamasin's hands slid beneath
his shirt, her fingers splayed to touch the sleek strength of him,
the bulge of muscle and bone.

In her frenzied exploration, she discovered a length of fabric
knotted loosely about his neck. *Avery's white silk scarf*—the
one for which she had traded Hunter's youth. Her fingers jerked
and fell away.

But Hunter roughly seized her hands, replaced them upon
his flesh, buried his face against her neck and murmured, "The
silk had your fragrance ... I wore it because it smelled of
you." And having said that, the groomsman, always intent and
bold, proceeded with his final claiming of the cottier's lass.

He was not languid about his lovemaking. She did not want
him to be—not now. Nothing mattered except that the groomsman was wholly hers, belonging to no one else for a few
groaning, gasping moments.

His penetration was an act of triumph; Tamasin gloried in
it. What Hunter gave, aside from the exquisite physical sensations that her young body craved, went far beyond anything
that Avery Hampton, with all his wealth and title, could ever

give. There was an inviolability about merging with the grooms-man, as she had always known there would be, something meant to be. She knew he realized it, too, as he drove himself with shared murmurs of half-pain, half-pleasure.

And when it was done she lay in his arms, and the water from the river soaked the cloak beneath them and wet their naked skin. They listened together to the sound of the water, to the sound of their own breathing. And after a while, Tamasin told him that she loved him.

To her dismay no low echo of the words came from his own lips where they pressed against her neck. Instead he said, "Brendan and I leave tonight to rejoin what's left of the Wexford army. We'll be heading for Killala. You'll go with us."

At first her heart leapt at the thought of belonging to him, of accompanying him, of being relieved of agonizing alone over his safety. But deep inside her heart, very deep, she experienced a doubt as to her own desires. Was she prepared to give up everything—all the luxury she had earned for herself—to follow a rebel officer, whose life, if he managed to keep it, would never be easy? She recalled Brendan's harrowed, hungry look, his frayed and dirty clothes, and knew what it would be like to follow a fleeing army.

And then, of course, there was Avery to consider. Could she leave him without a word, abandon him so completely after the life he had provided? He loved her in his own way.

Hardly daring to move, fearing Hunter would take away the strong arms that encircled her body, she whispered, "Not just yet, Hunter . . . I cannot leave just yet."

Instantly wary, his armored emotion warning him, Hunter loosened his arms. "You surely don't believe I'd leave you behind. We'll wed. Traveling with the army will be precarious, of course, but I'll manage to keep you safe. You can trust me to do that, can't you?"

"I trust you in all things, Hunter." Tamasin spoke carefully, afraid, growing cold even against the bare heat of his body, her words a breath against the rough edge of his jaw. "Don'

go back to the United Irish," she pleaded. Her tongue was
foolish as she added, "Leave Ireland. Get passage out of Dublin.
Avery can help arrange it—"

Hunter stood up in one fluid move. Pride, jealousy, and fury
resurfaced, bound together, and lashed out in the form of a
curse. "You dare to utter his name even while you're lying
with me?"

"I only thought to—"

"You thought to charitably ship me off to safety while you
stayed here with him in his fine house. That's what you thought
to do, didn't you? Damn it! *Didn't* you?"

"I—"

"Was this—" he interrupted, violently sweeping out an arm
to indicate the warm matted place where they had lain together,
"was this prompted by one of your fits of greed? Is that what
it was about? You needed me to supply what Avery Hampton
cannot? Bloody hell! I suspected it once, but was loath to
believe it of you." He snatched up his clothes.

Alarmed, icy, Tamasin instinctively reached out to him. "No,
Hunter—"

"Do you intend to come with me tonight or not?" he
demanded through his teeth. "Tell me now."

She lowered her head, unable to speak the words.

A low sound, a mingled laugh and groan, came from Hunter's
throat. Reaching down to retrieve her petticoats, which were
snagged upon a bramble and shivering in the breeze, he cast
them at her like an accusation.

"Of course you don't intend to come with me," he ground
out. "The bed of dirt and grass I'd provide wouldn't be bloody
grand enough, would it? *Would it?*"

Slowly, she moved her head back and forth, knowing it no
longer mattered what she said.

"To tell the truth," he said then, lightly, viciously, "I
enjoyed our little hour of fornication. Perhaps I even got more
out of it than you did. 'Tis the best I've ever had for less than
two shillings and a bottle of alehouse whiskey."

Tamasin suffered the insult, his baseness, refusing to answer because she knew he had said it to wound her. He had offered her his life, after all—what was left of it—and she had rejected the gift, just as one would push away a pauper's hand offering a precious last penny, but a penny nonetheless.

Hunter remained quiet for a moment, as dark as the tangled, thorny brambles surrounding him. She sensed her own throbbing sorrow had reached out, taken hold of him, salted the bleeding wound he already wore.

He wanted to say something in parting, she knew. But in the end, he kept the words—whatever they were—to himself.

Instead of speaking, he simply leaned down to snatch the silk scarf from the mud and toss it at her.

"A parting gift. A fitting one, wouldn't you say?" He turned on his heel and, glancing at her over one wide, rigid shoulder, added hoarsely, *"Oiche mhaith,* Damsel." *Good night. Goodbye.*

And while Tamasin sat doubled over clutching the soiled white scarf, her body still lovingly bruised by his, the grooms-man, the doomed rebel officer, parted the thorny green brambles. And went his way without her.

Chapter Twenty-Six

Over the next days Avery seemed to deteriorate in some indefinable way. A quick, haunted look brightened his eye, his hands shook, and a fevered flush settled across his cheeks. He appeared to have some malady of spirit that left him tired and restless.

In a wild need to entertain themselves, he and Rafael dashed from the fashionable Daly's Club to the Lottery Hall to Reilly's Tavern. They gambled, drank, laughed as if every moment of every day must be spent squeezing pleasure from all that Dublin—and their young lives—could offer. Once, they decorated the equestrian sculpture of William III in College Green with a cloak and sash. Another time they defied curfew and went swimming in the Liffey, slogging home in wet boots and bedraggled hats. They habitually stayed up half the night, drinking toasts. When one left the table to relieve himself, the other would drop bits of paper in his abandoned glass to signify how many rounds of the bottle he had missed and, upon returning, the absentee would be required to drink that number of glasses of salt water.

After these exhaustive bacchanalian bouts, Avery would come stumbling to Tamasin's bed, mumbling, anxious, clutching at her with desperate fingers. Always, she calmed him.

One particularly disquieting night, when he lay with his eyes red-rimmed and staring, she asked, "What is Rafael to you, Avery? Why do you fear him? What is his hold?"

Dazedly the baronet's son replied in a slurred voice, his mouth pressed wetly against her shoulder. "He is my nemesis," he murmured, "he is the inescapable shadow that follows just at my heels, waiting to consume me. Help me, Tamasin. Help me . . ."

Thoughtfully Tamasin lay beside him, staring at the choking fog that seemed to push at the windowpanes with ghostly fingers. After a while, when he slept, she eased out from under his heavy impotent body. Twice since midnight Avery had awakened, disoriented and babbling, to insist that someone stood beside the bed staring at him, menacing him. Throwing on a wrapper, her hair a black waterfall down her spine, Tamasin marched directly to Rafael's bedchamber, prepared to confront what seemed to be Avery Hampton's nightmare.

Without knocking or announcing herself, she threw open the Italian's door and entered. Evening clothes were tossed all over the Persian rug, a white stock hung snagged on a picture frame, and Rafael himself sat on his bed cinched in a purple silk dressing gown. His olive face was dark with a bluish beard shadow and, upon seeing Tamasin, his black eyes grew immediately and cleverly sensuous. She thought with malice that it had likely never occurred to him that he was anything less than a perfect copy of a Roman god.

He did not honor her by rising, but regarded the pair of generous breasts thrusting through her wrapper with a lazy and unflattering interest. "Is this merely a social call, Miss Cullen, or are you dissatisfied with your usual bed companion?"

She did not reply. The two of them were adversaries, both benefiting from a liaison with Avery Hampton for different reasons, both loath to allow the other total power over a man they considered malleable. Tamasin did not intend to permit Rafael the upper hand tonight, the chance to humiliate, then dismiss her before she had delivered what she had come to say.

"I know what you are." Her voice was cool and direct, most of its peasant brogue gone through careful practice. "I know precisely what you are. I know what intentions you hold toward Avery and to what lengths you will go to keep him under your thumb. And if you do not slink away like the rodent you are and find a victim elsewhere, I'm prepared to tell Sir Harry all about it."

The Italian observed her, his carved mouth lifting scornfully as he leaned back upon one elbow and drew up his knees to recline, relaxed, upon the bed. "And are you so certain Sir Harry will believe you, *care*—a peasant slut from the bogs?"

"When it comes to the best interests of his son, he'd prefer to believe a slut from the bogs than a perverse libertine."

"But I am a count, my dear," he replied smoothly, fingering the embroidered coverlet with one slender-boned hand. "Did you not know? So much higher up on the scale of class than a mere baronet. Sir Harry is impressed with such things, as are all twopenny Irish gentry who are not quite certain of their lineage and—" he lifted a brow, "reluctant to investigate it too closely."

"You are destroying Avery."

"One could say he is destroying himself. But he enjoys my company, and I—when he is not too overstrung—enjoy his. It is really none of your concern."

"I have made it my concern. And if you do not say your farewells to the Hamptons soon, I'll request an interview with Sir Harry. He will likely throw you out."

Rafael shifted slightly, still lounging so that the neck of his dressing gown fell open to reveal his smooth sculpted chest. "Play your hand then, Miss Cullen. And I shall play mine. But I warn you, I have played in the drawing rooms of dukes and generals. Playing is my life."

His bland confidence, the easy flow of his amusement, caused Tamasin's self-assurance to weaken. Refusing to let it show, she inclined her head in such a way to suggest condescension, and departed. Battle lines, such as they were, had been drawn upon more than one Irish front that night.

The next morning, a hot August Thursday overlaid with a salty haze, the newspaper reported a most astonishing, spine chilling event. Near a small port village called Killala in the distant province of Connaught, three frigates had been observed by the townspeople, who at first mistook them for British men-of-war. But as they shaded their eyes to get a better look at the launch boats, they saw not English sailors, but sun-tanned soldiers wearing curious blue and green uniforms. The sailors began to unload not only barrels of powder and crates of firelocks, but leaflets entitled "Liberty, Equality, Fraternity, Union!" Not an hour later, a French general strode up to the befuddled town bishop to announce in a Parisian accent, "Greetings. We have come to liberate you from the English yoke!"

As news of the invasion flew east on frantic wings, Dublin shuddered. But Cornwallis confidently responded to the foolish effrontery of Napoleon, who had sent only a thousand French soldiers to liberate all of Ireland. He calmly organized troops and, as the great English militia paraded through the capital toward the Grand Canal, ladies stood at casement windows and cheerfully waved, while gentlemen lined the streets and raised their hats.

Folding yesterday's *Evening Post,* Tamasin sank down before a breakfast tray laden with venison pastries, red currant jelly, and poached eggs. She was without appetite. Her stomach had been queasy for several weeks. Yet, knowing she should eat, she picked at the pastry and stared out the window, watching the activity on the street. Now that the parade of soldiers had passed, gentlemen shrugged off the beseeching hands of an army of bootblacks, most of whom were children begging a coin for their lampblack shine. University students hastened

along with books under their arms, and stray dogs nosed about
a pile of rubbish. A curricle driven by a dandy in a mustard-
colored jacket sped down the avenue at such a breakneck speed
that a poor woman selling mussels was almost knocked to the
ground by it.

Tamasin's chewing slowed, and she glanced away from the
disturbing scenes. Dispassionately, her eyes scanned the room
with its red Chinese wallpaper, its silver candle brackets, its
marble chimney pieces, and claret-hued rugs. The bedchamber
was beautiful. And yet, beneath it all—if one cared to look
closely enough—there were thorns on the roses, slight pale
scars on the surface of the hardwood, a stain here and there to
ruin the perfect plushness of the carpets.

The breeze and its oily city smell blended with her warm
chocolate, then rippled the pearl silk of her nightdress. She
shivered, stroking the costly fabric with hands that were now
as pampered as Eushanie's. She stroked up and down, closing
her eyes, trying in vain to evoke the sensual satisfaction that
fine textures had once so easily aroused.

She had paid a high price for luxury, she realized, for her
sumptuous, if imperfect, dream.

Tamasin put her hands to her temples, massaged them as if
to eradicate the burgeoning belief that she was surrounded by
depravity, by a lack of the vitality one could so easily find in
any field in Ireland. In the fields weathered hands cut peat and
slid bows over battered fiddles, people danced and sang and
drank with an honest, wholesome, and well-deserved pleasure.

With intolerable yearning, Tamasin thought about a particular pair of brown hands that had hefted stones, reined horses,
and now wielded a sword. She knew she had erred; she should
have allowed those fine, strong hands to lead her away from
Dublin and toward whatever existence Hunter Kinshella's destiny determined.

She reached for the sachet upon the dressing table, put it to
her nose, breathed in the scent of rose. Then she touched the
ruched camisole, beribboned bonnet, and soft kid shoes laid

across the bed ready to be donned. The thought of abandoning such luxuries now that she had grasped them made her ache. But that ache did not compare to the desolation of losing the groomsman. It was useless to reflect, of course, to wish, for she had lost her chance with Hunter. He had gone away to fight, to elude the King's men or do whatever necessary to try and keep his freedom a little longer. But she mourned him just the same, grieved until she grew as restless as Avery, pacing and waiting; waiting for *what* she wasn't sure. Perhaps the time had come to *act*. Foolishly or not.

That afternoon, with a low yellow sky overhead, the smell of beeswax and hothouse lilies strong, Avery burst into the house, his heels clicking against the marble while he bellowed for everyone to present themselves immediately.

Tamasin, Eushanie, and Rafael came hastening from all directions, astounded to see the baronet's son wearing a smart scarlet tunic decorated with silver lace, a sheathed dress saber, and a black cocked hat—the uniform of the British army.

"Avery!" Eushanie cried, clapping her hands, impressed as always by the romantic vision of a modern warrior.

"I have bought myself a commission," he declared, sweating in the woolen jacket and high stock. The hunted brightness in his eyes shone like a fever. "I'm *Lieutenant* Hampton now, ordered to depart within the hour for Tullamore."

Tamasin considered him. She suspected his decision to join the army had been a brash one, scarcely thought over and scarcely relished, but an attempt, nonetheless, to exorcise the demons that pursued him.

"I'd like to speak with you privately, Tamasin," he said, ushering her into the salon.

A few minutes later she stood in the center of the room, her slippers cushioned by a ruby carpet, her hands clasped across her skirts, and knew that Avery had something of import to say. He stood straight, soldierlike, and held his hands stiffly at his sides as if he were accustoming himself to his new uniform, his new stature.

Perhaps the effort proved too tiresome, for after a moment he wandered away, made a business of repositioning the silver inkwell on the Louis XIV escritoire. Outside, the traffic of the day continued as carriages, jaunties, and sedan chairs vied for passage down avenues lined with tall Georgian homes.

"You'll be waiting for me when I return," Avery stated, meaning it as a command even while his own self-doubt relegated it to a question. His voice softened, grew conciliatory. "I'll get you a house—allow you to chose it, if you like. Permit you to furnish it as you fancy. Perhaps near Blackrock, where you could look out at the sea everyday . . . ?"

It was the kindest tone he had ever used with her, one that nearly approached humbleness, and almost qualified as conversation between equals. With a sad, fond respect Tamasin observed the weary, somewhat forlorn line of Avery's back. Then she took a breath and squared her shoulders, feeling much like a soldier facing battle. "I can't promise to stay here, Avery." she said gently. The words brought her sorrow, but it was a sorrow born of maturity, and necessity.

He whirled about, the backbone of his ancestry stiffening, coming to his rescue. "What are you saying?" he snapped imperiously. "Of course you'll stay here. I have said that you shall."

"No, Avery. I don't belong here. I never did."

"Belonging has nothing to do with it."

"Yes, it does."

He strode across the carpet and took hold of her arms, the sweat of his hands dampening the thin fabric of her sleeves. "You belong where I put you, Tamasin. You've always looked to me to show you more of life, to provide you with something more than the rags you wore, the slop you ate. You craved what I could give you, sold yourself to me for it, and by God, you owe me for it. Don't think you'll be walking away and taking it with you now. I've been generous with you, Tamasin. Another man would have put you in the scullery and told you to be content with that, but I have raised your status. I won't give you a penny if you leave."

"I don't expect you to give me anything, Avery. I don't want you to."

Her calm voice, her unexpected resolve roused and frightened the baronet's son. Could it be that his hold over her, the hold that had never failed the ambitious cottier's lass, was failing now? Perspiration began to bead on his brow, and he glanced around furtively, first at the traffic outside, then at the closed mahogany doors. "What about me, Tamasin . . . ?" he hissed fiercely through his teeth, the words those of an angry and terrified boy who had pushed the dressed-up soldier aside. "What about *me?*"

The cry caused Tamasin's hands to tremble and her conscience to ache, for she knew Avery believed he needed her. But he needed something else, something she had come to realize she could never provide.

"I can't help you, Avery," she said in an even voice. "I *can't.* You once said you had made me who I was. Well, then, who am I? What am I? Nothing but a shadowy face in the darkness, a pair of arms that have no name. How have I helped you? Have you changed? Have you gotten what you sought to get from me? No." She shook her head, looked at him sadly. "I think not."

Walking forward, she touched his lapels with their edging of silver lace and pewter buttons. "You have to find your own way, Avery. Alone. Isn't that what *this* is all about?" Clenching the red wool sleeves in her hands, she shook them with the last measure of strength she had to give him.

For a moment Avery only stared at her face. Then his expression crumpled, his coppery eyes darted, and his mind grappled to understand itself while his heart searched for a purpose. "You have betrayed me," he muttered, bewildered, already drifting now that she had pulled the anchor up. "You've betrayed me. I gave you everything you wanted. You forced me to need you!"

"And that was wrong of me!" Tamasin countered.

She waited while he stalked to the window, and with his back turned, composed himself. He stiffened his shoulders, touched the saber at his hip as if for reassurance, and then cleared his throat, too emotional to speak for several moments. At last, when he was able to steady his voice, Avery said quietly, "It's Kinshella, isn't it?"

She saw no reason to lie and nodded. "Yes."

"Ah. He always seems to turn up. Strange, isn't it," he mused with a heavy sigh, "that we've never quite been able to rid ourselves of each other."

Outside, another regiment of British soldiers marched past the house to fife and drum, the pounding of their boots a magnificent cadence, their reflections captured in sequence on the panes of the window.

"You'll not have long with him, you know," Avery murmured, watching the long red ranks. "*He'll* not have long."

"I know."

"I could prevent you from going."

"I know that, too."

Taking out a handkerchief, Avery wiped his brow, then carelessly shoved it in his pocket, only to have it fall unnoticed to the floor. "Ah, well. Do what you must. Make your own mistakes. Go to him." He sighed. "But what is the point, Tamasin? What's the point when it's nearly over for Kinshella?"

She leaned to retrieve the handkerchief and gently tuck it back inside his pocket. "Hunter deserves to have someone by his side."

And I don't? Avery did not speak the words aloud, but Tamasin heard them. She looked away and answered him with fragile words. "Perhaps you need to learn to be alone with yourself, Avery."

Leaving the window, the baronet's son roamed to the desk again where he studied the flowers in a vase, then reached out a finger to touch their curling brown petals. "I've already decided to ask Rafael to leave," he said in a quiet, meaningful voice.

"I'm glad. 'Tis best, Avery. 'Tis best for you."

He turned to face her. The parade of soldiers had passed, and the plaintive cries of the bogwood sellers drifted through the open window to blend with the sounds of a ticking clock and Avery's shallow breaths. For a moment he regarded her, his throat convulsing. Then, struggling to affect a jocular tone, he laughed aloud. "Well, you haven't commented on these splendid trappings. Do I look like a soldier?"

Do I look like a man? he could have asked.

Tamasin smiled, her eyes full. "Yes. Yes, Avery. You look like a soldier. You'll make a splendid soldier."

That evening, as Tamasin packed a small bundle, taking only a change of clothes and pocket money—which she knew Avery would not begrudge despite his earlier bluster—Eushanie burst into the room.

Wild-eyed, she rushed forward, her fine-textured blondness more washed-out than ever, her hands white-knuckled where they clutched an old storybook. "The worst has happened, Tamasin!"

"Eushanie, what is it?"

The girl shut the door and leaned upon it as if barring entry to some dragon that had escaped the sword of her Sir Galahad.

"Papa has decided that I am to wed Rafael!"

"Sainted Mary," Tamasin breathed in dismay. When one golden egg had slipped out of his hand, it seemed that the Italian had seized another.

"Take me with you!" Eushanie cried, running to grab her friend's hands. "Take me with you. Wherever Hunter is, Brendan will be, too."

"How did you know I was leaving?"

"It wasn't difficult to see. Please, please, allow me to go."

Tamasin hesitated, searched Eushanie's imploring eyes for

a few long moments. The girl was prepared to elope with a man who cared nothing at all for her beyond the gold brooch or ivory comb she could occasionally press into his hand. Eushanie had never allowed herself to imagine Brendan as anything less than a faithful lover who would die for her if necessary. Her head dwelled so highly in the clouds that she saw him only as she wanted him to be, like a character in a children's story book.

"Eushanie—"

"I know what you're going to say," the girl cut in, speaking in a rush. "So I shall say it for you. You're going to tell me that Brendan Kinshella is no more sincere than one of the fairy-love talkers, that he possesses all the well-meaning guile of Cupid. You're going to say he is far beneath me in class and will surely break my heart. You would like to say—but won't because you're too kind—that no presentable man would look twice at a ugly woman unless she can provide him with money to throw away." Eushanie waylaid Tamasin's objections with a raised hand. "You're astonished that I *understand*, aren't you? That I am reasonable enough to admit Brendan's short-comings as well as my own."

To cover her astonishment Tamasin lowered her eyes and murmured, "You make me feel uncharitable, Eushanie."

"If so, I don't mean to." Eushanie pushed back her hair, her heavy bracelet tangling with the lace on her sleeve, its gold finding the faintest gleam of candlelight. "Can you blame me for wanting to play a princess just once, Tamasin, even if the ending does not exactly suit? Can you blame me for wanting to escape the prison that both my father's wealth and my unfortunate looks have made for me? I *do* know about unhappy endings, after all."

Moving to the mirror, she turned so that her square plain shape in its pearl-edged, overembellished gown was framed in the looking glass. "Truth to tell," she added in a softly honest but unembittered voice, "I never expected any other sort of ending, not for myself. Not really."

In the face of such candor Tamasin found no words with which to reply. The lot of our two lives, Eushanie's and mine, she thought, are not really so divergent. *The agony of love is both our life and our death, and we accept it gladly,* she thought. Was it the lot of all women, then, to follow men, to stand in the wings waiting to pick up the pieces—if there were any left—after war, after disillusionment, after the grand male designs had tried and failed? Who am I, Tamasin asked herself, to tell Eushanie not to hope, not to sacrifice her life for the imperfect man she sees—clearly, through undistorted glass— as her own ideal? Why am I, even now, packing my belongings to go in search of a beleaguered rebel soldier?

Tamasin raised her head, and very calmly asked, "Can you get horses for us, Eushanie? Can you get us an escort out of Dublin, do you think? Just as soon as it's light outside?"

Chapter Twenty-Seven

They set out in darkness on horseback accompanied by a pair of footmen, whose silence and cooperation Eushanie secured with two pieces of jewelry. Her remaining jewels were locked in their ivory casket. She packed them in a valise with her clothes, declaring that she and Brendan, if he could be persuaded to run away with her, would exist off the money a pawnbroker would give them for the emerald choker, the triple strand of pearls, the ruby ring, and the countless gold and silver bracelets that had once belonged to her mother.

They headed toward Killala. It was the port village where the French had landed, and several thousand of the United Irish army were marching there in order to join forces with the French General Humbert.

Tamasin and Eushanie traveled all day with their escorts, maintaining a grueling pace, meeting no trouble on the road. They stayed overnight at a village inn, and the following afternoon approached the town of Longford. They had not yet reached the outskirts when a gentleman traveler on a lathered horse waylaid them with news.

"Ten miles up the road," he told them excitedly, "a large army of rebels has captured a Protestant charity institution called Wilson's Hospital. They've turned out all the old men and charity boys there, wounded the chaplain, and stolen the arms and liquor. I estimate that there were several thousand rebels encamped in the place, waiting to meet up with the French. Rumors were circulating that the British army is on its way to foil the rendezvous."

As he spurred his horse and galloped on, both the Hampton footmen shook their heads and advised the ladies to give up their mad venture and return to Dublin at once.

"No," Tamasin said firmly. "If a battle hasn't yet started, we have a chance of finding the men we seek—provided they're camped at this Wilson's Hospital, which seems likely. But if we wait and a battle begins, there'll be chaos for days. Rebel armies are known to fall apart and scatter in all directions when they're routed. We'd have little hope of ever finding the Kinshellas in such a case."

The footmen hesitated. Both men had been reluctant from the start of the journey.

Afraid that they would dig in their heels and refuse to budge, Eushanie declared imperiously, "I have paid you men well. If you do not escort us to the rebel camp, we'll go on without you. As two women alone, well dressed and riding good horses, our safety would be severely jeopardized. We might fall into the hands of brutal men. Would you want our ravishment on your consciences?"

The older footman cleared his throat. "Begging your pardon, Miss, but the two of us can give you little protection, even as well armed as we are. The rebel army is reported to be made up mostly of savages. What's to prevent them from seizing our horses and arms and murdering us all?"

Weary of bickering, Tamasin nudged her horse toward Longford and spoke over a shoulder. "That's a chance we're forced to take. We only want time enough to declare ourselves under the protection of two of their rebel officers. I trust that when

Major Kinshella's name is mentioned, we'll be taken to him unmolested.''

"*If* he's there," one of the footmen murmured doubtfully. Thoroughly disgruntled, he and his counterpart resignedly spurred their mounts to follow.

Unfortunately, as it turned out, the foursome did not arrive in advance of the British forces. They were no more than a half mile away from the rebel camp when, with a sudden terrifying thunder, the government army swooped down from the hills in a well-ordered, murderous charge.

Tamasin had never seen nor imagined such a spine-chilling, spectacular sight, and for several moments, like her companions, could do little more than stare agog at the dreadful wonder of it. Hundreds of red-coated figures, smart, well-equipped veterans riding caparisoned chargers, descended upon the rebel camp like scarlet demons. Their crossbelts made bright white slashes over the fields, their drawn sabers gleamed, and their banners unfurled in vivid rectangles. The combined clamor of jingling military harness, booming cannon, pounding hooves, rattling artillery fire, and shouted commands startled the Hampton horses and almost deafened their mesmerized riders.

"Good God!" one of the footmen exclaimed, terrified, glancing wildly about for some sort of cover.

Almost paralyzed with fear for Hunter, Tamasin could do nothing but strain forward and fix her sights on the rebel troops. They were trying desperately to organize themselves, their officers dashing through the confused ranks bellowing orders, even while some of their ragged members deserted in vast numbers. Others rallied, many in homemade green uniforms, most in brown trustys. With rusty pikes and muskets they ran bravely out to meet the furiously coordinated British charge. Their flag, green with its Irish harp and cross, fluttered amid the mass of scrambling, straining figures. Before long the entire battlefield surrounding Wilson's Hospital was overlaid with the choking smoke of mortar fire and the pandemonium of full-fledged war.

The clash of a hundred steel swords rang, mingling with the grunts of men fighting hand-to-hand, the spitting of musketry fire, the cries of wounded and dying soldiers.

Within minutes, as Tamasin stared down upon it in frozen incredulity, the once-peaceful landscape became a panorama of utter bedlam and human destruction, a carnage so horrible she felt it could not possibly be real.

Imagining Hunter in the bloody foray, she closed her eyes momentarily and covered her ears, breathing hard with fear and shock, smelling the acrid smoke, the churned earth, the sweat of horseflesh, and the fresh blood of fathers and sons and lovers.

"The rebels will be butchered!" Eushanie screamed shrilly, noting the approach of government reinforcements. "Brendan may be in the midst of it! I must find him!"

The lady would have whipped up her quivering mount and galloped toward the battlefield if Tamasin had not managed to grab a rein and yank the horse's head around.

"Not yet, Eushanie!" she shouted, also feeling a sense of desperation, the instinctive need to do something other than sit and watch. "You can't find him now. 'Tis madness to try. We'll go together when it's over, search for Brendan and Hunter."

Until this point, the two footmen had hovered close to the women. But now the perimeters of the battlefield were widening. More tattered, desperate rebels began to desert and scurry in all directions. The servants insisted upon finding cover and keeping the valuable horses out of sight. A dense, distant grove of ash trees situated on a hillside provided both concealment and a commanding view of the battle.

The conflict stretched on for hours and hours. After a while, Tamasin could not estimate the number of fallen men, but could see that the vast majority of them were rebels who lay strewn like bloodied rag dolls over the emerald fields. The British, although smaller in number, were far superior in training, better equipped, and utterly ruthless with their well-honed sabers and accurate muskets. They showed no mercy at all as they hacked tirelessly through the flagging green and brown ranks.

Already hundreds of rebels had been captured, and as the remainder realized that imprisonment or immediate death was to be their fate, they began to flee in huge numbers. A few found themselves cornered, and in desperation attempted to swim across a nearby lake, their drowned bodies adding to the United Irish casualties. If evening had not begun to fall, the decimation of the rebel forces would have been entire.

In the haunted purple twilight, Tamasin and Eushanie left their horses with the footmen, who refused outright to venture onto the now-calm but gruesome battlefield.

Suspecting that the servants would desert, Tamasin took her valise and hid it in the undergrowth. Then, like shadows, the pair of women flitted through what remained of two formidable armies. They were scarcely noticed. Soldiers were used to seeing women pick through fallen bodies after war, either robbing them or searching for relatives. Besides, the business of burying and capturing was such an exhaustive task for the already weary British warriors that they had not the energy to pay attention to either scavengers or pretty faces.

Brown smoke rose from the ground, hovered over the blue of eventide. No longer did the hills roar with fury; now one heard only the occasional chime of a bridle bit, the snort of a tired horse, the low commands of officers and surgeons as they rounded up prisoners or carried the wounded to makeshift hospitals. But the most unnerving, the most eerie sound of all, was the collective moan of hundreds of broken, dying rebels who would not be—could not possibly be—tended by the meager staff of British military doctors.

Eushanie, as pale as the wounded men sprawled on the charred earth, walked close to Tamasin, searching every face. As they trod gingerly through a litter of packs, muskets, pikes, ammunition bags, and muddy helmets, the girl remained remarkably composed in spite of the blood on her hem. Perhaps she was at last able to be a true heroine in the horrible but still romantic place where brave men had fought and died.

In the end, Eushanie was the fortunate one, discovering Brendan whole and unharmed in the custody of a young British regular who was assigned to apprehend prisoners hiding in a small woodlet. The fresh-faced private, not more than eighteen, nodded politely when the two women approached through the lingering fingers of cannon smoke. He even tolerantly stood by while Eushanie threw her arms around Brendan and wept. Then, growing impatient, he diffidently reminded the distraught young woman of the circumstances.

"Sorry, Miss, but I must be taking your fellow to camp now. He'll likely be transported to Dublin at dawn with the others, if you'd care to follow the train of wagons then."

Straightening her shoulders, Eushanie almost visibly drew on her mantle of privilege and wealth. She slipped the ruby ring off her finger and held it out to him. "An exchange, soldier?" she asked steadily, watching his eyes widen.

Nervous, the young man glanced over his shoulder. For several seconds he regarded the group of red-coated men who moved quietly through the hazy woodlet retrieving the bodies of their fallen compatriots. Then he focused his eyes on the ruby ring again.

It would be worth a fortune to such a boy, Tamasin thought, for most of the British ranks were composed of unfortunates recruited from the slums and jails of London. Her instincts proved accurate. In the end, the temptation outweighed the young soldier's sense of patriotism. "Leave with him immediately, Miss," he advised, as he snatched the ring and carefully slipped it into the leather cartouche bag fastened at his belt. "If he's captured again, I'll not be able to help you. Travel north, the way's clear. Good luck to you."

Nodding to them curtly, he quickly strolled away and disappeared.

Brendan, standing with his hands bound, had remained quiet

during the exchange, and Tamasin now feverishly clutched at his sleeve. "Where's Hunter, Brendan?"

Weary almost beyond speech, powder-stained, barefoot, and barely able to stand, Brendan shook his shaggy head, not even able to muster a spark of his usual bonhomie. He was out of his element, near a breaking point, his nature too blithe and airy for the shocking realities of war.

"I haven't seen him since the start, lass," he murmured, his grief apparent. "I've wandered all about, calling for him, searching while trying to elude the blasted enemy. I last saw him riding into the midst of battle straight for a British colonel, his sword raised. Bloody reckless, he was. Damn him."

Nearby, a red-coated officer patrolled the woods, giving low orders to several of his men in the murky semidarkness. Brendan touched Tamasin's arm urgently, regaining a measure of his reason. "We cannot tarry longer, Tamasin," he hissed. " 'Twould be no point in it. I'd surely be captured again, and God knows what Eushanie would do if that were to happen."

"Go then," Tamasin whispered, her eyes fixed warily on the British officer. He was wandering closer, poking through the undergrowth with a saber, hunting for hiding rebels. "Go while you can. I'll stay. I'll find Hunter."

She embraced Brendan; his slight, hungry body seemed almost insubstantial in her arms. Then Eushanie pressed Tamasin's hand in gratefulness before allowing Brendan to lead her away through the smudged, steely darkness. An unsettling premonition settled over Tamasin as she watched them go, a flashing, clouded glimpse of the future; she believed she would never see her two friends again.

Alone, her stomach cramping with fear and her nostrils clogged with smoke, she continued her grim search. After an hour of fruitless trudging, she spied a riderless horse wandering on the distant fringes of the battlefield. Something about its long graceful stride, its height, its high-held tail pricked her memory, and she turned to follow the animal. She began to run, seized by a need to examine it, touch it. She wanted to study the horse's lines, its markings. She fancied suddenly that it was the thoroughbred from the lodge—the last racer, the only one the army hadn't managed to get. The one Hunter had kept for himself.

Stumbling toward it, then slowing for fear it would be startled and bolt, she experienced a sudden dread. It *was* the racer; Tamasin no longer doubted its identity. Hopelessness seized her. That the horse was roaming riderless could only mean that Hunter had fallen in battle. For the first time, that possibility—kept at bay until now—overwhelmed her, and she gasped with the horror of it.

Probably thirsty after its ordeal, the horse was walking toward the lake, slowly but steadily, its head bowed low. Wanting to stroke it, to run her hands over its saddle and reins, which were her last and only link with Hunter, Tamasin hastened forward. Then she halted in her tracks abruptly, squinted through the stifling darkness, and stared with trepidation.

The thoroughbred's head was lowered at a peculiar angle as it walked, the reins trailing the ground, but taut. It seemed to be dragging something heavy, something large . . .

"My God . . ." Tamasin breathed.

Stumbling forward, she grabbed the bridle and stopped the exhausted mount, then stared disbelievingly at the ground beside its muddy hooves. A bloodied, half-conscious Hunter Kinshella—through instinct or sheer stubbornness—had managed to hang on to the dragging reins.

"Sainted Mary help us," Tamasin prayed, falling down on her knees to touch the groomsman.

At first she could not pry his hard, muddy fingers loose from the reins, and sobbed despairingly as she realized that he was bleeding and close to death. It took her only a minute to complete a gruesome inventory in the darkness, to see that both of his legs had been injured by artillery fire.

Frenzied, she glanced around for help before realizing that she could neither call for assistance nor carry him back to the

British camp, for the soldiers there would either imprison him or execute him on the spot.

"Hunter!" she cried, cradling his head, afraid that he might already be dead. "God in heaven, I don't know what to do, where to take you." She stood up, glanced all about in a wild search for a place to hide the rebel officer.

Putting her hands under his arms, she began to drag him toward the lake and its tall concealing reeds, straining, struggling with the weight of his motionless body. She kept a watchful eye out for patrols as she pulled him along step by step, panting and gasping. At last she managed to get him through the dense bullrushes to the mossy shore and, after kneeling down to prop his head in her lap, frantically cupped handfuls of lake water and dribbled it over his mouth.

The coldness of the small measure she was able to get past his lips revived Hunter, and he stirred enough to demand more.

"*Augh-ishka,*" he babbled, shaking his head from side to side, distressed. "*Augh-ishka . . .*"

"I can't understand you, Hunter," Tamasin fretted, more concerned with the blood that was slowly, with a chilling inexorability, flowing from his wounded legs and pooling on the ground.

"*Augh-ishka . . .*"

Water-horse, he was saying. She had heard him mention the name before. What did it mean? Suddenly Tamasin recalled that an *augh-ishka* was a wild fairy horse from Irish legend that sometimes emerged from the sea to dwell on land. Hunter had once called the thoroughbred by that name.

"The stallion is here behind us, Hunter," she reassured him, touching his brow with a quivering hand. "He's drinking from the lake."

It was only then that the groomsman finally seemed to realize who she was, dimly remember what had happened to him and where he lay.

"Tamasin . . . ?"

She smoothed his damp hair, desperately afraid for his life, for his fate when morning came, if he survived that long. "Yes, 'tis Tamasin," she cried. "Oh, Hunter, tell me what I should do. I'm frightened. I don't know where to go for help."

But he lapsed into half-consciousness again, mumbling nonsense in Gaelic about *Tir-na-n-Og*, the favorite dwelling place of the fairies which few mortals had ever found.

"Geabhaedh tu an sonas aer pighin," he kept whispering, fiercely batting Tamasin's hands away when she tried to soothe him. *"Geabhaedh tu an sonas aer pighin."*

You'll get happiness for a penny there, he had said.

It made Tamasin cry to hear him say the words just as he had said them on the day she had traded his life for a white silk scarf.

Knowing his survival depended upon her ability to rouse him, on his being able to tell her what to do, she frenziedly splashed water over his face and immersed his hands in the lake. Then she began to shred her petticoats and wrap the strips around his injured legs. Her ministrations caused him pain and he struggled to sit up, cried out, then clenched his teeth and collapsed again, exhausted. The sharp pain had sobered him, however, enabling him to gather his wits and remember his situation and his danger.

"Have to think . . ." he breathed raggedly, closing his eyes and swallowing. "Think what to do. Brendan . . . ?"

"Alive and safe," Tamasin said quickly. "Eushanie rescued him, bribed a redcoat with her jewelry. God willing, they're on the road north by now."

Hunter exhaled with relief and clasped Tamasin's hands. He did not waste time considering his fate; he already knew what it would be. He did not dread dying. But he did dread imprisonment and would not suffer it. He felt for the pistol in his belt, assured himself it was still there. "Tell me how you came to be here, Tamasin," he gasped. "Why you came."

"For you, Hunter," she answered without pause, touching his powder-stained face, tenderly wiping the sweat away. "I came for you."

He savored the words, then asked, "What's happened on the battlefield? I don't hear musketry fire anymore."

"It's over. The rebels were routed, hundreds killed. The British are roaming about, picking up the wounded, searching for rebels. Hunter, I'm terrified! I don't know what to do to keep you safe."

Hysteria quivered in Tamasin's voice. She started when the wind gusted and caused the tall, thick reeds surrounding them to clack and clatter and scatter puffs of white duck feathers on the air. At the sound of her fear Hunter groped for her hand and pressed it, lending her strength even when he had scarcely enough to keep himself breathing.

"Where's the horse?" he asked.

"Here, close. Standing with its hooves in the water and its head hanging low. Too tired to move, by the looks of him."

"Good. Don't let him wander. He'll be noticed."

She nodded, then glanced with a chilling fear at Hunter's legs. "Can't we manage to get you atop the saddle? I could ride behind, take us somewhere, anywhere . . ."

"No, Tamasin." He shook his head. "A horse would be too conspicuous, call attention to us the moment we moved out of these reeds. Besides, our pace would be too slow. The stallion is spent." Hunter did not add that he hadn't the ability to stay in the saddle.

"What is to happen to us, then?" she breathed, afraid to know the answer. "What can we *do?*"

Hunter did not reply. He simply closed his eyes with his head pillowed in her muddied skirts, his teeth chattering with pain even though he held his jaws clamped. After a moment, he stared up at the stars, tiny pinpoints of light remotely winking, the same stars he had seen in boyhood over the green fields of Wexford. It suddenly galled him that his life might end here, within hours. He was only twenty-nine. He pressed Tamasin's hand to his cheek, needing her warmth and the strength of her spirit.

"I remember how you used to run barefoot over the fields,"

he whispered. He wanted to speak of the past aloud, to recall it vividly. "I remember how you used to stand on the hill behind your da's cabin, wrapped in that old black shawl of yours, and stare up at Hampton Hall—"

"No, Hunter," Tamasin pleaded, shaking her head and bowing over his face. She stroked his eyelids, the long rough line of his jaw. "Don't speak of that now, not anymore."

"Why?" He swallowed against the dryness of his throat. "Are you done with marble houses then?"

Sharp, bright tears filled her eyes and spilled over, wet her hands and his face. "Yes," she whispered. "Yes. Forever."

"Swear, then. Swear to me. Make a vow to me. I want to know that you'll never go back to the Hall. I want to hear you say that you'll never return to Avery Hampton."

"I won't. I swear I won't!" Tamasin said, her lower lip aquiver. "I'll never go back."

Hunter's face twisted, with pain or with relief she couldn't discern, and then he rested, fell into a light slumber, leaving her alone to listen to the distant sounds of the British army. At last they seemed to have given up their search for rebels in the darkness and settled down to grave digging. The faint, monotonous thud of scraping shovels became confused with the gently lapping water, the soughing of the reeds, the wind raking the tail of the poor winded horse.

As the hours marched silently, unstoppably toward dawn and its revealing pink light, Tamasin accepted the fact that there was no safe place to hide the groomsman. There was no escape, no hope for his survival without some source of help. If Hunter did not die here in her arms, then he would live no longer than it would take for the redcoats to capture, try, and hang him.

For long anguished moments, she sat in the muddy grass with his dark head cushioned in her lap. She stared out at the lake, whose water was so glassy that the moon seemed to be captured in its shivering silvered surface. The calamity into which she and Hunter had fallen seemed unreal all at once, impossible, the waste of the groomsman's life an outrage too unjust to be passively accepted. Earlier, Hunter had forced her to make a promise to him; she had done so willingly. And yet, now, her always active mind began to churn with frantic thoughts and remote possibilities. One thing became clear. Before her promise to him was scarcely an hour old, she must break it.

During the battle that day, she had glimpsed Avery Hampton's regiment in the chaos, recognized it by the blue facings on the bright, silver-laced uniforms. If the baronet's son had ridden with them and survived the foray, he would be encamped nearby, in the tents she had seen pitched while the British wounded were retrieved. If Avery were close, she would find him.

And yet, Tamasin delayed a moment to stroke Hunter's hair. She listened to his labored breathing, saw the slight rise and fall of his chest, and the ever-spreading darkness of blood as it seeped through the petticoat strips she had tied around his legs. She knew that going to Avery was a calculated risk; she could not be certain of his reaction. But she would beg, plead with him on her knees for Hunter's life, if necessary.

Easing out from under the groomsman's weight, gently leaving him sprawled in the damp matted grass, she prayed aloud to every saint she knew for his safety, then moved quietly toward the thoroughbred, who still stood with his front legs in the water and his head drooping. Gathering his wet, trailing reins, she stroked the hot neck crusted with dried lather, whispered soothing words, and slid a foot into the stirrup.

"Tamasin."

She tensed.

Hunter had awakened, was pushing himself up on his elbows. His hoarse voice was distressed, suspicious. "Where are you going?"

She steeled herself. No matter what he said to her, no matter what he did, she must ride away. Tamasin steadied her voice while her hands clenched the reins. "To the British camp to get help for you, Hunter. I'm going to the British camp. Avery is there.''

"Get away from the horse, Tamasin."

"I must go—"

"No!" Hunter struggled to stand, forgetting his wounds, attempting to push himself up with his arms. As he came to his feet and staggered forward, a wrenching snarl of pain tore through his throat. But he managed take another step, and another, his hands outstretched to stop her. "Get off that bloody horse! You'll not go to that bastard for me! *Damn you if you do!"*

Shutting her eyes against the picture of his agonized figure, Tamasin hauled herself up into the saddle. With hard heels she jabbed the reluctant horse, who managed to find an ounce more of valiance in his heart and move. Unable to bear the sight of the man she loved as he stumbled and fell to the ground, Tamasin jerked her head and looked ahead toward the faint, pale line of British tents.

She heard Hunter cry out behind her. She knew he believed that she had betrayed his honor. She knew he believed that she had betrayed *him* one final time.

Chapter Twenty-Eight

Lt. Avery Hampton tarried inside his military tent, a structure commodious enough to hold a cot, chair, and desk, lofty enough to allow two feet of space above his head. The candles upon the folding desk where he sat cast their fluttering light over the stretched canvas, highlighting a brass spyglass, the remains of a meal on a pewter plate, the steel spurs on his boots. Outside, where two sentries stood at attention, the sounds of an army camp after war—muffled voices, rattling tin plates, and the groans of wounded men hospitalized in a sea of tents.

Suddenly, one of the sentries asked permission to enter, and when it was granted, escorted a woman inside. Avery's eyes widened with surprise.

She was disheveled, filthy, with bloodstains on her gown and her hair hanging loose, but beautiful nonetheless.

"I'm not harmed, Avery," Tamasin said quickly, seeing that he was alarmed.

With a wave of his hand he dismissed the sentry. Then a slow smile spread across his face. He surmised that Tamasin had regretted her decision to leave him, after all. She had chased after him, risked life and limb wending through the battlefield in order to beg his forgiveness and regain her status under his protection. For a few, smug moments, Avery's desperate, always insecure vanity actually believed in the possibility.

"Have you come to keep me company in these unluxurious quarters?" he asked amiably, bowing low as if they stood together in a drawing room. Reaching to clasp her hand and raise it to his lips, he took pains not to brush against her bloodied skirts. "I warn you, there is no hot water, but we have a few amenities."

Tamasin cut to the point, her weariness and desperation so great her voice nearly failed. "I have come to request a favor, Avery."

Still thinking she meant to re-ensconce herself in his good graces, Avery released her hands, picked up a bread crust from his plate, and bit into it with a sudden renewed appetite. He would accept her apology, of course, after a mild chastisement, for he felt a great need for her. Despite his show of casual gallantry, his vitals were still a-tremble from his reaction to war. Today on the battlefield he had not precisely turned tail and run, but he had come close to it, riding up and down the fringes of the foray, keeping himself at a safe distance, nervously, ineffectually bawling commands. The screaming of horses, of men, the cannon blasts and musketry fire had unnerved him; the chaos had stripped him of what little courage he had managed to muster beneath the cover of his uniform.

He focused on Tamasin's capable hands, and felt his trembling subside. "A favor . . . ?" he repeated, loath to appear too eager, but suddenly ablaze with desire to lay his head down on her breast, close his eyes, and forget the horror of the day. "If you're here to make amends, I—"

"No," she cut in with quick impatience. "It's nothing to do with that. I need your help."

Her tone gave Avery immediate suspicion, and he examined her more closely, contemplating the dried bloodstains upon her skirts. He saw that they were not random splatters, but definite imprints, as if, perhaps, she had held a bleeding man in her arms.

His spiralling hope, his relief upon seeing the cottier's lass again plummeted all at once. He began to laugh, lightly at first, then heartily, the sound coming from deep in his belly as he threw his head back so far that the grime on his white stock showed. "Kinshella!" he managed to wheeze, holding his middle with both hands. "I should have known. God, I should have known."

"He's injured. I've hidden him. Patrols are everywhere, rounding up rebels, either killing them on the spot or hauling them to prison. I want you to help us escape, Avery. Please, God, help us! Help us to leave Ireland."

The baronet's son stopped laughing and stared at her, then shoved one cold hand in his pocket and roamed to the desk to finger the brass spyglass. He had thought about Tamasin Cullen since the moment he had marched away from her in his splendid new uniform. Indeed, her parting words had provided a rhythm for his feet in their shiny black boots. *Perhaps you need to learn to be alone with yourself, Avery.*

But he did not want to be alone. He wanted her, needed her strength and fortitude. He had joined the army for her as much as for himself, thinking to perform heroic acts, and through gaining some measure of self-liking, make her love him. Could she ever love him? Even knowing what he was, Tamasin Cullen had never condemned him, never scorned his weaknesses. And yet, Avery knew the cottier's lass was not meant for him. She was made for someone like Kinshella, someone built of the raw brawn and courage of an emerging Ireland.

"So," he said after a moment of painfully difficult reflection. "We are bargaining for the groomsman's life again, are we, Tamasin? Only, I didn't arrange the circumstances this time. He managed them on his own."

"I'm not asking to bargain with you."

Avery raised a brow. "Indeed? Well then, what *are* you asking, then?"

''A favor, as I said.''

''Why do you suppose I should grant it?''

Tamasin took a breath and regarded the baronet's son through the shifting gold gloom of the candlelight, seeing him as a man lost, but still powerful. His head was bowed in a sort of self-defeat that saddened her, so when she next spoke, her voice held all the gentleness that maturity and love had brought. ''Because, whether you care to admit it or not, Avery, we've marked each others' lives—all three of us. We've met equally along the way, too, every now and then. That should count for something, shouldn't it? Be worth something?''

''You're reminding me that I would not be here now, alive and well, but for Hunter Kinshella?''

''Yes. I'm reminding you. I must in order to save his life.'' Tamasin hesitated, then looked at Avery with full, direct eyes to emphasize the significance of what she had to say. ''And, I ask not only for Hunter, but in order to insure the future of his child.''

A rasping, unintelligible comment escaped Avery's lips at her announcement. ''His *child?*'' he hissed. For several seconds he stared at her in disbelief, and then laughed with no amusement whatever. Turning his back upon her, he shook his head in a sort of merciless self-mockery. ''Kinshella was in Dublin this summer, then. With you?''

''Yes,'' she admitted. ''Once—''

''Virile of him, wasn't it?'' Avery sneered, then closed his eyes and swallowed. After a moment he asked, ''Does he know?''

Tamasin shook her head, waiting while he ran a hand under his heavy chin and pondered the situation. She could see how deeply he was weighing his decision, his choices. He observed her, his eyes very clear and copper, the same eyes that had once commanded her in childhood. She recalled how a mere glance from them had sent her scurrying to do his bidding then. Strange, she mused, that they had lost their hold. They seemed only vulnerable eyes now.

At last, Avery broke his silence. He came close, took Tamasin's chin in his hand, and scrutinized her face with consuming gravity, with an unwilling need to imprint her features upon his memory. "This will be the last favor, Tamasin," he said with a quiet hardness. "I will not be available to you again—not ever, for any reason—for it is not in my nature to be generous for nothing, as you well know. Is that understood?"

"Yes," she breathed, relief and weariness robbing her lungs of air. "I understand."

One of the candles guttered and went out, the hot melted wax dripping onto the desk. The room seemed unbearably warm. Avery shrugged out of his scarlet tunic, shed it in the humid August night before tossing it upon the army cot. Then he sat down at the desk and, taking up a quill, scratched an inky trail of sepia across a yellow sheet of paper.

Even while he wrote, a disturbance ensued outside, punctuated by scuffling feet and contentious voices. The tent flap parted suddenly.

With his arms pinioned by the pair of sentries, Hunter Kinshella burst inside, resembling a cornered, wounded animal on the verge of madness.

He could hardly stand; only the support of the two men kept him upright. His clothes were the threadbare ones Tamasin had left him in, ripped and soiled. His hair was wet with perspiration, and his face darkened with powder stains. Both legs bled profusely through their makeshift wrap of bandages.

At first she was too stunned, too terrified, to move, knowing Hunter had just forfeited his chance—*their* chance of hope. He would either curse Avery to his face and be arrested, or refuse leniency—if by some miracle of grace the baronet's son remained forebearant and offered it. The end has come now, she told herself in a silent cry. *The end of us has come.*

"If you're writing out a pardon for me, you son-of-a-bitch," Hunter snarled at Avery, "you can stop and tear it up. I'll not take a damned pardon or anything else from you!" Blinking against the sweat rolling off his brow, breathing with difficulty as his blood dripped steadily on the ground, the groomsman turned cruel, accusing eyes on Tamasin. "What was the price *this* time?" he demanded.

"Hunter—"

"And who was paying? Did you sell me to Avery Hampton as you did before? For what, another bloody silk scarf? Or did you ask him for my life again? In exchange for what? What did you intend to *give* for me?"

"Hunter!"

"You've played with my life—my *life*—Tamasin!" the groomsman cried hoarsely, his eyes fierce with wrath. "You've made decisions, changed the course of it, stripped me of my own right to chose my fate. Now you're stripping me again. Damn it! What did you intend to do?" Hunter's face twisted. "You've already made a whore of yourself. What's left of you, Tamasin? God in heaven, *what's left?*"

A silence descended over the tent then, one so complete, so chilling and bright-edged that it seemed to quiver on the air. It was a silence that contained a man's heartbreak, his rage, his final bursting break of emotional honesty. The sheer sharp agony of it crossed the boundaries of time and class.

In embarrassment, the two sentries lowered their gazes. Their hands loosened a bit upon their captive, preferring not to touch anyone so harrowed with grief, so possibly close to death.

Avery released a breath almost gingerly, as if the hush were a thing that could be shattered like glass. His fingers still gripped the quill, and with an abrupt wave of his hand, he dismissed the guards. Gratefully they obeyed, filing out, leaving Hunter to stand alone on his shattered legs, which he managed to do by nothing more than stubborn will.

" 'Tis not a pardon I'm writing out, Kinshella," Avery snapped, his own voice tired and strained. "I haven't the power to grant you that. But this will get you passage out of Ireland." A trace of a smile, one from days long past, touched his pale lips. "There's not even a charge for it. The lady made it quite clear to me that I owed you a favor or two."

Tamasin stood behind Avery. Hunter's eyes jerked to hers, assessing, burning, and his tongue lashed out once more. "Have you decided to exile me again, Tamasin? Send me out of Ireland?"

He hobbled forward, one excruciating step, then another, his handsome face gray beneath its powder stains. Bracing his hands upon the desk in order to keep himself standing, he asked again through gritted teeth. "Have you? By God, look me in the eye and tell me that you have!"

"Hunter—"

He seized the paper and crumpled it then, hurled it at her feet.

She said nothing, but her heart hammered with grief.

Between them, Avery sighed. "I find your attitude very curious, Kinshella," he remarked, affecting his customary hauteur. "Don't you believe I'm indebted to you, that I owe you a favor? After all, you pulled me from a hole in the ground, and later from a burning barn and certain death—two occasions for which I will forever and heartily curse you. But you could not have known that, of course. And now you refuse to let me return the favor, to give you a simple if not so honorable ending. Why is that, groomsman?" he asked, pinning the other man with words. "Would you rather die on Irish soil than live on any other? Yes . . . ? Ah. Curious notion. Exceedingly curious. The ultimate act of patriotic honor, the kind one hears about in Eushanie's silly Irish legends. But," he lifted a shoulder insouciantly, "there it is, I suppose."

"Call the guards back," Hunter hissed. "And do your duty."

"In good time, Kinshella. We have a matter to discuss first." Avery indicated Tamasin with a hand and asked, "What about her?"

For a few seconds Hunter did not shift his gaze to Tamasin's face, but stared at the scarlet tunic draped over Avery's cot. It was a tunic like the one he had once been forced to wear, and its brilliant color appeared to shimmer and vibrate. Suddenly his brain seemed befuddled. He couldn't think clearly. But he remembered well what the two people in this room had once conspired to do to him.

Tamasin stared at the man she loved. His eyes were hard and glazed and full of pain. She knew she must speak at once, before the last shriveling moment of hope fled, before Hunter closed himself against her and let himself be taken away. She took a breath and when she spoke her words were measured and steady. "I am carrying your child, Hunter."

The words fell as stones.

Hunter lifted his lashes, his eyes narrowing, glittering beneath his wet black brows. After only a second or two of scrutiny, it became obvious that he did not believe what she had said. His legs, locked at the knees, quivered with the effort of sustaining his weight. The breeches were saturated bright red, and yet, still, he stood, the strong but not so common Irish laborer.

Demanding a confirmation of Tamasin's words, he turned hard eyes to Avery, who met his gaze and held it.

Very slowly, the baronet's son rose from his chair behind the desk and stood with straightened shoulders. Not a muscle moved in his face, not a twitch of disquiet touched his eyes. With no avoidance of the question in Hunter's expression, he said, "If she's carrying a child, I'm not the man who got it on her. What you've heard about me is true." His gaze stayed as steady as his voice. "Quite despicably true. Every word of it."

For several seconds Hunter measured the words, measured the man who had stated them. Then his eyes returned to Tamasin, but they could find no trace of treachery or deceit in her face. Hunter wanted to believe that Tamasin belonged to him, but he was afraid to believe. He distrusted her loyalty. His fledgling faith in the cottier's lass had been destroyed the instant he had seen her standing in Lt. Avery Hampton's tent.

"Oh, for God's sake, man," Avery snapped when Hunter's hesitation stretched. He waved an impatient hand at the groomsman. "Take her and get out of here. I'll see that you both get safely to Dublin and out of harbor. What do you think you'll be dying for if you stay in Ireland, anyway, Kinshella? The rebellion is over—*if* you've ever believed in it, which I'm inclined to think you haven't. Hampton Hall and the lodge are burned to the ground, and probably half of Wexford with them. Even if you could escape the noose—which you can't do without my help—what's left here for you? What's to become of Tamasin and your brat if you take yourself off to the gallows? Beggars both of them. And I'd not raise a finger to help.''

Avery turned his back as if the sight of the bleeding, fearless groomsman sickened him. "Get yourself out of Ireland and salvage what you can. I'll make leaving simple for you. After that, good riddance to you both.''

Chapter Twenty-Nine

The boat waited to abandon harbor, rocking in the hard glassy swells until she could lurch seaward propelled by wind-stretched canvas. Her destination was a port on the distant, unimaginable shores of America, one called Norfolk.

Tamasin knew nothing of the place, had never heard the name before, but the ship Avery had designated via a hastily scrawled letter happened to be bound in that direction, and so she had gratefully accepted it as a way of escape.

Not so Hunter. Had it been a vessel sailing for Hades, she thought, he could not have stepped aboard with any less reluctance in his eyes.

But step aboard he did. His punishing self-will astonished and alarmed Tamasin. She watched him walk on his injured legs up the plank to the deck, elbowing aside the sailors' helping hands through the companionway before ducking into the tiny cabin and collapsing exhaustedly upon a bunk.

Before they had left the military camp, Avery had secured clean clothes and the services of a surgeon, who had informed Hunter quite bluntly that he could not expect to be agile again,

and, indeed, would be fortunate if the legs did not soon warrant
a saw. Once aboard the ship Tamasin summoned the ship's
surgeon for his opinion, but when the poor fellow came to
change the bandages, Hunter grabbed his wrist, and in a voice
equal to a lion's roar, threatened his life. "I'll kill you if you
cut me," he said, his hand quivering with the strain of his
resolve.

The surgeon, accustomed to coarseness, but offended nonetheless, silently tended the wounds before hastening out. At
least the doctor was clean and neat, Tamasin thought, relieved
to be spared some heavy-handed barber who would do more
harm than good.

Finally alone with Hunter, she made nervous, murmured
attempts at conversation, talking about mundane things—
accommodations, the length of the journey, the amiability of
the crew—but he answered with little more than stony silence.

The rough, hurried transport to Dublin from the camp had
left him exhausted, and the pain tautened every muscle of his
body. But it was not only his body that suffered; his spirit, his
mind—every bone and organ that created the architecture of
the Irish groomsman—bled. Anguish seemed to seep from his
pores, and, as if some finely tuned intuition told him the precise
moment that the green blue shores of his country would forever
fade from his sight, he raised up from the bunk, hauled himself
upright with a hiss of breath, and watched through the porthole
as the ship rocked out of harbor. Watched without a word.

Tamasin stared at the back of the dark head she loved so
much. Beyond it, she could see the misty smudge of earth that
was Eire, his homeland, the one thing he had always wholly
loved. After a few moments, its dazzling green blent with the
blue sky above the water, and when it had become no more
than an etched impression behind dry red eyelids, Hunter turned
away from it.

For a long time afterwards, while the ship creaked and
bucked, Tamasin sat upon a sea chest with no will to move,
looking at the groomsman where he lay prone upon the bunk

with his back turned against her. She knew she had done him
a disservice. Twice she had exiled him. He would have stayed,
died with the others who had fought for Ireland, and been at
peace doing so, feeling it a fitting end. But she had forced his
honor by telling him of the child she carried. She had called,
one last time, upon his integrity, and he had acted. Now he
sped away with her toward some alien place less welcome to
him than death.

He shifted on his bunk, and although his back was still turned,
she realized he was not asleep.

"Fetch the captain," he said to her a moment later.

"T-the captain . . . ?"

"Aye." Hunter's voice was full of weary rue. "Ask him
when it's convenient to perform a marriage. I don't intend to
die, but if I should, you'll have no bastard of mine."

Simultaneously stung and startled, Tamasin opened her
mouth to speak, but no words came. What could she say? His
judgment was right; the child should be born in wedlock even
if its parents had not yet reconciled their conflicts. She was too
numb, too weary to contemplate any other aspect of their future.
The child must be provided for, considered above all else.
The rest, the course of their lives together, would have to be
determined step by step, league by league as the ship sailed
toward a new country, an uncertain home.

"Very well," she replied in a steady voice. "I'll bring the
captain to you."

When the bearded, taciturn captain arrived to perform the
short service, Hunter insisted upon standing. A groan broke
from his throat as he put weight upon his legs again, and his
complexion ashened during the few minutes it took for the
captain to hurriedly rush through the brief but binding cere-
mony.

Before leaving the army camp, Tamasin had retrieved the
valise she had hidden in the woodlet, and now wore a lavender
gown, the better of the two garments she had brought from the
Hampton home. As she stood beside Hunter and murmured her

vows, she wished she had kept her old black skirt and jacket—
not that the groomsman noticed. He scarcely glanced at her,
reciting the necessary words perfunctorily as if to get them
over as soon as possible.

Afterwards he made no attempt at civility while sharing a
cold repast with her, drinking a large quantity of wine with his
bread and cheese. It was as if he were loath to speak of their
destination, or of the child, or of their future, in case it should
scratch the surface of his carefully controlled emotion and rend
him open. He made no mention of their marriage either; nor
did he so much as touch her hand.

"We're going to a place called Norfolk, in Virginia. Have
you heard of it?" Tamasin ventured, desperate to engage in
conversation and break his silence.

Hunter nodded without looking up. "Aye."

"What . . . what do you think we should plan to do when
we arrive there?"

In answer to her question the groomsman glanced down at
his legs and gave her a mocking lift of one black brow. "I
would say our options are rather limited—or mine, anyway.
Wouldn't you?"

"It's not like you to engage in self-pity, Hunter," she said
in a quiet tone. "Or to be daunted by anything."

"Perhaps my sense of adventure has finally run out."

Tamasin wished he would unbend enough so that she could
tell him a secret she kept. But she did not want to risk his
wrath. If she were to inform him that Avery had sent Sir Harry's
thoroughbred along with them, given them the valuable animal,
Hunter might explode with fury. Insisting that the horse had
been ruined in battle and was no longer of any use, Avery had
declared that he would rather see it shipped to America with
the equally battered groomsman than shoot it. But Tamasin
knew that the horse—unlike Hunter perhaps—would eventually regain both its physical soundness and its heart. She knew,
too, that Avery had meant the thoroughbred as a gift, as a way
to help them survive without a more blatant offer of money.

It was the only thing she could remember the baronet's son ever giving without exacting something in return.

The unlikely newlyweds continued to sit together at a table folded down from the wall, a guttering candle and the remains of the meal between them. Believing it not only hardheaded of him not to lie down with his legs propped, but inadvisable, Tamasin murmured, "Won't you rest, Hunter?"

He poured more wine and gulped it. "In due time."

"The surgeon left some laudanum. Should I get it—?"

"No."

His belligerence was slowly eroding Tamasin's nerves and, raising accusing eyes, she snapped, "Why? Because you like to suffer?"

"Pain has a way of honing the senses, I've found."

"And a way of sharpening an uncivil tongue."

He nodded imperceptibly at her parry, his eyes an intent and cutting green. "As you say."

For a moment she watched his hands as they turned the stem of his wineglass. Then she blurted, "Are we not to make peace then, Hunter?"

His eyes glinted. "Are we at war?"

"Yes, we are. I think we have been for a very long while." Tamasin's voice was smoky, grave, one hand in her lap clenched around the other. " 'Tis time to end it."

Pulling himself up, not letting go of the back of the chair, Hunter shuffled two steps to the bunk and eased down, his body knotted with the strain of shifting his legs. As he laid his head back with teeth gritted, he quipped, "The trouble is, the end of a war suggests a victory for one side or the other, doesn't it?"

"I suppose."

"Well, then, *Mrs.* Kinshella, you have won yourself no victory by getting me."

He said nothing more, but turned away and shut her out.

A few minutes later, when he fell asleep, Tamasin cursed him aloud. "I'll not lie down with you, you self-pitying boor.

I'll sleep on the floor. Nay. I can't bear lying against such a stubborn back as yours, Hunter Kinshella.''

During the next several days she and Hunter scarcely spoke, exchanging only necessary words. He cared scrupulously for his wounds, requested that the surgeon call every morning and rewrap the dressing. On the fourth day, he lurched to his feet, forced himself to walk around the tiny cabin in slow, ambling steps. He grimaced as he labored, his eyes bright with the resolve not to accept the failure of his legs. But his face had regained its color, and freshly shaven, caused Tamasin to stare in wonder at its clean, hard symmetry.

Feeling unwelcome, an intruder into his personal struggle, Tamasin fled often to the deck, where she tarried for long hours staring out at the curlicue waves. She felt alone, abandoned by the man who was now her husband and bound to her for life. She thought of the child growing in her belly; she would welcome it, be glad to nurture it, hope that it had Hunter's eyes.

She pondered the nameless, elusive discord that stood between her and the groomsman. Over and over she questioned her judgement. Had she done the right thing, made the best decision in asking Avery's help, in telling Hunter about the child she carried? She knew that he would not have boarded this ship for her sake alone. Hunter did not trust her loyalty, not did he understand how much she loved him. Knowing that she had the wits and resourcefulness to make her own way in the world, he would have gone nobly and without guilt to his death as a rebel officer. But the child had changed that intent. Even Tamasin, with all her tenacity, would have had difficulty making a way for herself and an infant. Hunter had known that, and had claimed his responsibility.

Did he care for her? Tamasin didn't know. But, once, long ago, he had traded a fine, warm cathamore for a plain gold ring.

She contemplated the three of them—the groomsman, the cottier's lass, and the baronet's son. Even Avery, in the end, had found a measure of honor in his heart. Hunter, of course, was ruled by little else. And what, or who, ruled Tamasin Cullen? Had she ever really listened to her conscience, that inner voice of guidance that Father Dinsmore had always insisted she possessed? What was best, what was right? What did she *want?*

With a sigh, Tamasin considered, searching her heart, which was not the same heart, she thought, as the one that had kept the cottier's lass running over the fields after a dream. Now, she wanted no marble houses, no chocolates, no lace-edged fans. She wanted only Hunter Kinshella as he had been before she had interrupted the course of his life . She wanted. *Wanted.*

Staring out at the ocean until her eyes stung, at the cold aquamarine wilderness devoid of any landmarks, she twisted her hands, agitated, fretful. *"What stands between us?"* she whispered aloud, the wind stealing her voice away. "Something does, something apart from the events of war and Avery Hampton, apart even from this forced separation from Ireland. But what *is it?"*

As a fiery topaz sun lowered and poised on the horizon, as the breeze caught and fluttered the yellow sails, the answer came—dimly at first, then with growing clarity. It washed over Tamasin in a sudden, blinding, bright realization. Her hands balled. Whirling around, she ran for the companionway, bursting into the twilit cabin. She hardly glanced at Hunter where he sat on the bunk polishing the boots he couldn't yet wear. She was intent only upon the chest which contained her meager possessions.

Throwing it open, she scrabbled to seize the bundle of treasures inside, those fine, bright objects she had cherished long and out of habit. They offended her now, enraged her, and like a madwoman she began to tear at them. With rough and destructive hands, she worked loose the knot of the green and cream striped skirt until its contents spilled out in her lap. Then she pounded on the porthole above the bunk. When it swung open, wind whistled through, fresh and stinging, smelling of blue clouds.

The cabin was dusky with eventide, but her fingers knew intimately the textures of each of the objects of vanity that had sustained and driven her since childhood. Discovering a handkerchief, she tore it in two and thrust it out the porthole. She watched the pieces float away, two delicate wings on the air, dipping at last and forever into the water.

Her face contorted with emotion as she seized the pins, the gold felt hat, the feather, all the other debris of her ambition, and threw them out. The striped skirt she cursed, cramming it furiously through the porthole, watching it billow then sail away to be devoured by the waves. Then, galled even by the clothes she wore, she twisted out of the lavender skirt and jacket Avery's money had bought, and gave them to the sea.

Only the silk scarf remained. It was fitting, Tamasin thought, that it should be the last sacrifice, the most desecrated of all. She began to wad it, shred it, shove each frayed scrap out of the aperture until, slowly, a hand closed about her wrist. She battled it, until Hunter gripped her flailing arms and pinned them. He did not release her, but put his hard, warm arms around her until she was securely embraced, and after a moment she felt herself relax, drawn deeply down into a circle of safety, to the smell of Irish meadows and rain. Drawn home.

A great fearful sorrow swelled inside her, and she began to sob, strangling on her tears as she clutched, as for life, a pair of wide bruised shoulders that still carried their own weighty share of burdens.

"You've never forgiven me, have you, Hunter!" Tamasin cried in a burst of grief. Pressing her face against the curve of his brown, lean neck, suffering heartbreak, she accused, "You've never *forgiven* me!"

He squeezed his eyes shut, breathed raggedly against her hair and confessed, "No . . . no . . . I never have."

Accepting the honesty, she wept against him, feeling his pain and hers together. "I wanted your anger!" she railed. "I wanted

you to shout at me, call me vile names, punish me for my
wickedness in some way. And then I wanted you to forgive
me. I wanted to hear you say the words out loud—all of them,
the forgiveness and the pardon—so I would know it was over,
know that the past was gone.''

"The past was never gone, Tamasin,'' Hunter groaned. "You
wouldn't let it be. You always went back to him. You always
went back to Avery . . .''

"But the last time was for you, Hunter. For *you!* And still,
you have no forgiveness for me. You lie here every day staring
at my face, speaking as if you despise me. I don't know how
to atone, how to make up for the past, how to make you stop
hating me. You have hated me, haven't you?''

"Aye!'' he breathed in grief, his lips twisted against her
sweet, scented throat. "I have hated you, by God. I have.'' His
voice broke as he clasped her to his chest, rocked, put his
mouth against her ear. "But I always loved you, too, Tamasin
. . . I always loved you.''

The desolation in his voice made her cry, and he kissed her
until she responded, clung to him. And after the grief washed
over them in a sweeping wave, leaving them hot and empty,
needing the hollowness filled, the groomsman began to stroke
her arms.

He stroked slowly, tentatively, then put his hand upon her
breast above the lace of her chemise. She lay still and his
fingers slipped beneath the garment, then parted it, inched it
off her shoulders and down about her waist. Tamasin pushed
aside his coarser clothes, drew the shirt over his head, inhaled
a breath as the bareness of his chest came against hers at last.

"But we must put the past away,'' he whispered, "make it
nothing more than the scraps you've thrown out to sea. You've
done your part, lass. Aye. Now I shall do mine by making you
my wife.'' He kissed her face, her throat, her ears, trailed his
hand to her belly and let it linger there. She put her lips upon
his, opened her mouth, and he kissed it deeply, groaning. The
evidence of his need pressed hard against her thighs.

When he freed himself of his breeches, she opened, and he entered. She held him fast and he moved strongly, driven, until they both forgot, and remembered. There was a kind of expiation in what they did, in the contact of skin and sinew, in the great shuddering pleasure he found and she answered. For long moments, as the ship sailed further into its vacant blue, they held on to each other, connected, an island together. Their closeness gave them something real, now that Ireland was gone. And Hunter told her what it was. "Ourselves," he said in a clear, enduring tone. Then, more softly, with just a hint of the humor she so adored, "And a bit of happiness, Damsel. Don't you think? After all, I'm not the reluctant bridegroom you feared I was."

"Then show me," she answered, even as he bent his head. "Show me again."

Epilogue

"Mam! Mam! Look there! Can you see the birds? One, two, three of them! We must be nearing land."

The boy pointed to the dipping, veering gulls, long gray arrows in a dazzling turquoise sky. He was tall, bright, with a pixie smile that occasionally tugged at Tamasin's heartstrings, because it so resembled Brendan Kinshella's once golden grin. The boy also claimed his uncle's fair crown of hair, and often indulged in his own share of daydreams. But most of all, Tamasin thought with a poignant ache, studying his clean, eager profile as he leaned with outstretched arms into the wind as if to harness it, young Seamus was his father's child.

She moved to lay her hands upon his bright curls. "Where's your cap, Seamus? You didn't lose it?"

" 'Tis in my pocket, Mam. You fret so about everything. Where's Da?"

"Here," a voice behind them said.

Tamasin had never ceased to love the sound of it, to strain to catch the timbre of its brogue in the next room, or across the stable yard, or in the whispery blackness of a foreign night.

As her husband joined them at the rail, she looked up at
him, examined his face and expression, the taut, fine-strung
expectancy that corrugated his brow and made his mouth firm.
The years had not greatly changed Hunter Kinshella, she
decided, but the landmarks of hardship did show in his bearing,
in the iron of his jaw, in the sometimes faraway glint of his
green eyes. He was still exceedingly fine-looking, of course,
never having gained excess weight to soften the austerity of
his countenance or the lean angles of his horseman's body.
Indeed, he was not much different than the man who had once—
long, long ago—danced with her beside a hedgerow.

In a sudden wrenching tenderness, she touched his hand
where it lay atop the rail. He had been a good husband, a good
father, a good man.

As husband and wife, they had suffered their share of stormy
interludes, but, all and all, the fabric of life had not been too
badly frayed by anything but Hunter's unvoiced but inward
kind of restlessness.

Now, with a sigh, Tamasin glanced down at her husband's
legs. He had scarcely been able to shuffle off the ship upon
their arrival in America, walk down the bustling, unfamiliar
new streets beside her, but he had healed enough to ride as
expertly as ever.

Aye, when it had come to training racehorses, he had demon-
strated all the magical talents that his grandfather had once
possessed. In America, Providence rescued them; a shrewd
gentleman in Virginia had seen the groomsman's value and
hired him.

There had been Sir Harry's stallion, of course, never sound
enough to race again. After overcoming an initial, instinctive
resentment over Avery's peculiar generosity, Hunter had been
grateful to keep the thoroughbred, who had eventually sired
several swift colts before his death. The colts' winnings,
together with Hunter's resourcefulness, had provided a financial
nest egg that had finally purchased their passage back to Ireland.

A year ago Father Dinsmore had written to say that no one

cared about prosecuting rebel officers anymore. It seemed most
had forgotten the names and deeds of the United Irish soldiers;
the government no longer bothered to try them. Were he to
return to Ireland, the priest assured, the groomsman's leadership
of the ragged peasants would not be dredged up, although
almost everyone in Wexford still remembered Hunter Kinshella,
whose exploits had become legendary after the rebellion.

Conversely, the villagers did not seem to remember the baronet's son, or if they did, declined to speak of him. " 'Tis
strange," the priest had commented in his letter. "The people
here seem to have selective memories."

Of course, Tamasin and Hunter still recalled Avery Hampton
very well, although each of them in entirely different ways.

"Look, Da," young Seamus said in excitement, pointing
toward the water while scrubbing sea spray from his eyes.
"What's that out there? Could it be the water horse you told
me about when I was a wee lad?"

"An *augh-ishka*, you mean?"

"Aye. Tell me about it again, please, sir."

A haunted smile curved Hunter's mouth and he narrowed
his eyes, pretended to focus upon an imaginary, wild-maned
head plunging up from the waves. His voice was deep with a
magic in which Tamasin actually thought he believed, sometimes.

"An *augh-ishka*, Seamus, is a horse born of the sea," Hunter
explained. "Sometimes, when he has a mind to, the beast comes
prancing out of the water to run free and wild over the fields
of Ireland. If you can catch him, he'll make you a fine, fast
mount. But once you're astride," Hunter warned in mock sternness over a wagging finger, "you cannot let him glimpse the
sea again, or he'll return to it, dive into its depths with you
atop his back."

"If *I* ever caught the water horse," the lad asserted with his
chest puffed out, "I'd ride him to *Tir-na-n-Og*. And get happiness for a penny there. Right, Mam?"

Hunter slipped an arm about Tamasin's waist as she answered, "Yes, son. For a penny."

But Tamasin had already found happiness. She sighed, wishing she could see the same free, bright light in Hunter's eyes that she still remembered so clearly from the days of his childhood. All through the years in America, the groomsman had been driven by a restless discontent that had nothing to do with her. At times he had stared out over the Virginia fields, eastward, as if recalling his home and feeling a tugging, unquenchable desire to return to it.

Now, they had almost reached Eire's beloved shores again. Hope, Tamasin told herself, lay only a few leagues away.

She could not ponder the return to Ireland without thinking of Brendan and Eushanie. They had found their own happiness, more or less, years ago after the rebellion, having eloped straight from the battlefield. When Sir Harry's wrath had cooled, when he had had a chance to feel grateful that his uncomely daughter was permanently off his hands, he had given the couple an annuity and a half-decaying farmhouse in the South of England, which had probably given him cause for relief. "Out of sight, out of mind," she could imagine him muttering sourly with the inevitable glass of claret in his hand.

In her beautiful romantic hand, Eushanie wrote to Tamasin and Hunter frequently. She was the mother of eight golden-haired children, the wife of a man who probably had sired more than eight, scattering his unfaithful but charming seed across half the Surrey countryside. But aside from his carefree, rainbow-chasing follies, Tamasin suspected Brendan Kinshella loved Eushanie in his way; after all, where he had given her a romance, she had given him an income and, therefore, the means to idle in the sun and wager in the alehouse.

Tamasin turned her head, vainly trying to avoid the splash of saltwater that caught in her lashes; for a moment the water beads shimmered like diamonds in her eyes. *Avery.*

He had died two years after the rebellion had ended. "So young," Eushanie had written sadly. "His death was rather mysterious, although we believe he took too much laudanum. He always had such trouble sleeping, he told us, after the rebellion. And he was plagued by the most dreadful dreams. He used the drug to ease them, poor dear. I suspect he awoke in the night, tormented, befuddled, and poured too many spoonsful . . ."

Or just the right amount.

Tamasin blinked the water beads away and laid her head against Hunter's shoulder. He put his hand on her head, his fingers tense, restive with expectation.

Not an hour later, the ship docked off the shore of Wexford. Slowly, the three Kinshellas walked down the gangplank, Tamasin and Seamus matching Hunter's pace, finally stepping onto the cobbles of the little village. For a moment all three stood still, absorbing the sights, the smells, the sounds of Ireland.

Their homecoming was canopied by strips of cloud shadows chasing sunshine over gray stone and green valleys. It was all just as Tamasin remembered. Had it really been so many years? How clearly she recalled the green flag flying over Customs Quay, the hoards of barefoot Irish soldiers, the manacled gentlemen. And before that, the fairs, the markets, the feel of the dewy rain, the sounds of baying hounds and nickering horses.

"Let your Da go ahead, Seamus," she whispered in her son's ear, holding the boy back when he would have galloped down the narrow lane through scenery hardly changed in the years they had been away.

Reluctantly the boy complied, hanging back, trailing his father at a distance while, with anxious eyes, his mother followed Hunter's solitary walk up the hill.

Tamasin took a breath as she surveyed again the rough paths, the hedgerows, the cottages with their blue curls of peat smoke. Over the fields the mayflowers bloomed. Blue pink foxgloves rose like fairy spires in the ditches. Blackberry vines rambled through dense thorn thickets. Most affectingly, the emerald grass, fed with limestone and rain, lent its glorious sweet scent, and urged one to kick off shoes and stockings and simply run.

The threesome climbed a hill opposite the one upon which Hampton Hall had once so magnificently throned. The mansion, burned during the rebellion, was no more than a facade now, never rebuilt, its sooty stone frame slowly returning to the earth. Tamasin and her son lingered on the rise to regard it, their hands loosely intertwined, while Hunter halted his pace and stood staring intently toward the river. His tall enduring form seemed to blend with the landscape suddenly, make complete the picture of Eire.

"What's Da doing, Mam?" young Seamus asked curiously. "Why is he standing so still, acting so odd?"

Tamasin watched as Hunter removed his woolen cap and tucked it beneath an arm, then gazed out at the fields. She had seen him in the same pose once before, many years ago, as he stood on a rain-drenched drive, a soldier returned home. He was paying homage again, eloquently, wordlessly, to his homeland.

"What's he doing, Mam?" came the question again, more fretfully this time.

She swallowed, her voice not quite steady. "Well, he's rather like a knight standing before his queen, Seamus. Do you understand?"

Her son considered and nodded. He was well versed in knighthood, honor, and heroic deeds through his Aunt Eushanie's continual gifts of gilt-edged books. "Aye. But what will we do now we're here in Ireland, Mam? What will Da do for work now we've sold the horses?"

He'll be hefting stones, or exercising colts, or striding agilely, as he once had, across the rocky moors.

Tamasin managed a smile, her eyes misting over. "Does it matter, my darling? Nay, I think not. What matters is that your da has come home again." *The groomsman has his country,* she added silently. *He will thrive here.* With an abiding faith she finished aloud, "Someone will see his value, recognize hi worth.'' Her throat closed against a prickling of emotion. ''Just as I have.''

Just as I have.

She ran to him and he turned.

Hunter smiled, held her tightly. His heart was full.